Samuel J Eales, Dom. John Mabillon

Life and works of Saint Bernard, Abbot of Clairvaux

Translated and edit with additional notes

Samuel J Eales, Dom. John Mabillon

Life and works of Saint Bernard, Abbot of Clairvaux
Translated and edit with additional notes

ISBN/EAN: 9783742861214

Printed in Europe, USA, Canada, Australia, Japan

Cover: Foto ©Raphael Reischuk / pixelio.de

Manufactured and distributed by brebook publishing software (www.brebook.com)

Samuel J Eales, Dom. John Mabillon

Life and works of Saint Bernard, Abbot of Clairvaux

LIFE AND WORKS
OF SAINT BERNARD,

ABBOT OF CLAIRVAUX.

EDITED BY

DOM. JOHN MABILLON,

Presbyter and Monk of the Benedictine Congregation of S. Maur.

Translated and Edited with Additional Notes,

BY

SAMUEL J. EALES, M.A., D.C.L.,

Sometime Principal of S. Boniface College, Warminster.

VOL. I.

JOHN HODGES,

HENRIETTA STREET, COVENT GARDEN, LONDON.

1889.

CONTENTS.

PREFACE

ERRATUM.

Vol. I. p. 77, line 13, for " Clairvaux " *read* " Cîteaux."

entire disinterestedness, his remarkable industry, the soul-subduing eloquence which seems to have been equally effective in France and in Italy, over the sturdy burghers of Liége and the turbulent population of Milan, and above all the wonderful piety and saintliness which formed the noblest and the most engaging of his gifts—these qualities, and the actions which came out of them, rendered him the ornament, as he was more than any other man, the leader, of his own time, and have drawn upon him the admiration of succeeding ages.

We have to look at S. Bernard in more than one capacity. First and chiefly, he was a monk, for he lived in an age when the most elevated religious enthusiasm inevitably took the form of the monastic vocation. Nor is it difficult

PREFACE

TO

THE ENGLISH EDITION.

THERE are so many things to be said respecting the career and the writings of S. Bernard of Clairvaux, and so high are the praises which must, on any just view of his character, be considered his due, that an eloquence not less than his own would be needed to give adequate expression to them.

He was an untiring and transcendently able labourer; and that in many fields. In all his manifold activities are manifest an intellect vigorous and splendid, and a magnetic attractiveness of personal character which never failed to influence and win over others to his views. His entire disinterestedness, his remarkable industry, the soul-subduing eloquence which seems to have been equally effective in France and in Italy, over the sturdy burghers of Liége and the turbulent population of Milan, and above all the wonderful piety and saintliness which formed the noblest and the most engaging of his gifts—these qualities, and the actions which came out of them, rendered him the ornament, as he was more than any other man, the leader, of his own time, and have drawn upon him the admiration of succeeding ages.

We have to look at S. Bernard in more than one capacity. First and chiefly, he was a monk, for he lived in an age when the most elevated religious enthusiasm inevitably took the form of the monastic vocation. Nor is it difficult to see why this was necessarily the case. In the eleventh and twelfth centuries war, public or private, was the chief business of princes and nobles, and a constant incident of the daily life of the masses of the common people. But always when the world lives in a state of war, religion is driven to take the incorporated or associate (*i.e.*, the monastic) form by a kind of unconscious reaction, and indeed, in order to maintain its existence at all. Exaggerated forms generate each other in turn; and the idealized unworldliness of the monastic theory was the virtual protest, and a very needful one, against the coarseness and cruelty of the world as it stood. Monastic institutions satisfied, in fact, the conscience of the age, and were popular because they did so. Even so gifted a man as Bernard, we may venture to believe, would not have been nearly so influential had he been anything but a monk; because monachism was the expression, and the necessary expression, of the religious sentiment of those times. How deeply the monastic theory was graven into the consciousness of the twelfth century is shown by the practical paradox attempted, and actually accomplished for a time, in the welding together of characters absolutely contradictory—the soldier and the monk,—in the Knights Templars, the Knights of Calatrava and Alcantara, and other military Orders.

S. Bernard, then, was a monk and an ascetic, and as such the foremost in power and influence of his time. He was not only practically the founder of the great Cistercian Order, which was frequently called by his name,[1] but to him was owing in great measure, though not wholly, that general reform of the monastic Orders which restored for a time the austerity of the ancient discipline, and even sur-

---

[1] The monks of Abbeys dependent upon Clairvaux, were frequently called *Bernardines.*

passed it. So great was the enthusiasm which he inspired
that thousands of eager postulants, drawn from all classes,
crowded into the convents which were reorganized or
founded by him. Knights, nobles, ladies of the highest
rank, were among these ardent devotees, and that in large
numbers. Even reigning sovereigns, in not a few instances,
descended from their thrones before middle life was well
over and entered some convent. Clairvaux, while he presided over it, sent out parties of its monks to found new
monasteries, at the average rate of four every year, as may
be noted in our Table of Bernardine Chronology. At the
death of S. Bernard the number of Cistercian Abbeys
exceeded five hundred, and to such a degree did this
enthusiasm grow that in 1142 the kingdom of Portugal
declared itself a fief of the Abbey of Clairvaux. Under
the influence of S. Bernard the endurance of austerities
became a passion to be eagerly sought, not a penance re-
luctantly submitted to, and the heavier and sharper was the
Cross voluntarily borne, the greater was held to be its glory.

Not only was he the head of this great Order, but for a
whole generation his influence was paramount over the
Church. He was, more than any of the Popes who succeeded
each other at such short intervals, " the governing head of
Christendom,"[1] to whom every subject of importance was
sure to be, in some form, referred, and the expression of
whose view was equivalent to a judgment upon it. He had
received, in the view of his contemporaries, *unctio illa quæ
docet de omnibus.* His voice was the most trusted and
authoritative in Europe, though he was no Bishop nor
Archbishop, but only a simple Abbot. When, at the Council
of Etampes, he opened his mouth to declare to King Louis
VI. and all the prelates of France that Innocent, and he

---

[1] Milman, *Latin Christianity*, B. viii. p. 302.

alone, was the legitimate Pope, his words were taken as the
decision of the Holy Ghost, and unhesitatingly acted upon.
Henry I. of England, the Emperor Lothair of Germany, and
the Count of Aquitaine, yielded to the force of his arguments, or to the winning power of his remarkable per-
sonality, and acknowledged Innocent as Pope, abandoning
his rival.

It is no wonder that to those who looked on at these
astonishing facts, occurring one after another, the character
and the powers of the Abbot of Clairvaux should have seemed
truly Apostolic. They saw what in that age seemed marvellous in the extreme—a monk, poor, infirm, and obscure,
yet the counsellor, reverenced and obeyed, of sovereigns,
and even of Popes. Nor was there any adventitious or
worldly reason to account for this profound influence which
he exercised. In him the ascendency of a higher intellect,
of a nobler spiritual nature, a purer and more elevated
purpose, of a truly religious force, in short, was felt by all.
A halo of sanctity surrounded the head of the humble
Bernard, and whenever a difficult question of ecclesiastical
polity or of personal duty perplexed Prince, or Bishop, or
monk, the great Abbot of Clairvaux was constantly the
chosen referee. It would be easy to adduce instances of
this, even from the few specimens of letters to him which
are still extant, although the great mass of his correspondence has naturally perished.

As a *theologian* he was equally distinguished. Though
he was not unacquainted with the writings of the Fathers
and earlier commentators, his own expositions owe little to
these. They have an individuality that shows them to be
the utterances of a single mind. He treats all subjects on
the grand scale; refers all actions to spiritual standards,
and both illustrates and determines the question he is

treating by principles and sanctions drawn from the most
unexpected quarters, and frequently from the most awful
heights of authority. He has the imagination of a poet ;
and his works are full of word-pictures which glow and
sparkle like gems, even at the present day, through the
medium of the stiff and scholastic Latin in which they are
set. In his writings there are not a few of those

> jewels five-words-long
> That on the stretched forefinger of all Time
> Sparkle for ever.

Mysticism from his mouth drops most of its question-
able tendencies, and becomes a thing to charm the de-
votional mind, and to lift the thoughtful into new and
loftier regions of emotion. He is a mystic undoubtedly,
but after the manner of S. Ephrem Syrus and S. Gregory
the Great rather than of Eckart (b. 1260), Tauler (b. 1290),
or even of his contemporaries Hugo and Richard of S.
Victor, though these latter approach much nearer to him
than the former. It is essentially a pure and spiritual
mysticism that he inculcates, clear of all the actual sounds,
sights, and odours, celestial music, Elysian fragrance,
miraculous visitations, such as appear for example in the
writings of S. Theresa; though no doubt occasional ex-
travagances of language may be found in his writings,
particularly in his Sermons on the Canticles. Once, indeed,
he relates that the Saviour came down from heaven, and
entered into his soul; but he relates even this great distinction shown to him hesitatingly and with a reluctance and
modesty in every way honourable to him. And he takes
care to make it quite clear that this was a purely *spiritual*
event, attended by no outward manifestations : *" Ita igitur
intrans ad me aliquoties Verbum Sponsus, nullis unquam
introitum suum indiciis innotescere fecit, non voce, non*

specie, non incessa. Nullis denique suis motibus compertum est mihi, nullis meis sensibus illapsum penetralibus meis: tantum ex motu cordis sicut præfatus sum, intellexi præsentiam ejus; et ex fugâ vitiorum, carnaliumque compressione affectuum . . . percepi utcunque speciem decoris ejus." [1]

To a certain extent it is no doubt the case that besides being a mystical theologian, he was a mystic in another sense, that of being a *theurgist, i.e.,* one who claimed to exercise supernatural power. It is unquestionable that he is said by his biographers to have performed vast numbers of miracles. At some periods of his life, *e.g.*, during his progress through the cities of north Italy on behalf of Pope Innocent, and his preaching of the Second Crusade in the Rhineland, almost every action of his was regarded as miraculous, and every word he spoke as a prophecy. The possessed, the blind, the deaf and dumb, the fever stricken, and even the dying, he cured by the laying on of his hands. He worked marvellous cures with the sign of the Cross, with the sacramental Elements, with the touch of his vestments. He is said to have once performed thirty-six miraculous cures in a single day; and it was calculated that during this Rhineland mission he healed an average of thirty persons daily. One of the most striking—we had almost written of the most awful—instances in history of the magnificent power of a firmly-rooted faith, is the account of S. Bernard's confronting William, Count of Aquitaine, bearing in his hands the sacramental species, and thus breaking down his opposition to the religious peace of the State.

But this subject of S. Bernard's miracles we have only space just to mention here, and must hope to be enabled

---

[1] *Serm. in Cantica,* lxxiv, 5, 6.

to consider it at greater length in the *Life of S. Bernard,* which will, it is hoped, conclude this edition of his works.

For a similar reason we merely refer to Bernard in his capacity as the antagonist of the brilliant and able Peter Abaelard; as the mission-preacher among the simple countrymen of Languedoc ; or, lastly, as the Apostle of the Second Crusade, that unfortunate enterprise in which so many predictions were falsified, and so many lives hopelessly thrown away.

Bernard being such as he was, it is a matter of surprise that his works, almost alone among those of the Fathers, have never yet appeared in the English language. To the English reader the Sermons and Treatises of " The Last of the Fathers " are a rich mine, as yet unworked and almost unknown. Sundry versions of parts of the Works have been published by various persons at long intervals.

The following will be found (it is believed) a tolerably complete English bibliography of this subject :—

1. The Meditatons of Saint Bernard, translated by a Student of the Unyversity of Cambrydge. (Wynkyn the Worde [*sic*], Westmester, 1496, and again in 1545.)[1]

2. An Epistle called the golden epistle (T. Godfray, London), 1530. (?)

3.   "   "   "   Edited by Robert Whetford (Wynkyn de Worde, London), 1531. (?)

4. An Epistle called the golden epistle. (Rob. Wyer, London, 1531.)

5. A compèdius and a moche fruytefull treatyse of well liuynge. Translated by Thomas Paynell, London, Thomas Petyt. 8vo.[2]

6. How to Live Well. Translated by C. B. Tyrwhitt. Oxford. 1886.

[1] This is *Meditationes piissimæ*, not by S. Bernard.

[2] The date of this may be gathered approximately from the fact that it contains a dedication to the Princess Mary, daughter of K. Henry VIII., *i.e.,* between 1526 and 1553. There is another edition by John Byddell, n. d. 12mo. This is the *Liber de modo bene Vivendi, ad Sororem*, which is probably not by S. Bernard. Mabillon says of it that "it is consistent neither with the circumstances of Bernard nor those of his sister Humbeline."

7. Devout Meditations of S. Bernard, Or, his Book of the Soul, made English by G. Stanhope. 1701.

8. S. Bernard his Meditations, by W. P., M'r. of Arts in Cambridge. 1631.

9. A Monomachie of Motives in the Mind of Man. A. Fleming. 1582.

10. A Hive of sacred Honicombes. Translated by A. Batt. Doway, 1631.

11. Christian Doctrine and Practice in the Twelfth Century. (Small Books on Great Subjects.) London. 1841.

12. Flowers of S. Bernard, selected and translated. London. 1870.

13. The Virgin Mother of God. Selections from S. Bernard arr. and trans. by a Secular Priest. London and Derby. 1886.

14. Sermon on Cant. I, 5, on the death of his brother Gerard. 1858.

15. Sermons for the Seasons of the Church. Trans. by W. B. Flower. London. 1861.

16. Four Homilies on the Incarnation. Edinburgh. 1843.

17. Glories of the Virgin Mother. By a Catholic Priest. Boston (U.S.). 1869.

18. S. Bernard on the Love of God. Transl. by M. C. and C. Patmore London. 1st ed. 1881 ; 2nd, 1884.

19. The Holy War. Trans. by S. R. M[aitland]. Gloucester. 1827.

20. Letter of S. Bernard to Thomas of Beverley, on Conversion. Trans. by R. Collins. 1856.

21. The Mystic Vine.[1] Trans. by W. R. Brownlow. 1873.

22.   ,,   ,,   Translated by Samuel J. Eales, D.C.L. London. 1889.

23. A Legendary Psalter of S. Bernard. London : Percy Society. 1842.

24. Rhythmical Prayer to the Sacred Members of Jesus. Rendered into English Rhythm by C. M. Shapcote. London. 1879.

25. S. Bernard's Verses containing the unstable felicitie of this wayfaring world. (R. Edwards, Poet) 1596.

26. The same. R. Collier. 1867.

27. A joyful ballad of the Name of Jesus. Trans. by T. G. Crippen. London. 1867.

28. The Jubilee Rhythm of S. Bernard. Trans. by Alfred Edersheim, D.D. London. 1867.

BIOGRAPHIES.

29. Life of S. Bernard. Dublin. 1854.

30. Life of S. Bernard. Derby. 1858.

31. Biography of S. Bernard (Four Ecclesiastical Biographies), by J. H. Gurney. S.P.C.K. 1864.

32. Bernard of Clairvaux. A Biography, by T. M. Lindsay. 1882.

33. The Life and Times of S. Bernard. By Dr. Augustus Neander. Trans. from the German by Matilda Wrench. London. 12mo. 1843.

34. Life and Times of S. Bernard. By James Cotter Morison, M.A. London. 1884.

35. The Sweet Song of S. Bernard (*Jesu ! dulcis memoria*), newly translated by the Rev. George Peirce Grantham. London : *s.d.* 1886. (?)

---

[1] This is not by S. Bernard, though it has long been printed with his works.

It ought, however, to be mentioned here that it was at one time proposed by the Rev. Frederick Oakeley, then Fellow of Balliol College, Oxford, and the Rev. J. S. Brewer, of Queen's College, Oxford, to translate and publish a complete edition of the Works of S. Bernard. Their prospectus (which is now before the Editor) was issued, it is believed, about 1844; but events which speedily followed prevented its being carried out.

The present Edition may be regarded as a revival of that plan. One single aim has been, and will be, pursued throughout by the Editor: that of producing a translation as faithful and complete as possible; and the Notes have been confined to elucidations or illustrations of the text without any comment whatever from a doctrinal point of view. The following observations made by the two scholars just mentioned, in their original proposal, may be quoted here, as they exactly express the position taken up in the present Edition, and the reasons for it :—

> " It is to be distinctly understood that the various parties who may be concerned in this undertaking pledge themselves by the act no farther than to the opinion that it is, on the whole, desirable to promote acquaintance with the writings of this great Saint, and that in an unmutilated form. Any omission would seem to involve an expression of opinion both upon the part excluded and the part retained."

The Editor feels that the right course is: to avoid intruding the expression of his personal view of S. Bernard's writings, as they are one after another translated : to put before readers, to the best of his power, the exact equivalent of what his author wrote : and then to leave it to speak for itself. He can hardly hope that in so great a mass of translation some inaccuracies will not have crept in; but a certain degree of consideration will no doubt be given to one who presents these writings for the first time in English. Letters 127-173 and 175-298 (both inclusive), with their appendant notes, have been translated by the Rev. W. F. Cobb, B.A., T.C.D. All the rest, with the Prefaces, Chronology, and Notes, by the Editor, and he is also responsible for the whole. Notes which he has added are distinguished by the letter [E.], or by [Trans.].

The references to Scripture have been made accordant with the Authorized Version, and the wording of that Version has been generally adhered to. But S. Bernard, of course, quotes the Vulgate; and the Vulgate has many renderings peculiar to itself, upon which, not unfrequently, he founds his exposition or his argument, which would be deprived of much of its appropriateness, or even rendered altogether meaningless, by the substitution of other words in the quotation. When this is the case, a translation of the text of the Vulgate is given, distinguished by the note (VULG.).

Vols. I. and II. are occupied mostly with the General Introduction and the Letters, which it seemed imperative to give first. But the characteristic excellences of S. Bernard's writings will be put fairly before the reader in Vols. III. and IV., which will contain a mass of S. Bernard's Sermons for the Christian year, and will, it is hoped, be issued at the end of 1889.

SOLI DEO GLORIA.

SAMUEL J. EALES.

GENERAL PREFACE

OF DOM JOHN MABILLON

To his Second Edition of the

WORKS OF S. BERNARD.

I. After I had given the first-fruits of my studies to the works of S. Bernard, I never so far put out of my mind that first edition of them as to cease to think of completing, of perfecting, and if I saw the necessity, of entirely recasting it. Since I was at that time very young, and an unskilful beginner, when I set my hand to that first task, I did not think the work so perfect and correct in all respects, as that with longer experience and greater literary skill, I should not be able to find many passages in Bernard of which the text might be better established, and the meaning made clearer by more laborious notes. Wherefore, although in course of time, the direction of my studies had taken me far away from that great Doctor, yet my memory of the holy man and my affection for him remained so great, that whenever in reading and studying other authors, anything came before me which might later on be of use to me for settling the text of his works, or illustrating it, I carefully made note of it, and laid it aside in readiness for the preparation, in due time, of a second edition. During a long period my other labours altogether absorbed my attention so as to hinder my occupying myself with such a task ; but at length the taste for other literary occupations weakened, and in these times of continual wars, grew cold, and I was left with my S. Bernard only on my hands, as the occupation of that leisure which advancing age afforded, as it had been of the first years of my manhood. Gladly then,

by the indulgence of my Superiors, did I devote this leisure
to throwing fresh light upon an author who so well deserves
his high repute ; and I cannot refrain from saying that my
coadjutors, and I myself, have devoted all our care and
diligence to make this edition, not so much a reissue of the
former, as an entirely new, and as far as we could make it,
a perfected edition.

II. There will, perhaps, be some who disapprove of these
repeated editions, and blame them as being of more inconvenience than advantage in study.   Nor do I deny that it
would be very desirable that authors should, in the very
first edition, be presented in as near an approach to perfection as is possible to be attained.   But those who are
acquainted with that kind of labour are not ignorant of the
difficulty, not to say the absolute impossibility, of succeeding
in editing perfectly an author whose works are contained in
so great a number of ancient copies, scattered in places far
removed from each other, and presenting among themselves
so great a number of differences.   So that after much and
long labour in getting together a great number of copies,
and not only of complete volumes, but of leaves scattered
here and there, there is sometimes need of an Ædipus as
an interpreter to determine the text of the author in the
midst of a crowd of variant readings, to correct passages
which had been badly treated, to throw light upon obscuri-
ties, and to distinguish between works which are authentic
and others which are not.   To succeed in all these objects,
and to produce at the first attempt a perfect work, there
will be need of a genius and a degree of good fortune,
which I am far from possessing, nor do I know whether
anyone could claim to have it.   However that may be, I
prefer to ask pardon for the fault of rashness (if the fact be
so) in attempting my first edition, than either to increase
my fault by making excuses, or to leave my former edition
imperfect.   This is why I have thought it my duty to

undertake a new and more correct one, executed with
greater care. I have, then, collated anew the text of the
holy Doctor with the most ancient copies that I could
procure; and lastly, have bound myself with my companions once more to the wearisome labours of the printing
office, being cheered by an assured confidence that those
who are wise will welcome not ungratefully my plan and my
new labours, especially when they shall know the reasons
which have prompted the undertaking of this new edition,
and have understood fully the advantages which, as I hope,
it will offer.

§ I. OF THE DIFFERENT EDITIONS OF THE WORKS OF
    S. BERNARD: THE CAUSES, REASONS, ADVANTAGES,
    AND USEFULNESS OF THIS NEW EDITION.

III. In the first place, nothing shows more the value and
the merit of the works of S. Bernard, than the number of
editions which have appeared of them, both before and after
the invention of printing. The number of these is a proof
how eagerly the works of Bernard were procured by many
persons, and how much they were read and admired by all;
nor is this to be wondered at; for in his writings shines
forth an intellect endued with nobility, power, and elevation, united with gentleness, urbanity, and virtue. Eloquence is natural to him, an eloquence unpretending and
unforced, though not without ornament. His style is
nervous, his discourse vigorous, his language appropriate,
his thoughts elevated, his sentiments pious, his humour not
laboured, his whole discourse breathing of God and heavenly
things. The fire of his zeal burns not to consume, but to inflame with itself. He makes the point of his weapon felt, and
pierces, not to irritate but to move to action. He criticizes,
he blames, but so as to attract, not to excite antipathy.
He accuses, he threatens, he terrifies, but always in love,
never in anger. He soothes, but does not flatter; he

praises, but without extravagance. He urges, but with
kindness; he reproves, without being offensive; he charms,
he pleases, and he delights. His discourse, says Sixtus of
Sienna, is everywhere sweet, and yet fiery; it so delights and,
at the same time, inflames, that honey and milk seem to flow
together from his persuasive tongue, while jets of fire and
flame burst from his heart of fire. As for his knowledge, it
was far beyond the common, and was fed with the sap and
the very words of the Holy Scripture; and he so took into
his heart the sayings of the Fathers as to make them entirely
his own. He writes with such originality of Divine things,
of grace and free-will, of the office and of the proper
character of Bishops, of clerks, of monks, or of lay people,
that his teaching shows him to be, as it were, a fountain,
not a river or canal.[1]   Can we wonder if a man so gifted is
appreciated and his works sought out, read, and studied by
all the world ?   If editions of them without number appear,
and if learned and experienced men employ their labour
to augment, illustrate, and restore them to their original
integrity ?   If Rome herself, lady and mistress of the world,
which once received with veneration the instructions and
even the reprimands of Bernard; if Rome, I say, herself
suffered the Books *de Consideratione,* which were first presented to Eugenius III., which Nicolas V. caused to be
copied out with the greatest care, at length to be published from the Papal Press under Clement VIII., and
would have published the entire works of Bernard if Gerard
Voss had been willing to undertake to edit them ?   What
is less to be wondered at after this, is that in the capital of
France, of which Bernard is one of the greatest lights, he
has deservedly received the honour of the Royal Press.

IV. There are, however, other causes, some of them
proper and even necessary, why so many editions and col-
lations of the works of Bernard have been made. One,

---

[1] Which borrows its stream from elsewhere.—[E.]

and, indeed, the chief is, that the writings of the holy Doctor have been very widely scattered in various and very numerous MSS., of which not all could possibly find place in a first edition. These are brought to the light one after the other as fast as they fall into the hands or come to the knowledge of scholars.

The first edition appears to have been that which Peter Schœffer issued at Mayence in 1475 ; it contained Sermons *de Tempore*, those *de Sanctis*, also those *de Diversis*, and the Book *ad Milites Templi*, with some others, rightly attributed to Bernard.

About the same time appeared at Rouen, without any date, three Treatises of the blessed Father, viz., the Books *de Consideratione*, the *Apologia* to Abbot William, and the Book *de Præcepto et Dispensatione*.

In 1481 appeared at Brussels an edition, without name of editor or printer, which contained the Sermons *de Tempore* and *de Sanctis*, and certain of the Letters then published for the first time.

In 1494, at Paris, an edition containing three hundred and ten Letters, with the Sermons *in Cantica*, edited and corrected by Magister Rouald, Doctor in Theology.

The edition of Spires appeared in 1501. Two years later appeared that of Venice, but without the Letters, and already occupied to the extent of almost half by apocryphal writings and works of other authors.

Possevin places that of Brescia in the year 1495 ; it contained the Homilies on the *Missus est*, and some other Treatises.

The first edition of S. Bernard containing almost all his collected works is that of Paris, in 1508, called the *Seraphic* edition ; and is said at the commencement to comprise the works of S. Bernard the Doctor, mellifluous and devoted, compared then for the first time, and with the greatest care, with the originals in the library of Clairvaux, and arranged into a single volume by the care and industry of Magister John Bocard, and at the cost of John Lepetit, sworn librarian of the University of Paris.

Six years later, in 1515, Jodocus Clictoveus, of Nieuport, revised the preceding edition and republished it at Lyons, the printer being a German, John Klein, adding to it the Sermons *in Cantica* of Gilbert of Hoyland ; it was then many times reprinted both at Paris and at Lyons. In 1520 appeared another edition at Lyons by two monks of Clairvaux, Lambert Deschamps and Laurence of Dantzig, much more correct than all the others.

After these appeared many other editions, which I pass over without notice to come to that which Francis Comestor, of Arnay-le-Duc, a fellow of the College of the Sorbonne, undertook, to contain all the works of the holy Doctor, with an Epistle Dedicatory to Louis de Rie, Bishop of Geneva, in which he says that, in examining the ancient books, in which the library of the College of the Sorbonne was then very rich, he had happened upon an Appendix to the Book *de Diligendo Deo,* which was not found in any preceding edition, and afterwards upon a Treatise *de Amore Dei ac Dignitate Amoris ;* he printed these books with the works of S. Bernard, at the office of the Veuve Claude Chevallon in 1547.

This edition was reprinted many times, which, however, did not prevent Antoine Marcellin from publishing another at Bâle in 1552, which was printed by John Hervage. He prepared it, he says, with the greatest care, after consulting very ancient copies, and examined the whole works afresh and gave them in a different order, so that the Sermons were put in the first place, the Letters followed, then the Treatises, and lastly the writings attributed to S. Bernard, with some by other authors.

Before the edition of which we have just spoken, one appeared at Venice, of which mention is made by John

Guillot, of Champagne, in the preface he wrote for the edition of Nivelles, published at Paris in 1572, and in which he speaks of a collation of the various texts undertaken by the theologians of the Faculty of Paris, who corrected the latest editions as well according to their own knowledge as with the help of all the MSS. they could draw from the various libraries of France. So that, says Guillot, to attempt to correct again after so many scholars, and those of such mark, would be to try to cure a man already quite well, which did not all the same prevent his declaring that he had made many important corrections. He divided, also, into chapters, with analytic titles, the Books *de Consideratione,* addressed to Pope Eugenius, and the Book *de Præcepto et Dispensatione,* the text of which Henry Cuyck, of Guttenberg, had corrected by collation with seven MS. copies. He takes great care, also, to separate the authentic works of S. Bernard from those which are spurious, and to arrange the former in a more reasonable and convenient order. Nevertheless, Guillot leaves among the genuine works some spurious, either already included, or added for the first time; also Flowers collected from the works of S. Bernard.

But six years previously, in 1566, had appeared at Paris, the publishers being William Merlin and Sebastian de Nivelles, another edition; the Letter from the same Francis Comestor, who was lately mentioned with praise, to the Bishop of Geneva, being prefixed. It was enlarged by an *Appendix Hervagiana* published at Bâle by the successors of John Hervage, under the care of James Pamelius, of Bruges, who published also sixteen brief *Sermons* by S. Bernard, the *Parable concerning Christ and the Church,* a book of *Soliloquies,* and some other writings attributed to Bernard.

The same year Louis le Mire, of Rosay, caused to be printed at Paris, by Charlotte Guillard, another *Appendix* which he had received from Francis Comestor.

I pass over a great many other editions which appeared during this epoch. Indeed, scarcely a year passed without its being signalized by the appearance of one. The finest of all is that which appeared in 1586 under the sign of the *Ship*, with a Letter Dedicatory from John Guillot, to the Reverend Father Guy de Chartres, Abbot of Clairvaux, and a preface from the same to the reader.

In 1575 Hubert Lescot, Regular Canon, made a translation into French of the greater number of the Sermons and Treatises of S. Bernard, but without the Letters. These latter were added in 1622, having been translated by Philip le Bel, Doctor of the Faculty of Paris, according to what is stated in the latest version by the Reverend Father Gabriel, de S. Malachi des Feuillants.[1]

V. As for the editions of S. Bernard which have appeared in our age, it would almost be a never-ending task to enumerate them, nor is it at all necessary. Two only I am glad to note, that of Edmund Tiraquellius, a monk of Cîteaux, in the year 1601, the other of Jean Picard in 1609, with notes, some additional Letters, and an Epistle Dedicatory of Tiraquellius to R. P. Edmund de la Croix, Abbot of Cîteaux, and also a Letter and Preface of Guillot. This edition of Picard appeared also in the same year at Antwerp, printed by John Keerberg, and after that was reprinted many times; until, in 1641, appeared the best and most accurate of all, that of James Merlon Horst, a most pious and learned man. That edition threw all others into the shade, and was reprinted frequently.

VI. It will be well to say a few words respecting the mode in which this worthy man has prepared his edition. In the first place he expresses his wonder that since of all the Fathers of the Church there is none whose works are more frequently read than Bernard, he should be at the

---

[1] This is a reformed Cistercian Order founded by Jean de la Barrière, Abbot of Feuillans, with the permission of Gregory XIII. The habit is white.—[E.]

same time that one of whom the editions had been up to
that time most neglected, so that they seemed to become
worse and more defective the more they were multiplied,
as if that Father either did not need any care at all, or
was unworthy of it. He declares that this was the cause
which had moved him to set his hand to cure this evil. He
had submitted the whole of the works to exact and severe
criticism, and divided them into six volumes, of which the
first contained the *Letters;* the second the Sermons *de
Tempore* and *de Sanctis;* the third the Sermons *in Cantica;*
the fourth various *Treatises;* the fifth those writings which
are not by S. Bernard; and the sixth, those of the two
disciples of the Holy Doctor, Gilbert and Guerric. It is he,
also, who divided the Treatises into chapters and sections,
and has prefixed analytical summaries to each Letter and
Treatise. He spared neither labour nor expense to procure
all the editions of S. Bernard which he could find in the
libraries of different countries, although he was not successful in obtaining some of the works of that Father, of
which Possevin and others have given a list. Besides
these a great many introductions are added, the life of S.
Bernard in seven books, with various Elogia of the Saint,
and a chronology. Finally, he has inserted lengthy Notes,
besides those shorter ones which are inserted in the margin
throughout the work, with very full Indexes of the places of
Scripture, of subjects, and of the names mentioned by S.
Bernard. The reader cannot help recognizing the immense
labour with which he has endeavoured to make his edition
absolutely accurate. Unfortunately the work of the printer
has not altogether corresponded to his wishes. This learned
man was preparing an edition more complete and more
careful still when he died, on the 20th April, 1644.

VII. Nevertheless it cannot be questioned that Horst
was happily enabled to bring that first edition to a degree
of perfection as complete as was possible to a man who,

though learned, diligent, and most studious of his author,
was working alone: so that his edition was received with
both hands (as the saying is), approved and very often
reprinted in various countries and places.   But our illustrious Claude Cantelou, having collated, at the order of our
superiors, the text of Horst with many MSS. in France,
discovered in his work certain faults which required to be
corrected by the aid of our Codices, and he published the
corrected text of the Sermons *de Tempore* and *de Sanctis*
in a new form. He was preparing with the same care to
publish the rest of the works of S. Bernard, when he died,
and left his work for me to continue.   I was then a young
man ; a novice and inexperienced in the literary art, and it
would never have occurred to me to put my labour and knowledge into comparison with those of the learned Horst, if
our Superior General, the Reverend Abbot Bernard Aude-
bert, of pious memory, had not overcome my scruples and
my reluctance to continue the work of Cantelou after his
death.   I obeyed, however, though unwillingly, and with
the useful and valuable help of James Lannoy, who put at
my disposal all the originals of S. Bernard's works which
existed in the library of Cîteaux, of which he was abbot, I
succeeded at length in producing an edition in larger
and also in smaller size of S. Bernard, as perfect—I do
not say as it might and ought to have been, but as good
as my young inexperience was able to make it, or rather
as the selfishness of the printer, who showed himself
more careful to serve his own interests than those of
the public, would allow it to be.

VIII. But with time and experience in that kind of labour,
I accumulated, day by day, more materials which would be
of use for another and much improved edition of Bernard,
and I continued, as I have said, diligently to collect these, in
order that when time and leisure should permit, I might
make such an edition more correct, more elegant, and more

perfect. But when I set myself to the work I found myself confronted by another difficulty, arising from the unhappy state of the laws which ruled the press, and from which I extricated myself at last in any way I could, as if taking refuge in any harbour attainable from a storm, and in a manner which there is no need to detail here.

IX. Although it is entirely foreign to my habit and to my intention to extol my own work, yet it is proper here to show, in the first place, in what respects this latest edition differs, as well from that of Horst as from my former one. I have, first, had the advantage of being able to collate a number of ancient MSS. which I had not seen at the time of my former edition, both those which I consulted and studied in the provinces that I traversed, and in the Colbertine Library, where Stephen Baluze, a man born to help and develop learned pursuits, had assembled a great many copies since my first edition had appeared. I have thus been able out of the various readings to select and restore to the text those which seemed most to accord with the manner and sentiments of Bernard, which pursuit requires an extensive acquaintance with old books, a tact acquired by habitude only, and a riper judgment than the general run of educated persons suppose, who regard us as collectors of spiders' webs when they see the importance that we attach to those things which they regard as trifles; but, let that class of men think what they please respecting me; I do not desire the applause of men for my work, but to render service to the Church and to the literary fraternity.

X. Nor have I employed the resources of criticism only in restoring the text, but also in separating the general writings of Bernard from the suppositious and spurious writings which had made their way among the genuine, as well in the edition of Horst as in my former one. Thus I have expunged two Letters of Bernard Brito which Horst had placed among those of our Bernard; I have rejected four or five Sermons from those *de Tempore* and *de Sanctis ;* I have rejected also a Book of Declamations, and some others which were shown by clear signs and arguments not to be from the pen of Bernard.

XI. For that work of criticism I have found of great assistance, not only the writers of the Lives of S. Bernard, and chiefly Geoffrey, which contain a list of the principal works of the holy Doctor, but also the old MSS., the citations of ancient authors, and, most of all, the ancient Collection from the writings of Bernard, which is called *Book of Flowers, Florilegium* and *Bernardinus,* first edited at Paris in 1503. It is much to be preferred to another collection which was made in 1571 by a Canon Regular named Hubert Scutépuits, and intruded by John Picard into his edition of Bernard. That first Collection is far more ancient, and an old MS. copy at Cîteaux has supplied to us the name of the author, for we find in it these words, with an inscription following :—" Here begins a prologue of Bernardinus, which Dom Willermus, monk of S. Martin of Tournay, has extracted and compiled from the books and sayings of the holy Bernard, Abbot of Clairvaux." That prologue begins thus :—" As I was not greatly occupied in any pursuit," etc., as in the editions in which the name of the author is wanting ; but it is easily inferred that he must have lived in the thirteenth century, from the age of the MSS. in which this Collection is found. The Collector does, indeed, praise certain Treatises as being Bernard's, which are not his, viz., the Letter to the Brethren of Mont Dieu, Meditations, and Book of Declamations ; but, nevertheless, his authority is of considerable weight, especially in recognizing the Sermons of Bernard. Thus every time that a doubt arises on any passage of his writings, as in the Sermons *de Diversis,* it seemed advisable to note these citations out of Bernardinus. Nor is it wonderful that both the Letter to the Brethren of Mont

Dieu, the Declamations, and the Meditations are brought
forward in that Collection under the name of Bernard, since
S. Bonaventure makes the same mistake as to that much-
praised epistle, and the Books of Declamations and Meditations appear to be centos out of the writings of Bernard, as
I shall point out in the proper places.

XII. Besides criticism of the books, I have made some
changes in Horst's arrangement, both of the volumes and
of the treatises. He had placed the Sermons *de Tempore*
and *de Sanctis* after the *Letters ;* then came the Sermons
in Cantica and, lastly, the *Opuscula* and the *Treatises.* It
appeared to me better that the *Opuscula* and the *Treatises*
should follow the *Letters,* since the former are, for the
most part, written in the form of letters, or have even been
transferred out of that class to rank among the latter.
From this order it results that the Sermons *de Tempore*
and *de Sanctis* fall into the third place, and those *in Cantica*
into the fourth. In the fifth place I have added the
Sermons of Gilbert on the same subject, being a continuation of those of Bernard. As to the fifth and sixth volumes,
I will speak more at length in the Preface to Vol. v. or
even in those to the earlier volumes.

XIII. In order that all the genuine works of Bernard
might be contained in one volume, I have placed at the end
of Tome vi. or Vol. ii. the Books of his Life and Actions,
which Horst had put at the beginning of his first volume,
so that neither should the allied works of Bernard be
separated from each other, nor the size of the volumes be
made very unequal. At the end of the first and of the
second volume I have placed very full indexes, the former.
of the genuine works of Bernard, the latter of those not by
him.

XIV. The more lengthy notes and observations with
which the Letters and other works of S. Bernard had been
enriched by Horst, or formerly by myself, have been thrown

together at the end of each Tome. To the first Tome a short *Chronology* is prefixed, which may serve to throw light upon the notes and provide a solid framework into which they may be fitted. Such is the character of the improvements that I have introduced into this new edition of Bernard.

XV. To come in particular to the examination of Tome i., which contains the Letters of Bernard, I have devoted no little labour to correcting, arranging, illustrating, and adding to them.

For corrections I have consulted the MSS. in various libraries; of the Vatican, of the Colbertine, those of S. Peter at Ghent, and of Orval in Belgium; besides those which I used in my former edition. From one MS. at Corbey I have restored certain inscriptions of some importance. By the aid of that MS., and of two others in the Colbertine of good rank, bearing the numbers of 1410 and 2476, and containing the *Opuscula* of S. Bernard, with which I have collated the same *Opuscula*, I have added for each Letter marginal notes, which briefly explain any historical facts referred to.

XVI. Respecting the order of the Letters, I have long hesitated whether to retain the received order or to adopt a new one. There were reasons for each course. The antiquity of the existing order was a reason for retaining it, for it appears to have been adopted while Bernard was still living, at least as far as the first 310 Letters, of which the last is addressed to Arnold, Abbot of Bonneval; while as for the others, which were scattered here and there, it was not until later that they were united to the great body of Letters; nor all at once, but only at intervals, as they came to the knowledge of the editors or collectors. Then one other reason was in favour of the ancient order, viz., that in it the order of time was, on the whole, preserved; whereas it was to be feared that more inconvenience than usefulness would follow any change of the received order, because of the numerous citations of the Letters numbered on that ancient method, without mentioning the fixed and solemn order of the ancient copies. What, on the contrary, strongly made for the opposite course was the intolerable confusion of certain Letters which were arranged at a considerable distance before those to which they were the replies. From this results the farther inconvenience that the parts of a subject are by this faulty arrangement detached from each other. In these difficulties it seemed best, on the whole, to take a middle way, and while retaining the received order for the first 310 Letters, to arrange the re- mainder in order of time, noting in the margin the number by which each had previously been marked. When in con- sequence of this new arrangement it happens that a Letter ought to follow some other, we warn the reader to defer it until the other has been first read; in that manner we have both respected the old order, and avoided the confusion that a new one would have caused.

We have said that the old order, in which we read the Letters of S. Bernard, seems to have been established even in the lifetime of their author; we find the proof of this in William, formerly Abbot of S. Thierry, who died before Bernard. For he, in the first book of his Life of the Holy Doctor, evidently written during the life of Bernard, reports that his Letter to his relative Robert (n. 50), which had not been wetted in the midst of a shower of rain, "was not unjustly placed first by his brethren in the volume of his Letters because of so great a miracle." The author of the third Life, who is no other, as we think, than Geoffrey, his secretary, relates that that arrangement was made by him.

XVII. The order of the Letters is, nevertheless, not quite uniform in all the old copies, although in most of them there is no great difference up to Letter 310. There are not quite so many as this in some copies, from which we gather that there were, not one collection of the Letters only, but many. In the three Vatican MSS. these Letters are included. Of these the finest, No. 662, contains 296, in nearly the same order as that of the editions; the last of these is the Letter addressed to the Irish Brethren on the death of the blessed Malachi. In another MS., No. 664, there is the same order in 282 Letters; of which the last is that to Hugh, Knight of the Temple. The third, No. 663, contains 240 Letters, arranged in an order entirely different; so that the first of that collection, addressed to Cardinal Haimeric, is the 313th in previous editions, and the last, addressed to Pope Eugenius on the subject of the Bishop of Autun, is the 275th. In all the other MSS. the order is pretty nearly the same as in the printed collections, with the exception of the MS. at S. Peter of Ghent, in which the collection is divided into three parts, the first containing 100 Letters, the second 164, the third 76; in which the last is from John of *Casa Mario* to Bernard, and that preceding it, from Bernard to Rorgon of Abbeville. And perhaps in no other MS. are more Letters of Bernard collected than in that of Ghent; and Willermus, the monk of Tournay, must have had this MS., or one similar to it, under his eyes in writing his *Bernardinus,* which was just now praised, since he quotes the Letters as of the first, second, or third part. But in the MS. at Clairvaux of the Cistercian Order there are 307 Letters, and in that at Orval 306; each of these having in the last place the Letter to Abbot Arnold, which was certainly the last which Bernard wrote. It was without doubt the former of these two collections that John of Salisbury (Letter 96) begged Peter de Celles to send to him, as he thanks him "for the Letters of the blessed Bernard" in the following one.

XVIII. To speak now of the Letters added in this edition (which are in the last place to be treated of), we ought to premise that in the first edition of the Letters of Bernard which appeared at Brussels in 1481 and at Paris in 1494, there were only 310 Letters, of which the antepenultimate is hat to Arnold, Abbot of Chartres, the penultimate to the Irish Brethren on the death of the holy Bishop Malachi, and the last to Guy, Abbot of Moustier-Ramey. But the edition of 1520, executed by two monks of Clairvaux, as we have said above, contained in all 351 Letters, of which the last is addressed to the novice Hugh, who was afterwards Abbot of Bonneval. The Letter to Arnold is the 310th, and that to the Irish the 311th. The reason for this difference is that in the former edition two Letters are wanting, viz., the 84th, which is the second to Simon, Abbot of S. Nicholas, and the 147th, to Peter, Abbot of Cluny. Jodocus Clictoveus, in his edition of 1515 and those following, has only 350 Letters in all; he has omitted that to the novice Hugh, which was inserted by Antonio Marcellino into the edition of Bâle of 1552, and in all those which followed up to that of John Picard. This last editor added seventeen new Letters to those already known, but without arranging them in order. Two of these Letters are placed at the head of those which he drew from the MS. of Pithon; the others were not published till long after. He had found them in his library at S. Victor.

Horst omitted certain Letters which had been wrongly included, and so reduced the number to 366; to which he added two spurious Letters of Bernard de Brito, seventeen genuine from certain English MSS., and one of the Abbot Fastred to finish his volume, which brought the number to 386.

I had myself included eleven new Letters in my first edition, and in this the number has risen to 482. This includes not only the twenty-eight Letters of Bernard recently discovered in Germany, and added in the form of an Appendix to an edition of Horst published at Cologne, but also some other Letters of the Saint found elsewhere, and some Letters addressed to him, or written concerning him, which seemed necessary for full understanding of those which he himself wrote.

I have divided all these Letters into three parts, of which the first comprises the 310 former Letters retaining their ancient and common order; the second to the 454th comprises the rest of the genuine epistles of Bernard; the third the doubtful, the spurious, and those written by others. These are the chief matters which have occupied my attention in editing the first Tome; other things the diligent Reader will easily observe.

XIX. I may state here that the Works of Bernard, which Horst complained were lying hidden in various libraries, are not from the pen of the Saint; a fact which I have been able to ascertain. Thus the book on the Hexæmeron is by Arnold, Abbot of Bonneval in the Chartrain; the Commentary on the Penitential Psalms by Innocent III.; the Exposition of the Psalm *Afferte* (Ps. xxix) by Richard of S. Victor; another upon Ps. l. by Urban II. A Commentary on the Epistles of S. Paul is, according to Possevin, by Bernard of Clavone, an Augustine monk. A Commentary on the Apocalypse has been wrongly attributed by Caramuel to Bernard, which Commentary, being placed in a MS. next following some works of Bernard, under the title of " cujusdam " (of a certain author), Caramuel read " ejusdem " (of the same author), and so ascribed it to Bernard, like the preceding. I am convinced that with the exception of certain Letters which have not been yet brought to light, there remain no important works of Bernard unpublished. These are :—A Letter to Hugh, Abbot of Pontigny, as appears from the first paragraph of Letter 33, addressed to the same Abbot; two to Innocent II. against Peter of Besançon, from Letter 195; one to the same on behalf of Peter of Pisa, from the end of Letter 213. We learn also from the commencement of Letter 253 that he had addressed

many Letters to the same Pontiff on behalf of the introduction of Premonstratensian monks into the Monastery of S.
Paul at Verdun. There is also in Letter 203, to Atto,
reference made to a Letter to Ansellus, sub-deacon of
Troyes; in the beginning of Letter 223, to Joscelin, to an
apologetic Letter to Suger; in Letter 233, to the same, to
two Letters to John de Buzay; in the end of Letter 284 to
Pope Eugenius, to another addressed to the same Pope in
favour of the Bishop of Claremont. The monk Hermann
of Tournay speaks also of a Letter which Bernard wrote to
Pope Eugenius on behalf of a monastery at Tournay (No.
115).[1] The Letter formerly numbered 358, now 376, makes
mention of an encyclical Letter against duels, addressed to
the Archbishops of Rheims and Sens, the Bishops of
Soissons and Autun, and the Counts Theobald and Raoul.
Furthermore, Peter the Venerable repeats, in his Letter numbered 388 among those of Bernard, some words of a Letter
which the holy Doctor had written on behalf of a certain
English abbot, " as if judgment were subverted," etc., which
I do not remember to have read in any of Bernard's Letters.

XX. Ordericus Vitalis also mentions a Letter of Bernard
to Natalis, Abbot of Rebais, on behalf of the monks of
Utica, whose abbot, named Guarin, was begging for the
relics of S. Evroult from Abbot Natalis :—" Geoffrey declared that he had the intention of going to Clairvaux, and
asked him to go thither with him, to which he consented
willingly. They came them both together to Clairvaux
with all their attendants. They were received hospitably by
the brothers of that community, who strictly observe the
Rule of S. Benedict. They asked to see Dom Bernard,
the Abbot of that monastery, and having spoken with him
and asked of him many questions, they found in him great
wisdom. He replied to all their questions, treated
eloquently of the Holy Scriptures, and satisfied all their

[1] *Spicileg.* Tom. ii. p. 483.

wishes. When he heard of the cause of the Religious of Utica, he kindly came to the aid of Abbot Guarin, and wrote a persuasive Letter to the community of Rebais. . . . Abbot Guarin presented this Letter of the venerable Bernard to these Religious, who received it with pleasure, and willingly determined to comply with the request made." Thus writes Ordericus in his sixth book.

XXI. Furthermore, Ademar of Angoulême says in his *Chronicle,* when treating of the origin of the Carthusians: —" This Order, as Bernard bears witness, holds the first place among ecclesiastical Orders, not on account of its antiquity, but by the power of its sanctity. Wherefore he calls it the most beautiful column of the Church," which words are not found in any of the published works of S. Bernard.

XXII. Finally, John Picard cites from John de Manburg in his treatise *Concerning the manner of life of Regular Canons,* a letter addressed by Bernard to Fulk, from which Manburg has quoted these words :—" Instead of wearing black or grey furs round the neck, they wear furs coloured purple like women." If these words were quoted from any Letter of Bernard it has not been yet published, but in the second Letter from Bernard to Fulk, par. 11, there are to be found expressions similar in sense, although not exactly alike in words. It is the same in the passage which Picard cites also from Manburg as being still inedited. It is contained in substance in the *de Consideratione,* B. iv. n. 12, concerning the qualities requisite for a Cardinal.

This is all that it seems necessary or interesting to say by way of preface to this new edition of the Letters of S. Bernard.

§ II. Of the Sanctity and Learning of Bernard, and his Authority in the Church.

XXIII. Before proceeding farther it will be well to consider the two titles which are commonly bestowed upon

Bernard, viz., that he is called *Doctor Mellifluus* (the sweet-tongued or honied-worded Doctor), and the *Last of the Fathers*, though not unequal to the first. The title of *Doctor* has been yielded by the Church to those whose teaching has been approved by its general voice, particularly when that teaching is united with sanctity of life. She gives the name of *Fathers* to those whom their sanctity, their teaching, and at the same time their antiquity, unite to distinguish; teaching, I mean, of the Holy Scripture and of the tradition of the Church, rather than of philosophical reasonings.

Therefore holy men illustrious by their teaching may be called Doctors immediately after their death, but the name of Fathers is reserved for those whom a certain antiquity long since acknowledged renders venerable, at the same time that they are distinguished by a method of treating the subjects on which they have touched, quite different from the method of philosophical deduction. Each of these titles of honour Bernard has deservedly obtained.

As for the first, it was bestowed upon him by Pope Alexander III., even in the very Mass of his canonization, when he read the Gospel reserved exclusively for the holy Doctors, and commencing by these words : " *Ye are the salt of the earth,*" etc. (S. Matt. v. 13). Pope Innocent III. confirmed that title of honour in eloquent words in the Collect which he composed for the Festival of S. Bernard, and in which he is called " The Blessed Abbot Bernard and Illustrious Doctor."[1]

The appellative of *Mellifluus* (whose words are sweet as honey) is more recent, and the holy Doctor was first called by it by Theophilus Reynauld in a singular little book which is entitled the " Gallic Bee " (*Apis Gallicana*). The first editors of his works who gave him that title on the first page of their volumes are—first, the editor of the

---

[1] *Doctor Egregius.*

edition of Lyons in 1508, then Jodocus Clictoveus in 1515,
and also the two monks of Clairvaux, whom I have already
highly praised ; and Horst restored the use of the same
name after it had fallen into neglect; but among all his
praises the very best is this : That merely his name at the
head of his works is a title sufficient to recommend them.
There can be no praise beyond that for an author ; but if
there is any other epithet that befits Bernard, it is surely
this of θεοδίδακτος (taught of God), bestowed upon him by
other authors; since the knowledge with which he was
endued seems to have been not so much acquired by
human powers as infused into him from above.

XXIV. That he was, notwithstanding, wanting neither in
labour nor industry in reading and studying both sacred and
profane authors is clear from the manner in which he sometimes quotes them. Without doubt, he had learned and
studied profane authors in his youth and when he was still
in the world ; and these would sometimes come back to his
memory in his old age. As to theological subjects, he
studied them with care and industry when he became a
monk. How extensive and profound his knowledge of them
was may be gathered, in the first place, from two of his
Sermons *in Cantica,* the 80th and 81st, where he discourses
in terms so just and so elevated upon the image of God, in
the word and in the soul, and on the homogeneity of the
Divine Nature, that no one before or after him has sur-
passed them. A similar remark must be made upon his
Letter (190) to Pope Innocent, in which he sets forth
wonderfully the satisfaction which Christ has obtained for
us by His suffering ; and his knowledge of the Canons, as
shown in those famous Books *de Consideratione,* is incomparable. Hence is confirmed that saying of Leo the Great :
" The true love of that which is just contains within itself
both the precepts of Apostles and the authority of Canons."
Finally, the holy Doctor was versed in the Holy Scriptures,

by continual perusal of them, to such a degree, and his
writings show so plainly everywhere his use of that knowledge, that, to employ the words of Sixtus of Sienna, they
may be called truly *centos* from the sacred volumes, so
studded are they everywhere with phrases drawn from the
Old and New Testament as to form a jewelled mosaic, so
skilfully and aptly introduced, that they might be thought
to be suggested by the subject. And if it is not becoming
to make use of the Holy Scripture in that way at all times,
and upon every subject, yet it can hardly be disapproved
when treating of sacred things. Upon this point may be
adduced the words of the Apostle Peter: *If any man speak
let him speak as the oracles of God* (1 S. Peter iv. 11). It
may be said, indeed, that Bernard sometimes employs
various texts of Scripture in a sense unfounded and far
from literal, so that he seems rather to play upon the words
quoted, than to expound their real sense; but it is easy to
reply that, there being in Scripture manifold senses, the holy
man believed that he might choose that sense which seemed
to him proper to edification, especially when he was not
treating of any doctrine of the faith, but only proposed to
himself to enlarge upon some pious thought, and thereby
to attract the attention and delight of his hearers.

XXV. That S. Bernard was not only versed in Holy
Scripture, but also had a knowledge of the writings of the
holy Fathers, as extensive as his numerous occupations had
permitted him to obtain, no one will doubt who has
diligently perused his writings. He names them from time
to time, and praises their sayings; and their teaching is
to be found throughout all his works. Thus, when he says
that he has only had "the oaks and beeches of the forest
for masters" (*Life*, B. i. n. 23), he must be understood to
speak in the sense that he himself suggests to Cardinals in
the fourth Book *de Consideratione*, n. 12, viz., that "in every
matter we ought to count more upon prayer than upon

one's own industry or labour," which Geoffrey has rightly
applied to Bernard in this very matter (*Life*, B. iii. 1). But
how greatly he profited from the reading of the Fathers,
especially from S. Augustine, is shown easily by his Treatise
de Gratia et Libro Arbitrio, which is a kind of learned and
able summary of Augustine's teaching on that subject. He
joins Ambrose to Augustine in his Letter 11, or rather his
Treatise addressed to Hugo of S. Victor ; and he adds that
from these two columns of the Church he will not easily be
drawn away. He praises Athanasius in his tenth Treatise
against Peter Abaelard ; and not unfrequently Gregory the
Great also. Finally, in terminating his Homilies *de Laudibus Virginis,* he acknowledges that he has borrowed many
things from the Fathers. It is a wonderful thing indeed that
the holy man, though suffering under so many complaints
and such weak health, though distracted by so many cares
and duties, not only those belonging to the community (and
these could have been neither few nor light in so numerous
a household of monks as that over which he presided), but
also, and chiefly, public affairs, about which he was consulted, should yet have been able either to read so many
books or to succeed in the composition of works so eloquent
and so learned ; so wonderful indeed that no one can doubt
that, beyond the noble nature and rare intelligence with
which he had been gifted at his birth, a certain assistance of
Divine wisdom must have been bestowed upon him to enable
him to speak, act, teach, and write as he did. Thus Geoffrey
reports that he had " sometimes acknowledged that when in
meditation or prayer he had seemed to see the whole Scripture placed and opened before his eyes " (*Life*, B. iii. n.
7). But he was accustomed to say that he ascertained
better the meaning of the Scriptures " by drinking from
the original fountain itself, than from the streams running
from it, that is, the expositions of the text; yet he used
to peruse pious and orthodox expositors, not with the idea

of preferring his own opinion to theirs, but in order to form his own upon theirs; and following faithfully the track made by them, he too used to quench his thirst at the fountain whence they had drank before him" (*Ibid.* i. 24). This reverence of the holy Doctor towards the ancient Fathers shines forth everywhere in his writings, as in Letter 98, n. 1, Serm. v. *in Cantica,* n. 6, and elsewhere. He had leisure to devote himself to the study of them, during the long continued malady under which he suffered, and which obliged him during the early years of his office of Abbot to withdraw himself from the society of his brethren, and to live as a private person in the monastery. He only did this at first, according to the account of Abbot William, in obedience to the express command of William, Bishop of Chalons, and of the Abbots of his order; but afterwards the progress of the disease made it impossible for him to do otherwise (*Ibid.* i. 33, 40). Abbot William saw him when he was relieved of the management, internal and external, of the monastery, " rejoicing to be able to think of nothing but God and the salvation of his own soul, and enjoying, as it were, the delights of Paradise." Then the holy man discoursed to him of the *Canticles,* as he did at greater length later on. When Bernard had recovered a little health, he devolved a part of the administration of the monastery upon his brother Gerard, which left him sufficient leisure for the study of the Holy Scripture, and in his twenty-first Sermon *in Cantica* he attributes to that leisure all the progress that he had made in his spiritual studies. We learn from Sermon 51, n. 3, on the same subject, that these were his occupations; prayer, reading, composition, meditation, and such like. It was in such pursuits that the blessed Father spent the fifteen years of his life which elapsed from the foundation of Clairvaux to the schism of Peter Leonis, at which period, being brought into connection with great public events and questions of considerable difficulty, he so acquitted himself with regard to them as to excite the admiration with which the whole of Europe, not to say the whole world, afterwards regarded him.

XXVI. It was not without reason, therefore, that Nicholas Lefèvre, a great man and preceptor of Louis the Just, was accustomed to say, as we are told by Francis Balbus in his Life, that while he had the highest admiration for all the Fathers, he especially admired the divine (*divus*) Augustine, whose works he habitually reåd, and among more recent writers the divine Bernard, whom he called the Last of the Fathers, and certainly as there is none of the ancients who went before him who merited better than Bernard the praise of being second to Augustine, so there is none of those who came after him; since in none is there either a sanctity made more illustrious by actions and even by miracles, a doctrine more pure, a severer respect for tradition, an eloquence more splendid in speech and in writing, or finally, an influence more widely diffused or more powerful.   To use the words of William, " What man is there to whose will as well the highest secular authority, as the highest ecclesiastical, deferred, and to whose advice it humbled itself ?   Proud kings, princes, and tyrants, soldiers, and even robbers so fear and éven reverence him, that the saying may seem to have been fulfilled, which we read in the Gospel that the Lord spoke to His disciples : *Behold I give you power to tread upon serpents and scorpions,* etc. (S. Luke x. 19).   But among spiritual persons . . . there is in him an authority of quite a different kind.   For just as it is said by the Prophet concerning those sacred Living Beings, that when there was a Voice from the firmament that was over their heads, *they stood and let down their wings,* so at the present time everywhere in the world, men of spiritual faculty when they hear him speak or teach are silent themselves, and yield the precedence to him, submitting their senses and their intellect to his. One sees a proof of this in his writings, etc." (*Life*, B. i. n. 70). Rightly, therefore, says the Monk Cæsar Heisterbach, that his authority was so great "that the purple-clad Fathers of the Church, the kings and princes of the world, used to speak through the mouth of Bernard alone, as through an oracle recognized by the whole world (*De Miraculis*, B. xiv. c. 17). This estimation in which the holy Doctor was held has continued even to our own day, as is shown by the testimonies of illustrious men concerning him, among whom Bartholomæus à Martyribus, the pious Bishop of Braga, a student and admirer of Bernard, ought to hold no small place.

XXVII. What drew to him, in his life-time, so great authority in the eyes of all, was his extraordinary humility, even in the midst of honours. He himself ranked this virtue higher than any (*De Laudibus Virg.*, Hom. iv. n. 9). This is what Ernald says: "His life is full of things admirable and worthy of praise. Some admire his teaching, others his character, others his miracles, and I," he says, "render honour to all these. But there is something which I place above them all, and to which I render more willing admiration ; it is that being a vessel of election, and boldly upholding the Saviour's name before nations and kings, seeing himself obeyed by all the princes of the world, and the Bishops in every nation listening for his opinion, his advice, by a singular privilege, reverenced by the Roman Church herself; nations and kingdoms being sub-jected to him, as if by a general delegation ; and when his actions and his words were supported even by miracles, which is a thing still more glorious, he was never thrown off his balance, never thought of himself more highly than he ought. On the contrary, he always thought humbly of himself, considered himself not the author, but the in-strument, of mighty works; and when in the universal judgment he was raised above all, he was the lowest of all in his own" (*Life*, B. ii. n. 25). " His heartfelt humility overcame in him the elevation forced upon him, nor was the whole world able to do so much to exalt him, as he to keep himself humble " (*Ibid.*, iii. 22). Nor did such profound sentiments of humility lower him in the opinion of others, but on the contrary raised him the more, and "the more modest and humble he showed himself, the more important were the services he rendered to the people of God in the knowledge of their salvation " (*Ibid.*, iii. n. 8).

XXVIII. To the sanctity of the Father Abbot responded in his sons the sentiments of piety and perfection of life, which redounded to his glory. The entire Roman Court was a witness to this, when it accompanied Pope Innocent to Clairvaux. " The Bishops wept and the Pontiff himself. All wondered at the gravity of demeanour in that community on an occasion so solemn, so happy for them. Their eyes were fixed upon the ground, nor wandered in curiosity around the assembly. It might have been thought that their eyes were closed; they saw no one, although they were themselves seen by all. The Roman[1] saw nothing that was precious in that monastery; no costly furniture met the eye. They saw nothing in the chapel but the bare walls. The only thing that ambition could envy was the characters of the brethren, and this was not a costly treasure for the brethren, since piety is not diminished when it is shared by another" (*Ibid.*, B. ii. 6). It was on these columns that the authority of Bernard was reared, and by these guards that it was protected. " But the sweetness of his character tempered the austerity of his life, and his sanctity preserved his authority, as if he had brought from heaven to make visible among men a marvel of purity more than human, and sought for in the presence of God" (*Life*, B. iii. 21 ; B. i. 28). His sanctity and purity

[1] Pontiff.

were attested by miracles which were so remarkable and famous that his enemies themselves acknowledge them, so numerous and frequent that Bernard himself was struck with wonder, as Geoffrey testifies (*Life*, B. iii. 20).

XXIX. As his influence was so great we cannot wonder that he was able, as William reports, " to revive the ancient religious fervour in the monastic order" (*Life*, B. i. 42), and, according to the narrative of Geoffrey, "to correct the corrupted manners of Catholics, to restrain the violence of schismatics, and to confound the error of heretics " (*Life*, B. iii. 12). With what power he did all these things is shown by the history of his life, by his own writings, and, most of all, by his Letters.

§ III. WITH WHAT SUCCESS BERNARD LABOURED IN REFORMING THE LIVES OF THE CLERGY, THE MONKS, AND THE LAY PEOPLE.

XXX. This holy man grieved over and deplored the morals of his age, which were everywhere corrupted, and particularly those of the ministers of the Church, of whom he brought many to a better life. Such was the influence of his words and of his preaching that he altogether renewed the appearance of the Church and of the clergy, particularly in France, and restored it to its ancient virtue and earnestness. It was to him that the elevation of Eugenius, a very holy man, to the See of Rome was due; and he instructed and animated in him all Roman Pontiffs . to the right and legitimate administration of the duties of their charge by the admirable books which he put forth *de Consideratione*. Among Bishops he recalled Henry of Sens and Stephen of Paris from living as courtiers, to a manner of life worthy of their Episcopal order; many also of his own Religious he caused to be elevated to the Episcopate to serve as an example to other Bishops (*Life*, B. ii. 49). To all of the clerical order he has given salutary warning in his sermon addressed to clerics *de Conver-sione.*

Concerning the Episcopal office and character, Letter 42, to Henry, Bishop of Sens, may first be consulted. It is counted among the Treatises and placed now in Vol. ii. Rightly, therefore, in the History of the *Bishops of Verdun*, is Bernard spoken of as "he on whose counsels'the Church of France, and the Realm of France, too, are firmly founded at the present day" (*Spicileg.*, Vol. ii. p. 311).

XXXI. He had, in speaking, an extraordinary charm, "of which his pen, however elegant it might be, could not repro-duce the warmth and sweetness." God had bestowed upon him the gift of speech, equally learned, pleasing, and persuasive. "He knew how to adapt what he had to say to the need of the hearer, whether consolation was needed or entreaty, exhortation or blame; he knew when and by whom each was required, and this is apparent even now in reading his writings, though they are far from having the same effect as his words had upon those who heard them" (*Life*, iii. 7). If his writings are able to produce such an impression upon the reader, how much greater must his words have done upon those who heard them? It is not wonderful, therefore, that God should have done so many and such great things by his means for the salvation of men of his time.

XXXII. But who could possibly recount all the efforts that he made to resuscitate the ancient fervour of the monastic orders? Some idea of this may be formed by going through his admirable letters and writings upon this subject, his Book *de Præcepto et Dispensatione*, his *Apology* to Abbot William, and various Sermons. In these he encourages monks to retain with care, and to re-establish with zeal, the original institutions of the Fathers of monachism, that is, works of penitence, mortifications, modesty and humility, poverty, contempt of the world, love

of solitude and silence, and zeal for continual advance, upon
which he saw that the whole monastic life turned and
depended. Hence Peter the Venerable calls him, not undeservedly, "the strong and milk-white column, on which
the edifice of the monastic order is supported," and "the
brilliant star, whose glowing and luminous rays give light,
as it were—that is, by his example and his preaching—not
only to monks, but the whole of the Latin Church in his
time" (*Letter* 228, n. 30).

XXXIII. Laurence of Liége, in his *Lives of the Bishops
of Verdun*, compares the Orders of Cîteaux and of Prémontré to the two Cherubim which shadowed the Mercy
Seat ; one of those, that of Cîteaux, under the guidance of
Bernard, that Abbot of holy memory, recalled to the original
rule of Apostolic life the monastic Order which in his time
had almost lapsed. "That Order of Cîteaux," he continues,
"spread, in the space of three years, into as many as two
hundred abbeys of great reputation, merit, and number of
Religious, and began to be diffused even among the
barbarous Sarmatians and the farthest Scythians" (*Spicileg.*,
V. xii. p. 325). So powerful and widespread was the reputation of Bernard for sanctity and that of his disciples !
Hence it came about that Bernard himself was held to be,
as it were, the founder of the Cistercian Order, of which he
was, in fact, the child and scholar. In his time the Cistercian
Order took the name of Clairvaux from his monastery, and
men began afterwards even to call the Order by the name
of S. Bernard, although Innocent VIII. had forbidden that in
his letter of union between the two monasteries of Clairvaux
and Cîteaux. Hence in the letter of Albero, Bishop of
Verdun, cited by Laurence of Liége, of whom we have
spoken above, the abbots of Trois-Fontaines, and of
Caladia are regarded as being of the Order of Clairvaux
(*loc. cit.*, p. 222), and Peter de Celles speaks of "the Order
of Cîteaux or Clairvaux" in B. i. Letter 24. So in a letter

of Samson, Bishop of Rheims, he makes mention more than
once of the Order of Clairvaux (Letter 435). It is true
that by these words, "the Order of Clairvaux," the single
monastery at Clairvaux with those dependent upon it is
intended rather than the whole Order.

XXXIV. It does not seem necessary to explain in this
place how austere and rigorous was the life of the
Religious of Cîteaux or Clairvaux under Bernard, since that
is shown with the greatest exactness in the letters and
writings of Bernard, as well as in his *Life*, especially in
B. i. 5, in which the first inhabitants of Clairvaux are said
to have served God "in poorness of spirit, in hunger and
thirst, in cold and nakedness, and in many watches; frequently they had no food except the leaves of the beech tree
boiled, and bread made of barley, vetches, and millet."
Bernard himself in his Letter to Robert (n. i.) says that the
delicacies of the Monks of Cîteaux were "vegetables, beans,
pottage, and coarse bread with water." Fastred makes
similar statements in his Letter, which may be read among
those of Bernard. Stephen of Tournay declares (Letter 72)
that "so great is their frugality in food that they use only
these two dishes—either beans or pulse from the field, cabbage or vegetables from the garden. As for fish they use
it so rarely that scarcely more than the name of it is known
among them." Many more details are given by the same
author and by Peter of Celles. This austerity of the
Order was kept up not only to the end of the twelfth
century, as appears from Peter of Blois (Letter 82), but
even beyond the middle of the thirteenth, according to
James de Vitry, who says of them : "Meat they do not eat
except in severe illness, and they commonly abstain even
from the use of fish, eggs, milk, and cheese." (*Hist.
Orient. et Occid. c.* 13.) We see the same severity of life
revived even in our own day in France in the pious monks of
Notre Dame de la Trappe, and in those who have imitated

them, who by the purity and austerity of their life, by
their love of solitude, their silence, their labour, and other
religious virtues, show that to be possible in fact, which we
read of, but scarcely believe, of Bernard and his disciples.

XXXV. James de Vitry adds in the following chapter that
women, who by reason of the weakness of their sex had
not dared "from the beginning of the Order" to carry
austerity to such a degree of severity, did at length
imitate this example. Even in the lifetime of Bernard the
female sex was not altogether a stranger to the rigorous
observance of the Rule; as we learn from Hermann, a
monk of Laon, who says in his Book of the *Miracles of
the B. Virgin* (B. iii. c. 17) that there was near Laon a little
convent of virgins of the Cistercian observance, which the
Bishop Bartholomew had founded, in which the nuns,
under their Abbess Guiberga, "had renounced the use of
garments of linen and the use of furs, and used only tunics
of wool, which they had spun and woven themselves;"
and that they cultivated the earth, clearing the woodland
with axe and hoe, tearing out brambles and thorns,
labouring with their own hands, seeking in silence their
daily bread, and imitating in all respects the life of the
monks of Clairvaux.

XXXVI. It would be too long to adduce the names of all
the illustrious persons, of both one and the other sex,
whom we know to have been induced by Bernard to enter
the monastic life. Of such were Henry, son of Louis VI.
King of France, Ermengarde Duchess of Brittany, Adelais,
Duchess of Lorraine, and innumerable men and women
besides, but it is no less true and admirable that he
persuaded men who remained in the world to adopt a pious
and religious habit of life. Beyond all princes Count
Theobald attached himself to him, put himself and all his
resources at the disposal of the monastery of Clairvaux,
put his very soul into the hands of the Abbot, and, laying

down his princely dignity, showed himself among the
servants of God as a fellow-servant and not a lord, so that
he would obey in all things whatsoever the lowest in the
house had demanded of him (*Life*, ii. 52.)   Abbot Ernald,
from whom we have quoted these words, is a witness how
much so great a prince was able to do at the advice and
entreaty of Bernard, both in constructing, endowing, and
assisting monasteries, in relieving the poor, and in the
discharge of his high duties as sovereign, and Bernard's
Letters testify to the same thing. We learn also from the
118th Letter of Bernard that Beatrice, a lady as distinguished by her piety as her birth, was glad to emulate
the pious example of Theobald.   Lastly, I may cite as an
example how great was the influence which Bernard
exercised in correcting the lives of men; the conversion of William, Duke of Aquitaine, whom he changed
from a determined schismatic to be a most obedient
and pious prince. To sum up all in a few words
with Geoffrey: "What crimes has he not condemned;
what hatreds has he not composed; what scandals has he
not put an end to; what schisms has he not extinguished;
what heresies has he not confuted!" But these two last
subjects, viz., the schisms and the heresies, require from us
special description.

§ IV.   OF THE SCHISM OF ANACLETUS, WHICH WAS
PUT AN END TO BY S. BERNARD.

XXXVII. Although Baronius and other ecclesiastical
historians have written much concerning the schism which
after the death of Honorius II., in 1130, arose between
Innocent and Anacletus, there still remain points requiring a
fuller explication, which I shall endeavour to supply from
my reading of ancient documents, so as to illustrate the
Letters of Bernard upon this subject. And that we may
proceed in due order we have first to inquire who or what

before the schism were Gregory, Cardinal of S. Angelo,
and Peter Leonis (for these were the original names of
Innocent and Anacletus). Then we will examine with care
the election of Innocent, its circumstances and conditions,
and the opposition of Anacletus, and, lastly, the consequence following from all these facts.

XXXVIII. Peter Leonis, a Roman of the Leonine family,
was at first a monk at Cluny, and was by Paschal II. (if we
may believe Onuphrius) created Cardinal deacon, with the
title of SS. Cosmas and Damian; afterwards he was created
by Callistus II. Cardinal presbyter of S. Maria *trans Tiberim*,
title of Callistus, in 1120. We learn from the Chronicle of
Maurigny "that this Peter was son of Peter who was son of
Leo. But Leo, when he made his *passover*,[1] that is when
he was converted from Judaism to Christianity, was baptized
by Leo (Leo. IX.) and had the honour to receive his name."
"This man," that is to say the convert Leo, "because he
was very learned, attained to great honour in the Court of
Rome. He had a son named Peter who afterwards acquired
great power and reputation. About that time began
between the Sovereign of Germany, who was by succession
from Charles the Great Patrician of Rome, and the Roman
Church, that most violent quarrel respecting investitures.
In the war which followed that man Leo showed himself so
strenuous in arms, so provident in counsel, and so faithful
to the Roman Church that the Pope honoured him with a
particular friendship, and confided to him, with the defence
of the other fortifications of Rome, the guard of the Tower
of Crescentius, a kind of strong castle which resembled a
second Rome, and which is constructed on the right bank
of the Tiber and at the head of the bridge which is thrown
across the river. From thence his greatness was wonderfully increased; his reputation became every day higher,
and he grew continually in riches, possessions, and honours."

[1] *Pascha.* There is a kind of play upon the word here.—[E.]

I have quoted this passage in full, since our view of what was done will depend in great measure upon the descent of Peter, his Jewish origin, his power, and to recall the name of the tower of Crescentius (which they call the Castle of S. Angelo), in which Anacletus found a safe asylum. The author of this Chronicle continues : " Among the numerous children of each sex of which this kind of Antichrist boasted must be counted this Peter of whom we are speaking now ; he is reported in a letter to have been called by some 'the precursor of Antichrist.' " I believe, however, that he was not called thus until after the great event of his life and the consequences which followed from it. " He repaired," continues our author, " to France, and pursued his studies in Paris ; and when he was returning into his own country he assumed the monastic habit at Cluny, that very rich and holy community. After having practised there for a certain time the rules of a religious life, he was recalled to the Court of Pope Paschal II. at the request of his father ; and was made Cardinal in the time of Pope Callistus with the same Gregory who afterwards became Pope Innocent II. Then he was sent into France to hold councils at Chartres and Beauvais." There is no mention here of the title of Cardinal deacon, which, according to Onuphrius, he had received from Pope Paschal. On this matter the authority of the Chronographer of Maurigny is the better, as he was a contemporary of Peter Leonis.

XXXIX. Gregory was, it is said, created Cardinal deacon, with the title of S. Angelo, by Urban II., then sent into Gaul as Legate by Callistus II. with Peter Leonis in 1124, and proceeded with him to Séez, in Neustria, as Ordericus reports.[1] This is how Vincent describes the legation :—" The most excellent Cardinals, Gregory and Peter Leonis, between whom later on there was a schism as to the Papacy, having been sent into France, performed

[1] Ord., xii. p. 8;7.

their commission at Limoges, and during that time made a
visit to the man of God, Stephen."[1] Duchesne reports
that they both attached their signatures to the constitution
of Abbot Suger in 1125 as Legates in these terms :—" I,
Peter, Cardinal presbyter and Legate of the Apostolic See,
approve and confirm. I, Gregory, Cardinal deacon of S.
Angelo and Legate of the Apostolic See," etc.[2] At the
same time Bernard wrote many epistles to a certain
Cardinal deacon named Peter, who was also Legate ; they
are numbered 97 and following. This Peter I once
supposed, with Manrique, to have been Peter Leonis. But
since that Peter to whom Bernard writes appears to have
been Cardinal deacon, not presbyter, these letters cannot
have been addressed to Peter Leonis, who was at that time
Cardinal priest, as we gather from the story of Onuphrius
and from some other writers, as well as from the signature
of Peter himself, which I have reported above, and from the
testimony of Suger, which I am about to adduce. Perhaps
this Peter, Cardinal deacon and Legate, to whom Bernard
addressed the Letters we have referred to, was the same
who came into Gaul by the command of Pope Honorius
against Pontius, the deposed Abbot of Cluny, and his
supporters ; of which step Peter the Venerable speaks
thus :—" The venerable Pope Callistus of whom I have
written above had then departed this life, and Pope
Honorius was his worthy successor. He at the news of
the violent disputes at Cluny sent as Legate *de latere* the
lord Cardinal Peter, with whom was joined Hubald, Primate
of Lyons, and he condemned with a terrible anathema
Pontius and all his supporters, who were then called
Pontians." But it is not easy to decide of what title this Peter
was Cardinal, for there were more Cardinals of that name
about that time besides Peter Leonis, namely, Peter, Bishop
of Porto ; Peter of Pisa, of the title of S. Susanna ; Peter

[1] *Life of Stephen de Grandmont*, B. ii. 49.   [2] Chesnius, iv. p. 547.

of Burgundy, of the title of S. Marcellus ; Peter, Cardinal of
S. Æquitius, who was promoted in 1125 in the first creation
of Cardinals by Honorius ; Peter, Cardinal presbyter of S.
Anastasia in the following year ; and, lastly, Peter, Cardinal
deacon, of the title of S. Adrian, two years later. But the
Letters of Bernard seem to have been written before the
creation of these two.[1]

XL. In the meantime Pope Honorius died, in the middle
of February, 1130. The Chronicle of Maurigny makes this
date 1129, since it counts the year in the French manner,
beginning from Easter. " Then," says the same author,
" the Cardinals who were present at Rome with the
Chancellor Haimeric, and had been present at the last
moments of Honorius, set over themselves a certain
Gregory," him, that is to say, whom we have just now
mentioned, " a man distinguished for knowledge and piety,
and clothe him, a little too hastily as is said by some, in
the Pontifical insignia. They say that this was done by a
dispensation, so that they might frustrate the intrigues of
a certain Peter who seemed to be aspiring to the Papacy
by secular means. This was Peter, son of Peter, son of
Leo," and so on as I have related above concerning him.
Suger explains the circumstances very clearly in his Life of
Louis the Fat, where he says : " At the death of Honorius
the elder and wiser dignitaries of the Roman Church, for
the purpose of avoiding any tumult in the Church,
agreed that this important election should take place in
common, according to the Roman custom, in the Church of
S. Mark, and not elsewhere." But " those Cardinals whom
duty or personal intimacy retained around Honorius, not
daring to assemble in that place through fear of the Roman
population, who were in a state of tumult, elected as
Pontiff, before the decease of Honorius was generally
known, Gregory, Cardinal deacon of S. Angelo, a person of

[1] Milman (*Lat. Christ.* iv. 300 note) expresses a doubt whether S. Bernard's
correspondent was not, after all, Peter Leonis, notwithstanding Mabillon's
argument : but apparently without reason.—[E.]

high character. But those who favoured the party of
Peter Leonis, having invited others according to the agreement in the Church of S. Mark, assembled there ; and
when the death of the lord Pope was known they elected
by vote the same Peter Leonis, Cardinal presbyter, with the
consent of many Bishops, Cardinals, clergy, and Roman
nobles, and thus was this pernicious schism caused. The
election of Innocent was, therefore, the first in date,
but it was made hastily and without the attendance of all
the electors. But," continues Suger, " as the party of
Peter Leonis prevailed at Rome, both by the influence of
his family and by the favour of the Roman nobility," Innocent
left Rome, embarked for France, and " sending messengers
to King Louis," entreated his assistance. Therefore Louis
summoned at Etampes " a Council of Archbishops, Bishops,
Abbots, and Religious in order to inquire not so much
concerning the election as concerning the person elected."
This Council declared for Innocent, under the influence of
Bernard, in whose judgment the whole of the Council
coincided by their vote, as Ernald declares (*Life*, B. ii. c.
1). In consequence of this Suger, as he himself reports,
was commanded by the King to go to meet Innocent at the
Abbey of Cluny, whose Abbot, Peter the Venerable, had,
with his monks, declared for Innocent, although Anacletus
had formerly been a monk there, as I shall note afterwards
upon Letter 126. The King himself, with the Queen and
his children, went to meet the Pope as far as the Benedictine Abbey of Fleury, where " he prostrated himself at his
feet, as if doing reverence at the sepulchre of Peter."
Following his example, Henry, King of England, came likewise " to Chartres to meet Innocent, and devoutly prostrated
himself at his feet " and promised him obedience for himself and his subjects. But Innocent " in the course of his
visitation to the Church of France arrived in Lorraine.
The Emperor Lothair came to meet him in the city of
Liége with an enormous attendance of Archbishops,

Bishops, and dignitaries of his realm, and in the midst of the great square before the cathedral church, as if he had been the Pope's equerry, approaching him respectfully on foot in the midst of his procession, he kept off with one hand the crowd with a rod, and with the other he led by the bridle the white horse on which the Pope was mounted, like a servant conducting his lord. Then, as the ground was sloping, he supported and almost carried him, and thus greatly increased the dignity of His Paternity (the Pope) in the eyes of all." All this took place in 1130. Although Suger says nothing here of Bernard, we know from Ernald that he was a constant companion of Innocent's journey throughout France.

XLI. Before going on to other subjects it will not be out of place to remark here what took place at Liége. The Annals of Magdebourg, or Saxon MSS., inform us under the year 1131 : " The Sunday before Mid-Lent, March 22nd, was held at Liége a very distinguished assembly of Bishops and Princes, thirty-six in number, in presence of the Apostolic lord Innocent, of the Emperor Lothair, with the Empress, where many wise decisions were made for the good both of the Church and of the State. There also Otto, Bishop of Halberstadt, who had been deprived of his See three years before, was restored to it by the intercession of the Emperor and the Princes. Ernald reports that in that assembly was brought forward also the question of investitures, which at length Lothair, by the influence of Bernard, restored to the Church. This Council was preceded by a synod at Wissembourg, as one of the authors of the Annals of Magdebourg contemporary with these events asserts. There was in the month of October a Council of sixteen Bishops assembled at Wissembourg by the Emperor, at which was present the Archbishop of Ravenna, as Legate of the Apostolic See, where Gregory, who as Innocent had prevailed over Peter Leonis in the election of a Pope, was recognized and confirmed by the Emperor Lothair, and all there present.

XLII. After the assembly at Liége Innocent returned into France (as Suger relates) and passed the feast of Easter at S. Denis. "Three days after Easter he went to Paris, and then when he had spent some time in visiting the churches of France, and in supplying his penury from their abundant wealth, he chose to take up his abode at Compiègne." Some time after (Suger declares) he held a Council at Rheims, the opening of which Dodéchin fixes on October 19th, and in which Louis the Younger received on the 25th of the same month the insignia of royalty from the hands of Innocent, as Robert, who has continued the Chronicle of Sigebert, states. The Saxon MS. Annals report under 1131, "Pope Innocent on the Feast of S. Luke having again assembled together many of the clergy and laity," that is after the Synod at Liége, "held at Rheims another assembly for some days, over which he presided." Suger adds that having dismissed this Council the Pope made some stay at Autun, and at length returned into Italy with Lothair.

XLIII. Ernald (*Life*, ii. c. 1) places the Council at Rheims before that at Liége, and writes that Innocent proceeded from Liége to Clairvaux, and after a short delay in France returned to Rome in the company of Lothair. But it is quite clear that the synod at Rheims was later than that at Liége, as well from the narrative of Suger as from the Saxon Annals, and especially from the Chronicle of Maurigny, in which the journey of Innocent is carefully described. The chronicler, in fact, relates that Innocent, after having been recognized at Chartres as legitimate Pope by King Henry of England, "resolved to proceed to the Court of Lothair, Patrician of Rome, Emperor, and as his first stage on leaving Chartres was at Maurigny," which is a Benedictine Abbey in the neighbourhood of Etampes, and in his company, besides

Bishops and Cardinals, was " Bernard, Abbot of Clairvaux,
who was the most famous preacher of the Divine Word at
that time in the whole of France," and Peter Abaelard,
Monk and Abbot, who is called " a religious man, who holds
an excellent school of theology." When the Pope had
consecrated the Church of Maurigny, " on the third morning
he departed with his company and proceeded to his conference, which was at Liége . . . then, returning to Gaul,
he remained a long time at Autun until the time drew near
for the meeting of the Council, which had been summoned
to assemble at Rheims on the Festival of S. Luke the
Evangelist; then having gained over to his cause Geoffrey
Martel of Tours . . . he returned to Paris, passing by
Orleans and Etampes." In the meantime he heard of the
death of Philip, whom his father had associated with him
in the kingdom. Profoundly grieved by this news he sends
as his legates *a latere* to console the King two venerable
Bishops, "Geoffrey of Châlons, and Matthew of Albano."
Then proceeding to Rheims he solemnly anointed Louis as
King in a fully-attended synod. He received at the same
time letters of obedience and fidelity from the Emperor
Lothair and from Henry, King of England, as well as from
Hildefonso the Elder, King of Hither Spain, and Hildefonso
the Younger, King of Farther Spain. Besides this, it filled
the Pontiff with great joy to receive " a letter from the most
excellent hermits of the Chartreux, which was borne by a
certain venerable Abbot of the Cistercian Order, and read
in full Council by Geoffrey, Bishop of Chartres." This
Abbot was Hugo, of Pontigny, as the letter bears witness,
which the same Chronicler inserts at the end of his second
volume. At the commencement of the third he adds that "a
little after the Council of Rheims Innocent returned to Rome,
but because Peter, his unjust rival, had drawn to his own
side the greater part of the city, Innocent was able to
obtain only the Church of S. Peter, which is the seat of the

dignity of the holy priesthood, but Peter occupied as his residence the palace of the Lateran, to which belongs Imperial dignity." Upon this matter there is a letter of the Emperor Lothair in the *Spicilegium*, Vol. vi., in which Norbert, Archbishop of Magdebourg, has the title of Chancellor. He was acting as the deputy of Bruno, of Cologne, who had not proceeded into Italy with the Emperor (Chron. Saxon.) But Innocent for the sake of the City of Rome withdrew to Pisa, where he remained until the death of Peter, which took place in 1137.

XLIV. In the meantime Peter, or Anacletus, left no means unattempted to bring over persons of influence to his side. Among Bishops, Gerard of Angoulême adhered to him, who since he had fulfilled the functions of legate under the two last Popes had it much at heart to obtain the same honour from Anacletus also. He gained over to Anacletus William, Count of Poitou. Furthermore, Anacletus, in order to bring over Roger, Duke of Apulia, to his party, gave him his own sister in marriage and crowned him King of Sicily, as Ordericus states (B. xii. p. 498). Among the letters of Peter Leonis, in which he takes upon him the name of Pope, which have been preserved in the MS. of Casinum, and published in part by Baronius, there is one in which he complains vehemently of the Abbot of Farfa, whom, because he was opposed to himself, he has, as he says, " stricken with the sting of the Church," *i.e.*, " condemned with a sentence of excommunication."

XLV. All these troubles and divisions which we have detailed, perhaps at greater length than was necessary, gave much occupation to Bernard, who wrote letter after letter in every direction to bring over schismatics to Innocent and to keep those who were faithful to their duty. He undertook various journeys also for the same cause, as we infer from the following epistles and from his *Life* (B. ii. 6 and 7).

XLVI. We now have to speak of Gerard, Bishop of Angoulême, of whom Arnulf, then Archdeacon of Séez, and afterwards Bishop of Lisieux, has left us a portrait in the treatise which he wrote against him, and which our brother Achery has published in Vol. ii. of the *Spicilegium.* "He was Norman by birth; the poverty of his parents obliged him to leave his father's house, and was at length elected Bishop of Angoulême by a chance," as there was a division among the electors, and his election offered "a certain means of escape" from the difficulty in which they were. Then he began to confer the dignities of his Church upon his nephews, born in a low condition,[1] to shut his eyes to crimes and leave them unpunished, to seek and to obtain the dignity of legate from the Pontiff, to act haughtily, to convoke Councils and synods in a spirit of ostentation. Arnulf adds that when Innocent was elected, Gerard at first favoured him, but not having been able to obtain the dignity of legate from him he threw himself into the party of Peter Leonis, by whom a new commission as legate was granted to him, embracing all the countries between the Alps and the ocean of the west. And it was added that "wherever he should set his foot there he should have the power of legate." When he was reinvested with this dignity he endeavoured to gain over the Kings of England and the two Spains to the party of Anacletus, but without success. He deposed the Bishops of Poitiers and Limoges and replaced them by unworthy men. He imposed himself, Gerard, upon the See of Bordeaux, being at once Bishop and Archbishop, which Ernald also states (*Life*, B. ii. c. 5). Then Arnulf says, addressing Gerard, and enumerating the partisans of Anacletus, "that unbelieving troop whom you follow compose all the supporters of Peter Leonis; it is not yet purged from the leaven of Jewish corruption, and that tyrant, whom Sicily, the nurse of tyrants, sustains . . . it

[1] *Obscuro loco.*

has in its ranks only the Count of Poitou, a man devoted to pleasures, a man sensual, not capable of comprehending spiritual mysteries, given over to the error because of the refusal of a request unlawful to be granted." These are the supporters of Anacletus. "While to our side," continues Arnulf, "we have the adhesion of the Emperor, every king, every prince, every man almost who is worthy to bear the Christian name. But in that universal consent, those whose adhesion is most significant to my eyes, whose authority strikes me, influences me, and commands my obedience, are the men to whom it has been given to know the mysteries of the kingdom of God, and whose conversation seems to be already in heaven; such are they in truth who dwell among the perpetual snows of the Chartreuse, and they who, shining forth from Cîteaux or Cluny, fill all the world with the rays of their light." Thus speaks Arnulf to Gerard, whom, nevertheless, others praise, but the authority of Arnulf ought to weigh most with us. "I have written nothing," he says, "but what I either myself knew personally or have received on good authority, or which is not, at least, affirmed by public report." There is more respecting Gerard in the notes to Letter 127. Gerard died in 1136. Then Geoffrey, Bishop of Chartres, received the command of Innocent to traverse the whole of France, and especially Aquitaine, and to destroy with his own hands all the altars which Gerard, the author and supporter of that rebellion, or which Gilo, Bishop of Tusculum, or their accomplices had consecrated in the time of the schism, "with benediction and unction of chrism," as we read in the Chronicle of Maurigny, B. iii. But we are lingering too long upon these matters. Those who wish to learn more respecting the sentiments, life, and character of Innocent and Anacletus may consult the treatise of Arnulf just quoted. There is a letter of Paschal II. respecting the Legation of Gerard to be found in *Spicileg.*, B. iii., and in

B. iv. an account of the Synod of Laon, at which he presided in 1109.

XLVII. It may be seen (as we have already said) by the
Life and in the Letters of Bernard how many journeys he
accomplished, and how much trouble he went through in
the long and unhappy time of that schism. Thus he thrice
travelled into Italy upon this account, and it was thanks to
his efforts, that the schism was terminated by the death of
Anacletus in 1138. For although the schismatics gave him
a successor in the anti-pope Victor, it was "not so much in
órder to prolong the division as to find, by delay, a suitable
opportunity to reconcile themselves with Pope Innocent,"
and, in fact, Victor himself came by night "to the holy
man"—that is, to Bernard—"and he induced him to lay
aside the insignia of Papal dignity which he had assumed,
and conducted him to the feet of Innocent" (*Life*, ii. 47).
Such was the end of this long and calamitous schism.

XLVIII. In sign of gratitude for so great a service, which
was due principally to Bernard, Innocent freed by his own
authority the possessions of the Cistercian Order from the
tithes payable upon them, without even consulting those to
whom the tithes belonged. From these new divisions arose,
which caused no little trouble and annoyance to Bernard.
The monks of Cluny, in particular, complained loudly against
this exemption, which deprived them, without compensa-
tion, of a great part of their revenues, and their irritation
rose to such a point that the monks of Gigny destroyed to
the very ground a neighbouring monastery of the Cistercians
named Moiremont. The detailed account of this melancholy event will be found in two Letters numbered 229 and
283, the former from Peter the Venerable, and the latter
from Bernard, and in the notes upon these. Nor was this
contest immediately closed, but in process of time extended
into other countries also.

XLIX. We may infer this from Letter 82, which Peter of

Blois wrote in the name of Richard, Archbishop of Canterbury, "To the Abbot and the Convent of Cîteaux;" for in this letter, after beginning with praises of the Cistercians, he goes on to say that "their reputation is in one respect stained by their refusal to pay to other monks and to the clergy the tithes which are due from them," the writer continues, "and whence comes this injurious exemption that you should be freed from the payment of tithes, to which your lands were liable before they came into your hands, and which have hitherto been paid, not with respect to the persons holding them, but by the necessary liability of the land? If those lands had passed into your possession, wherefore is the right of another person over them in this respect to be endangered? For, in common fairness, when the lands passed to you they passed with the burden that was upon them." And when the privilege accorded to the Cistercians by Pope Innocent was brought forward as an argument against him, he replies that such a privilege "might be borne with for a while, since necessity had been the cause of its introduction at a time when the Order"—that is, of Cîteaux—"was happy in its poverty, and gladly shared with the poor its scanty resources." But now that its possessions were multiplied, "even beyond all measure," such a privilege must be considered rather to minister to the ambition of the Order than to be a means of assistance to piety. "Furthermore, whatever may be the extent of the privileges of the Roman Church, they cannot be made use of to usurp unjustly that which belongs to another." At length, if the Cistercians shall show themselves pertinacious and unyielding in this matter, Richard threatens that he will bind in the bond of anathema all persons "who shall either give or sell anything to the Cistercians" to the hindrance of the right of tithes, and that he will appeal to the throne of the Supreme Judge "that none may absolve from the bond of this excommunication." He goes even

farther still, since he- threatens to invoke the help of the
secular arm in favour of the spiritual power, and to confis-
cate all that shall have been sold or given to the Cistercians
against the decree which he has pronounced.   This is what
we read in the letter of Peter of Blois.

L. Geoffrey, Prior of Vigeois, makes similar complaints
on the same subject in his *Chronicle* (*Labbe*, *Biblioth.* ii.
p. 328), in which, after praising the Cistercians because
they gave many alms from the proceeds of their own labour,
because they sang their offices in choir, according to the
Rule, and for many other good actions, he yet notes this
against them, that they took the lands and refused to pay
the tithes due to others; without counting this, that they
indiscreetly threw into obscurity the memory of certain
saints.   He wrote this about the close of the twelfth century, at which time the tempest raised by the exemption
from tithe decreed by Innocent in favour of the Cistercians
had not yet subsided.

§ V. Concerning the Errors of Peter Abaelard
    and of Gilbert de la Porrée, and S. Bernard's
    Refutation of them.

LI. This circumstance added no little to the glory of
Bernard, that he had no others as adversaries than the
partisans of error or heresy, nor did he attack the men so
much as their errors. Chief among the former class must
be reckoned Peter Abaelard and Gilbert or Gislebert de la
Porrée. Among heretics, the worst was Henry and his
followers, who were called Henricians from him. We shall
treat here of the two former, and of Henry and his followers
in the next paragraph.

LII. Peter Abaelard gives a vivid description of himself
in his history of his calamities; afterwards Otto, Bishop of
Frisingen, has sketched him with a kindly pen. You have
an epitome of his life in my Notes to Letter 187 of Bernard,

where the defenders and supporters of Abaelard are refuted. Here we need only give a summary of what Bernard did against him. Then we shall show by the words of his defenders themselves how unjust those are towards the truth, who declare themselves in his favour in the controversy, rather than in that of S. Bernard.

LIII. First, we will commence by observing that long before his collision with Bernard he had been cited by Conon, Legate of the Holy See, to the Council held at Soissons in 1121; and in it, his Book on Theology, in which erroneous propositions were contained, was committed to the flames, the author being confined in the monastery of S. Medard. When he was dismissed thence, he proceeded to disseminate his views in all directions, and grievously resenting the imputation of being a heretic, which was thrown upon him by many people, and of which he suspected that Bernard was the origin, he cited him to the Council of Soissons, in 1140, or it might be said, dragged him thither, so unwilling was Bernard to come.

There, in presence of the Bishops and other illustrious clergy of the second order, Abaelard himself was heard a second time and confuted by Bernard, his doctrine examined and again proscribed, but the author was left unpunished, because he had appealed to the Apostolic See. But as he heard that the sentence of the synod had been approved by Innocent II., he desisted from his appeal, and on the advice of Peter the Venerable retired into the monastery of Cluny, and at last made a pious ending of his days in a monastery at Chalons sur Saône.

LIV. Bernard wrote against Abaelard various Letters, of which the most important is one to Pope Innocent (Letter 190), which is placed eleventh among the Treatises. In this letter Bernard names briefly the chief heads of the errors which he had found in the writings of Abaelard, and logically refutes them. In this edition I place, following the Vatican MS., at the head of this Letter, or rather Treatise, fourteen propositions extracted by Bernard from the writings of Abaelard which were submitted to Innocent at the same time as the Letter.   I shall treat at length the whole of this controversy in an Admonition prefixed to this particular Treatise.   For the present I content myself with adding some particulars respecting the defenders of Abaelard.

LV. In the first place must be quoted Abaelard himself, who in his Apology complains that many errors had been imputed to him "by malice," and particularly that he had said "the Father is all powerful, the Son powerful, and the Holy Spirit without power," which words he repudiates as " not merely heretical, but diabolical," and affirms that they cannot be found in his writings.   But of this and other heads of accusations I shall speak in observations on Treatise 11.   Abaelard confesses, however, in the course of his Apology, that he had written "some things that he ought not, by error;" but protests that he had written nothing "through malice or through pride," and adds that if through his much speaking, some expressions had escaped him which were to be regretted, he was always prepared "to correct, or altogether retract, what he had spoken ill ; " and finally, that he was a son of the Church, and "received what she receives, and rejected what she rejects."   Well and good ; I have no wish to prove Abaelard to have been a heretic; it is sufficient for the cause of Bernard to show that he erred in certain respects, and this indeed he himself does not deny.

LVI. But how far does the testimony of Otto of Frisingen tell against the holy Doctor or in favour of Abaelard ?   He says that " Bernard had a fervent jealousy for the Christian religion, and was credulous from his habitual gentleness of character," so that he had little love for those *Professors* who attached too much importance to their human reasonings

and their worldly wisdom, "and if anything was reported
of such persons which seemed to show that they were out
of harmony with the Christian faith, he listened willingly to
it" (Otto, B. i. c. 47). But this judgment is rather praise
than blame for the holy Doctor, since there is nothing
more in the duty of a Catholic Doctor than to repress as
soon as possible men of that class, who attach too much
value to their philosophical reasonings, especially when
they devise new terms of philosophy, which may easily lead
into error incautious persons. I may adopt the words of
William, that "the excess of zeal which is blamed in him will
be itself praiseworthy to pious minds . . . happy is he to whom
the only crime which can be imputed is that which others
are accustomed to consider as doing them honour" (*Life*,
B. i. 41). But Otto himself, although he favours Abaelard,
yet acknowledges that he had weakened too much the
distinctions between the Three Persons of the holy Trinity,
not having followed good precedents, "and that because of
this he was considered a Sabellian heretic in the provincial
synod of Soissons." How then can it be wondered at, if
repeating the same errors a second time he was regarded
with extreme suspicion by lovers of the orthodox faith?

LVII. I need not say much of Berengarius of Poitiers,
who wrote an Apology for Abaelard, who had been his
teacher, against the synod of Soissons and against Bernard
himself; as well because he was a man of little or no
authority, as because he, when he returned to a better mind,
was unwilling to continue to be "the defender of the propositions objected to Abaelard because, although they might
not be unorthodox, yet they sounded distinctly suspicious,"
and he would have suppressed his book if he had been able,
as he declares in his letter to the Bishop of Mende. And
although we have no longer all the books of Abaelard in
which he had disseminated his errors, yet in those which
remain there is no lack of "difficult and dangerous"

passages, as the Paris theologians have detected, and have placed at the head of his works a kind of antidote to destroy the effect of the more dangerous of these. It would have been very desirable that the Apologetic Preface should have been expunged from thence. But enough has been said of Abaelard.

LVIII. The condemnation of Gilbert de la Porrée, Bishop of Poitiers, excited no less angry feeling against Bernard than that against Abaelard. According to Otto of Frisingen, Gilbert "was born at Poitiers, studied there, afterwards became a teacher, and from a teacher he finished by being Bishop of the same city. From his youth he subjected himself to the training of the most renowned masters, and relying more on their knowledge than his own intellect, he acquired from them learning solid and profound" (Otto, B. i. c. 46), while praise of his knowledge was enhanced by the gravity of his character. These masters were, "first, Hilary of Poitiers, then Bernard of Chartres, and finally two brothers named Anselm and Ralph, both of Laon." This Hilary was no other, I think, than the great Bishop Hilary of Poitiers, whose authority, as Geoffrey declares, Gilbert abused. Bernard of Chartres is not otherwise known to me than by the testimony of Otto; as for Ralph of Laon, he was well known to Guibert, to a monk named Hermann, of Laon, and to Geoffrey, the secretary of S. Bernard, as was also his brother Anselm, Dean of Laon. In his Commentaries on the *Psalms,* on the *Epistles* of S. Paul, and upon Boethius, he indulges in philosophical speculations concerning the Divinity and other truths of religion beyond what is permissible. Otto states that "there were among other opinions which were objected to him four propositions concerning the Divine Majesty, namely:—That the Divine Essence is not God; that the properties of the Persons are not the Persons themselves; that the Divine Persons cannot be predicated in any proposition ; that the Divine Nature is not incarnate." I will speak more fully upon these in later chapters. Minor errors also were objected to him, namely, that "no one except Christ had any merit, that no one should be baptized except those ordained to salvation," and other opinions of that kind which Geoffrey reports. (Treatise against the opinions of Gilbert, in the Appendix.)

LIX. Gilbert having given utterance to all these errors in a sermon which he preached to an assembly of his clergy, his two Archdeacons, Arnold and Calo, report the matter to Eugenius III., who was then at Sienna, in Tuscany, and was coming into France. He remitted the examination of the cause to France. In the meantime the Archdeacons obtain the support of Bernard for their side. An examination was made of the accused doctrines at Auxerre and at Paris, and they were condemned at a Council at Rheims in 1148. Otto reports briefly what was done in each of these assemblies, but Geoffrey, the secretary of Bernard, gives a more detailed account. He even wrote a short history of the proceedings respecting them at the Council of Rheims, and forty years later he wrote a letter on the subject to Henry, Cardinal Bishop of Albano. Both his letter and this history will be found at the end of Vol. vi.

LX. I have found no particulars respecting this assembly at Auxerre, of which only Otto makes mention ; but there are, on the contrary, many details given of the proceedings of that at Paris. Geoffrey states that it was held "at the Festival of Easter," and therefore it must have been in 1147 ; since we learn from Otto that the Council assembled at Rheims "during the Lent" of the following year, and the Appendix to Sigebert fixes it as the 22nd March. "Gilbert appeared then before the Pope, the Cardinals, the Bishops, and other venerable and learned men, to explain himself on the points upon which he was accused. The debate lasted for several days. There appeared against him two celebrated doctors, Adam de Petit-Pont, a very acute reasoner, and recently made Canon of the Cathedral of Paris, and Hugh de Champ-fleury, Chancellor of the King, who affirmed upon their oath that they had heard from the mouth of Gilbert certain of the incriminated propositions. In the midst of the discussion which followed upon this, it was declared that Gilbert had said amongst other things that ' I confess that God the Father is God in one sense, and Father in another sense ; yet not both God and Father in the same sense.' Joscelin, Bishop of Soissons, was particularly indignant at this declaration. All this took place on the first day. Another time he was accused of having in a *prosa*[1] con-cerning the Holy Trinity said that the ' three Persons were three individuals.' The Archbishop of Rouen (Hugh the Third of that name) made the matter worse by saying that it would have been better to say that God is one individual." This is the account which Otto, Bishop of Frisingen, gives of the Council of Paris (Otto, B. i. c. 51-52).

LXI. Geoffrey relates it a little differently, and makes the synod at Viterbo which was held upon the same subject to have preceded it. He mentions but one informer against Gilbert to the Pope, the Archdeacon Arnold, upon whom he bestows the cognomen *Pince-sans-rire* [= *qui non ridet, i.e.,* a dry joker]. But in the meeting at Paris he opposes Bernard to Gilbert as his only adversary, " whose concern it was wherever he might be to defend every interest of our Lord Christ. When Gilbert was required to produce his Commentary on Boethius, in which were contained some suspected propositions, he replied that he had it not at hand. But he denied that he had ever taught or believed ' that the Divine Nature was not God,' etc., and

---

[1] Sequence, *i.e.,* a species of rhythmical introduction to the Gospel in the Liturgy. The laws of metre were not strictly observed in it.—[E.]

he called in witness of this two of his disciples, Rotold, then Bishop of Evreux, and afterwards Archbishop of Rouen, and the Magister Ivo of Chartres, another person without doubt than the illustrious Bishop of Chartres of that name." I think that this man was a regular Canon of the Abbey of S. Victor, near Paris, and afterwards created Cardinal by Innocent II., to whom Bernard's Letter 193 was addressed. To put an end to these altercations the Pope orders that the book in question should be brought to a future Council "which he proposed to hold during the same year at Rheims;" and although it was deferred to mid-Lent of the following year, it was none the less held within a year from the meeting at Paris, since that was held, as we have said above, during the preceding Easter.

LXII. "In the meantime the *Exposition* of Boethius by Gilbert was, by order of the Pope, sent to Godescalc, then Abbot of Mont S. Eloi, near Arras, and afterwards Bishop of the same town, in order that he might examine it; he noted in it many suspicious propositions, to each of which he opposed the teaching of the holy Fathers extracted from their works. Alberic, Bishop of Ostia and Legate in Aquitaine, would have brought forward the most ample information regarding the life and conduct of Gilbert if he had not been removed by a premature death a little before these discussions. At length, at the Council of Rheims," came on the discussion of the propositions noted by Godescalc; but as he was not a practised speaker the book of Gilbert, and also the passages of the holy Fathers noted by Godescalc, were delivered by the lord Pope to S. Bernard. The Council contained Bishops from the four realms of France, Germany, England, and Spain. Among these were personages of great renown and of no little learning, Geoffrey de l'Oratoire, Archbishop of Bordeaux, whose suffragan Gilbert was; Milo, Bishop of Térouanne; Joscelin, Bishop of Soissons; and Suger, Abbot of S. Denis, to whom

Louis, King of France, when setting out for Jerusalem, had committed the administration of his entire realm; and, indeed, says Otto, he did this according to the prerogative of that community (Otto, B. i. c. 55). Geoffrey, although he did not approve the teaching of Gilbert, was favourable to his person.

LXIII. At the first session of the Council Gilbert called his clerks to bring in various enormous volumes, complaining that his adversaries had quoted against him only mutilated texts. Then Bernard spoke thus: "What need is there to delay longer about expressions of that kind? The origin of this scandal arises from nothing else but this—that a great many persons believe that you think and teach that the Divine Essence or Nature, the Divinity, Wisdom, Goodness, Greatness are not God, but the Form in which God is. If this is what you believe, avow it openly or deny it." He dared to affirm, that all this was the Form of God and not God Himself. Then Bernard replied: "Behold! here we have what we were seeking; let that confession be written down." So the supreme Pontiff directed; and then Dom Henry of Pisa, who was then sub-deacon of the Roman Church, and who at a later time became a monk at Clairvaux, the Abbot of S. Anastasius, and finally Cardinal priest, with the title of SS. Nereus and Achilles, brought at his command pen, ink, and paper. But while he was drawing up the record of that avowal of Gilbert, the latter cried out, addressing himself to Bernard: "And do you write also that the Divinity is God." To this Bernard replied: "Let it be written with an iron pen, with a point of diamond." After much disputation on one side and the other, the Cardinals declared that they would reserve their judgment. At this the Bishops murmur greatly because the Cardinals reserved to themselves alone the decision of the cause, and charged Bernard that he should draw up articles of faith in an opposite sense to those for which Gilbert was accused, fearing lest (since there were many supporters of Gilbert among the Cardinals) the Council should be dissolved without any decision. Therefore Bernard did this. Then the Bishops subscribed these articles, and sent them by Hugh, Bishop of Autun, Milo, Bishop of Térouanne, and Abbot Suger to the Pope, begging him to confirm them, which Eugenius did without difficulty. At length Gilbert, being summoned before the assembly which had met in the noble palace called Tau (the palace of the Archbishop of Rheims was thus called because of the shape of the battlements, which recalled the form of the Greek letter T), he abjured spontaneously all the errors contained in each of his propositions. The Pope condemned them all likewise, with the book of the author of them, and strictly forbade that anyone should dare to read or transcribe that book until the Roman Church had corrected it. Gilbert having said that he would make the corrections that the Pope required, the Pope refused permission for him to do so. This is in brief summary the account of Geoffrey.

LXIV. The account of Otto gives some details which are wanting in that of Geoffrey, and in some respects does not agree with it. Thus, he places the examination of Gilbert as having been entered upon "when the synod was finished and the decrees promulgated;" then he says that it was "after the week of Mid-Lent, and when the time of the sacred Passion of the Lord was beginning to draw on, that Gilbert was brought up for judgment; and that when he had read from the books of the orthodox Fathers passages in his defence, it was Pope Eugenius, who was fatigued with all these quotations, and not Bernard, as Geoffrey asserts, who required that Gilbert should say simply "whether he believed that the supreme Essence was God," and that he, wearied by the lengthened reading, replied, without consideration, "Not," which avowal the secretary of the Council immediately caught up from his mouth. After the

dismissal of the assembly he says that Gilbert employed the
rest of the day and the following night in assuring himself
of the support of his friends among the Cardinals, of whom
he had no small number.

LXV. The next morning the record of the proceedings
was read, and the Bishop was called upon to reply; but he
at length so explained his view that, if the Name of God
were taken to denote His very Nature, he allowed that it
was God; but if it were understood to denote a Divine
Person, then he could not subscribe to that, for fear (he
said) that if he did so, without qualification, he might be led
to allow that, whatever might be affirmed of either Person,
the same might equally be affirmed of the Divine Essence;
and so " be led on to say that as the Person of the Son had
become incarnate and had suffered, so the Divine Essence
had also been incarnated and had suffered." He supported
this distinction by passages drawn from the works of the
Fathers Theodoret and Hilary, and also by the authority of
a Council of Toledo: "and when the Abbot of Clairvaux
wished to determine the sense of this last authority, and
employed certain words which were not pleasing to the
Cardinals," Gilbert demanded that they might be written
down, to which Bernard agreed, using the words which
Geoffrey records, "Let them be written with a pen of iron
and point of diamond." At length the holy Abbot assembled with the Bishops, and, together with them, drew up a
profession of faith opposed to the propositions of Gilbert,
which act of the clergy of France so grievously offended
the sacred college of Cardinals that they complained of the
matter to the Pope, both against the Bishops and against
Bernard himself, because they had ventured by drawing up
their profession of faith without even consulting the
Cardinals, to put the last touch, as it were, to the final
sentence, which office belonged to the Roman See. Bernard being at length called upon by the Pontiff to give

satisfaction to the Cardinals, replied, with deference and humility, that neither he himself, nor the lords the Bishops had made any definition with respect to the articles in question ; but having been challenged by the same Bishop of Poitiers to write down his profession of faith, he had not been willing to do that alone, but had simply taken the Bishops as witnesses of his views to give more authority by their witness to that which was asked of him. At this explanation so full of humility and modesty, the previous indignation of the Cardinals was appeased, on condition, however, that the writing just read having been drawn up without reference to the Curia, should not be taken for a Creed in the Church, as being deficient in the needful weight of authority. "And thus no decision could be arrived at concerning the three propositions, because of the excitement which had before been raised." Otto declares that this was not strange, and he adds that Gilbert differed from the other Bishops on a fourth point also, " since they professed that the Divine Nature was Incarnate but in the Son." But Gilbert, "that the Person of the Son was incarnate not without his Nature. The Roman Pontiff spoke only on the first point, and defined that in theology no separation can be made between the Nature and the Person, and that the Divine Essence should be called God not only in an *ablative* sense,[1] but also in a nominative sense."[2] Gilbert reverently accepted the decision of the Pope, restored his Archdeacons to favour, and returned to his diocese " in full honour, and in the completeness of his powers."

LXVI. In all these accounts it is evident that Otto strongly favoured Gilbert, therefore it is not to be wondered at that at the end of his account he should add that it is doubtful whether " in this matter the Abbot of Clairvaux, being subject as a man to the weakness of human nature,

[1] *i.e.*, by way of abstraction or predicate apparently.—[E.] [2] *Nomen.*

was not deceived, or whether the Bishop, being a very learned and accomplished man, did not simply escape the judgment of the Church by cleverly concealing his real meaning." But Radevic relates that Otto, when very near his death, caused his book to be brought in which he had written this, and delivered it to certain religious men, "that whatever he had said on behalf of the opinions of Magister Gilbert which might do harm to anyone might be corrected according to their judgment."[1]

Rightly does Geoffrey refer his readers with respect to the whole of this disputation to the Sermons of Bernard *in Cantica,* especially to Sermon 80, in which the holy man does not hesitate to declare that those are heretics who persist in defending the opinion of Gilbert, although he refrains from mentioning the name of the author because of his submission.

§ VI. Of the Henricians and of other Heretics who were Refuted by Bernard.

LXVII. Gilbert and Abaelard, who had fallen into theological errors by a perverse employment of philosophy, Bernard overcame by reason and authority. He overcame equally by his actions and his example many heretics who at that time infested the various provinces of France. These were, in Flanders, Tanchelm, a native of Antwerp; in Provence, Peter de Bruys, whose followers were called Petrobrusians; and in Aquitaine Henry. Others there were, but withoût any well-known leader, in Lorraine and in the districts about Cologne, whom we will therefore call Colognians. To these may be added all the followers of Arnold of Brescia.

LXVIII. It appears from the *Life of S. Norbert* that he opposed Tanchelm and his eager assaults, and that Frederick, Bishop of Cologne, "hindered their advance and

---

[1] *Radevicus,* B. ii. c. 11.

their attacks " in the diocese of Maestricht : and on this subject there is a letter in Tengnagel from this Church to the same Frederick about "the seducer Tanchelm," which gives an account of his heresy and its origin. Peter the Venerable also laboured against the Petrobrusians, and wrote a treatise in order to refute them. The zeal of Bernard for the Christian cause was exercised chiefly against the heresy of the Henricians, which he industriously harassed by speech and writing. His Letters 240 and 241 should be read on this subject, and the *Life of Bernard*, by Geoffrey, B. iii. c. 6, to all of which we will add some further information from other sources.

LXIX. Henry, whom the holy man, and Geoffrey after him, calls "an apostate monk," is also called "a false hermit" in the Acts of the Bishop of Mans (*Analecta*, Vol. iii.), where his character and his perverse actions are accurately described. In what place he was born the words used do not indicate precisely. "About the same time," that is to say, under Bishop Hildebert, "a certain hypocrite appeared on the confines of these regions whose depraved character and whose detestable doctrines rendered him worthy of the punishment of being thrown to scorpions in the manner of parricides." He under a feigned show of learning and sanctity committed horrible excesses. He was wont to boast that he could recognize at the first glance the faults of all men, even those which were unknown to anyone. He sent to Mans two of his disciples, who arrived in the suburbs of the city on Ash Wednesday. "They bore, according to the custom of their master, staves and a banner of the Cross, and resembled penitents in all respects by the colour of their garments, and by their kind of life. The inhabitants of Mans, being deceived by these appearances, welcomed them as if they had been angels. Even the Bishop Hildebert received them kindly, and as he was on the point of setting out " on a journey to

Rome," he " enjoined his archdeacons amongst other things
to permit the pseudo-hermit, Henry, to enter peaceably into
the town and to preach to the people," which he had afterwards reason bitterly to repent.   Perhaps it may be inferred
from this that Henry was originally from the neighbourhood
of Mans, where he commenced to disseminate the venom
of his perverse doctrine.   If he had made himself known
elsewhere already, Hildebert, who was a prelate both
learned and vigilant, would not so easily have given him
access into his city.   But it may possibly be the case that
he had come from a distant region, perhaps from Italy, as I
am about to explain.

LXX. Scarcely had Henry entered into the city than
"the common people, as they were accustomed to do,
applauded his novelties."   Many of the clerks also supplied
him with food, and prepared for him a platform from
whence he might address the great crowds of people,
which he did with "marvellous eloquence."   The effect of
his addresses was to excite the anger of the people against
the ecclesiastics of the town.   They were treated "like
heathens and publicans, so that great threatenings were
uttered against their domestics, nor would anyone buy anything from them or sell anything to them."   They even
went so far as "to determine not only to pull down their
houses and pillage their goods, but also to stone them or
to hang them to the gibbet, had not the sovereign and the
nobles resisted their wicked intentions."

LXXI. When the turn which things had taken was but
too late perceived, the clergy of Mans forbade, by a written
notice, the preaching of Henry and his followers.   Wherefore Henry, the return of Hildebert being made known,
"retired into the village of S. Carileph," by no means desist-
ing from his endeavours, but breaking out into more violent
proceedings day by day.   When Hildebert, on his return
from his Roman journey, wished to give his benediction to

the people, they being led away by the preaching of the heretic, treated him with great disrespect. Then he went to meet the deceiver, demanded of him "whether he had received sacred Orders, and if so, what?" He replied that he was a deacon; and having been bidden to depart out of that province, "he fled secretly, and would have spread his serpentine venom and troubled other regions in like manner, but that happily his reputation preceded him." All that we have said upon this subject is from the Acts of Hildebert.

LXXII. During this time, two disciples of Henry, Cyprian and Peter, renounced their errors, as an encyclical letter of Hildebert (n. 78) declares. In this their master is thus depicted: "This was Henri, a principal snare of the devil and well-known soldier of antichrist. Taken captive by his appearance of religion and knowledge, these two brothers long adhered to him, until both the turpitude of his life and the errors of his doctrine became evident to them. When they had become convinced that his ways were not right, their eyes were opened as to their condition, and they came to present themselves to us. He had so infested our diocese with his doctrines, that our clergy had scarcely the liberty to oppose and confute them even within the walls of their Churches." It was thus that Hildebert was convinced, though very late, of the danger to which he had exposed himself by an incautious approbation of un- known teachers, who under an appearance of piety corrupt the minds of their hearers.

LXXIII. It is clear from what precedes, that this Henry infested the diocese of Mans long before he approached the neighbourhood of Toulouse, whence Bernard expelled him: since the journey to Rome, which Hildebert undertook while he was yet Bishop of Mans and during the time of which that wicked deceiver sowed the tares among the people of Mans, must have taken place before 1125, in

which year Hildebert became Archbishop of Tours. But
Bernard, on the other hand, did not go into the neighbourhood of Toulouse before 1147. In his Letter 241, which he
wrote from Toulouse to Count Hildefonsus, the holy man
expresses himself in these terms : " Inquire if you please, in
what manner he has departed from the city of Lausanne, from
Mans, from Poitiers, and from Bordeaux." It appears that
such was the itinerary of that apostate in his wanderings.
He began to preach at Lausanne, from whence he went to
Mans ; perhaps he had come to Lausanne from Italy, from
which rubbish of this kind, relics of the Manichæans, passed
over into every part of France. Such were those heretics
called *Cameracenses* who had come out of Italy and were in
1025 condemned at the Council of Arras. About the same
time some of them were burnt at Orleans, and indeed the
Exordium Cisterciense (*Life*, B. vii. c. 17) calls the
Henricians by the name of Manichæans, where it is
reported that the legate of the Pope and other Bishops
assembled at Toulouse with our Saint, " in order to confute
the heresy of the Manichæans." The most illustrious Bishop
of Meaux, in the excellent work which he has written concerning the Variations of Heretics, has clearly shown (B. xi.)
in what manner these heretics and their followers merited
the name of Manichæans since they shared their errors.

LXXIV. The same Henrician heretics spread also in the
diocese of Périgueux, under the leadership of a certain
Pontius, as I learn in a letter from Heribert, in Vol. iii. of
my *Analecta*, where the peculiar tenets of those Pontians
are set out. This explains why Bernard repaired to the
people of Périgord or to Perigueux, as appears from Part iii.
of Book vi., which is that of his miracles ; it is related in
Par. 4, that he found many Arians at Toulouse, and put them
to flight as he had done the heretic Henry. Not only this,
but the same Henry having been previously condemned in
a Council at Pisa, is said to have been committed to

Bernard in order that he might become a monk at Clairvaux. But he, after he had received a letter from Bernard to the inmates of Clairvaux, preferred to persist obstinately in the error which he had once taken up, rather than to return in this brief and easy manner to the way of salvation.

LXXV. Bernard depicts Henry in vivid colours in his Letter 251 already quoted. He represents him as a man well-educated and having an appearance of piety, but given over to gaming and to bad women. He enumerates as his errors these: He made no account of priests and persons in holy Orders, he abolished sacraments and festivals, and refused baptism to infants. Of another class was that heretic, who is mentioned by Hildebert in his Letter 51, who rejected intercessions of saints, and endeavoured, without success, to draw Hildebert himself into giving patronage to his sect. But whether those heretics whom Bernard addresses himself to confute in his Sermons 65 and 66, *super Cantica*, are the same as the Henricians we must now inquire.

LXXVI. I was myself at one time of the opinion that they were the same, but the discovery of a letter of Evervinus, Abbot of Steinfeld, which was the occasion of these two Sermons, made me change my opinion. Those heretics were, in fact, from Cologne, and, though they shared in some points the errors of the Henricians, they differed from them in many respects. Evervinus divided the heretics from Cologne into two classes. One class pretended that they alone constituted the Church, since they only walked in the footsteps of Christ. In respect of food they forbade the use of milk and whatever was made of it. In their sacraments they covered themselves with a veil. They asserted that they consecrated every day their food and their drink to be the Body and Blood of Christ, and that other people in their sacraments were far distant from the truth. Besides the baptism of water they employed another in fire and the spirit by the imposition of hands alone. Our baptism they rejected, as also marriage. Finally they declared that whomsoever was chosen or baptized among them had the power of baptizing others whom he thought worthy, and of consecrating upon their altar (*mensa*) the Body and Blood of Christ.

LXXVII. The others refused to the priests of the Church as living in a worldly manner the power of consecrating and of administering the other sacraments, baptism excepted, which latter they used to confer, not on children, but on adults alone. Every marriage contracted between persons who had ceased to be virgin they regarded as fornication. Lastly, they rejected the prayers of saints, fasting, and other bodily mortifications ; also purgatory and prayers for the dead.

LXXVIII. The Henrician heretics and those of Cologne, therefore, were of similar views, inasmuch as they held in hatred the ministers of the Church, the sacraments, the baptism of infants, and marriage. They differed only in a few particulars which arose from a certain variety of disposition than from opposing principles. In one word, they were different branches, but they sprang from the same root. I have no doubt that these heretics of Cologne were produced from the workshop of Tanchelm. He was a layman, as Abaelard asserts, who disseminated his errors in Flanders, and especially at Antwerp, and at length arrived at such a point of madness that he used to call himself the Son of God, and caused a temple to be built to himself, it is said, by the people whom he had seduced. For this reason there was founded by the Bishop of Tournay, under whose jurisdiction that place then was, a company of twelve clerics in the Church of S. Michael at Antwerp, in order that they should combat these impious dogmas, which church was afterwards given over to S. Norbert. What were the perverse dogmas of Tanchelm I learn from a Letter

of the Church at Maestricht to Frederick, Bishop of Cologne,
"Concerning the seducer, Tanchelm." He used to say
that "the Churches of God ought to be considered places
of prostitution; that what was done by the priest's office at
the table of the Lord was absolutely nothing; that the sacraments ought to be called pollutions, and that their efficacy
came to them from the holiness and the merits of the
ministers who performed them," all of which agree perfectly well with the wild fancies of the heretics previously
named. A certain presbyter, Evervacher, "apostatizing
from his priestly dignity, adhered to the service of that
execrable man and followed him to Rome." The same
person did much harm afterwards to the Church at
Maestricht. The whole clergy of that city returned thanks
to Frederick because "he hindered the progress and success"
of Tanchelm, from which it is to be inferred that his errors
had penetrated even into the diocese of Maestricht, and as
far as Cologne, as is evident from the Letter of Evervinus,
and that those heretics of Cologne arose from the same
author.

LXXIX. Hugo Metellus, who was then a canon regular
of Toul, is a witness in his Letter to Henry, Bishop of that
city, that a scourge of the same kind had crept in upon the
soil of Toul. "There are hiding in your diocese," he says,
" or rather are beginning to show themselves, men who are
destructive, who would be more truly called by the name of
savage beasts, since they live in a similar way, for they
condemn Marriage, they abhor Baptism, they make a
mockery of the Sacraments of the Church, and they abhor
the very name of Christian." These were, without doubt,
the miserable and ill-omened disciples of the heretics of
Cologne.

LXXX. To the Henricians succeeded, or rather were
added, men of the same stamp, who called themselves
Cathari, that is to say, *the pure;* whose errors Bonacursus,

who was at first their master at Milan, has laid bare and
confuted in a book which has been published in *Spicilegium,*
B. iii. These have much affinity with the tenets of the
Manichæans, as also with those of the other heretics whom
we have mentioned above. It is to the Cathari that Gilbert
of Hoiland seems to make allusion in his Sermon 36, *in
Cantica,* n. 6. " There shoot up," he says, " in these days
certain trees which our Heavenly Father hath not planted,
trees whose origin is not from our Libanus. These are the
men who boast of their endurance in labour, their patience
under injuries, and their endurance of poverty. They seem
to be cedars, but they are not those of Libanus. Their
heart and conscience is defiled." Ecbert, Abbot of Schönoue,
also wrote Sermons against the Cathari, which still remain.

LXXXI. Bonacursus associates the Passagiens and the
Arnoldists with the Cathari, the former because they declared
that all the rites of the Mosaic Law ought to be observed.
They equally denied the divinity of the Son and of the
Holy Ghost, and rejected the authority of all the Doctors of
the Catholic Church, as they did also and chiefly that of the
Roman Church. The latter—that is, the Arnoldists- -
thought that " the Sacraments of the Church ought to be
avoided because of the corruption of the clergy."

LXXXII. They took this name, I imagine, from that
factious man Arnold, who, under pretext of restoring
liberty and the Republic at Rome, desired all the temporal
rights of the Pontiff to be abrogated, and to leave him only
the power over spiritual things with tithes and free will
offerings. He was born at Brescia, and was a clerk of the
Church of that town. He had been a disciple of Peter Abaelard, and had a strong liking for new and singular opinions,
as Otto of Frisingen testifies. After having studied in
France he returned to Italy, and assumed the habit of the
Religious, the better to deceive the unwary ; which, however, did not prevent him from being a hater of monks, and

f

especially of the clergy. While he flattered laymen, he used to say that neither clerks who had property; nor Bishops who had rights of temporal lordship, nor monks who held lands, could possibly be saved, but that all these things pertained to the sovereign. Besides this, he is said not to have held correct opinions respecting the Sacrament of the Altar, nor the Baptism of infants" (*Otto Fris.*, B. ii. 20). Thus he was infected with the errors of the Petrobrusians and Henricians. Innocent II. expelled him from Italy and obliged him to retire to Zurich in Switzerland. Having heard of the death of Innocent, he returned to Rome at the beginning of the pontificate of Eugenius, and, finding the city ill-disposed towards the new Pontiff, he blew upon the flame of sedition. This reached so great a height that the Cardinals were maltreated, some of them wounded, and Eugenius himself driven from Rome. Bernard undertook the cause of the Pontiff, and wrote to the Romans a magnificent Letter on this subject (Letter 243). He addressed another in the same sense to the Emperor Conrad, whom the Romans had endeavoured without success by a Letter, given by Otto (B. i. 28), to draw over to their side. Thus our Saint was never found wanting to any needful work, nor to any necessity of the Church; he seemed to have been born only to labour for the common interest of the Christian Republic. At last Arnold was apprehended, attached to a post by order of the prefect of that Rome which he had so greatly flattered, and his body reduced to ashes, "so that his remains might not be held in veneration by the foolish populace." Much more respecting him may be read in Otto and in the Notes from that author to Letter 195 of Bernard.

§ VII. OF THE CRUSADE PREACHED BY S. BERNARD AND ITS UNHAPPY ISSUE.

LXXXIII. One of the last labours of Bernard was the preaching of an expedition into the Holy Land, which enterprise was for him the source of great labour and anxiety, as may be easily understood both from his Life and his writings. Otto of Frisingen attributes to Louis the Younger, King of France, the idea of this expedition. He felt himself strongly influenced by the idea of making a voyage to the Holy Places, as his brother Philip, who was "bound by the same vow," had been prevented by death from fulfilling it. He imparted his design to the chief noblemen of his court, and they determined to take the advice of Bernard on that subject. The holy abbot being then summoned, was of opinion that a matter of such great importance should be referred "to the consideration of the Roman Pontiff." Eugenius sanctioned and greatly approved the project, and "committed to the Abbot of Clairvaux full power of preaching and of exciting the zeal of all to this enterprise, since he was regarded as a prophet or apostle among all the peoples of France and Germany." Bernard obeyed the Apostolic letter, "and having raised the minds of very many persons to a high pitch of enthusiasm for the expedition beyond the sea, he gave the Cross at Vézelay to King Louis, to Thierry, Count of Flanders, to Henry, son of Theobald, Count of Blois, and to other barons and nobles."

LXXXIV. In the meantime a certain monk, named Ralph, whilst preaching the Crusade also in Germany, excited the Christians to commence by the murder of the Jews. Bernard repressed his zeal by a Letter, and he himself undertook to preach the Crusade in the east of France, that is to say, in that region of Germany which borders on the Rhine. Then the Emperor Conrad summoned a general assembly at Spires, whither Bernard proceeded, and, "by the working of many miracles, both in private and public, he persuaded the Emperor Conrad and his nephew Frederick and other princes and illustrious persons to take the Cross." Frederick, Duke of Suabia, whom his son had greatly displeased by taking the Cross, he succeeded in appeasing; he ordered the monk Ralph to return to his cloister, and in his place he gave to Conrad, who was travelling through Bavaria, Adam, Abbot of Eberach, to help him in urging on the departure of the expedition. There is extant a Letter of Bernard (n. 363) on this subject addressed to the peoples of the East of France; it is followed by a Letter addressed to Henry, Archbishop of Mayence, to beg him to repress the zeal of Ralph. "Thus," continues Otto, "not only the whole of the Roman Empire, but also the neighbouring realms, Western France, England, Pannonia, and many other peoples and nations, rose to take the Cross on hearing of this expedition, and almost the entire West became peaceful, so that it was regarded as a crime not only to excite private quarrels, but also for any one to bear arms in public."

LXXXV. So great an impression upon the whole of the West is to be ascribed to the preaching of Bernard; but when the success of the expedition did not answer to the hopes and prayers of the people, all the obloquy of the ill-success was thrown upon him also, as is customary with mortals who judge of things according to their issue; nor was there anything that ever caused greater grief to Bernard than that, not for his own sake, but for the cause of God. Thus he says at the commencement of Book ii. *Of Consideration:* "If it is needful for one of two things to happen, I prefer that the murmurs of the multitude should be against me rather than against God It would be a happy thing for me if the world would deign to use me for a shield to ward off blows directed against Him. Willingly do I accept the detraction of evil tongues," etc. The unfortunate issue of that enterprise threw such a gloom over the minds of almost all that the holy Doctor pronounced him happy "who had not been scandalized by it." But how great was the sorrow of Bernard himself appears both from Letter 288, which he wrote upon that subject from his bed of suffering, caused probably by grief of mind, and from the Letter of John, Abbot of Casa Mario, to Bernard himself, which is now numbered 386 among those of Bernard, in which the author tries to console our Saint, whom he had heard was deeply afflicted on account of the unfortunate issue of the expedition.

LXXXVI. Yet there were not wanting those who came forward to defend Bernard, among whom must be reckoned, and not in the last place, Otto, Bishop of Frisingen, who was not in the habit of greatly favouring Bernard. He makes a digression in his Book *de Gestis Friderici* (chap. lx.) to excuse the failure of that expedition, in which he himself had taken part. At the end of an excursus, philosophical rather than historical, he thus concludes in favour of Bernard : " Yet if we should say that that holy Abbot was inspired by the Spirit of God to rouse us to that enterprise, but that we, disobeying the salutary commandments of God by our pride and our licence, have deservedly compromised both the success of the undertaking and the safety of those engaged in it, we should say nothing contrary to ancient examples and arguments." Yet one thing, he adds, namely, that " the spirits of the prophets are not always subject to the prophets," desiring, no doubt, to indicate by these words that it is not absolutely certain that Bernard had spoken by the inspiration of the Holy Spirit respecting that expedition, when he conjectured what the event of it would be.

LXXXVII. And yet Bernard himself, at the beginning of B. ii. *de Consideratione,* written to Pope Eugenius, when trying to defend that enterprise from calumny, does not hesitate to say that he was impelled from above to what he did. " We have spoken of peace," he says, " and there is no peace ; we have promised success, and behold confusion." Then he adds these words in his own defence :

" Can it be said that I acted rashly or lightly in that matter ?
I have run, indeed, in it not (as the Apostle says) as uncertainly, but at your bidding, or rather at the bidding of
God, through you." And a little farther on he supposes his
adversaries to reproach him thus : " How do we know that
your word comes from the Lord ? What sign doest thou
that we may believe thee ? " And addressing himself to
Eugenius he replies thus : " I have nothing to reply to that ;
modesty constrains me to be silent. Do you reply for me
and for yourself according to what you have heard and seen."
In which words he, without doubt, makes a modest reference to the miracles done by him for the confirmation of his
preaching.

LXXXVIII. But of all his apologists Geoffrey, his disciple,
best vindicates his master from reproaches (*Life,* B. iii. c.
4). He first remarks that Bernard was not the original
author of the enterprise ; " in fact, the proved necessity of
the Crusade had already won over the minds of many
persons when he was called into counsel once and again by
the King of France, and entrusted with the matter also,
by letters from the Pope ; nor did he consent to open his
mouth upon this subject nor to give advice to the people
until he was bidden by the express communication of the
Pontiff himself to lay the matter before peoples and princes
as the tongue of the Roman Church." His preaching,
undertaken by him as a matter of obedience, was at length
confirmed from on high by so many and so great miracles
and signs that " it would be very difficult to relate them or
even to enumerate them." Finally, that if the Eastern
Church did not obtain freedom by that expedition, at all
events the Church on high attained a joy proportioned to
the number of those who, by their death, " rendered up
their souls to Christ in the fruit of penitence and purified
by many tribulations." And, indeed, this was the very
truth which John, the holy Abbot of Casa Mario,

signified to Bernard had been made known to him by revelation.

LXXXIX. But why do we delay in justifying Bernard? His authority has long been so great in the eyes of all, even of the heterodox, that his life, his extraordinary sanctity, and his teaching are approved by the general opinion and praise of all.

XC. So much it seemed proper to me to say by way of Preface to this new edition of the Works of S. Bernard. If it shall seem careful and accurate to the learned, my friends and the companions of my studies, Dom Michael Germain, D. Thierry Ruinart, and also D. Edmond Martène, who have expended their labour upon this edition with much love and industry, will have the praise. For myself I ask but one reward, as I have proposed to myself but one end, that the fruit of my labour should be, if only in some small degree, serviceable and useful to the admirers of S. Bernard, to the Church, and to the entire Christian world.

To this preface in the fourth edition, from which we have translated, the following note is appended :—

Such, with the exception of a few words, were the prefatory observations made by D. John Mabillon to his second edition of S. Bernard, which we reproduce in preference to others, inasmuch as it is considered of higher value by the studious. In the year 1719 appeared a third edition, with various additions, respecting which we read at the end of Mabillon's preface as follows :—

" D. Massuet had made a beginning of labour upon this edition, and would have proceeded with it had not an untimely death put a period to his studies. To him are owing, in Vol. i., two recently discovered Letters, Nos. 418 and 419, a third drawn from the *Miscellanea* of Baluze, No. 425, and also two charters, whereof the former is for the monasteries of Lisieux and S. Êvre, and the other for the monastery of S. Amand de Boisse. In the second volume there will be found new : The third book of the Epistle to the

Brethren of Mont Dieu, and the *Admonitio* of D. Massuet, in which
he claims the entire Epistle, which was ascribed to William of
S. Thierry, as having been written by Guigo, fifth Prior of the
Grande Chartreuse. Also another *Observatio* of the same writer
which assigns the Treatise *de Contemplando Deo*, and that *de Natura
et Dignitate Amoris* to William of S. Thierry. Lastly, the Letter
of Tromund, monk of Clairvaux, respecting the canonization of
S. Bernard, which has not before been published."

In this fourth edition we have not omitted these additions, and
we have furthermore included thirty-six Letters of S. Bernard which,
after the above editions were completed, D. Martene transcribed
from MSS., viz., thirty-four from the Vedastine, one from that of
Anchin, and another spurious one from Verdun, and first made
public in his *Amplissima Collectio Veterum Scriptorum*, etc.,
Tom. I., pp. 725-744. Of these the first is numbered in the
common order of the Letters, 420, and the thirty-fifth,
454, the spurious one, 455. Also a Hymn of the holy Doctor,
which in the same Collection (Tom. i. p. 746) D. Martene has
brought forward from the Aldenberg MS., and as it is in the praise
of S. Malachi, it finds an appropriate place in Vol. ii., after the
Life of that Bishop. In order that this new edition might be the
more correct, I have consulted not only three examples of Mabillon,
but also some older copies.

BERNARDINE CHRONOLOGY.

A.D.

1091. The fourth year of Pope Urban II., the 35th of the Emperor Henry IV., the 31st of Philip I., King of France, BERNARD was born in the castle called Fontaines, near Dijon, in Burgundy. His father was Tescelin Sorus, lord of Fontaines; his mother Alith, daughter of Bernard, lord of Montbar. His paternal house was lately, by the gift of Louis XIII., King of France, granted to the Feuillant Fathers for a convent.

1098. B. Robert, Abbot of Molêsmes, taking with him twenty-one monks of the same house, withdrew into the desert of Cîteaux, and there founded a new monastery, in the Diocese of Chalons, about five leagues from Dijon, with the approval and help of Walter, Bishop of Chalons, and Hugh, Archbishop of Lyons.

1099. Death of Urban II. He is succeeded by Paschal II., who had been a monk of Cluny.

B. Robert, on the complaints of the monks of Molêsmes, is commanded by the Pope to return to Molêsmes. He is succeeded at Cîteaux by Prior Alberic. This year the Church is dedicated to the honour of B. V. M.

1100. This year the monks John and Ilbodus are sent to Rome with commendatory Letters. Paschal II. confirms the foundation of Cîteaux, and confers privileges upon it.

1101. Abbot Alberic institutes a stricter observance of the Rule of S. Benedict.

1102. Odo, Duke of Burgundy, founder of Cîteaux, dies, and is buried in the Abbey Church. In the same year his son Henry puts on the monastic habit there.

A.D.

under the presidency of Conon, Bishop of Præneste,
Legate of the Holy See, in which Peter himself was
obliged to commit his book on the Trinity to the
flames. William of Champeaux, Bishop of Chalons,
died this year.

The monastery of Foigny founded, in the Diocese of
Laon, to whose Abbot, Rainald, Bernard wrote Letters
72-74.

1122. Peter Maurice de Montboisier, called the Venerable,
an Auvergnat, and a very dear friend of Bernard, was
made Abbot of Cluny.

1123. About this year Peter, Abbot of Ferté, was chosen
to be Bishop of Tarentum, being the first of the
Cistercian Order to become a Bishop, and was succeeded by Bartholomew, brother of Bernard.

Suger elected Abbot of S. Denys in succession to
Abbot Adam.

1125. Death of the Emperor, Henry V., and a disputed
succession.

In the same year a severe famine in France and
Burgundy, which gives extensive exercise to the charity
of Bernard.

1126. Otto, afterwards Bishop of Frisingen, a well-known
chronicler, enters upon the monastic state in the community of Morimund.

1127. About this time Stephen, who from having been
Chancellor had become Bishop of Paris, was reclaimed
by the admonitions of Bernard from living the life of a
mere courtier to a more faithful fulfilment of the duties
of his office. He was harshly treated and persecuted by
King Louis, but was at length restored to favour by the
efforts of Bernard. Henry, Archbishop of Sens, who
not long after fell under the royal displeasure for a
similar cause, was also defended by him. See Letter
45 and notes.

The monastery of Igny, fourth daughter-house of
Clairvaux, was founded in the Diocese of Rheims. The

A.D.

first Abbot was Humbert, who not long after resigned
his post through love of quiet, and returned to Clairvaux, for which Bernard, then in Italy, wrote him a
letter of severe reprimand (Letter 141). The second
Abbot was Guerric, a man famed alike for his piety
and his writings.

1128. A Council held at Troyes, under Matthew, Bishop of
Albano, at which were present Stephen, Abbot of
Cîteaux, Bernard, of Clairvaux, and other Abbots of the
same Order. In it a white habit (to which Eugenius
III. afterwards added a red cross) was prescribed for
the Knights of the Temple, and a Rule drawn up to
govern the Order.

Regny founded in Diocese of Auxerre.

1129. The same Legate holds a Council at Chalons; where
by the advice of Bernard, Henry, Bishop of Verdun,
was deposed from his See and another Bishop appointed.

Monastery of Ourcamp (Ile de France), in the
Diocese of S. Cloud, founded by the Bishop Simon.

1130. Death of Pope Honorius II. and schism in the
Church, caused by an election to the Papacy disputed
between Gregory (Innocent) and Peter Leonis (Anacletus). Bernard energetically supported the cause of
Innocent for eight years.

In the same year Bernard firmly refused the vacant
Archbishopric of Genoa. Also Baldwin, in a Council
held at Clermont, was admitted to the College of
Cardinals; he was the first Cistercian to be raised to
that rank.

1131. Pope Innocent is magnificently received at Liège,
having come into France late in the former year.
Bernard induces Lothair to abandon his demand for
the cession of investitures, and the Pope crowns him
King of Germany in the same place. The Imperial
diadem is to be conferred in Rome two years later.
After this he crowned the young Prince Louis in place

A.D.

of his dead brother; then consecrated a church at
Cluny; and after that visited Clairvaux and other
churches, Bernard accompanying him everywhere. In
this year also Bernard was elected to the Bishopric
of Châlons, but firmly declined it.

In this year was the murder of Thomas, Prior of S.
Victor, at Paris, by the nephews of Theobald Notier,
Archdeacon of Paris. In this year were founded the
following daughter houses :—

Moreruela, in Castile.

S. John of Tarouca, in Portugal.

Longpont, in the Diocese of Soissons.

Charlieu, in the Diocese of Besançon.

Bonnemont, in Savoy; Diocese of Geneva.

Rievaulx, in England; Diocese of York.

1132. Bernard proceeded into Italy after departure of Pope
Innocent; reconciled the Pisans and Genoese, and
modestly but decidedly rejected the Archbishopric of
Genoa, once more offered to him.

At this time arose that great controversy between
the Cluniacs and Cistercians, arising out of the
exemption of the latter from tithes by Pope Innocent.
See Letters 228, 283.

In this year were founded :—

Vaucelles, in Diocese of Cambrai (Letter 186).

Fountains (*Tres Fontes*), in England, Diocese of
York (Letters 92, 94).

1133. S. Bernard, since the forces of Innocent were not
sufficient for taking Rome (the Emperor Lothair had
supplied him with 2,000 soldiers only), wrote to
Henry, King of England, to beg help. But at length
Innocent obtained entrance into Rome, and crowned
Lothair in the Lateran Church. When Lothair returned
home Innocent was obliged to retire to Pisa, whence
Bernard was sent into Germany to reconcile Conrad
to the Emperor Lothair. At this time the holy Abbot
sent the congratulatory Letter to the Pisans, because

A.D.

they had resisted the attempts of Anacletus to win
them over to his party (Letter 130). On this journey
took place the conversion of Mascelin (*Life*, iv. 3),
and also of the Duchess of Lorraine.

1134. A Council was held at Pisa, at which Bernard attended
by command of Pope Innocent, having made peace
between Lothair and Conrad. He had great difficulty
to avoid accepting the Archbishopric of Milan, which
was pertinaciously pressed upon him.

He founded a monastery of his Order at Chiaravalle
(*Chara-Vallis*), near Milan. Then he proceeded to
Paris and Cremona to reconcile those cities ; but not
having succeeded at Cremona, he notified their obstinacy to Innocent (Letter 318).

In the meantime, after the Council, Norbert, founder
of the Præmonstratensian Order, departed this life ;
also Stephen, Abbot of Cîteaux, who was at length
succeeded by Raynald, son of Milo, Count of Bar-sur-
Seine.

There were founded this year Hemmerode, in the
Diocese of Trèves, and Vauclaire (*Vallis-Clara*), in
that of Laon. The first Abbot (of the latter) was Henry
Murdach, to whom Letter 321.

1135. Bernard, after his return through Milan from Italy,
was enabled to accomplish the transfer of Clairvaux to
a more convenient site (*Life*, ii. 5). Scarcely had he
settled there than he was sent, with Geoffrey, Bishop
of Chartres, into Aquitaine, to reclaim William, Count
of Poitou, and other schismatics led away by Gerard,
Bishop of Angoulême (c. 6). A little after his return
he undertook his Exposition of the Canticles, at the
request of another Bernard, viz., Desportes, Prior of
the Chartreuse (Letters 153, 154).

This year were founded :—

Buzay, in the Diocese of Nantes, by Ermengarde,
Countess of Brittany, whom he had recalled from
worldly vanity during his journey just mentioned

A.D.

(Letters 116, 117). The first Abbot was John, to whom Letter 232.

Hautecombe, in the Diocese of Geneva.

Grâce de Dieu, in Diocese of Saintes.

Eberbach, in Diocese of Mentz.

1136. Guy, the eldest of Bernard's brothers, died away from Clairvaux, according to his brother's prediction (*Life*, ii. 12), namely, at Pontigny.

This year were founded :—

Balerne, Diocese of Besançon ; first Abbot, Burchard, to whom Letter 146.

Maison Dieu, on the Cher, in Diocese of Bourges ; the first Abbot was Robert, cousin of Bernard, to whom Letter 1.

Auberive, Diocese of Langres.

There was also adopted the Abbey *des Alpes*, in the Diocese of Geneva ; Guarine, the Abbot, and afterwards Bishop of Sion, urging the transfer (Letter 253).

1137. Bernard is summoned into Italy for the third time by Innocent, the cause of Anacletus being still supported by his great partisan Roger of Sicily.

In this year were founded :—

Di Columba, Diocese of Placentia, in Italy.

Bocchia, Diocese of Vesprin in Hungary (although this is referred by some to 1153).

There was also adopted the monastery of *Valparaiso* (formerly *Bellus-Fons*), in Spain.

1138. The Emperor Lothair II. died this year, and was succeeded by Conrad, Duke of Franconia, his former rival.

Also the Antipope Anacletus. The successor to him elected by the Cardinals of his party, Cardinal Gregory, called Victor, resigned the Papal insignia into the hands of Bernard, and submitted to Innocent, thus closing the schism, in great measure through the zeal and prudence of Bernard. "But the holy Abbot, leaving

A.D.

the Roman Court without delay, returned into France, nor would he bring back anything with him by way of gift or recompense, beyond a tooth of S. Cæsarius, and other relics of saints " (*Life,* iv. 1). His brother Gerard died this year. He now resumed his work on the Canticles, which had been interrupted.

In this year Rainald, Archbishop of Rheims, died ; and after two years Samson, Bishop of Chartres, was made his successor, Bernard himself having declined the dignity.

This year was founded the monastery of Nisors, Diocese of Lyons, over which was set Alberic, to whom Letter 173.

There was adopted also that of Dunes, Diocese of Bruges. The first Abbot was Robert, who afterwards succeeded Bernard at Clairvaux. To him Letter 324.

1139. Lateran Council assembled at Rome. In this year Malachi, Primate of Ireland, visited Clairvaux on his way to Rome. He left there six of his companions to be trained in the Cistercian Rule, that they might introduce it into Ireland.

1140. A Council held at Sens, in which the errors of Abaelard are condemned. He retired to Cluny, and two years later died at the monastery of S. Marcellus, Châlons, where he had gone for medical treatment.

There were founded this year :—

Clairmarais, Diocese of S. Omer.

Blancheland, Diocese of S. David's, Wales.

Ossera, Diocese of Orense, Gallicia.

Rivour, Diocese of Troyes, over whom was set Alan, afterwards Bishop of Autun, compiler of a Life of S. Bernard.

Also Pope Innocent handed over to the monks of Clairvaux for reorganization the monastery of S. Anastasius, at Aquæ Salviæ; and there was set over it Bernard of Pisa, a disciple of S. Bernard, who afterwards was called to the Roman See as Eugenius III.

A.D.

Also were adopted that of Benchor,[1] conveyed by Archbishop Malachi ; and of Casamaria in Veroli, Italy.

1141. Pope Innocent laid King Louis under an interdict because he refused to receive the Archbishop of Bourges, whom, however, he did at length receive, and then was absolved from an oath which he had unreasonably taken (Letter 218 onwards).

In this year the same King Louis attacked Theobald, Count of Champagne, and laid waste his territories (Letters 217, 220, 222, 223).

At this time occurred the death of Humbeline, sister of Bernard (*Life*, i. 6).

This year was founded the Abbey of Mellifont, in the Diocese of Armagh, Ireland, by the efforts of Archbishop Malachi. It consisted of the companions whom he had left at Clairvaux for training, with some others (Letters 356, 357).

1142. Ivo, cardinal presbyter, was sent into France to pronounce sentence against Ralph, Count of Vermandois, who having repudiated his former wife Eleanor, niece of Count Theobald, had married Petronilla, the daughter of William, Duke of Aquitaine, sister of the Queen (Letters 216, 217, 220, 221).

Alfonso, King of Portugal, gave himself as tributary, and his realm to be a fief of the Abbey of Clairvaux, and assigned to it a payment of fifty double Marabotines of fine gold.[2]

In this year died Hugo of S. Victor, called a second Augustine for his own age, an intimate friend and admirer of Bernard (Letter 70).

About this time were founded :—

Melon, Diocese of Tuy, in Gallicia.

Sobrado, Diocese of Compostella.

Haute Crète, Diocese of Lausanne, in Savoy.

[1] Ancient name of Bangor co. Down.
[2] The Abbey actually tried in 1578 to make good its claim under this charter.
—[E.]

A.D.

1143. Pope Innocent died in this year, and was succeeded by Guido de Castello, called Celestine II., to whom Letters 234, 235.

Founded this year:—

Alvastern, Diocese Linköping, Sweden.

Nidal, in the same (some writers put this four years later).

Belle Perche, Diocese of Montauban.

Meyra, in Gallicia; Diocese of Luçon.

1144. Pope Celestine died.

Bernard succeeded in making peace between King Louis and Count Theobald (Letters 220 and onwards should be read).

In this year died Bartholomew, Abbot of Ferté, brother of S. Bernard. Also Stephen of Châlons, Cardinal Bishop of Praeneste, a member of the Cistercian Order, a man of great sanctity, to whom Bernard wrote various Letters.

Founded:—

Beaulieu, in Diocese of Rhodez.

1145. Pope Lucius died this year, and was succeeded by Bernard, Abbot of Aquas Salvias, as Eugenius III. (Letter 237 and onwards). At this time Bernard was consulted by King Louis respecting a Crusade, and devolved the decision upon the Pope.

Founded:—

La Prés, in Diocese of Bourges.

1146. Council held at Chartres to consider of the Crusade, to which Peter the Venerable was invited (Letter 364), but was not able to come, as we collect from his reply (B. vi., L. 18). Bernard was, by the direction of Eugenius, chosen as chief advocate of this warfare. He exhorted the peoples of Germany, of Eastern France, the Bavarians, the English, etc., both by letters and by preaching, to take the Cross, and was greatly assisted by many miracles (Letters 363-365, and Book of the Miracles of S. Bernard).

A.D.

Founded :—

Boxley, in Diocese of Canterbury, England.

Villars, in Diocese of Namur, Brabant. This foundation the Auctarium Gemblacense fixes in the
following year in these words :—" Twelve monks
with their Abbot, Laurence, and five lay brethren
(*conversi*), sent by B. Bernard from Clairvaux into
Brabant, erected the monastery at Villars."

1147. Pope Eugenius was driven from Rome by Arnold
(Letter 242), and took refuge in Gaul, being received
in Paris with great honour by King Louis, who had
taken the Cross in the previous year, on Palm Sunday,
and with him his brother, Robert and Geoffrey, Count
of Mellent. The King set off into Syria against the
Saracens on June 14.

In a Synod at Etampes the administration of France
was committed to Suger, Abbot of St. Denys, Gilbert
being present.

Bernard, with Alberic, Cardinal Bishop of Ostia and
Legate, and Geoffrey, Bishop of Chartres, proceeded
into Aquitaine against the heretic Henry (General
Preface, and Letter 241).

In this year Alfonso, King of Portugal, having taken
the city of Santarem by the intercessions of S. Bernard,
sent letters asking for monks to be sent that he may
found a monastery of the Cistercian Order in his
kingdom.

Founded :—

Alcobaça, Diocese of Lisbon, in Portugal, by the
before-mentioned king.

Vauricher, in Diocese of Bayeux.

Margan, in Wales.

Espina, in Diocese of Palancia, in Castile, by Sanchia,
the sister of King Alfonso (Letter 301).

Also the monastery of Grandselve, in Diocese of
Toulouse, of the Order of S. Benedict, was adopted, its
Abbot, Bernard, passing over himself with the whole
house (Letter 242).

A.D.

1148. This year Pope Eugenius was present at a general
council of the Cistercian Order, and consecrated a new
cemetery for them. Taking leave of the brethren, not
without tears, he returned into Italy.

After the departure of Eugenius from France,
S. Malachi, Primate of Ireland, who was on his way
to Rome, to apply to the Pontiff for the pallium,
happily departed this life at the place he most wished,
namely, Clairvaux, and at the time also, namely, on the
very day of the solemn commemoration of all the
departed. His memory began to be held famous
immediately upon his death (see the Epistle Consolatory, 374, to the Irish ; also his Life, by S. Bernard ;
and two Sermons delivered at the time of his burial).
The new building for the Abbey of Clairvaux was completed at the very time that S. Malachi was lying at
the point of death, and the bones of the venerable
Fathers which at first had slept in the old monastery
were translated from the old cemetery to the new on
the Festival of All Saints (Sermon i. on S. Malachi, n.
1). His canonization is in the Chronicle of Clairvaux
(given by Chifflet), referred to 1192.

In the same year died the blessed Humbert, Abbot
of Igny. (For proof of this date see note on a Sermon
delivered by Bernard on his death.)

Founded :—

Cambroane, in the Diocese of Cambray. The first
Abbot was Fastrade, from Clairvaux, which latter
Abbey he was the head of after Robert.

Also was adopted Alne, in the Diocese of Liège, previously a Benedictine Abbey, and afterwards a house
of Regular Canons.

Also in this year Serlo, Abbot of Savigny, submitted
his own abbey and thirty other monasteries depending
upon it ; viz., the Benedictine Abbey of Savigny, in
the Diocese of Avranches, to Clairvaux, during the
meeting of the great Chapter of Cîteaux ; and four also

A.D.

were adopted from Stephen, the founder and father of
the rising community of Obazin, in the Diocese of
Limoges.

1149. In this year King Louis returned to France after the
unsuccessful issue of the Crusade (see Letter 386;
Lib. de Consideratione, ii. 1; and *Life*, iii. 4). When
making preparations for a new expedition he was dis-
suaded by the Cistercians, as Abbot Robert reports in
his Chronicle, under A.D. 1150.

In the same year Henry, brother of King Louis
(Chronicle of Tours), who had before been Treasurer
of S. Martin at Tours and afterwards had put on the
monastic habit at Clairvaux, was made Archbishop of
Beauvais (see Letter 307 and notes).

Founded this year :—

Font-Morigny, Diocese of Bourges.

Aubepierre, Diocese of Limoges.

Lonway, Diocese of Langres.

Looz, Diocese of Tournay.

Also adopted, Boulancourt, a house of Regular
Canons, in the Diocese of Troyes.

1150. Bernard sends Book ii. of his *de Consideratione* to
Pope Eugenius, now, after many conflicts, in possession of Rome, and makes it include an apology for the
recent design of a Crusade. He receives a consolatory
letter from John, Abbot of Casa Maria, in the town of
Véroli (now Letter 386 among those of Bernard).

1151. Abbot Rainald, of Cîteaux, died towards the end of
the preceding year, and was now succeeded by
Goswin, Abbot of Bonnevaux, in Poitou (Letter 270).

This year died Hugo, Bishop of Auxerre. Respecting the election of his successor, see Letters 261, 274,
and onwards.

Also Suger, Abbot of S. Denys, to whom, when on
his death-bed, Bernard wrote Letter 266.

Founded the Monastery of Hesron, in Diocese of
Roskild, Denmark.

A.D.

1152. This year died Theobald, Count of Champagne, a man of distinguished piety, the friend and patron of S. Bernard. He was buried in the monastery of Lagny, on the Marne, of which he was patron (*advocatus*). Bernard wrote to him Letter 271 not long before his death.

Adopted this year the Abbey of Moreilles, in Diocese of Maillezais. Also (about this time) Armentera, in Diocese of Compostella, Gallicia.

Founded :—

Abbey of Clermont, in Diocese of Mans.

1153. Pope Eugenius died this year.

Not long after died the holy Doctor Bernard, worn out with many labours for God and the Church. Though his strength was consumed by violent disease since the middle of the winter, as he writes in Letters 288, 307, 308, he had succeeded in making peace between the townsmen of Metz. He rested in peace himself at length, on the 18th of August, at nine o'clock a.m., in his sixty-third year, in the fortieth year of his monastic profession, and in the thirty-eighth year of office as Abbot. Bernard was succeeded by Robert, Abbot of Dunes.

In this very week Ascalon, the strongest city in Palestine, was taken by the Christians, according to the frequently repeated promise of the Saint (*Life,* iii. 4).

Founded this year monasteries at :—

Peyrouse, Diocese of Périgueux.

Mores, Diocese of Langres.

And adopted :—

Abbey of Monte Ramo, in Diocese of Orense, in Gallicia.

LIST AND ORDER OF THE
LETTERS OF S. BERNARD, ABBOT.

---

[1] This is the Treatise *De Moribus et Officio Episcoporum.*

---

[1] Placed among the Treatises.

LETTER I. (*Circa* 1119.)

*He recalls, with wonderful gentleness, and affection more
than fatherly, Robert, his relative ; who, induced either by
shrinking from a very severe Rule, the attraction of a freer
life, or the blandishments and cunning suggestions of
others, had withdrawn from the Cistercian Order to the
Cluniac.*

1. I have waited long enough, my dear son Robert, perhaps too long, [hoping] that the grace of God might deign
to visit both your soul and mine, inspiring you with salutary
contrition and me with joy for your repentance. But since
my hope is so far not fulfilled, I am no longer able to hide
my grief or express my anxiety. Thus, though wounded, I
am obliged to call upon my assailant; despised, to ask for
the pity of him who contemns me ; though injured, to make
satisfaction to my injurer; and in fine, against all rule, to
beseech him who ought to beseech me. Extreme grief
does not deliberate or observe limits, is not ashamed, does
not fear loss of dignity; it disregards measure, and rule,
and order. The powers of the mind are wholly occupied in
relieving itself, by any means, of what causes it pain, or in
obtaining what it suffers to be without. But you say : I
have not injured nor despised anyone, but rather, being
scorned and injured in many ways, I have fled from my
enemy. Whom have I injured in fleeing from injuries ? Is
it not better to withdraw from the persecutor than to resist
him ?—to fly the striker than to strike back ? Truly, I allow
it. Not to contend have I begun to write, but to bring con-

tention to an end. The pursuer—not the fugitive—is to be blamed for a flight from persecution. I pass over what has been done. I do not ask why or how. I do not discuss whose is the fault, and I wish to bury all remembrance of wrongs. Such [discussions] are wont to arouse, not to soften, differences. I speak only of what is more to my heart—unhappy that I am—to be deprived of you, and not to see you, death for whom would be to me life, and without whom life is death! I do not ask why you went away. I complain only because you have not returned. I speak not of the causes of your departure, but of the delay of your return. Return only, and there shall be peace. Return, and it shall suffice, and I will sing with joy, *He was dead and is alive again; he was lost and is found!* (S. Luke xv. 32).

2. Surely it was my fault that you departed. I was rigid to a delicate youth; I was severe, and treated harshly a sensitive mind. When you were here you were wont, as far as I remember, to murmur against me, and since, as I have heard, you do not cease to blame me, though absent. It shall not be laid to your charge. I might, perhaps, allege that it was my duty to restrain the passions of petulant youth, and that those harsh beginnings of strict discipline are needful in early years, as the Scripture bears witness: *Chasten thy son with a rod, and thou shalt deliver his soul from death* (Prov. xxiii. 13); and, again, *Whom the Lord loveth he chasteneth, and scourgeth every son whom he receiveth* (Heb. xii. 6), and that *More wholesome are the wounds of a friend than the kisses of an enemy* (Prov. xxvii. 6). But let it be, as I said, that it was by my fault you went away; only let there be no contention about the offence to hinder the amends for it. I have, perhaps, sometimes and in some matters acted unwisely towards you, but never have I been ill-disposed. Therefore, spare the penitent, or at least have consideration for one who speaks frankly to you. If you fear for the future you shall find me not what I was, because I think that you are not what you were. A changed person yourself, you shall find

me changed, and him whom you before feared as a master you may safely embrace as a companion. Therefore, whether you withdrew by my fault, as you think and I do not dispute, or by your own, as many think, although I do not maintain it, or by our common fault, as I incline to think, if for this reason you demur to return, you alone shall be without excuse. Would you be free from all blame? Return. If you acknowledge your fault, I forgive it. Do you also forgive me where I acknowledge mine, otherwise either you are too indulgent to yourself, when you are conscious of your fault and yet will not acknowledge it, or you are too unmerciful to me, whom you will not forgive even when I make amends.

3. Now, if you are unwilling to return, seek some other excuse wherewith to flatter your conscience, for henceforth there will be no reason for you to dread the severity of my rule. You need not fear that I shall be too severe to you when you are here, seeing that I abase myself with my whole heart to you when absent, and am bound to you by entire affection. I practise humility, I promise love, and do you still fear? You have fled from a stern [ruler] ; return to a gentle one. Let my lenity recall you, since my severity drove you away. See, my son, how I wish to recall you—not in fear again and in the spirit of servitude, but in the spirit of filial adoption, in which you may call and not be disappointed, *Abba, Father!* (Rom. viii. 15). Though you have caused me so great grief I use not threats and terrors, but caresses and entreaties. Others would, perhaps, employ different means ; would lay before you your offence, would remind you of your vow, and awake in you the fear of judgment· They would reproach you with disobedience, with apostacy in abandoning a coarse garment for a fine habit, a diet of vegetables for dainties, and, in fine, poverty for riches. But I know that you are more easily induced by love than compelled by fear, and I have not thought it needful to goad the unresisting, to terrify the frightened, to confound still more him who blushes. But would it not seem an unheard-of thing that a youth, modest, simple, and retiring, should

have dared to violate his vow, to leave the place of his profession against the will of his brethren, the authority of his
master, the obligation of his rule ? Yet it is not more strange
than that the piety of David should have been beguiled
(2 Sam. xi.), the wisdom of Solomon mocked (1 Kings xi.),
the strength of Samson rendered vain (Judges xvi.). What
wonder that he who deceived our first parents and expelled
them from Paradise should have seduced an inexperienced
young man in the midst of a desert solitude ! Add to this
that he has not been led away by beauty, as the elders of
Babylon (Hist. of Susan., 8), nor by the love of money, as
Gehazi (2 Kings v. 20), nor by ambitious desires, as Julian
the Apostate, but holiness deceived him, religion seduced
him, the authority of his elders led him astray.   Do you ask
how ?

4. A certain great Prior was sent forth by his superiors :
and he, a wolf disguised in sheep's clothing, was admitted
into the sheepfold. He attracts, he allures, he flatters ;
the preacher of a new Gospel, he commends drunkenness,
condemns frugality ; voluntary poverty he calls misery ;
fasts, vigils,. silence, the labour of the hands, he styles
folly ; but, on the contrary, sloth he names contemplation ; gluttony, loquacity, inquisitiveness, in short, every
kind of excess, he calls discretion. What, he says, does
God delight in our sufferings? Where does Scripture
bid anyone to slay himself? What sort of religion is
it to dig the earth, to cut wood, to carry manure? Is it
not the declaration of the Truth, *I will have mercy and
not sacrifice* (S. Matt. ix. 13, Ezek. xxxiii. 11, S. Matt.
v. 7). Why has God created food if it is not permitted to
eat it ? or given us bodies if we must not sustain them ?
And then, *He that is evil to himself, to whom will he be
good* (Ecclus. xiv. 5). *What wise man ever hated his own
flesh ?* (Eph. v. 29).

5. Thus with such pleadings a too credulous youth is
seduced ; he follows his deluder, he is led to Cluny ; he is
shorn, shaven, washed ; in place of his worn, cheap. rustic
clothes he is clad in new, fashionable, and costly ones, and

thus he is taken into the convent. And with what honour, triumph, and observance! He, a youth, is set above his equals, above his seniors; the entire brotherhood favours, compliments, congratulates him; they all rejoice as victors when they divide the spoil. O, good Jesus! how many things are done for the destruction of one poor soul! Whose heart, however firm, would not grow soft? whose inner eye, however spiritual it might be, would not be confused? Among such distractions who could consult his conscience, who could either recognize truth, or maintain humility?

6. Application is made on his account to Rome. Apostolic authority is approached; and that the Pope may not refuse his consent, it is suggested to him that [the youth when] an infant was offered to that monastery by his parents. There was no one to contradict this; judgment was given upon a mere statement, and against the absent. Those who did the injury are justified, those who suffered it put off altogether, and the offender absolved without making satisfaction. Too mild a sentence of absolution is confirmed by a cruel privilege, which, when reported, encouraged and rendered secure the ill-assured victim of bad advice. And among these things a soul may perish for which Christ died, because the Cluniacs choose! Profession is made upon profession, vows which will not be loosed and cannot be kept, and since the first agreement is made invalid, a pretext is found for a second, and sin heaped upon sin.

7. May He speedily come who will right wrongs judicially done and put to shame unlawful oaths, who will right those that suffer wrong, will judge the poor in justice, and contend with equity for the meek of the earth! To Thy tribunal, O, Lord Jesus, I appeal; to Thee I commit my cause, O, Lord God of Sabaoth, who judgest justly, and triest the reins and the hearts (Jer. xi. 20), whose eyes, as they cannot deceive, so they cannot be deceived. Thou seest who seeks the things which are Thine, and who seeks his own (1 Cor. xiii. 5). Thou knowest with what gentleness I have succoured him in all his temptations, with what

groanings I have wearied for him the ears of Thy Holiness, how troubled I used to be by his faults and escapades. And now I fear that it was in vain. For I think, as far as I have tried, that it is for the profit neither of the mind or body of a young man, by himself sufficiently eager and inexperienced, to apply to the one such stimulants, to the other such incentives to vanity. Therefore, Lord Jesus, be Thou my judge; let my sentence come forth from Thy presence, let Thine eyes look upon the thing that is equal (Ps. xvii. 2).

8. Let them see and judge which ought rather to stand good, the vow of a father respecting his son or that of the son respecting himself, especially when he has made the vow even more perfect. Let them see how Thy servant, our law-giver Benedict,[1] would have decided; whether what was done respecting a young infant, without his knowledge, or what he himself afterwards did advisedly of his own accord, when he was of an age to speak for himself, should hold good. It is clear that he was promised only, not given. The petition which the Rule prescribes was not made on his behalf by the parents, nor his hand with the petition folded in the covering of the altar, so that he might be offered before witnesses. A [piece of] ground is shown which is said to have been given with him and for him. But if they received him with the ground, why did they not keep him as well as the ground? Did they, perhaps, require more than its fruit, or value the land more than this soul? Otherwise, if offered to the monastery, what was he seeking in the world? If he were to be brought up for God, why was he abandoned to the devil? Why was Christ's sheep found a prey to the wolf? From the world you came, Robert, yourself being witness, not from Cluny, when you came to Citeaux. You requested admission, you

---

[1] According to the Rule of S. Benedict (Cap. lix.) the simple promise of the parents to devote a child to the Order was not binding. There must have been a solemn offering of the child, according to prescribed forms, during which he was clad in the monastic habit.

It does not appear whether there had been any such formal offering of the young Robert. — [E.]

begged, you entreated; but were put off for two years, on account of your tender age, though you were most unwilling to wait. Which time being patiently and blamelessly fulfilled, you begged with many prayers and even (if you remember) tears, and at length obtained, the wished-for favour and the entrance [into the Order] which you had so desired. After this, being patiently proved for a year, according to the Rule, and your demeanour being resolved and without reproach, you were professed at your own wish; then first you discarded the secular dress and put on the religious habit.

9. O, foolish boy! who has enchanted you that you should not fulfil the vows of your own lips? Shall you not be justified or be condemned out of your own mouth? Why are you careful about your parent's vow and forgetful of your own, forgetting that out of your mouth, not of his, you will be judged? Who can flatter you with talk about an apostolical absolution, while the Word of God itself holds your conscience bound? *No one,* He says, *putting his hand to the plough, and looking back, is fit for the kingdom of God* (S. Luke ix. 62). Question your own heart, your intention; let your conscience answer you why you fled, why you deserted your Order, your brethren, your place, and me; me, who am near you in blood and still nearer in spirit. If you are now living more severely, more correctly, more perfectly than before, then you may be confident that you have not *looked back,* and glory with the Apostle who says : *Forgetting the things that are behind and pressing forward unto the things that are before, I press unto the mark* (Philipp. iii. 13). But if it is otherwise, be not high-minded, but fear; because whatever indulgence you give to yourself in food, in unnecessary dress, in idle words, in unregulated and inquisitive licence, beyond what you have promised and have observed here, this beyond doubt is a looking back, a wandering from the path ; in short, an apostacy.[1]

[1] A stern declaration indeed against monks who, seeking greater laxity, held lightly the obligations of their Rule. See Letters 313, 382, and Serm. iii. on Ps. xc.

10. And these things I say to you, my son, not to distress you, but to warn you, for though you have many teachers in Christ, you have not many fathers (1 Cor. iv. 14). For (if you should deem it of any value) both by word and by my example have I begotten you to religion. Does it please you that another person should glory in you, who has laboured not at all for you and in you? Like as to the harlot before Solomon, so it has happened to me: namely, to her whose little son had been secretly taken away by another, who had overlaid and destroyed her own (1 Kings iii. 20).

11. Now for what advantage to you, or for what need of yours, have our friends endeavoured to do this? For as for me, if I had ever offended them in anything (which I am not conscious of having done), I would at once have made full amends. But it is strange if I have not sustained the worse reprisal; if (that is to say) I have been able to do them some such injury, as I have now endured from them. For I protest that they have taken, not the bone of my bones nor flesh of my flesh, but the very joy of my heart, the fruit of my spirit, the crown of my hope, and (as I verily feel) the half of my soul. And why? Perhaps they pitied you, and not bearing to see the blind leading the blind, they took you to their own leading, that you might not perish under mine. But could not you be saved, unless I were despoiled? And would that you may be saved even without me! But is your salvation likely to be more advanced by nicety of dress, and abundance of dainties, than by frugality of dress and living? If soft and warm garments, fine and costly cloths, full sleeves, an ample hood, a thick and soft coverlet, and fine linen[1] make a saint, why should not I also follow the

---

[1] Bernard notes here the different kinds of clothing which were in use among the Cluniacs, and which the Cistercians had rejected as contrary to the Rule. We may see in the little "Exordium Cisterciense" that they had rejected "frocks, furred tunics, linen shirts, drawers, cowls; also mattresses, and bed-clothes." Also in "The Book of Institutes," c. 15, "hoods lined with wool" are rejected. We see in the MS. *Customs of Cluny*, by Bernard of Cluny, c. 30, that among other things it was permitted to a monk of that monastery to have as articles of dress "two frocks, two hoods, two shirts, and three furred tunics," and for the

example? But these are the comforts of the sick, not the weapons of combatants. For *those who wear soft clothing are in kings' houses* (S. Matt. xi. 8). Wine and fine flour, mead and fat things, fight for the body, not the soul. With broiled meats the flesh, not the soul, is made fat. Many brethren in Egypt long served God without using even fish.[1] Pepper, ginger, cumin, sage, and a thousand kinds of things pickled, delight indeed the palate, but inflame the passions. And do you place security in these things? or suppose that you can spend your youth safely thus? Salt, with hunger, is sufficient condiment to one who lives soberly and prudently; but if hunger is not waited for, it becomes needful to excite it with I know not what potions.

12. But what shall he do, you say, who cannot live otherwise? I know that you are delicate and would not be able

bed "a pillow, a sheet, a counterpane, a blanket, and a rug." The frocks differed from the hoods both in form and material, because the hood had only a narrow cowl, and either no sleeves at all or very narrow ones. The frock, on the contrary, had very ample sleeves and hood, and it was made of costly cloth, which was called *froccus* or *floccus* (whence the name *frock*). Among our-selves the hood is still commonly called *floccus*. The Cistercians call it generally *coulle* (say cowl), because of their repugnance to frocks. The "*coopertorium silvestre*" of which S. Bernard speaks was a kind of outside wrap made of the skins of animals hunted in the forest. In his Apology, addressed to William, n. 24, Bernard of Cluny attacks the "*cattinum*" and "coverings which do not permit you to remain uncovered, either of lamb's skin or cat's skin, that of hares, nor in short, of any other kind of higher price."—See *Life*, B. iv. c. 36.

[1] It appears by this that the monks of Cîteaux used fish only rarely, and when upon a journey (see *Life*, B. vii. c. 20), nor eggs, as will be seen from what follows. We learn the practice with regard to eggs from a Letter of Abbot Fastred, printed at the end of those of S. Bernard. A novice, in distaste of all food during his last illness, "felt a desire for a cooked egg," but he observed abstinence to the end. The same author tells us that "vegetables were cooked without oil or fat," and Bernard himself speaks of "broths made with flour . . . . with oil and honey added," not butter, which he eat "with scruple" to warm his stomach. In this letter and the following one, which is from Peter d. Roya, we see that the monks of Clairvaux drank a kind of beer, sometimes pure water, "rarely wine," and even then mixed with much water, which Humbert used for his infirmities, but only out of obedience (Bernard, Serm. on Saints, n. 4; *Life*, B. i. n. 46; Serm. 30 on the Canticles). Joannes Eremita (*Life of Bernard*, B. ii. n. 10) speaks of the vine as being held under malediction at Clairvaux.

to endure a harder life, but that is only because you are accustomed to these things. But what if you could make yourself able? Do you ask how? Rise, gird yourself, shake off sloth, use your powers, move your arms, open those folded hands, do something useful, and you will soon find that you have appetite for what takes away hunger without pampering the palate. Many things which, when idle, you turn from, after labour you will take with relish. Cabbage, beans, pottage, coarse bread,[1] with water, are little appetizing, I allow, to an idle person, but they seem great delicacies to one who has laboured. Having become unaccustomed to tunics,[2] you are perhaps afraid to take to wear them again, as being too cold in winter and too hot in summer; but have you ever read, *He who fears the hoar frost the snow shall fall upon him?* (Job vi. 16). Idleness produces distaste, exercise, hunger. You fear watchings, fastings, and the labour of the hands; but these things are trifles to him who meditates on the everlasting burnings. Then the remembrance of the outer darkness causes you not to shudder at solitude. If you remember that every idle word shall be called in question (S. Matt. xii. 36), silence will not greatly displease you. That eternal weeping and gnashing of teeth, if brought before the eyes of the heart, will render hard mat or soft couch the same thing to you. Finally, if you have faithfully kept watch the whole time of the night which the Rule prescribes, with Psalms (Rule of S. Bened., cap. ix. seqq.), hard indeed will be the couch on which you will not sleep soundly.

13. Rise, soldier of Christ, shake off the dust, return to the battle whence you have fled, fight more bravely after your flight, and you shall conquer the more gloriously. Christ has indeed many soldiers who have set out bravely, stood

---

[1] The *Life* (B. ii. n. 6) shows us what kind of bread was used at this time at Clairvaux. Fastred, in his letter cited above, says that it was made of oats.

[2] The monks of Cîteaux wore their tunics immediately upon the skin, without any garment of wool or linen between, but not the goats' hair *cilicium* (*Life*, B. i. n. 39).

fast and overcome, but few, who having turned back from flight and dared anew the peril which they had evaded, have put to flight the enemies from whom they had fled. And because every rare thing is precious, I rejoice that you should be of those who shall appear the more glorious the rarer they are. But do not think that because you have fled from the fight, you have escaped from the hands of the enemy. The adversary overtakes you with more pleasure when flying than he resists you when combating, and strikes more boldly at your back than he attacks face to face. Are you securely taking your morning slumbers, when at that time Christ rose from the dead; and thus unarmed, at once more timid yourself and less formidable to enemies? A multitude of armed ones have surrounded your house, and you are sleeping? Already they ascend the mound, they pull down the palisade, they rush in at the postern door. Is it safer for you that they should find you alone than with others— naked in your bed than armed and in the field? Rise up, seize your arms, and fly to your fellow soldiers whom you have deserted. Let fear itself join you again to those from whom it parted you. Why do you, O, effeminate warrior, shrink from the weight and hardness of your weapons? The adversary pressing on you and the darts flying around will make the shield, the cuirass, and the helmet seem to be no burden. Even the bravest soldiers have fears when the trumpet sounds before the combat, but when they are in the thick of the fight, the hope of victory and the fear of being overcome renders them intrepid. But what can you fear when the unanimity of your brethren and fellow combatants fortifies you on all sides, when the Angels stand beside you, when Christ, the leader of the war, will go before you, cheering His own on to victory, and saying, *Be of good cheer ; I have overcome the world !* (S. John xvi. 33). If Christ be for us, who can be against us? (Rom. viii. 31). You can fight safely when you are sure of victory. Safe, indeed, is warfare with and for Christ, for, though wounded, prostrate, trampled on, killed, if possible, a thousand times, yet, if only you do not fly, you shall not lose the victory.

Flight, flight alone can take it from you. Woe to you if, in declining the fight, you lose at once the victory and the crown ; which may God avert from you, my dearest son, since your condemnation will be the greater, if I have rightly charged you in this my letter.[1]

[1] This Letter was dictated by Bernard in the open air, " in the midst of rain without rain," as says William, Abbot of S. Thierry (*Life of S. Bernard*, B. i. c. 2), and because of this marvel was placed before the other Letters. The place where this took place, close to Clairvaux, was marked by a little oratory in memory of it. It was written by William, afterwards first Abbot of Rievaulx, in England, to whom some refer, but wrongly, those praises with which Gilbert of Hoiland, in his Sermon 41 (*in Cantica*), commemorates a certain Abbot of Rievaulx, without doubt the successor of William, by name Aelred, who died, according to Pitsæus, in 1166. For it can hardly be the case that this William of Rievaulx, who died 1146, was praised by Gilbert in that sermon, which is in the form of a funeral oration, as if he were recently dead. Now Gilbert himself undertook the continuation of his explanation of the Canticles only after the death of S. Bernard, which happened in 1153, and in Sermon 30 he mentions the schism excited by the Emperor Frederick against Alexander III. in 1159.

Robert, to whom this Letter was addressed, is called a relative of Bernard in this Letter, n. 9, and in Letter 32, n. 3. Joannes Eremita, an author of that time, speaks thus of him in his *Life of S. Bernard*, B. i. c. 2, n. 5 :—" He was nephew of the same matron," namely, Alith, mother of S. Bernard, " of whom we are going to speak, and son of her sister. It was to him that the blessed Bernard addressed the first of his Letters." He is said to have lived sixty-seven years as a monk. Peter Chifflet, a monk of the Society of Jesus, in an appendix to his dissertation on the illustrious origin of S. Bernard, suggests that the mother of Robert was Diana, wife of Otho de Châtillon de Montbar, and in that case Robert would have been called the nephew of S. Bernard, either by the mere fancy of the person who collected his Letters, or by a mode of speaking once common, which allowed the children of two brothers or of two sisters, as well as those of a brother and of a sister, to be called nephew, provided that it was the younger alone who received that title from his cousin older than himself. And it is sufficiently clear that this was the relation of Robert to S. Bernard, as well from this Letter as from B. i. of the Life, c. 2.

As to the date of this Letter, it seems to have been written about 1119. It would appear that Robert made his solemn profession among the Cistercians in 1113. When the monks of Cluny heard of this they had recourse to an underhand proceeding to bring him back to them. The Exordium Cisterc. Dis. 3, c. 9, thus refers to this :—" In the meantime the Cluniac brothers, hearing that the young man had given himself to the Cistercian Order, were exceedingly indignant. . . . As they did not presume to demand him publicly, being overawed by the reputation of the blessed Bernard, they resorted to a more crafty proceeding. A certain Prior was sent," etc. In the meantime S. Bernard long concealed his feelings, as he says in the commencement of this Letter, but at length, not being able to restrain his grief, he wrote this Letter, which did not, however, bring Robert back, as he complains in Letter 32, until he was sent back by Peter the Venerable.

That Robert made his profession in 1116 is apparently shown thus : Almost all writers, both within and without our Order, think that Robert was one of those thirty friends whom Bernard withdrew from the world and took with him to Cîteaux, which, indeed, Bernard himself seems to indicate in these words of this Letter :—" For (if you should deem it of any value), both by word and my example, have I begotten you to religion." Then, on account of his extreme youth, his admission to Cîteaux was put off for two years, after which he was received to make his novitiate, as Bernard asserts also in n. 8, and Bernard entered Cîteaux in 1113, to which date, if the two years of waiting and one of probation be added, we have 1116 as the date of Robert's profession.

This argument is much strengthened by the authority of the Exordium already cited, where it is said that Robert was admitted to his probation at Cîteaux before Bernard was set over Clairvaux, that is to say, before 1115, in which year Clairvaux was founded, for the Exordium speaks thus :—" Dom Robert, formerly Abbot of Maison Dieu and a relative of the blessed Bernard according to the flesh, in his youth had taken upon him the light and easy yoke of the Lord at Cîteaux. But afterwards, when that most reverend man of God, Bernard, was made Abbot of Clairvaux, he was trained up under him in that monastery in spiritual discipline." From this it appears that the departure of Robert from Clairvaux, or rather his being decoyed away, is to be attributed to the design and the influence of Pontius, Abbot of Cluny from 1109 to 1122, and that it was not under the government of Peter the Venerable, who succeeded Pontius after Hugo II. had been abbot for three months only, as appears from the Chronicle of Cluny. It is very certain that Peter, who was a great lover of peace and uprightness, would not have been likely to send a prior to Clairvaux to draw away a young man, or, even if that be thought possible, the sending back of Robert would not have been counted among the benefits and offices of charity which he had done to S. Bernard, for he would not have been able to confer a benefit in repairing an injustice, for he writes thus in a certain epistle to Bernard (B. 6, ep. 35) :—" Why, then, my dear friend, do you not wish to give me, at least for a month, one of your monks, when I have given up to you, induced by love towards you, Robert your relation, Garnier, and certain others, not for a month, but permanently ? "—from which it is to be remarked in passing, not only that Robert returned to Clairvaux, but that he was sent back by Peter in the beginning of his abbacy at Cluny. He was sent later on by Bernard as Abbot to Maison Dieu, in the Diocese of Dijon.

LETTER II. (*Circa* A.D. 1120.)

TO A YOUTH NAMED FULK, WHO AFTERWARDS WAS ARCHDEACON OF LANGRES.

He gravely warns Fulk, a Canon Regular, whom an uncle had by persuasions and promises drawn back to the world, to obey God and be faithful to Him rather than to his uncle.

To the honourable young man Fulk, Brother Bernard, a sinner, wishes such joy in youth as in old age he will not regret.

1. I do not wonder at your surprise ; I should wonder if you were not surprised that I should write to you, a countryman to a citizen, a monk to a scholastic,[1] there being no apparent or pressing reason for so doing. But if you recall what is written—*I am debtor both to the wise and to the unwise* (Rom. i. 14), and that *Charity seeketh not her own* (1 Cor. xiii. 5)—perhaps you will understand that what it orders is not mere presumption. For it is Charity which compels me to reprove you; to condole with you, though you do not grieve; to pity you, though you do not think yourself pitiable. Nor shall it be unserviceable to you to hear patiently why you are compassionated. In feeling your pain you may get rid of its cause, and knowing your misery begin to cease to be miserable. O, Charity, good mother who both nourishest the weak, employest the vigorous, and blamest the restless, using various expedients with various people, as loving all her sons ! She blames with gentleness, and with simplicity praises. It is she who is the mother of men and angels, and makes the peace not only of earth but of heaven. It is she who, rendering God favourable to man, has reconciled man to God ; she, my Fulk, makes those brethren, with whom you once shared pleasant bread, to dwell in one manner of life in a house (Ps.

---

[1] Either a canon holding a prebend of theology or simply a student—here probably the former. But see n. 7.—[E.]

lxviii. 6). Such and so honourable a parent complains of being injured, of being wounded by you.

2. But in what have I injured, you reply, or wounded her? In this, without doubt, that you whom she had taken in her maternal bosom and nourished with her milk, have untimely withdrawn yourself, and having known the sweetness of the milk which can train you up for salvation, have rejected and disdained it so quickly and carelessly. O, most foolish boy! boy more in understanding than in age! who has fascinated you to depart so quickly from a course so well begun? My uncle, you will say. So Adam once threw the blame of sin upon his wife, and his wife upon the serpent, to excuse themselves; yet each received the well-deserved sentence of their own fault. I am unwilling to accuse the dean; I am unwilling that you should excuse yourself by this means, for you are inexcusable. His fault does not excuse yours. But what did he do? Did he use violence? Did he take you by force? Nay, he begged, not insisted; attracted you by flatteries, not dragged you by violence. Who forced you to yield to his flatteries? He had not yet given up what was his own. What wonder that he should reclaim you, who wast his! If he demands a lamb from the flock, a calf from the herd, and no one disputes his right, who can wonder that having lost you, who are of more value in his sight than many lambs or calves, he should reclaim you? Probably he does not aim at that degree of perfection of which it is said, *If any one has taken away thy goods, seek them not again* (S. Luke vi. 30). But you, who had already rejected the world, what had you to do with following a man of the world? The timid sheep flies when the wolf approaches; the gentle dove when she sees the hawk; the mouse, though hungry, dares not leave his hole when the cat is prowling around; and yet you, *when thou sawest a thief thou consentedst with him* (Ps. l. 18). For what else than a thief shall I call him who has not hesitated to steal that most precious pearl of Christ, your soul?

3. I should wish, if it were possible, to pass over his fault,

lest the truth should obtain for me only hatred and no result. But I am not able, I confess, to pass a man untouched, who up to this very day is found to have resisted the Holy Spirit with all his power. For he who does not hinder evil when he can, even although the evil purpose may be frustrated, is not clear of that purpose. Assuredly he tried to damp my fervour when it was new, but, thanks to God, he did not succeed. Another nephew of his, Guarike, your kinsman, he much opposed, but what harm did he do? On the contrary, he was of service. For the old man at length unwillingly desisted from persecution, and as the youth, his nephew, remained unsubdued, he was the more meritorious for his temptation. But, alas! how was he able to overcome you, who was not able to overcome him? Was he stronger or more prudent than you? Assuredly those who knew both before preferred Fulk to Guarike. But the event of the combat showed that men's judgment had erred.

4. But what shall I say concerning the malice of an uncle who withdraws his own nephews from the Christian warfare to drag them with himself to perdition? Is it thus he is accustomed to benefit his friends? Those whom Christ calls to abide with Him for ever this uncle calls back to burn with him for evermore. I wonder if Christ is not reproving him when he says, *How often would I have gathered* thy nephews *as a hen gathers her chickens under her wings and thou wouldest not? Behold thy house is left unto thee desolate* (S. Matt. xxiii. 37). Christ says, Suffer the little children to come unto Me, for of such is the kingdom of heaven (S. Matt. xix. 14). This uncle says, Suffer my nephews to burn with me. Christ says, They are Mine; they ought to serve Me. But their uncle says, They ought to perish with me. Christ says, They are mine, I have redeemed them. But I, says the uncle, have brought them up. You, indeed, says Christ, have fed them, but with My bread, not thine; while I have redeemed them not with thy blood, but Mine own. Thus the uncle, according to the flesh, struggles against the Father of spirits for his nephews,

whom he disinherits of heavenly possessions while he
desires to load them with earthly.   Yet Christ, not considering it robbery to draw to Himself those whom He has
made and redeemed with His own blood, has done when
they came to Him, what He had before promised, *Him who
cometh unto me, I will in no wise cast out* (S. John vi. 37).
He opened gladly to Fulk, the first who knocked, and made
him glad also.   What more ? he put off the old man and
put on the new, and showed forth in his character and life the
canonical function which had existed in name alone.   The
report of it flies abroad, to Christ, a sweet savour; and
the novelty of the thing diffused on all sides brought it to
the ears of his uncle.

5. What then did the carnal guardian, who lost the carnal
solace of the flesh which he had brought up and loved after
a carnal fashion ?   Although to others the event was *a
savour of life unto life* (2 Cor. ii. 16), not so to him.
Wherefore ?   Because *the carnal man receiveth not the
things of the Spirit of God, for they are foolishness unto
him* (1 Cor. ii. 14).   For if he had the spirit of Christ he
would not so greatly lament on account of the flesh that which
he rejoiced over on account of the spirit.   But because he
relishes earthly things, not those which are above, he is sad
and troubled, and reflects thus within himself :   What do I
hear?   Woe is me ! from what hope have I fallen ! Ought he
to do anything without my advice and permission ?   What
right, what law, what justice, what reason is it, that him,
whom I have nourished up from infancy, another person
should have the good of when grown up ?   Now that my
head is white, alas ! I shall spend the remainder of my life
in grief, because the staff of my old age has deserted me.
Woe is me ! if this night my soul is required of me, whose
shall those things be which I have prepared?   My store-
houses are full, disgorging this one into that, my sheep
fruitful, abounding in their goings forth ; my oxen fat, and
for whom shall these remain?   My lands, my meadows,
my houses, my vases of gold and of silver, for whom have
they been amassed?   Certain of the richer and more

profitable honours of my Church I had acquired for myself;
the rest, although I could not have them, I hoped that Fulk
should. What then shall I do? Because of him shall I
lose so much? For whatever I possess, without him, I
reckon as lost. Rather than that I will both retain them,
and recall him if I can. What is done cannot be undone;
what is heard cannot be concealed. Fulk is a Canon Regular,
and if he returns to the world will be remarked and disgraced. But it is better to hear that about him than to live
without him. Let integrity yield to convenience, shame to
necessity. I prefer not to spare the ingenuousness of a
youth, rather than to undergo miserable melancholy.

· 6. Adopting then this counsel of the flesh, forgetful of
reason and law, as it were a lion prepared for prey, and as a
lioness robbed of her whelp, raging and roaring, not
respecting holy things, he burst into the dwelling of the
saints, in which Christ had hidden his young soldier from
the strife of tongues, who was one day to be adjoined to the
company of Angels. He demands that his nephew be
restored to him; he loudly complains that by him he had
been wrongly deserted; while Christ resists, saying, Unhappy man, what are you doing? Why do you rob?
Why persecute Me? Is it not enough that you have taken
away your own soul from Me, and the souls of many others
by your example, but you must tear him also from My
hand with impious daring? Do you not fear the
coming judgment, or do you despise My terrors?
Upon whom do you wage war? Upon the terrible One,
who takes away the spirit of princes (Ps. lxxvi. 12). Mad-
man, return to thyself. Remember thy last end and sin
not, call to mind with salutary fear what you are.
And thou, O youth, He says, if thou dost assent and
agree to his wishes thou shalt die the death.[1] Remember that Lot's wife was, indeed, delivered from Sodom

[1] Bernard usually shows himself very doubtful of the salvation of those who,
having been called by God to the religious state, had not yielded to their vocation, and much more of those who, having entered it, though not made profession, had returned to the world. See Letters 107 and 108. But Fulk had
actually made profession.

because she believed God, but was transformed in the
way because she looked back (Gen. xix. 26). Learn in
the Gospel that he who has once put his hand to the plough
to him it is not permitted to look back (Luke ix. 62). Your
uncle, who has already lost his own soul, seeks yours. The
words of his mouth are iniquity and guile. Do not learn,
my son, to do evil (Ps. xxxvi. 4). Do not turn aside to
vanities and falsehoods (Ps. xl. 4). Behold in the way in
which you walk he hides snares—he has stretched nets.
His discourses are smooth as butter, and yet they are sharp
spears (Ps. lv. 21). See, my son, that you are not taken
with lying lips and a deceitful tongue. Let divine fear
transfix your flesh, that the desire of the flesh may not
deceive you. It flatters, but under its tongue is suffering
and sorrow ; it weeps, but betrays ; it betrays to catch the
poor when it has attracted him (Ps. x. 9). Beware, I say,
My son, that you do not confer with flesh and blood (Gal. i.
16), for *My sword shall devour flesh* (Deut. xxxii. 42).
Despise entreaties and promises. He promises great things,
but I greater ; he offers more, but I most of all. Will you
throw away heavenly things for earthly, eternal for temporal ?
Otherwise it behoves you to dissolve the vows which your
lips have pronounced. He is rightly required to dissolve
who was not forced to vow, for, although I did not repulse
you when you knocked, I did not oblige you to enter.
You cannot, therefore, put aside what you promised of
your own accord. Behold each of you I warn, and
to each give salutary counsel. Do not you, He says
to the uncle, draw back a regular to the world, for in so
doing you make him to apostatize. Do not you, a regular,
follow the secular life, for in so doing you persecute
Me. If you seduce a soul for which I died you make yourself an enemy of My cross. *He who does not gather with
Me scatters* (S. Matt. xii. 30). How much more he who
scatters what has been gathered ? And you, if you consent
to him you dissent from Me, for *he who is not with Me is
against Me* (*ibid.*). How much more is he who was with
Me against Me if he deserts ? You, if you lead astray a boy
who has come to Me, shall be adjudged a seducer and pro-

faner, but you, if you destroy what you had built, shall make
yourself a deceiver. Both of you must stand at My tribunal
and by Me be judged—the one for his prevarication, the
other for the leading astray; and if the one shall die in his
iniquity his blood shall be required at the hand of his
seducer (Ezek. iii. 18). These and similar warnings Thou,
O Christ, didst invisibly thunder to each, I appeal to their
conscience as witness. Thou didst knock at the doors of
the mind of each with kindly terrors. Who would not fear
them and recover wisdom in fearing, unless it were one
like *the deaf adder, that stoppeth her ear and refuseth to
hear the voice of the charmer, charm he never so wisely*
(Ps. lviii. 4, 5), who either does not hear, or pretends that
he hears not?

7. But how far do I draw out this letter, already
too long, before speaking of a thing that is worthy
only of silence? In what circuitous paths do I approach the truth, fearing to draw the veil from shame!
I say with shame. That what is known to many I
cannot conceal if I would. But why with shame? Why
should I be ashamed to write what it did not shame them
to do? If they are ashamed to hear what they shamelessly did, let them not be ashamed to amend what they were
reluctant to hear. Alas! neither fear nor reason could keep
back the one from seduction, nor shame or his profession
the other from prevarication. What more? A deceitful
tongue fits hasty words; it conceiveth sorrow, and brings
forth iniquity. Your Church received its scholar, whom it
had better have been without. So formerly Lyons recovered,
without credit, by the zeal and pertinacity of its dean, its
canon whom it had well lost, the nephew of the same dean.
Just as the one snatched Fulk from S. Augustine, so the
other Othbert from S. Benedict. How much more beautiful
that a religious youth should draw to himself a worldly old
man, and so each should be victorious, than that the worldly
should draw back to himself the religious, in which each is
vanquished! Oh, unhappy old man! Oh, cruel uncle! who,
already decrepit and soon about to die, before dying have
slain the soul of your nephew, whom you have deprived of

the inheritance of Christ in order that you might have an
heir of your sins. But he who is evil to himself, to whom
is he good? He preferred to have a successor in his riches
rather than an intercessor for his iniquities.

8. But what have I to do with Deans, who are our in-
structors, and have acquired authority in the Churches. They
hold the key of knowledge, and take the highest seats in the
synagogues. They judge their subjects at their will, they recall fugitives, and when they are recalled scatter them again
as they choose. What have I to do with that? I confess
that because of you, my Fulk, I have exceeded somewhat the
degree proper to my humility in speaking of these, since I
wished to be indulgent to your fault, and make your shame
little in comparison. I pass over these that they may not
have ground to rail, not at the blame, but at him who blames,
for they would rather find fault with my presumption than
occupy themselves with their own correction. At all events
it is not a prince of the Church that I have undertaken to
reprimand, but a young student, gentle and obedient.
Unless, perhaps, you show yourself to be a child in sense,
not in malice, and object to my boldness, saying, What has
he to do with me? What do the faults which I commit
matter to him? Am I a monk? And to this I confess I
have nothing to answer, except that I counted, in addressing
myself to you, on the sweetness of character with which
you are endowed by nature, and that I was actuated by the
love of God, to which I appealed in the first words of my
letter. It was in zeal for Him that, pitying your error and
your unhappiness, I was moved to interfere beyond my
custom in order to save you, although you were not mine.[1]
Your serious fall and miserable case has moved me thus to
presume. For whom of your contemporaries have you seen
me reprimand? To whom have I ever addressed even the
briefest letter? Not that I regarded them as saints, nor
had nothing to blame in them.

9. Why, then, you will say, do you blame me especially,
when in others you see what you might, perhaps, more

[1] i.e., not owing me obedience as a monk.

justly find fault with? To which I reply: Because of the excessiveness of your error, of the enormity of your fault, for although many others live loosely, without rule and discipline, yet they have not yet professed obedience to these. They are sinners indeed, but not apostates. But you, however honourably and quietly you may live, although you may conduct yourself chastely, soberly, and religiously, yet your piety is not acceptable to God, because it is rendered valueless by the violation of your vow. Therefore, beloved, do not compare yourself with your contemporaries, from whom the profession which you have made separates you, nor flatter yourself so much because of your self-restraint in comparison with men of the world, since the Lord says to you, *I would thou wert hot or cold* (Apoc. iii. 15, 16). Here is plainly shown that you please God less, being lukewarm, than if you were even such as those are, entirely cold towards Him. For them God waits patiently until their cold shall pass into heat, but you He sees with displeasure to have fallen away to lukewarmness, after having been fervent in warmth. And because I have found thee lukewarm, He says, *I will vomit thee from My mouth* (*ibid.*), and deservedly, because you have returned to your vomit and rejected His grace!

10. Alas! how have you so soon grown weary of the Saviour, of whom it is written, *Honey and milk are under His tongue* (Cantic. iv. 11). I wonder that nourishment so sweet should be distasteful to you, if you have tasted how sweet the Lord is. Or perhaps you have not yet tasted and do not know how sweet is Christ, so that you do not desire what you have not tried; or if you have, then your taste is surely depraved. He is the Wisdom of God who says: *He who eats of Me shall always hunger, and he who drinks of Me shall never cease to desire to drink again* (Ecclus. xxiv. 29). But how can he hunger or thirst for Christ who is full of the husks of wine? *You cannot drink of the cup of Christ and of the cup of demons* (1 Cor. x. 21). The cup of demons is pride, detraction, envy, debauch, and drunkenness, with which when your mind and body are saturated, Christ

will find in you no place. Do not wonder at what I say. In
the house of your uncle you are not able to drink deep of the
fulness of the house of God. Why, you say? Because it is a
house of [carnal] delights. Now, as fire and water cannot be
together, so the delights of the spirit and those of the flesh
are incompatible. Christ will not deign to pour His wine,
which is more sweet than honey and the honeycomb, into
the soul of him whom He finds among his cups breathing
forth the fumes of wine. Where there is delicate variety of
food, where the richness and splendour of the service of the
table delights equally the eyes and the stomach, the food of
heaven is wanting to the soul. Rejoice, O, young man, in
thy youth! but then, when temporal joy departs in time to
come, everlasting sorrow will possess thee! May God preserve you, His child, from this. May He rather destroy the
deceiving and perfidious lips of those who give you such
advice, who say to you every day, Good, good! and who
seek your soul! They are those with whom you are dwelling, and who corrupt the good manners of a young man by
their evil communications (*colloquia :* otherwise counsels,
consilia).

11. But now how long before you will come out from
their midst? What do you in the town who had chosen the
cloister, or what have you to do with the world which you
had renounced? The lines have fallen to you in pleasant
places, and do you sigh after earthly riches? If you wish
to have both together, it will be said to you soon, *Remember,
my son, that you have received your good things when you
were in life* (S. Luke xvi. 25). *You have received,* He said,
not you have seized; so that you may not shelter yourself
under the vain excuse, that you are content with what is
your own, and do not seize what belongs to another. And,
after all, what are those goods which you call yours? The
benefices of the Church? Certainly; you do well in
rising to keep vigil, in going to Mass, in assisting at the
day and night offices, so you do not take the *præbend*
of the Church without return. It is just that he who
serves the Altar should live from the Altar. It is granted

therefore to you that if you serve well at the Altar you should live from it, but not that you should live in luxury and splendour at its expense, that you should take its revenues to provide yourself with gilded reins, ornamented saddles, silver spurs, furs of all kinds, and purple ornaments to cover your hands and adorn your neck. Whatsoever you take from the Altar, in short, beyond necessary food and simple dress, is not yours, and it is rapine and even sacrilege. The Wise man prayed for necessary sustenance, not for things superfluous (Prov. xxx. 8). The Apostle says, *having food and clothing* (1 Tim. vi. 8), not food and magnificent dress. And a certain other saint says, *if the Lord shall give me bread to eat and raiment to cover me* (Gen. xxviii. 20). Take notice, to *cover me.* So then let us too be content with raiment to cover us, not with luxurious and costly clothing which is worn to please women, and makes the wearers like them. But you say : Those with whom I associate do this ; if I do not do as others, I shall be remarked for singularity. Wherefore I say, go forth from the midst of them ; that you may not either live with singularity in the eyes of the town or perish by the example of others.

12. What do you do in the town at all, O effeminate soldier? Your fellow soldiers whom you have deserted by flight are fighting and overcoming ; they knock and they enter in, they seize heaven and reign while you scour the streets and squares, sitting upon your ambling courser, and clad in purple and fine linen. These are the ornaments of peace, not the weapons of war. Or do you say, *Peace, and there is no peace* (Ezekiel xiii. 10). The purple tunic does not put to flight lust, and pride, and avarice, nor does it protect against other fiery darts of the enemy. Lastly, it does not ward off from you the fever which you more fear, nor secure you from death. Where are your warlike weapons, the shield of faith, the helmet of salvation, the breast-plate of patience? Why do you tremble? there are more with us than with our enemies. Take your arms, recover your strength while yet the combat lasts; Angels are spectators and helpers, the

Lord himself is your aid and your support, who will teach your hands to war and your fingers to fight (Psalm cxliv. 1). Let us come to the help of our brothers, lest if they fight without us they vanquish without us, and without us enter into heaven; lest, last of all, when the door has been shut it be replied from within to us knocking too late, *Verily I say unto you, I know you not* (S. Matthew xxv. 12). Make yourself known then and seen beforehand, lest you be unknown for glory and known only for punishment. If Christ recognizes you in the strife, He will recognize you in heaven, and as He has promised, will manifest Himself to you (S. John xiv. 21). If only you by repenting and returning will show yourself such as to be able to say with confidence *Then shall I know even as also I am known* (1 Corinthians xiii. 12). In the meantime I have by these admonitions knocked sufficiently at the heart of a young man modest and docile ; and nothing remains for me now than to knock by my prayers also, for him, at the door of the Divine Mercy, that the Lord may finish my work if my remonstrances have found his heart ever so little softened, so that I may speedily rejoice over him with great joy.

. . ——————— .

LETTER III. (*Circa* 1120.)

To the Canons Regular of Horricourt.[1]

Their praises inspire him with more fear than satis-faction. They ought not to put any obstacle in the way of the religious profession of certain regular canons of S. Augustine, whom he has received at Clairvaux.

To the Superior of the holy body of clerics and servants of God who are in the place which is called Horricourt, and to their disciples: the little flock of the brothers of Clairvaux, and their very humble servant, Brother Bernard, wish health, and power to walk in the Spirit, and to see all things in a spiritual manner.

[1] The title of this letter follows a MS. at Corbey. It does not appear who these regular canons were.

Your letter, in which you have addressed to us an exhortation so salutary and profitable, brings us convincing
proof of your knowledge and charity, which we admire, and
for which we thank you. But that which you have so
kindly prefixed by way of praise of me is, I fear, not
founded on experience, although you have thus given me an
excellent occasion to practise humility if I know how to
profit by it. Yet it has excited great fear in me, who know
myself to be far below what you imagine. For which of us
who takes heed to his ways can listen without either great
fear or great danger, to praises of himself so great and so
undeserved ? It is not safe for any one to commit himself to
his own judgment or even to the judgment of another; for
He who judgeth us is the Lord (1 Corinthians iv. 4). As
to the brothers concerning whose safety we recognize that
your charity has been solicitous, that we should return them
to you unharmed; know that by the advice and persuasion
of many illustrious persons, and chiefly of that very distinguished man William, Bishop of Châlons,[1] they have taken
refuge with us, and have begged us with earnest supplication to receive them, which we have done. Though they
have quitted the rule of S. Augustine for that of S. Benedict in order to embrace a stricter life, yet they do not depart from the rule of Him, who is the one Master in heaven

[1] This was William of Champeaux, a friend of S. Bernard, who died in 1121.
He had given up teaching before he was a Bishop in order to withdraw into the
Monastery of S. Victor, near Paris. Hildebert, then Bishop of Mans, congratulates him on this in a Letter which has been printed without a title, but which in
the MS. of S. Taurinus of Evreux is inscribed to William of Champeaux. In
the Chronicle of Maurigny it is said that "when the Cardinal legate Conon came
in 1120 to that monastery, near Etampes, he had with him as helper the great
William of Châlons, who had presided over schools of the highest rank (that is
of theology), and then, having a zeal for God, shone in the knowledge of the
Divine Scriptures above all the bishops of Gaul." He attained to the see of
Châlons in the year 1113. It was this William who consecrated S. Bernard
abbot, and had such a high regard for him, that when the Saint had fallen into
serious illness he undertook his cure. Robert Hoveden, in the first part of his
Annals, writes thus under the year 1121: "William of Champeaux, Bishop of
Châlons, eight days before his death having put on the monastic habit (that is,
when taken with mortal illness, according to the custom of those times), departed
this life." He was buried at Clairvaux in a chapel which he had built.

and in earth; nor do they make void that first faith which they promised among you, and which, indeed, they promised, first of all, in baptism. They being such, therefore, and having been so received, we are far from thinking that your sense of right will be injured by our having received them, or that you ought to take it ill if we retain them; yet if they desist from their resolution during the year of probation which the Rule requires, and desire to return to you, be assured that we shall not detain them against their will. In any case, most holy brethren, you would be wrong to resist, by an ill-considered and useless anathema, the spirit of liberty which is in them; unless, perchance (which may God avert!), you study more to promote your own interests than those of Jesus Christ.

LETTER IV. (*Circa* 1127.)

TO ARNOLD, ABBOT OF MORIMOND.[1]

He recalls Abbot Arnold, who had rashly left his monastery and was wandering abroad, to the care of it.

To the Lord Abbot Arnold, Brother Bernard, Abbot of Clairvaux, desires the spirit of compunction and prudence. 1. First of all I have to inform you that the Abbot of

---

[1] Morimond was the fourth (or, as some writers say, the third) daughter house of Cîteaux. It was in the Diocese of Langres, and was founded in 1115. The first abbot was this Arnold, a young man of great promise, of a noble family of Cologne, and brother of Frederick, then Archbishop of Cologne. After he had been at the head of it for ten years, being molested by his secular neighbours and harassed by the disobedience of his monks, he deserted the monastery, taking some monks with him. The four chief of these were Adam (to whom Letter V. was addressed), Everard, Henry, and Conrad. At this time Stephen, Abbot of Cîteaux, was detained in Flanders by the affairs of the Order; but Bernard exerted himself to recall the fugitives by letters to Arnold, Adam (Ep. vi.), and also to Bruno, a nobleman of Cologne, who afterwards succeeded Frederick, to beg him to take steps for their return. But to no purpose, for Arnold died in Belgium in 1126. After this Bernard wrote again to Adam, threatening him with excommunication unless he submitted, which he seems happily to have effected; and the Cistercian writers commonly suppose this man to be the Adam who presided over a monastery of the Order and died at length in the odour of sanctity.

Cîteaux has not yet returned from Flanders, whither he had gone, passing by this place a little before your messenger came to us, and because of this he has not yet received the letter which you charged to be presented to him, and hitherto is ignorant of the great novelty which you have presumed to undertake. He would be happy, I consider, to be ignorant of such deplorable rumours as long as possible. As for yourself, that you should forbid me to write to you, and should declare useless the efforts I should have made to try to dispose you to return, because you say that your course is irrevocably taken, makes me despair. Perhaps, indeed, I ought not in reason to obey you in this; but in truth, the grief I feel will not suffer me to keep silence; and more, if I knew for certain where I should meet you, I would rather have come to you, than have sent this letter, to try if I should have more success in person than my letter is likely to obtain. Perhaps you smile at my unfounded confidence, inasmuch as you are conscious of your own strength of purpose, and hope that no force, no prayers, no persistence would be able to bend it. But I am not distrustful of His power who said: *All things are possible to him that believeth* (S. Mark ix. 22). And I do not hesitate to apply to myself that saying: *I can do all things in Him who strengtheneth me* (Philip. iv. 13). Although I myself am not ignorant of the obstinacy of your stony heart, yet would that I could now take you aside to plead with you, whether successfully or not. Then I would put before you face to face not only in words but in looks and in countenance what I have in my heart against you, whether uselessly or not, I cannot tell. Then I would fall at your feet, I would embrace your knees; and falling upon your neck would kiss that head which is so dear to me, and which has borne many years with me the gentle yoke of Christ. Weeping, I would beg and entreat you with all my energy, by Jesus Christ, to spare His Cross by which He has redeemed those whom you, as far as in you lies, are destroying; has collected those whom you are dispersing. You are destroying, I say, those whom you desert, and dispersing those whom you take with you, for each of whom I fear an equal peril, though of a different kind. And, lastly, spare also us your friends to whom you have left nothing but grief and tears, although undeserved. If it had been permitted to me, I could have influenced you, perhaps, by the feelings of the heart, though not by reason; and the tenderness of a brother would, perhaps, have softened that iron heart which now refuses to yield even to the fear of Christ. But, alas! even this opportunity you have taken away from us.

2. O, powerful support of our Order! Listen patiently, I beg, to your friend, though absent, who cannot bear your entire departure, and who feels with you to the very marrow your sufferings and dangers. Do you not fear, O, great support of our Order, that by your fall its entire ruin will surely and speedily follow? But I, you say, do not fall; I know what I am doing, I have a good conscience. Be it so. I believe you in what you say of yourself, but what of us, who by your departure must groan under the heavy weight of scandal, and trembling expect still heavier perils to come? Or do you know all that, and yet pretend not to know? How do you pretend that you have not made ruin for yourself when you have drawn ruin upon many others? You were not placed in this post to do what was useful to yourself, but rather that which was useful to others; then ought you not to seek not the things which are your own, but those which are for Jesus Christ? How, I ask, will you depart in safety, who have taken away by your departure every kind of security from the flock committed to you for ever? Who will protect them from the attacking wolves, who will console them in tribulations, provide for them in temptations, and resist for them the roaring lion who seeks whom he may devour? They will be exposed, without doubt, to the bites of the wicked, who devour the flock of Christ as bread. Alas! what will be the fate of those new plantations of Christ, which, by your hands, He had set in divers places, in the spots of horror and solitude? Who will dig around, who nourish them,

surround them by a hedge, and cut back with care the greedy
shoots which exhaust their strength? Either, when the
wind of temptations shall blow, these ill rooted ones shall
easily be rooted up, or growing up among thickets of
thorns will be choked by them, as there is none to clear
them away, and thus will bring forth no fruit.

3. This being so, consider what is this good which you
have done, and whether it can be called good, in the midst
of such evil consequences. However worthy the fruits of
penitence that you flatter yourself you will make, will they
not be necessarily choked in the midst of thorns? Do you
not, in fact, sin, even if you offer rightly, if you do not
rightly divide the victim?[1]

Will you say that you rightly divide when you trouble
yourself only about your own soul, and deprive those sons
who were committed to you of a father's care? O, unhappy ones, and to be pitied; the more that they see themselves orphaned even while their father lives! Then,
farther, ought you not to have doubted whether you were
doing well, even for your own soul, to venture on a step so unexampled without the advice of your brethren and co-abbots,
without the permission of your father and master? It must
also raise against you the indignation of many, that you have
led away with you weak youths and delicate young men. Or, if
they were strong and robust, then they were indispensable to
the house now desolate; but if (as I have said) weak and
delicate, they will not be fit to endure the fatigues of a
hard and laborious journey. And we cannot believe that
your remaining over them is because you wish still to direct
their souls, since we know that you propose to lay down the
burden of the pastoral charge of them, and henceforth to live
for yourself alone. And, furthermore, it would be unfitting
that without being called you should presumptuously
resume in one place a burden which against rule you have
rashly laid down in another. But you know all these

---

[1] In Gen. iv. 7 the LXX. reads: οὐκ ἐὰν ὀρθῶς προσενέγκῃς ὀρθῶς δὲ μὴ διέλῃς
ἥμαρτες; *if thou didst offer rightly, but didst not rightly divide, hast thou not
sinned?*—[E.]

things, and I do not wish to press upon you superfluous
words; but, in conclusion, I faithfully promise that if you
ever give me the opportunity of converse with you I will
strive to find for you a means of doing as far as may be
with permission, and therefore in peace of mind, what you
are now attempting lawlessly and with peril.   Farewell.

LETTER V. (A.D. 1125.)

TO A MONK ADAM.

*Bernard exhorts him not to adhere to Arnold, the
Abbot of Morimond, nor make himself the companion of
his journey, or rather wandering.*

1. Your humility, which is well known to me, and the
circumstances of peril in which you stand, oblige me to
address you earnestly and reprehend you in plain words.
O, foolish one! who has bewitched you to withdraw so
hastily from the salutary rule of life in which you equally
with me (God is witness) were lately agreed? Consider
your ways, O foolish one, and turn your steps towards the
testimonies of the Lord.   Do you not remember that you
first dedicated the first fruits of your conversion at
Marmoutiers;[1] then that you were put under my poor
direction at Foigny,[2] and that you made your final profession at Morimond?   Was it not there again that at my
suggestion you frankly renounced the journeying, or rather
wandering, suggested to you by Abbot Arnold, and you
saw clearly that company with him was forbidden to you
if he himself was not able to go forth lawfully? What
then? Can you say that he departs in a lawful manner
who has left a lamentable scandal amongst those committed
to him, not waiting for the licence of his superior?

2. But to what purpose, you may ask, are all these
details? That I may show you your manifest inconstancy;

---

[1] The monastery of Marmoutiers was near Tours. See Letter 397.
[2] In the Diocese of Laon. See Letter 72.

that I may show you clearly that you say both Yes and No; that I may force you to recognize and blush for your errors, and to learn, though late, from the Apostle that *we must not believe every spirit* (1 S. John iv. 1). Learn from Solomon to have many friends, but to choose one counsellor among a thousand (Ecclus. vi. 6) ; learn from the example of the Forerunner of the Lord not to wear soft clothing nor to be blown about with every wind of doctrine, like *a reed shaken with the wind* (S. Matt. xi. 7, 8) ; learn from the Gospel *to build thy house upon a rock* (S. Matt. vii. 24) ; learn also with the disciples not to forget the wisdom of the serpent with the simplicity of the dove (S. Matt. x. 16) ; and both from these as from a great many other testimonies of Scripture you may get to understand how greatly that seducer has deceived you, who, since he was not able to arrest the beginning of good in you, envied your perseverance, considering without doubt that it would be sufficient for his malicious purpose if he could take away from you this one and only virtue which would assure you the crown. I beg you, therefore, by the bowels of the mercy of Christ, that you wander abroad no more, or at least not before you come to speak with me at a place convenient to us both, and consider what remedy may be found for the very great evils which from your departure we either feel have happened or feel will happen. Farewell.

LETTER VI. (A.D. 1125.)

TO BRUNO OF COLOGNE.[1]

Bernard begs him to take means for bringing back certain wandering monks of Morimond to their monastery.

To the very dear and most illustrious lord Bruno, Brother Bernard, called Abbot of Clairvaux, wishes health, and whatever good the prayers of a sinner can bring.

---

[1] Afterwards Archbishop of Cologne. See Letters 8, 9.

Since the day when we had the pleasure to become acquainted at Rheims I trust I have retained some small share in your remembrance; and because of this I do not write to you timidly, as to a stranger, but freely and confidently, as to a well-known and familiar friend.

1. Arnold, Abbot of Morimond, has lately quitted his monastery and scandalized our entire Order by his breach of rule, because he neither waited for the advice of his brother abbots before carrying out a plan of so doubtful a nature, nor for the licence or assent of the Abbot of Clairvaux, under whose authority he was. But being a man under authority and having soldiers under him, while he proudly threw off the yoke of his superior, he still more proudly kept his own yoke upon those subjected to him. Thus of a great multitude of monks, whom uselessly traversing sea and land he had gathered together, not for Christ, but for himself, abandoning a few only, and those the simpler and least fervent, he has taken the better and more perfect as sharers of his error. Among whom, three whose withdrawal has much troubled me, he has dared to win over and take away with him, namely, Everard our[1] brother, Adam, whom you have known well, and that noble youth Conrad, whom some time ago, not without scandal, he carried off from Cologne. Whom, if you would kindly take the trouble, I feel sure that you would be able to recover.

2. Concerning Arnold himself, I have long known his obstinacy and unbending mind, and I do not wish to trouble you with useless efforts to recall him. But I have heard that Everard, Adam, and some of the other brethren of the same company, are now staying in your neighbourhood. If that is the case, it would be well if you would go yourself at once to see them, would win them over by entreaty, convince them by reason, and strengthen in them the simplicity of the dove with the wisdom of the serpent. Make them understand that obedience should not hold them to a man who has not himself been obedient; that

[1] Otherwise, your.

they cannot lawfully follow a superior who is unlawfully
wandering abroad; nor be drawn away to desert the Order
they have professed for the sake of a man who has dis-
regarded its Rule; that the Apostle bids us not to hesitate
to declare anathema even an angel from heaven, who
should preach another gospel; and that by the same
Apostle they are taught *to withdraw themselves from any
brother that walketh disorderly* (2 Thess. iii. 6). Who
may teach you also *to be not high-minded nor trust in
uncertain riches* (1 Tim. vi. 17), until Christ shall claim for
Himself His true disciple, proved by his renunciation of all
things. Farewell.

LETTER VII. (A.D. 1126.)

To the Monk Adam.[1]

1. If you remain yet in that spirit of charity which I either
knew or believed to be with you formerly, you would
certainly feel the condemnation with which charity must
regard the scandal which you have given to the weak.
For charity would not offend charity, nor scorn when it
feels itself offended. For it cannot deny itself, nor be
divided against itself. Its function is rather to draw
together things divided; and it is far from dividing those
that are joined. Now, if that remained in you, as I have
said, it would not keep silent, it would not rest uncon-
cerned, nor pretend indifference, but it would without doubt
whisper with groans and uneasiness at the bottom of your
pious heart that saying, *Who is offended, and I burn not*
(2 Cor. xi. 29). If, then, it is kind, it loves peace, and
rejoices in unity; it produces them, cements them,
strengthens them, and wherever it reigns it makes the
bond of peace. As, then, you are in opposition to that
true mother of peace and concord, on what ground, I ask

---

[1] The MS. in the Royal Library is inscribed: *De Discretione Obedientiæ: Of
Discernment in Obedience.* This Letter was written after the death of Abbot
Arnold, which took place in Belgium in the year 1126.

you, do you presume that your sacrifice, whatever it may
be, will be accepted by God, when without it even
martyrdom *profiteth nothing* (1 Cor. xiii. 3) ?   Or, on what
ground do you trust that you are not the enemy of charity
when breaking unity, rending the bond of peace, you
lacerate her bowels, treating with such cruelty their dear
pledges, which you neither have borne nor do bear ?   You
must lay down, then, the offering, whatever it may be,
which you are preparing to lay on the altar, and hasten to
go and reconcile yourself not with one of your brethren
only, but with the entire body.   The whole body of the
fraternity, grievously wounded by your withdrawal, as by
the stroke of a sword, utters its complaints against you and
the few with you, saying : *The sons of my mother have
fought against me* (Cant. i. 5).   And rightly ; for who is not
with her, is against her.   Can you think that a mother, as
tender as charity, can hear without emotion the complaint,
so just, of a community which is to her as a daughter ?
Therefore, joining her tears with ours, she says, *I have
nourished and brought up children, and they have rebelled
against me* (Isa. i. 2).   Charity is God Himself.   *Christ is
our peace, who hath made both one* (Eph. ii. 14).   Unity is
the mystery even of the Holy Trinity.   What place, then,
in the kingdom of Christ and of God has he who is an
enemy of charity, peace, and unity ?

2. My abbot, perhaps you will say, has obliged me to
follow him—ought I then to have been disobedient ?   But
you cannot have forgotten the conclusion to which we came
one day after a long discussion together upon that scandalous project which even then you were meditating.   If you
had remained in that conclusion, now it might have been
not unfitly said of you, *Blessed is the man who hath not
walked in the counsel of the ungodly* (Ps. i. 1).   But let it
be so.   Sons ought, no doubt, to obey a father; scholars a
teacher.   An abbot may lead his monks where he shall
please, and teach them what he thinks proper ; but this
is only as long as he lives.   Now that he is dead, whom you
were bound to hear as a teacher and to follow as a guide,

why are you still delaying to make amends for the grave
scandal that you have occasioned ?   What hinders you now
to give ear, I do not say to me when I recall you, but to our
God, when He mercifully does so by the mouth of Jeremiah,
*Shall they fall and not arise ?   Shall he turn away and
not return ?* (Jer. viii. 4).   Or has your abbot, when dying,
forbidden you ever to rise again after your fall, or ever to
speak of your return ?   Is it necessary for you to obey him
even when dead—to obey him against charity and at the
peril of your soul ?   You would allow, I suppose, that the
bond between an abbot and his monks is by no means
so strong or tenacious as that of married persons, whom
God Himself and not man has bound with an inviolable
sacrament—as the Saviour says : *What God hath joined
together let no man put asunder* (S. Matt. xix. 6).   But the
Apostle asserts that when the husband is dead the wife is
freed from the law of her husband (Rom. vii. 2), and do you
consider yourself bound by the law of·your dead abbot, and
this against a law which is more binding still, that of
charity?

3. These things I say, yet I do not think that you ought
to have yielded to him in this even when living, or that thus
to have yielded ought to be called obedience.   For it is of
that kind of obedience that it is said in general : *The Lord
shall lead forth with the workers of iniquity those who
deviate in their obedience* (Ps. cxxv. 5, VULG.).   And that
no one may contend that obedience to an abbot, even in
things evil, is free from that penalty, there are words elsewhere still more precise : *The son shall not bear the
iniquity of the father, and the father shall not bear the
iniquity of the son* (Ezek. xviii. 20).   From these, then, it
appears clearly that those who command things evil are not
to be obeyed, especially when in yielding to wrong commands, in which you appear to obey man, you show yourself plainly disobedient to God, who has forbidden everything that is evil.   For it is altogether unreasonable to
profess yourself obedient when you know that you are
violating obedience due to the superior on account of the

inferior, that is, to the Divine on account of the human. What then? God forbids what man orders; and shall I be deaf to the voice of God and listen to that of man? The Apostles did not understand the matter thus when they said, *We must obey God rather than men* (Acts v. 29). Does not the Lord in the Gospel blame the Pharisees: *Ye transgress the commandment of God on account of your traditions* (S. Matt. xv. 3). And by Isaiah: *In vain they worship Me*, he says, *teaching the commands and doctrines of men* (Is. xxix. 13). And also to our first father.[1] *Because thou hast obeyed thy wife rather than Me, the earth shall be rebellious to thy work* (Gen. iii. 17). Therefore to do evil, whosoever it be that bids, is shown not to be obedience, but disobedience.

4. To make this principle clear, we must note that some actions are wholly good, others wholly evil: and in these no obedience is to be rendered to men. For the former are not to be omitted by us, even if they are prohibited [by men]: nor the latter done, even though they are commanded. But, besides these, there are actions between the two, and which may be good or evil according to circumstances of place, time, manner, or person, and in these obedience has its place, as it was in the matter of the tree of the knowledge of good and evil, which was in the midst of Paradise. When these are in question, it is not right to prefer our own judgment to that of our superiors, so as to take no heed of what they order or forbid. Let us see whether it be not such a case that I have condemned in you, and whether you ought not to be condemned. For clearness, I will subjoin examples of the distinction which I have just made. Faith, hope, charity, and others of that class are wholly good; it cannot be wrong to command, or to practise them, nor right to forbid them, or to neglect the practice of them. Theft, sacrilege, adultery, and all other such vices are wholly evil; it can never be right to practise or to order them, nor wrong to forbid or avoid them. The law is not made for

---

1 *Protoplastus*, the first formed. Tertullian, *Exhort. ad Castit.*, cap. 2, and *Adv. Jud.*, c. 13, calls Adam and Eve *Protoplasti.*—[E.]

things of this kind, for the prohibition of no person has
the power to render null the commandments given, nor the
command of any to render lawful the things prohibited.
There are, finally, things of a middle kind which are not in
themselves good or evil; they may be indifferently either
prescribed or forbidden, and in these things an inferior
never sins in obeying. Such are, for example, fasting,
watching, reading, and such like. But some things which
are of this middle kind often pass the bounds of indiffer-
ency, and become the one or the other. Thus, marriage is
neither prescribed nor forbidden, but when it is made may
not be dissolved. That, therefore, which before the nuptials
was a thing of the middle kind obtains the force of a thing
wholly good in regard to the married pair. Also, it is a
thing indifferent for a man in secular life to possess or not
to possess property of his own; but to a monk, who is not
allowed to possess anything, it is wholly evil.

5. Do you see now, brother, to which branch of my
division your action belongs? If it is to be put among
things wholly good it is praiseworthy: if among those
wholly evil it is greatly to be blamed: but if it is to be
placed among those of the middle kind you may, perhaps,
find in your obedience an excuse for your first departure,
but your delay in returning is not at all excusable, since
that was not from obedience. For when your abbot was
dead, if he had previously ordered anything which was not
fitting, the former discussion has shown you that you were
no longer bound to obey him. And although the matter is
now sufficiently clear by itself, yet because of some who
seek for occasion to object when reason does not support
them, I will put the matter clearly again, so that every
shade of doubt may disappear, and I will show you that
your obedience and your leaving your monastery were
neither wholly good nor partly good, but plainly wholly
evil. Concerning him who is dead, I am silent; he has
now God alone for his judge, and to his own Lord he
either stands or falls; that God may not say with righteous
anger, " Men have taken away from me even the right to

judge." However, for the instruction of the living I discuss, not even what he has done, but what he has ordered; whether, that is to say, his order ought to have been obligatory, inasmuch as a widespreading scandal has followed upon it. And I say this first; that if there are any who followed him when he wrongly left his cloister, but who followed in simplicity, and without suspecting any evil, supposing that he had license to go forth from the Bishop of Langres and the Abbot of Cîteaux (for to each of these was he responsible); and it is not incredible that some of those who were of his company may so have believed; this, my censure, does not touch them, provided that when they knew the truth, they returned without delay.

6. Therefore my discourse is against those only, or rather for those, who knowingly and purposely put their hands into the fire; who being conscious of his presumption, yet followed him who presumed, without caring for the prohibition of the Apostle, and his precept, to withdraw from every brother who walks disorderly (2 Thess. iii. 6). Despising also the voice of the Lord himself, *He who gathereth not with me scattereth* (S. Matt. xii. 30). To you, brethren, belongs clearly and specially that reproach spoken by Jeremiah, which I recall with grief : *This is a nation that obeyeth not the voice of the Lord their God* (Jer. vii. 28). For clearly that is the Voice of God pointing out His enemy from the work that he does, and, as it were, showing him with a stretched finger to ward off simple souls from his ungodly example : *He who is not with Me*, He says, *scatters;* ought you to have followed a disperser ? And when God invites you to unite with Him, ought you rather to follow a man who wishes to disperse you ? He scorned his superiors, he exposed his inferiors to danger, he deeply troubled his brethren, and yet ye seeing a thief joined yourself with him ! I had determined to be silent concerning him who is dead, but I am obliged, I confess, to proceed still a little further, since I cannot blame your obedience, if his command is not shown to be altogether improper. Since the orders and the actions of the man were similar to each other, it seems

impossible to praise or to blame the one without the other. Now it is very clear that orders of that kind ought not to have been obeyed, since they were contrary to the law of God. For who can suppose that the institutions of our Fathers are not to be preferred to those of lesser persons, or that the general rules of the Order must not prevail over the commands of private persons ?   For we have this in the Rule of S. Benedict.[1]

7. I should be able, indeed, to bring forward the Abbot of Cîteaux as a witness, who, as being superior to your abbot as a father to a son, as a master to a disciple, and, in a word, as an abbot to a monk committed to his charge, rightly complains that you have held him in contempt because of the other.   I might speak also of the Bishop, whose consent was not waited for, a contempt which was inexcusable, since the Lord says of such and to such: *He who despises you despises Me* (S. Luke x. 16).   But as to both these might be opposed and preferred the authority of the Roman Pontiff as more weighty ; by whose license it is said that you have taken care to secure yourselves (the question of that license shall be discussed in its proper place), [see below, No. 9], I rather bring forward such an one as you dare not set yourself against.   Most surely He is the Supreme Pontiff, who by His own blood entered in once and alone into the Holy Place to obtain eternal redemption (Heb. ix. 12), and de- nounces with a terrible voice, in the Gospel, that none should dare to give scandal to even the least of His little ones (S. Matt. xviii. 6).   I should say nothing if the evil had not proceeded farther.   An easy forgiveness would follow a fault which has no grave consequences.   But at present there is no doubt that you have preferred the commands of a man to that of God, and have thus scandalized very many.   What man of any sense would say that such an audacious act was good, or could become good, by the direction of any man, whatever his dignity ?   And if it is not good, nor can become good, without doubt it is

[1] Reg. Cap. 71.

wholly evil. Whence it follows that since your withdrawal was to the scandal of many, and by this contrary to the law of God, since it is neither wholly good nor even of a middle kind, it is, therefore, wholly and altogether evil; because that which is wholly is always such, and that of a middle kind can become so.

8. How then can either the permission of your abbot avail to make that permissible which is (as we have already shown beyond question) wholly evil, since (as we have said above) things of this kind, that is things purely evil, can never be rightly ordered nor permissibly done? Do you see how futile is the excuse you draw from obedience to a man when you are convicted of a transgression against God? I hardly suppose that you would resort to that reply of the Lord respecting the scandal given to the Pharisees, *Let them alone, they be blind leaders of the blind* (S. Matt. xv. 14), and that as He attached no value to their objections, so you attach no value to ours; for you know that there is no comparison in this respect between Him and you. But if you make comparison of persons, you find that on one side it is the proud Pharisees who are scandalized, on the other the poor of Jesus Christ; and as to the cause of the scandal, in the one case it is presumption, in the other truth. Again, as I have shown above, you have not only preferred a human to a Divine command, but that of a private person to a public rule, and this alone would suffice for proof; but the custom and Rule, not only of our Order, but of all monasteries, seems to cry out against your unexampled innovation and unparalleled presumption.

9. You had then just reason to fear, and were rightly distrustful of the goodness of your cause when, in order to still the pangs of your consciences, you tried to have recourse to the Holy See. O, vain remedy! which is nothing else than to seek girdles, like our first parents, for your ulcerated consciences, that is, to hide the ill instead of curing it. We have asked and obtained (they say) the permission of the Pope. Would that you had asked not his permission, but his advice; that is to say, not that he would permit you to do

it, but whether it was a thing permitted to you to do! Why, then, did you solicit his permission? Was it to render lawful that which was not so? Then you wished to do what was not lawful; but what was not lawful was evil. The intention, therefore, was evil, which tended towards evil. Perhaps you would say that the wrong thing which you demanded permission to do ceased to be such if it was done by virtue of a permission. But that has been already excluded above by an irrefragable reason. For when God said, *Do not despise one of these little ones who believe in Me*, He did not 'add also, Unless with permission; nor when He said, *Take care not to give scandal to one of these little ones* (S. Matt. xviii. 6-10), did He limit it by adding, Without licence. It is then certain that except when the necessary interests of the truth require, it is not permitted to anyone to give any scandal, neither to order it, nor to consent to it. Yet you think that permission is to be obtained to do so. But to what purpose? Was it that you might sin with more liberty and fewer scruples, and, therefore, with just so much the more danger? Wonderful precaution, marvellous prudence! They had already devised evil in their heart, but they were cautious not to carry it out in action except with permission. They conceived in sorrow, but they did not bring forth iniquity until the Pope had afforded his consent to that unrighteous birth. With what advantage? or, at least, with what lessening of the evil? Is it likely that either an evil will cease to be or even be rendered less because the Pope has consented to it? But who will deny it to be a bad thing to give consent to evil? Which, notwithstanding, I do not in any way believe that the Pope would have done, unless he had been either deceived by falsehood or overcome by importunity. In fact, unless it had been so, would he weakly have given you permission to sow scandal, to raise up schisms, to distress friends, to trouble the peace of brethren, to throw into confusion their unity, and, above all, to despise your own Bishop? And under what necessity he should have acted thus I have no need to say, since the issue of the matter sufficiently shows. For I see with grief that you have gone forth, but I do not see that you have profited in doing so.

10. Thus, in your opinion, to give assent to so great and weighty evils is to show obedience, to render assistance, to behave with moderation and gentleness. Do you, then, endeavour to whitewash the most detestable vices under the name of virtues? Or do you think that you can injure virtues without doing injury to the Lord of virtues? You hide the vainest presumption, the most shameful levity, the cruellest division under the names of obedience, moderation, gentleness, and you soil those sacred names with the vices hidden under them. May I never emulate this obedience: such moderation can never be pleasing to me, or rather seems to resemble molestation; may gentleness of this kind ever be far from me. Such obedience is worse than any revolt: such moderation passes all bounds. Shall I say that it goes beyond them or does not come up to them? Perhaps it would be more adequate to say that it is altogether without measure or bound. Of what kind is that gentleness which irritates the ears of all the hearers? And yet I beg you to show some sign of it now on my behalf. Since you are so patient that you do not contend with anybody, even with one who tries to drag you away to forbidden ground, permit me, too, I beg of you, to treat with you now somewhat more unrestrainedly. Otherwise I have merited much evil from you if you think that you must resent from me alone what you are accustomed to resent from no one else.

11. Well, then, I call your own conscience to witness. Was it willingly or unwillingly that you went forth? If willingly, then it was not from obedience. If unwillingly, you seem to have had some suspicion of the order which you carried out with reluctance. But when there is suspicion, there consideration is necessary. But you, either to display your patience or to exercise it, obeyed without discussion, and suffered yourself to be taken away, not only without your own volition, but even against your

conscience.   O, patience worthy of all impatience!   I
cannot, I confess, help being angry with this most ques-
tionable patience.   You saw that he was a scatterer and
yet you followed him; you heard him directing what was
scandalous and yet you obeyed him!   True patience consists in doing or in suffering what is displeasing to us, not
what is forbidden to us.   A strange thing!   You listened
to that man softly murmuring, but not to God openly protesting in such words as these, like a clap of thunder from
heaven, *Woe to him through whom scandal cometh* (S. Matt.
xviii. 7).   And to be the better heard, not only does the
Lord Himself cry aloud, but His Blood cries with a terrible
voice to make even the deaf hear.   Its pouring forth is its
cry.   Since it was poured forth for the children of God who
were scattered abroad that it might gather them together
into one, it justly murmurs against the scatterers.   He whose
constant duty it is to collect souls together hates without
doubt those who scatter them.   Loud is His voice and piercing
which calls bodies from their graves and souls from Hades.
That trumpet blast calls together heaven and earth and the
things that are with them, giving them peace.   Its sound
has gone out unto the whole world, and yet it has not been
able to burst through your deafness!   What a voice of
power and magnificence when the words are spoken:
Let the Lord arise and let His enemies be scattered (Ps.
lxviii. 2).   And again: *Disperse them by Thy power, O
Lord, my protector, and put them down* (Ps. lix. 12).   It
is the blood of Christ, brother Adam, which raises its voice
as a sounding trumpet on behalf of pious assemblies
against wicked scatterers; it has been poured forth to
bring together those who were dispersed, and it threatens
to disperse those who scatter.   If you do not hear His
voice, then listen to that which rolls from His side.   For
how could He not hear His own blood who heard the blood
of Abel?

   12. But what is this to me? you say.   It concerns one
whom it was not right for me to contradict.   The disciple
is not above his master; and it was to be taught, not to

teach, that I attached myself to him. As a hearer, it became me to follow, not to go before, my preceptor. O, simple one, the Paulus of these times! If only he had shown himself another Antony,[1] so that you had no occasion to discuss the least word that fell from his lips, but only to obey it without hesitation! What exemplary obedience! The least word, an iota, which drops from the lips of his superiors finds him obedient! He does not examine what is enjoined, he is content because it is enjoined![2] And this is obedience without delay. If this is a right view of duty, then without cause do we read in the Church: *Prove all things, hold fast that which is good* (1 Thess. v. 21). If this is a right view, let us blot out of the book of the Gospel *Be ye wise as serpents,* for the words following would suffice, *and harmless as doves* (S. Matt. x. 16). I do not say that inferiors are to make themselves judges of the orders of those set over them, in which it may be taken for granted that nothing is ordered contrary to the Divine laws, but I assert that prudence also is necessary to notice if anything does so contradict, and freedom firmly to pronounce against these. But you reply, I have nothing to do with examining what he orders; it is his duty to do that before ordering. Tell me, I pray you, if a sword were put into your hand and he bade you turn it against his throat, would you obey? Or if he ordered you to fling yourself headlong into the fire, or into the water, would you do it? If you did not even hinder him from such acts as these to the best of your ability, would not you be held guilty of the crime of homicide? Come, then, see that you have done nothing

---

[1] Antony, who was called by S. Athanasius "the founder of asceticism," and "a model for monks," is called "Abbas," though he was more properly a hermit, and always refused to take oversight of a monastery. He was born at Coma, in Upper Egypt, about A.D. 250. The Paulus here mentioned was a disciple of Antony. He was remarkable for his childlike docility, on account of which he was surnamed Simplex, and notwithstanding a certain dulness of intellect seems to have shown sometimes remarkable discernment of character.—[E.]

[2] This clause is wanting in some MSS.

but co-operate in his crime under the pretext of obedience. Do you not know that it has been said by a certain person (for you would not, perhaps, give credence to me) that it would be better to be sunk in the depths of the sea than to give scandals (S. Matt. xviii. 6). Why has He said this unless that He wished to signify that in comparison to the terrible punishments that are reserved for the scandalous, temporal death would seem scarcely a punishment but an advantage? Why, then, did you help him to make a scandal? For you did so in following and obeying him. Would it not have been better, according to the declaration of the Truth I have quoted, to hang a millstone from his neck and so to plunge him in the depth of the sea? What then? You that were so obedient a disciple, who could not bear that he, your father and master, should be separated from you for a single instant, for a foot breadth (as it is said), you have not hesitated to fall into the ditch behind him with your eyes wide open, like another Balaam? Did you think that you were labouring for his happiness when you showed toward him an obedience more hurtful for him than death? Truly, now, I experience how true is that saying : *A man's foes shall be they of his own household* (Micah vii. 6). If you see and feel this, do you not groan if you perceive what you have done? And if you do perceive, do you not tremble? For, indeed, your obedience (it is not my judgment, but that of the Truth Himself) has been worse for him than death.

13. If you are now convinced of this, I do not know how you can help trembling and hastening to repair your fault. Otherwise what conscience of wrong will you carry hence to that terrible tribunal where the Judge will not need witness, where the Truth will scan even purposes, and penetrate in search of faults to the hidden places of the heart, where, in short, that Divine look will try the most secret recesses of minds, and at the sudden shining of that Sun of justice all the windings of human souls will be spread open and give to the light whatever, whether good or evil, they were hiding? Then, brother Adam, those who commit

a sin, and those who consent to it will be punished with equal chastisement. Then thieves and the associates of thieves will listen to a similar sentence; the seducers and the seduced will undergo an equal judgment. Cease, then, to say again, What is it to me ? Let him see to it. Can you touch pitch and say I am not defiled ? Can you hide fire in your bosom and not be burned ? Can you have your portion with adulterers without resembling them in some respect ? Isaiah did not think so, for he reproached himself not only because he was himself unclean, but also because he was the companion of the unclean : *Because*, he says, *I am a man of unclean lips and I dwell in the midst of a people of unclean lips* (Isaiah vi. 5). For he blames himself not because he dwelt among sinners, but because he has not condemned their sins. For, so he says : *Woe is me because I have been silent* (Isaiah vi. 5, VULG.). But when did he consent to the doing of evil, that he blames himself not to have condemned it in others ? And did not David also feel that he was defiled by the contact of sin when he said : *With men that work iniquity, and I will not communicate with their chosen friends* (Ps. cxl. 4, VULG.). Or when he made this prayer : *Cleanse me O Lord from my secret sins, and spare Thy servant from the offences of others* (Ps. xix. 12-13, VULG.). Wherefore he strove to avoid the society of sinners in order not to share in their faults. For he says farther : *I have not sat in the council of vanity, and I will not enter into the company of those who do unjustly* (Ps. xxv. 4-5, VULG.). And then he adds : *I have hated the congregation of evil doers, and will not sit with the wicked* (*ibid.*). Finally, hear the counsel of the wise man : *My son, if sinners entice thee, consent thou not* (Prov. i. 10).

14. Have you, then, against these and innumerable other and similar testimonies of the truth, thought that you ought to obey *anybody ?* O, odious perversity ! The virtue of obedience which always wars on behalf of truth, is arrayed against truth. Happy the disobedience of brother Henry, who soon repenting of his error and retracing his steps, has

the happiness of not persisting longer in such an obedience. The fruits of disobedience are sweeter and to be preferred [to this] ; and now he tastes them with a good conscience in the peaceable and constant practice of the duties of his profession in the midst of his brethren, and in the bosom of the Order to which he has devoted himself ; while some of his former companions are breaking the hearts of their ancient brethren by the scandals they are making ! Whose disobedience of slackness and omission, if the choice were given me, I would even prefer, with his sense of penitence, than the punctilious obedience of such as these, with scandal. For I consider that he does better for the keeping unity in the bond of peace who obeys charity, though disobedient to his abbot, than those who so defer to a single man as to prefer one to the whole body. I might boldly add even this, that it is preferable to risk disobedience to one person than to endanger the vows of our own profession and all the other advantages of religion.

15. Since, not to speak of other obligations, there are two principal ones to be observed by all dwellers in a monastery, obedience to the abbot and stability or constancy. But one of these ought not to be fulfilled to the prejudice of the other, so that you should thus show yourself constant in your place as not to be above being subject to the superior, and so obey the superior as not to lose constancy. Thus if you would disapprove of a monk, however constant in his cloister, who was too proud to obey the orders of his superior, can you wonder that we blame an obedience which served you as the cause or occasion for deserting your place, especially when in making a religious profession constancy is vowed in such a way as not to be at all subordinated to the will of the abbot under whom a monk may be placed.

16. But perhaps you may turn what I say against me, asking what I have done with the constancy which ought to have kept me at Cîteaux, whereas I now dwell elsewhere. To which I reply, I am, indeed, a Cistercian monk professed in that place, and was sent forth by my abbot to where I

now dwell, but sent forth in peace without scandal, without disorder, according to our usages and constitutions. As long, therefore, as I persevere in the same peace and concord in which I was sent forth, as long as I stand fast in unity, I do not prefer my private interests to those of the community. I remain peaceful and obedient in the place where I have been posted. I say that my conscience is at peace, because I observe faithfully the stability I have promised. How do I compromise my vow of stability when I do not break the bond of concord, nor desert the firm ground of peace? If obedience keeps my body far distant from Cîteaux, the offering of the same devotions and a manner of life in every way similar hold my spirit always present there. But the day on which I shall begin to live, according to other laws (which may God avert), to practise other customs, to perform different observances, to introduce novelties and customs from without, I shall be a transgressor of my vows, and I shall no longer think that I am observing the constancy that I promised. I say, then, that an abbot ought to be obeyed in all things, but saving the oath of the Order. But you having made profession, according to the Rule of S. Benedict, where you promised obedience, you promised also constancy. And if you have, indeed, obeyed, but have not been constant by offending in one point, you are made an offender in all, and if in all, then in obedience itself.

17. Do you see, then, the proper scope of your obedience? How can it excuse your want of constancy, which is not even of weight to justify itself? Everyone knows that a person makes his profession solemnly and regularly in the presence of the abbot. That profession is made, therefore, in his presence only, not at his discretion also. The abbot is employed as the witness, and not the arbiter of the profession ; the helper of its fulfilment, not an assistant to the breach of it ; to punish and not to authorize bad faith. What, then? Do I place in the hand of the abbot the vows that I have taken, without exception ratified by my mouth and signed by my hand in presence of God and

His Saints? Do I not hear out of the Rule (Rule of S. Benedict C. 58) that if I ever do otherwise I shall be condemned by God, whom I have mocked? If my abbot or even an angel from heaven should order me to do something contrary to my vow, I would boldly refuse an obedience of this kind, which would make me a transgressor of my own oath and make me swear falsely by the name of my God, for I know, according to the truth of Scripture, that out of my own mouth I must either be condemned or justified (S. Luke xix. 22), and because *The mouth which lies slays the soul* (Wisd. i. 11), and that we chant with truth before God, *Thou wilt destroy all those who speak falsehood* (Ps. v. 6), and because *everyone shall bear his own burden* (Gal. vi. 5), and *everyone shall give account of himself to God* (Rom. xiv. 12). If it were otherwise with me, with what front could I dare to lie in the presence of God and His angels, when singing that verse from the Psalm: *I will render unto Thee my vows, which my lips have uttered* (Ps. lvi. 13, 14).

In fact, the abbot himself ought to consider the advice which the Rule gives, addressing itself to him in particular, "that he should maintain the present Rule in all respects," and also, which is universally directed, and no exception made, "that all should follow the Rule as guide and mistress, nor is it to be rashly deviated from by any" (Rule of S. Bened. capp. lxiv. 3). Thus I have determined to follow him as master always and everywhere, but on the condition never to deviate from the authority of the Rule, which, as he himself is witness, I have sworn and determined to keep.

18. Let me, briefly, treat another objection which may possibly be made to me, and I will bring to a close an epistle which is already too long. It seems that I may be reproached with acting otherwise than I speak. For I may be asked, if I condemn those who have deserted their monastery, not only with the consent of their abbot, but at his command, on what principle do I receive and retain those who from other monasteries, who, breaking their

vow of constancy and contemning the authority of their
superiors, come to our Order? To which my reply will be
brief, but dangerous; for I fear that what I shall say will
displease certain persons. But I fear still more lest by
concealing the truth I should sing untruly in the Church
those words of the Psalmist: *I have not hid my righteous-*
ness within my heart: my talk hath been of Thy truth and
of Thy salvation (Ps. xl. 12). I receive them, then, for this
reason, because I do not consider that they are wrong to
quit the monastery, in which they were able, indeed, to
make vows to God, but by no means to perform them, to
enter into another house where they may better serve God,
Who is everywhere, and who repair the wrong done by the
breach of their vow of constancy by the perfect performance
of all other duties of the religious life. If this displeases anyone, and he murmurs against a man thus seeking his own
salvation, the Author of salvation Himself shall reply for
him: *Is thine eye evil because* he *is good?* (S. Matt. xx.
15). Whosoever thou art who enviest the salvation of
another, care rather for thine own. Dost thou not know
that *by the envy of the devil death entered into the world?*
(Wisd. ii. 24). Take heed, therefore, to thyself. For if
there is envy there is death; surely, thou canst not both be
envious and live. Why seek a quarrel with thy brother,
since he seeks only the best means of fulfilling the vows
which he has made? If the man seeks in what place or in
what manner he may best discharge what he has promised
to God, what wrong has he done to you? Perhaps, if you
held him your debtor for a sum of money, however small,
you would oblige him to compass sea and dry land until
he rendered you the whole debt, even to the last farthing.
What, then, has your God deserved from you that you are
not willing for Him, too, to receive what is due? But in
envying one you render two hostile; since you are trying
both to defraud the lord of the service due from his
servant, and to deprive the servant of the favour of his
lord. Wherefore do you not imitate him, and yourself
discharge what is due from you? Do you think that your

debt, too, will not be required of you? Or do you not
rather fear to irritate God against you the more by wickedly
saying in your heart, He will not require it?

19. What, you say to me, do you then condemn all who
do not do likewise? No; but hear what I do think about
them, and do not make futile accusations. Why do you
wish to make me odious to many thousands of holy men,
who, under the same profession as I, though not living in
the same manner, either live holily or have died blessed
deaths? I do not fail to remember that God has left to
Himself seven thousand men who had not bowed the knee
before Baal (1 Kings xix. 18). Listen to me, then, man
envious and calumnious. I have said that I think men
coming to us from other monasteries ought to be received.
Have I blamed those who do not come? The one class I
excuse, but I do not accuse the other. It is only the
envious whom I cannot excuse, nor, indeed, am I willing to
do so. These being excepted, I think that if any others
wish to pass to a stricter Rule, but fear to do so because of
scandal, or are hindered by some bodily weakness, do not
sin, provided that they study to live a holy, pious, and
regulated life in the place where they are. For if by the
custom of their monastery relaxations of the Rule have
been introduced, either that very charity, in which they
hesitate to remove to a better on account of causing
scandal, may, perhaps, be an excuse for this; according
to that saying *Charity covers a multitude of sins* (1 Peter
iv. 8), or the humility in which one conscious of his
infirmity regards himself as imperfect, for it is said *God
gives grace unto the humble* (S. James iv. 6).

20. Many things I have written, dear brother, and,
perhaps, it was not needful to use so many words, for an
intelligence such as yours, quick in understanding what is
said, and a will well-disposed to follow good counsel.
But although I have written specially to you, yet so many
words need not have been written on your account, but for
those for whom they may be needful. But I warn you, as
my own former and intimate friend, in few words and with

all confidence, not to keep longer in suspense, at the great peril of your own soul, the souls of those who are desiring and awaiting your return. You hold now in your hands (if I do not mistake) both your own eternal life and death, and theirs who are with you ; for I judge that whatever you decide or do they will do also. Otherwise, announce to them the grave judgment which has been rightly passed with respect to them by all the Abbots of our Order. Those who return shall live, those who resist shall die.

LETTER VIII. (A.D. 1131.)

To Bruno,[1] Archbishop elect of Cologne.

Bernard having been consulted by Bruno as to whether he ought to accept the See of Cologne, so replies as to hold him in suspense, and render him in awe of the burden of so great a charge. He advises him to seek counsel of God in prayer.

1. You seek counsel from me, most illustrious Bruno, as to whether you ought to accept the Episcopate, to which it is desired to advance you. What mortal can presume to decide this for you ? If God calls you, who can dare to dissuade you, but if He does not call you, who may counsel you to draw near ? Whether the calling is of God or not who can know, except the Spirit, who searcheth even the deep things of God, or one to whom God Himself has revealed it ? That which renders advice still more doubtful is the humble, but still terrible, confession in your letter, in which you accuse your own past life gravely, but, as I fully believe, in sincerity and truth. And it is undeniable that such a life

------

[1] Bruno, son of Engelbert, Count of Altena, was consecrated, in 1132, by William, Cardinal Bishop of Præneste, and succeeded Frederick in the See of Cologne. In the year 1136 he proceeded into Italy with the Emperor Lothair, and died in that year. He was buried in the church of S. Nicholas, at Bari, in Apulia. A short time after his death his tomb was violated, as was that of Duke Raoul, by Roger, Prince of Sicily ; their bodies were dragged through the street, and mutilated with cruelty more than barbarous. The chronicler Otto of Frisingen calls him " a learned man."

is unworthy of a function so holy and exalted. On the
other hand, you are very right to fear (and I fear the same
with you) if, because of the unworthiness you feel, you
fail to make profitable use of the talent of knowledge committed to you, unless you could, perhaps, find another way,
less abundant, perhaps, but also less perilous, of making
increase from it. I tremble, I confess it, for I ought to say
to you as to myself what I feel: I tremble, I say, at the
thought of the state whence, and that whither, you are
called, especially since no period of penitence has inter-
vened to prepare you for the perilous transition from the
one to the other. And, indeed, the right order requires
that you should study to care for your own conscience
before charging yourself with the care of those of others.
That is the first step of piety, of which it is written, *To pity
thine own soul is pleasing unto the Lord* (Ecclus. xxx.
23). It is from this first step that a well-ordered charity
proceeds by a straight path to the love of one's neighbour,
for the precept is to love him as ourselves. But if you
are about to love the souls that would be confided to
you as you have loved your own hitherto, I would prefer
not to be confided rather than be so loved. But if you
shall have first learned to love yourself then you will know,
perhaps, how you should love me.

2. But what if God should quicken His grace and multiply
His mercy upon you, and His clemency is able more quickly
to replace the soul in a state of grace than daily penitence?
Blessed, indeed, is he *unto whom the Lord will not impute
sin* (Ps. xxxii. 2), for who shall bring accusation against the
elect of God? If God justifies, who is he that condemns?
This short road to salvation that holy thief attained, who
in one and the same day both confessed his iniquities and
entered into glory. He was content to pass by the cross
as by a short bridge from the religion of death[1] unto the
land of the living, and from this foul mire into the paradise
of joy (S. Luke xxiii. 43). This sudden remedy of piety
that sinful woman happily obtained, in whose soul grace of

[1] Unlikeness.

a sudden began to abound, where offences had so abounded. Without much labour of penitence her sins were pardoned, because she loved much (S. Luke vii. 37-50), and in a short time she merited to receive that amplitude of charity which, as it is written, *covers the multitude of sins* (1 S. Peter iv. 8). This double benefit and most rapid goodness also that paralytic in the Gospel experienced, being cured first in the soul, then in the body.

3. But it is one thing to obtain the speedy forgiveness of sins, and another to be borne in a brief space from the sins themselves to the badges (fillets) of high dignities in the Church. Yet I see that Matthew from the receipt of custom was raised to the supreme honour of the Apostolate. But this again troubles me, because he did not hear with the other Apostles the charge, *Go ye into all the world and preach the Gospel to every creature* (S. Mark xvi. 15), until after he had done penitence, accompanying the Lord whithersoever He went, bearing long privation and remaining with Him in His temptations. I am not greatly reassured, though S. Ambrose was taken from the judge's tribunal to the priesthood, because he had from a boy led a pure and clean life, though in the world, and then he endeavoured to avoid the Episcopate even by flight and by hiding himself and many other means. Again, if Saul also was suddenly changed into Paul, a vessel of election, the Doctor of the Gentiles, and this be adduced as an example, it entirely destroys the similarity of the two cases to observe that he, therefore, obtained mercy because, as he himself says, he sinned ignorantly in unbelief.[1] Besides, if such incidents, done for good and useful purposes, can be cited, it should be, not as examples, but as marvels, and it can be truly said of them, *This is the change of the right hand of the Highest* (Ps. lxxvii. 10).

4. In the meantime let these provisional replies to your

---

[1] 1 Tim. i. 13. But surely the inference that the writer should have drawn was that S. Paul's sudden transformation was combined with and to be attributed to his Baptism : " cui prorsus innovato per Baptismum omnia vetera sint dimissa."—[E.]

queries suffice. If I do not express a decisive opinion, it is because I do not myself feel assured. This must needs be the case, for the gift of prophecy and of wisdom only could resolve your doubt. For who could draw clear water out of a muddy pool? Yet there is one thing that I can do for a friend without danger, and with the assurance of a good result; that is to offer to God my petition that He will assist you in this matter. Leaving, therefore, to Him the secret things of His Providence, of which we are ignorant, I will beg Him, with humble prayer and earnest supplication, that He will work in you and with respect to you that which shall be for His glory, and at the same time for your good. And you have also the Lord Norbert,[1] whom you may conveniently consult in person on all such subjects. For that good man is more fitted than I to explain the mysterious acts of Providence, as he is nearer to God by his holiness.

LETTER IX. (A.D. 1132.)

TO THE SAME, THEN ARCHBISHOP OF COLOGNE.

He exhorts Bruno, then recently created Archbishop of Cologne, to fear.

I have received with respect the Letter of your Grace, and have attended with care to what you have enjoined. If I have succeeded, you will have proof. But enough respecting that. Permit me in the same spirit of charity to say what follows. If it is certain that all those who are called to the ministry, are chosen also to the Kingdom, certainly the Archbishop of Cologne is secure of his own salvation. But if Saul was chosen to the kingdom, and Judas to the priesthood, by no other than God Himself, and it cannot be disproved that Scripture asserts this, then it is needful for even the Archbishop of Cologne to fear. But if that declaration holds good even in our own time (and it is true that it does)

---

[1] The founder of the Præmonstratensian Order. See respecting him Letter lvi.

that not many noble, not many powerful, not many wise are called by God (1 Cor. i. 26), has not the Archbishop of Cologne a triple cause for fearing? Let us, then, who are raised to high dignities, study not to be high-minded, but to fear, and condescend to those of low estate. *Have they made you chief?* it is said, *be among them as one of the rest* (Ecclus. xxxii. 1); and again, *The greater thou art, the more humble thyself in all things* (Ecclus. xxx. 18). It is the counsel of the wise, and listen to that of Wisdom Himself, who says *He that is greatest among you, let him be as the younger* (S. Luke xxii. 26). We know from other passages that those who have authority will have to meet a strict judgment (Wisd. vi. 5). Fear, then, ye that are powerful. The servant, also, that knoweth his Lord's will, and doeth it not, he shall beat with many stripes (S. Luke xii. 47). Fear, then, ye that are learned. Let the noble fear, for the Judge of all is not an acceptor of persons. That triple bond of necessary reason for fear will be very difficult to break through. Do I seem hard because I do not flatter, because I inculcate fear, which is the beginning of wisdom, upon a friend? May it be granted to me always so to benefit my friends; that is, by inspiring into them a salutary fear, rather than to deceive them by flattery. To that He incites me who says: *Happy is the man who feareth alway* (Prov. xxviii. 14); and He deters me from flattery who says: *O My people, they who flatter thee cause thee to err* (Is. iii. 12, VULG.).

LETTER X. (A.D. 1132.)

To the Same.

He incites Bruno to a just zeal for the punishment of crime.

The duty of your office, and the injunction of the Holy See, lay upon you a double obligation to punish a crime so enormous. Yet I think it not superfluous that the admoni-

tion of a friend should be added in a matter of such importance. I wish the one whom I regard as father and friend
to be admonished of this, to punish in every case that
requires it, and with a due degree of severity; so that you
should not only visit an offence that is before you with a
just chastisement, but should also restrain the hearer from
rashly imitating it.

LETTER XI. (Circa A.D. 1125.)

To Guigues,[1] the Prior, and to the other Monks of the Grand Chartreuse.

*He discourses much and piously of the law of true and
sincere charity, of its signs, its degrees, its effects, and of
its perfection which is reserved for Heaven (Patria).*

Brother Bernard, of Clairvaux, wishes health eternal to
the most reverend among fathers, and to the dearest among
friends, Guigues, Prior of the Grande Chartreuse, and to
the holy Monks who are with him.

1. I have received the letter of your Holiness as joyfully
as I had long and eagerly desired it. I have read it, and the
letters which I pronounced with my mouth, I felt, as it
were, sparks of fire in my heart, which warmed my heart
within me; as coming from that fire which the Lord has sent
upon the earth (S. Luke xii. 49). How great a fire must
glow in those meditations from which such sparks fly forth !

---

[1] His name was de Castro, and he was a Frenchman by birth. He was the
fifth General Prior of the Grand Chartreuse from B. Bruno, and the first writer
of the Statutes. He was held in much affection by Bernard, as appears both
from this Letter and from Book III. of the Life of St. Bernard, c. 1. Peter
the Venerable speaks of him in Letter 388 thus : " He was in his time the flower
and glory of religion." In the fortieth Letter of Book IV., addressed to Basil,
successor of Guigues in the rule of the Grand Chartreuse, he says :—" I had
determined to renew with you those old and sacred meetings of your predecessor,
Guigues, of happy memory, held frequently with me, in which I used to be so
fired by the flashes, as it were, of wisdom proceeding from his mouth that I was
of necessity almost lost to the perception of all human things." He rendered
his soul to the Lord, not without report of sanctity, in (or about) the 27th year of
his priorate, the year 1137, but in the 53rd year from the founding of the Order.

This, your inspired and inspiring salutation, was to me, I confess, not as if coming from man, but like words descending surely from Him who sent the salutation to Jacob. It is not for me, in fact, a simple salutation given in passing, according to the custom and usage of men, but it is plainly from the very bowels of charity, as I feel, that this benediction, so sweet and so unhoped for, has come forth. I pray God to bless you, who have had the goodness to prevent me with benedictions of such sweetness, that confidence is granted to me, your humble servant, to reply, since you have first written ; for though I had meditated writing, I had hitherto not presumed to do so. For I feared to trouble, by my eager scribbling, the holy quiet which you have in the Lord, and the religious silence which isolates you from the world. I feared, also, to interrupt, even for a moment, those mysterious whispers from God, and to pour my words into ears always occupied with the secret praises of heaven. I feared to become as one who would trouble even Moses on the mountain, Elias in the desert, or Samuel watching in the temple, if I had tried to turn away ever so little, minds occupied with divine communion. Samuel cries out : *Speak, Lord, for Thy servant heareth* (1 Sam. iii. 10). And should I presume to make myself heard ? I feared, I say, lest presenting myself out of season before you, as it were to David engaged in flight, or abiding in solitude, you might not wish to listen, and might say, " Excuse me, I cannot hear thee now ; I prefer rather to give ear to words sweeter than thine." *I will hear what the Lord God will say unto me ; for He shall speak peace unto His people, and to His saints, and to those who are converted at heart* (Ps. lxxxiv. 9, VULG.). Or, at least, this : *Depart from me, ye evil-disposed, and I will study the commandments of my God* (Ps. cxix. 115). For could I be so rash as to dare to arouse the much-loved spouse sweetly resting in the arms of her bridegroom as long as she will ? Should I not hear from her on the instant : Do not be troublesome to me ; *I am for My Beloved, and My Beloved is for Me ; He feedeth among the lilies* (Cant. ii. 16).

2. But what I do not dare to do, charity dares, and with all confidence knocks at the door of a friend, thinking that she ought by no means to suffer repulse, who knows herself to be the mother of friendships; nor does she fear to interrupt for an instant your rest, though so pleasant, to speak to you of her own task. She, when she will, causes you to withdraw from being alone with God; she, also, when she willed, made you attentive to me; so that you did not regard it as unworthy of you, not merely to benignantly endure my speaking, but more, to urge me to break the silence. I esteem the kindness, I admire the worthiness, I praise and venerate the pure rejoicing with which you glory in the Lord, for the advances in virtue which, as you suppose, I have made. I am proud of so great a testimony, and esteem myself happy in a friendship so grateful to me as that of the servants of God towards me. This is now my glory, this is my joy and the rejoicing of my heart, that not in vain I have lifted up mine eyes unto the mountains whence there has now come to me help of no small value. These mountains have already distilled sweetness for me ; and I continue to hope that they will do so until our valleys shall abound with fruit. That day shall be always for me a day of festival and perpetual memorial, in which I had the honour to see and to receive that worthy man, by whom it has come about that I should be received into your hearts. And, indeed, you had received me even before, if I may judge by your letter ; but now with a more close and intimate friendship, since, as I find, he brought back to you too favourable reports concerning me which, doubtless, he believed, though without sufficient cause. For, as a faithful and pious man, God forbid that he should speak otherwise than he believed. And truly I experience in myself what the Saviour says : *He who receives a righteous man in the name of a righteous man shall receive a righteous man's reward* (S. Matt. x. 41). I have said, the reward of a righteous man, because I am regarded as righteous, only through receiving one who is righteous. If he has reported of me something more than that, he has spoken not so much according to the truth of

the case as according to the simplicity and goodness of his heart. You have heard, you have believed, you have rejoiced, and have written, thereby giving me no little joy, not only because I have been honoured with a degree of praise and a high place in the estimation of your Holiness, but also because all the sincerity of your souls has made itself known to me in no small measure. In few words, you have shown to me with what spirit you are animated.

3. I rejoice, therefore, and congratulate you on your sincerity and goodness as I congratulate myself on the edification which you have afforded to me. That is, indeed, true and sincere charity, and must be considered to proceed from a heart altogether pure and a good conscience and faith unfeigned, with which we love our neighbour as ourself. For he who loves only the good that himself has done, or, at least, loves it more than that of others, does not love good for its own sake, but on account of himself, and he who is such cannot do as the prophet says : *Give thanks unto the Lord, because He is good* (Ps. cxviii. 1). He gives thanks, indeed, perhaps, because the Lord is good to him, not because He is good in Himself. Wherefore let him understand that this reproach from the same prophet is directed against him : *They will praise thee when thou doest well unto thy own soul* (Ps. xlix. 18). One man praises the Lord because He is mighty ; another because He is good unto him ; and, again, another simply because He is good. The first is a slave, and fears for himself ; the second mercenary, and desires somewhat for himself ; but the third is a son, and gives praise to his Father. Therefore both he who fears and he who desires are each working for his own advantage ; charity which is in him alone who is a son, seeketh not her own. Wherefore I think that it was of charity that was spoken, *The law of the Lord is pure, converting the soul* (Ps. xix. 7), because it is that alone which can turn away the mind from the love of itself and of the world and direct it towards God. Neither fear nor selfish love converts the soul. They change sometimes the outward appearance or the actions, but never

affect the heart. No doubt even the slave does sometimes the work of God, but because he does it not of his own free will he remains still in his hardness. The mercenary person does it also, but not out of kindness, only as drawn by his own particular advantage. Where there is distinction of persons, there are personal interests, and where there are personal interests there is a limit of willingness, and there, without doubt, a rusting meanness. Let the very fear by which he is constrained be a law to the slave, let the greedy desire, with which the mercenary is bound, be a law to him, since it is by it that he is drawn away and enticed. But of these neither is without fault or is able to convert the soul. But charity does convert souls when it fills them with disinterested zeal.

4. Now, I should say that this charity is faultless in him who has become accustomed to retain nothing for himself out of that which is his own. He who keeps nothing for himself gives to God quite certainly all that he has, and that which belongs to God cannot be unclean. Thus that pure law of the Lord is no other than charity, which seeks not what is advantageous to herself, but that which profits others. But law is said to be of the Lord, either because He Himself lives by it or because no one possesses it except by His gift. Nor let it seem absurd what I have said, that even God lives by law, since I declared that this law was no other than charity. For what but charity preserves in the supreme and blessed Trinity that lofty and unspeakable unity which it has ? It is law, then, and charity the law of the Lord, which maintains in a wonderful manner the Trinity in Unity and binds It in the bond of peace. Yet let no one think that I here take charity for a quality or a certain accident in God, or otherwise to say that in God (which God forbid) there is something which is not God; but I say that it is the very substance of God. I say nothing new or unheard of, for S. John says *God is love* (1 S. John iv. 16).

It is then right to say that charity is God, and at the same time the gift of God. Therefore Charity gives charity, the

:substantial [1] gives the accidental. Where the word signifies the Giver it is a name of the substance, and where the thing given, it is a name of the accident. This is the eternal law, Creator and Ruler of the Universe. Since all things have been made through it in weight and measure and number, and nothing is left without law, not even He who is the Law of all things, yet He is Himself none other than the law which rules Him, a law uncreated as He.

5. But the slave and the mercenary have a law, not from God, but which they have made for themselves—the one by not loving God, the other by loving something else more than Him. They have, I say, a law which is their own and not of the Lord, to which, nevertheless, their own is subjected; nor are they able to withdraw themselves from the unchangeable order of the divine law, though each should make a law for himself. I would say, then, that a person makes a law for himself when he prefers his own will to the common and eternal law, perversely wishing to imitate his Creator; so that as He is a law unto Himself, and is under no authority but His Own, so the man also will be his own master, will make his own will a law to himself. Alas! what a heavy and insupportable yoke upon all the sons of Adam, which weighs upon and bows down our necks, so that our life is drawn near to the grave. Unhappy man that I am, who shall deliver me from the body of this death? (Rom. vii. 24) with which I am so weighed down that unless the Lord had helped me, my soul would almost have dwelt in the grave (Ps. xciv. 17). With this load was he burdened who groaned, saying: *Why hast Thou set me as a mark against Thee, so that I am a burden to myself?* (Job vii. 20). Where he says, *I am made a burden to myself*, he showed that he was a law unto himself, and the law no other than he himself had made it. But when, speaking to God, he commenced by saying, *Thou hast set me as a mark against Thee*, he showed that he had not escaped from the Divine law. For this is the property of that eternal and just law of God, that he who would not be

---

[1] Mabillon reads *substantiva*, but another reading is *substantia*.—[E.]

ruled with gentleness by God, should be ruled as a punishment by his own self; and that all those who have willingly
thrown off the gentle yoke and light burden of charity
should bear unwillingly the insupportable burden of their
own will.

6. Thus the everlasting law does in a wonderful manner,
to him who is a fugitive from its power, both make him an
᾿ adversary and retain him as a subject; for while, on the
one hand, he has not escaped from the law of justice, by
which he is dealt with according to his merits, on the other
he does not remain with God in His light, or peace, or
glory. He is subjected to power, and excluded from
happiness. O Lord, my God, *why dost Thou not take away
my sin, and pardon my transgression?* (Job vii. 21). So
that throwing down the heavy weight of my own will, I
may breathe easily under the light burden of charity; that
I may not be overborne any longer by servile fear, nor
allured by selfish cupidity, but may be impelled by Thy
spirit, the spirit of liberty, which is that of Thy' children.
Who is it who witnesses to my spirit that I, too, am. one of
Thy children, since Thy law is mine, and as Thou art, so
am I also, in this world? For it is quite certain that those who
do this which the Apostle says *owe no one anything except
to love one another* (Rom. xiii. 8) are themselves as God is
in this world, nor are they slaves or mercenaries, but sons.
Therefore neither are sons without law, unless, perhaps,
some one should think the contrary because of this which is
written, *the law is not made for a righteous man* (1 Tim.
i. 9). But it ought to be remembered that the law promulgated in fear by a spirit of slavery is one thing, and that
given sweetly and gently by the spirit of liberty is another.
Those who are sons are not obliged to submit to the first,
but they are always under the rule of the second. Do you
wish to hear why it is said that law is not made for the
righteous? *You have not received*, he says, *the spirit of
slavery again in fear.* Or why, nevertheless, they are
always under the rule of the law of charity? *But ye have
received the spirit of the adoption of sons* (Rom. viii. 15).

Listen, now, in what manner the righteous man confesses
that at the same time he is and is not under the law.
I became, he says, *to those which were under the law as
being under the law, although I myself was not under the
law : but to those who were without law, I was as being
without law, since I was not without the law of God but in
the law of Christ* (1 Cor. ix. 20, 21). Whence it is not
accurately said the righteous have no law, or the righteous are
without law, but that the law was not made for the righteous;
that is, it is not, as it were, imposed upon unwilling
subjects, but given freely to willing hearts by Him to
whose sweet inspiration it is due. Wherefore the Lord
also beautifully says, *Take My yoke upon you* (S. Matt. xi.
29). As if He would say, I do not impose it upon you
against your will, take it if you are willing; otherwise you
will find not rest, but labour, for your souls.

7. The law of charity, then, is good and sweet, it is not
only light and sweet to bear, but it renders bearable and
light the laws even of slaves and mercenaries. But it does
not destroy these, but brings about their fulfilment, as the
Lord says, *I am not come to destroy the law, but to fulfil*
(S. Matt. v. 17). The one it moderates, the other it
reduces to order, and each it lightens. Charity will never
be without fear, but that fear is good ; it will never be
without any thought of interest, but that a restrained and
moderated one. Charity, therefore, perfects the law of the
slave when it inspires a generous devotion, and that of the
mercenary when it gives a better direction to interested
wishes. So, then, devotion mixed with fear does not
annul those last, but purifies them, only it takes away the
fear of punishment which servile fear is never exempt from;
and this fear is *clean and filial, enduring for ever* (Ps.
xix. 9). For that which is written, *perfect love takes away
fear* (1 S. John iv. 18), is to be understood of the fear of
punishment, which is never wanting, as we have said, to
slavish fear. It is, in fact, a common mode of speech
which consists in putting the cause for the effect. As for
cupidity, it is then rightly directed by the charity which

is joined with it, since ceasing altogether to desire things
which are evil, it begins to prefer those which are better,
nor does it desire good things except in order to reach
those which are better; which when, by the grace of God,
it has fully obtained, the body and all the good things
which belong to the body will be loved only for the sake
of the soul, the soul for the sake of God, and God alone for
Himself.

8. However, as we are in fleshly bodies, and are born
of the desire of the flesh, it is of necessity that our desire,
or affection, should begin from the flesh; but if it is rightly
directed, advancing step by step under the guidance of
grace, it will at length be perfected by the Spirit, because
*that is not first which is spiritual, but that which is
natural, and afterwards that which is spiritual; and it is
needful that we should first bear the image of the earthly
and afterwards that of the heavenly* (1 Cor. xv. 46, 49).
First, then, a man loves his own self for self's sake, since
he is flesh, and he cannot have any taste except for things
in relation with him; but when he sees that he is not able
to subsist by himself, that God is, as it were, necessary to
him, he begins to inquire and to love God by faith. Thus
he loves God in the second place, but because of his own
interest, and not for the sake of God Himself. But when, on
account of his own necessity, he has begun to worship Him
and to approach Him by meditation, by reading, by prayer,
by obedience, he comes little by little to know God with a
certain familiarity, and in consequence to find Him sweet
and kind; and thus having tasted how sweet the Lord is,
he passes to the third stage, and thus loves God no longer
on account of his own interest, but for the sake of God
Himself. Once arrived there, he remains stationary, and I
know not if in this life man is truly able to rise to the
fourth degree, which is, no longer to love himself except for
the sake of God. Those who have made trial of this (if
there be any) may assert it to be attainable; to me, I
confess, it appears impossible. It will be so without doubt
when the good and faithful servant shall have been brought

into the joy of his Lord, and inebriated with the fulness of the house of God. For being, as it were, exhilarate, he shall in a wonderful way be forgetful of himself, he shall lose the consciousness of what he is, and being absorbed altogether in God, shall attach himself unto Him with all his powers, shall thenceforth be one spirit with Him.

9. I consider that the prophet referred to this when he said: *I will enter into the powers of the Lord: O, Lord, I will make mention of Thy righteousness only* (Ps. lxxi. 16). He knew well that when he entered into the spiritual powers of God he would be freed from all the infirmities of the flesh, and would have no longer to think of them, but would be occupied only with the perfections of God. Then, for certain, each of the members of Christ would be able to say of himself, what Paul said of their Head: *If we have known Christ according to the flesh, yet now henceforth know we Him no more* (2 Cor. v. 16). There no one knows himself according to the flesh, because *flesh and blood will not inherit the kingdom of God* (1 Cor. xv. 50). Not that the substance of flesh will not be there, but that every fleshly necessity will be away; the love of the flesh is to be absorbed into the love of the spirit, and the weak human passions which exist at present will be absorbed into powers divine. Then the net of charity, which is now drawn through a great and vast sea, and does not cease to bring together from every kind of fish, at length drawn to the shore, shall retain only the good, rejecting the bad. And while in this life charity fills with all kinds of fishes the vast spaces of its net, suiting itself to all according to the time, making, in a sense, its own, and partaking of the good and evil fortunes of all, it is accustomed not only to rejoice with them that rejoice, but to weep with them that weep. But when it shall have reached the shore [of eternity], casting away as evil fish all that it bore with grief before, it will retain those only which are sources of pleasure and gladness. Then Paul will no longer be weak with the weak, or be scandalized with those who are scandalized, since scandal and weakness will be far away. We ought

not to think that he will still let fall tears over those who
have not repented here below; and as it is certain that
there will no longer be sinners, so there will be no one to
repent.   Far be it from us to think that he will mourn and
deplore those whose portion is everlasting fire with the
devil and his angels, when in that City of God which the
streams of that river make glad (Ps. xlvi. 4), the gates of
which the Lord loves more than all the dwellings of Jacob
(Ps. lxxxvii. 2), because in those dwellings, although the
joy of victory is sometimes tasted, yet the combat always
continues, and sometimes the struggle is for life; but in
that dear country there is no place for adversity or sorrow,
as in that Psalm we sing: *The abiding place of all those
who rejoice is in Thee* (Ps. lxxxvii. 7, VULG.), and again :
Everlasting joy shall be unto them (Is. lxi. 7).   How, then,
shall any remembrance be of mercy, where the justice of
God shall be alone remembered?   There can be no feeling
of compassion called into exercise where there shall be no
place for misery, or occasion for pity.

    10. I am impelled to prolong this already lengthy dis-
course, dearly beloved and much longed-for brethren, by
the very strong desire I have of conversing with you ; but
there are three things which show me that I ought to come
to an end.   First, that I fear to be burdensome to you ; that
I am ashamed to show myself so loquacious; third, that I
am pressed by domestic cares.   In conclusion, I beg you
to have compassion for me, and if you have rejoiced for the
good things you have heard of me, sympathize with me
also, I pray, in my too real temptations and cares.   He
who related these things to you has, no doubt, seen some
few little things, and has valued these little things as great,
while your indulgence has easily believed what it willingly
heard.   I felicitate you, indeed, on that charity which
believes all things (1 Cor. xiii. 7).   But I am confounded
by the truth which knows all things.   I beg you to believe
me in what I say of myself rather than another who has
only seen me from without.   *No man knoweth the things
that are in a man save the spirit of man which is in him*

(1 Cor. ii. 11). I assure you that I do not speak of myself by conjecture, but out of full knowledge, and that I am not such as I am believed and said to be. I feel assured of this, and confess it frankly; that so I may obtain your special prayers, and thus may become such as your letter sets forth, than which there is nothing I desire more.

LETTER XII.

To the Same.

He commends himself to their prayers.

To the very dear Lord and Reverend father Guigues, Prior of the Grande Chartreuse, and to the holy brethren who are with him, Brother Bernard of Clairvaux offers his humble service.

In the first place, when lately I approached your parts, I was prevented by unfavourable circumstances from coming to see you and to make your acquaintance; and although my excuse may perhaps be satisfactory to you, I am not able, I confess, to pardon myself for missing the opportunity. It is a vexation to me that my occupations brought it about, not that I should neglect to come to see you, but that I was unable to do so. This I frequently have to endure, and therefore my anger is frequently excited. Would that I were worthy to receive the sympathy of all my kind friends. Otherwise I shall be doubly unhappy if my disappointment does not excite your pity. But I give you an opportunity, my brethren, of exercising brotherly compassion towards me, not that I merit it. Pity me not because I am worthy, but because I am poor and needy. Justice inquires into the merit of the suppliant, but mercy only looks to his unhappiness. True mercy does not judge, but feels; does not discuss the occasion which presents itself, but seizes it. When affection calls us, reason is silent. When Samuel wept over Saul it was by a feeling of pity, and not of approval (1 Samuel xv. 13). David shed tears

over his parricidal son, and although they were profitless, yet
they were pious. Therefore do ye pity me (because I need
it, not because I merit it), ye who have obtained from God
the grace to serve Him without fear, far from the tumults of
the world from which ye are freed. Happy those whom
He has hidden in His tabernacle in the day of evil
men ; they shall trust in the shadow of His wings until the
iniquity be overpast. As for me, poor, unhappy, and
miserable, labour is my portion. I seem to be as a little
unfledged bird almost constantly out of the shelter of its
nest, exposed to wind and tempest. I am troubled, and I
stagger like a drunken man, and my whole conscience is
gnawed with care. Pity me, then ; for although I do not
merit pity I need it, as I have said.

LETTER XIII. (A.D. 1126.)

To the Lord Pope Honorius.

*He begs that the election of Alberic[1] to the See of
Chalons-sur-Marne may be ratified.*

To the supreme Pontiff Honorius, a certain brother, a
monk by profession, and by his life a sinner, sends his
humble duty.

It is said that over you the prayer of a poor man has
more power than the will of the powerful. The thought of
this singular nobleness in you, as well as the suggestion of
charity, impels me to write without fear to your Highness.
I speak to you, my lord, with regard to the Church of

---

[1] Alberic had a school in Rheims. " A man most illustrious for his knowledge of literature and his sound judgment," says Robert de Monte of him. Peter
Abaelard, his rival, calls him " Remensis," and " a disciple of William de Champeaux" (*Hist. Calamit. suar.* cap. 5). He is said to have been a " fellow
scholar" with Abaelard (*Epist. Heloissæ*, ii.), but became a strong opponent of the
novel speculations of the latter, and it was by his efforts in great measure in the
Council of Soissons that Abaelard was obliged to commit to the flames his Book
on the Trinity.

The letter and commendation before us does not seem to have been successful
in its purpose. But it appears that Alberic succeeded to the See of Bourges at
the death of its Bishop, Ulgrinus, some time after 1128.

Chalons, and I neither am able, nor ought I, to conceal from you as far as my ability extends, the danger to which it is exposed. In fact, being in its neighbourhood, I feel already that the peace of this Church will speedily be profoundly troubled, if your Holiness should not be able to assent to the election of that distinguished man, that is, of Magister Alberic, which has united the suffrages of the whole clergy and the people in an equal vote. On that subject, if you should deign to inquire or to care for my opinion, I would say that that man is of a faith irreproachable, that his doctrine is sound, and that he has shown prudence both in divine and human things ; and I hope that in the House of God (if by Him he should be chosen) he would be a vessel of honour, and would be of service not only to that house, but to the whole of the Gallican Church. It is now for your wisdom to judge, whether I am right in asking from you the giving of a dispensation from which such good effects may be expected.

LETTER XIV. (*Circa* A.D. 1126.)

To the Same Pope Honorius.

He commends the cause of the Church of Dijon to the Pontiff.

To the Supreme Pontiff HONORIUS, Brother BERNARD, called to be Abbot of Clairvaux, wishes health, and all that the prayers of a sinner can do in his behalf.

God, whom we venerate in you, knows the respectful fear with which I write to you. But charity, who governs both you and me, makes me bold so to do. Being requested by the Church of Dijon,[1] I have undertaken to make request

---

[1] This was the convent of monks of St. Benignus, at Dijon, which, as he says in the following Letter, he held in great affection, because of the antiquity of their house. It was in the Church of that house that the father and mother of Bernard were buried. It was not until long after that they were taken up to be carried to Clairvaux. The writers of that age, including Bernard, as we see in this and many others of his Letters, use the words *Church* and *Monastery*

on its behalf. But I almost doubt what I ought precisely to ask for it. For, as it is unjust to try to obtain anything contrary to justice, either by entreaty or by purchase, so it is superfluous before one who loves justice to make great efforts on behalf of that which is just. But although I do not know precisely what request it is best to make, yet I have full confidence that your kindness will not be unfruitful, especially in the cause of Religious.[1] And, indeed, I know not what your Holiness may think good to decide after a careful examination of the matter, but I can bear witness that I have heard, and frequently do hear, that the Abbey of Dijon has possessed by long and uncontested tenure that[2] which the people of Luxeuil are contesting with them, so that the older inhabitants of the neighbourhood are astonished, and indignant at the unfounded claim.

LETTER XV. (*In the same year as the preceding.*)

TO HAIMERIC THE CHANCELLOR.

To the illustrious lord HAIMERIC, Chancellor of the Apostolic See, BERNARD of Clairvaux wishes health, and the grace to follow the Apostle, *forgetting the things which are behind, and looking forward to those which are before.*

Our friends are not ignorant of your friendship for me, and if I were desirous of keeping the fruit of so great felicity to myself they would show themselves jealous. The monks of Dijon are very dear to me, because of the ancient associations of that Church. I beg you to let them experi-

indiscriminately to denote a convent of monks. See Letters 39, 60, 339, 392, 394, 395, etc., while it is not rare to find the word *Monastery* employed for *Church*. The Church of S. Benignus is simply called the Church of Dijon, because it is the principal Church of the town.

[1] Bernard and other writers not unfrequently use this name to designate monks, as in Letters 45 and 202, and in Sermon 26, *de Diversis*, n. 2. Gregory the Great long before uses the same term (Book i. Ep. 59).

[2] The dispute was respecting two little chapels of Clermont and of Vignory, and was not closed until a decision of Stephen, Archbishop of Vienna, assisted by some other Bishops. (Perard in *Burgundicis Monumentis*, pp. 224 and 228.)

ence that affection, whether yours for me or mine for them
is not without its influence. Justice, nevertheless, being
done in all respects, against which it is not right, even for
a friend, to desire anything.

LETTER XVI. (*The same year as the preceding.*)

To Peter, Cardinal Presbyter.

To his very dear lord PETER, Cardinal Presbyter, Brother
BERNARD, Abbot of Clairvaux, wishes health everlasting.

I have no cause to plead with you ; yet the cause of the
monks of Dijon, because they are Religious, I regard as
mine. Take their cause in hand as if it were mine; yet
so mine that it may be also that of justice. I believe, however, that their cause is just; and the whole country testifies
with me.

LETTER XVII. (*Circa* A.D. 1127.)

To Peter, Cardinal Deacon.[1]

*He excuses himself that he has not come when sum-
moned, and replies respecting some of his writings which
are asked for.*

To the venerable lord PETER, Cardinal Deacon of the
Roman Church, Brother BERNARD wishes health and entire
devotedness.

That I have not come to you as you commanded has been
caused not by my sloth, but by a graver reason. It is that,
if you will permit me to say so with all the respect which
is due to you, and all good men, I have taken a resolution

---

[1] This Peter is without doubt another person from Peter Leonis, who was
equally legate, but Cardinal Presbyter. He seems to be the same whom Pope
Honorius II. sent into France at the beginning of his pontificate as legate
à latere against Ponce and his followers, as Peter the Venerable declares in his
second book *On Miracles*, c. 13. Or he may have been Peter de Fontaines, a
compatriot of S. Bernard, created Cardinal A.D. 1120, on the title of S. Marcellus, by Pope Callixtus II.

not again to go out of my monastery, unless for precise
causes ; and I see at present nothing of that kind which
would permit me to carry out your wish, and gratify
my own by coming to you. But you, what are you doing
with respect to that promise of coming here which your
former letter contained ? We are awaiting it still. What
the writings were, which you had before ordered to be prepared for you [otherwise, *for us*] and now ask for, I am
absolutely ignorant, and, therefore, I have done nothing.
For I do not remember to have written any book on morals
which I should think worthy of the attention of your
Excellency.[1]

Some of the brethren have drawn up in their own way
certain fragments of my instructions as they have heard
them. Of whom one is conveniently near to you, viz.,
Gebuin, Precentor and Archdeacon of Troyes. You can
easily, if you wish, obtain of him the notes drawn up by him.
Yet if your occupation would leave you the time, and you
should think fit to pay to your humble sons the visit which
you promised, and which they have been expecting. I would
do all in my power to give you satisfaction, if I have in
my writings anything which could please you, or if I were
able to compose any work which should seem worthy of you;
for I greatly esteem your high reputation. I respect that
care and zeal about holy things which I have heard of in
you, and I should regard myself as very happy if these un-
polished writings, which are a part of my duty, should be in
any respect agreeable to you.

[1] Bernard gives usually the title of *Excellency* to Cardinals. Sometimes he
calls them *Holiness*.   But the name of *Excellency* is also given to the secular
princes as to the Pope, and even to Bishops.

LETTER XVIII. (*Circa* A.D. 1127.)

TO THE SAME.[1]

He protests against the reputation for holiness which is attributed to him, and promises to communicate the treatises which he has written.

1. Even if I should give myself to you entirely that would be too little a thing still in my eyes, to have recompensed towards you even the half of the kindly feeling which you express towards my humility. I congratulate myself, indeed, on the honour which you have done me; but my joy, I confess, is tempered by the thought that it is not anything I have accomplished, but only an opinion of my merit which has brought me this favour. I should be greatly ashamed to permit myself in vain complacency when I feel assured that what is loved or respected in me is not, indeed, what I am, but what I am thought to be; for when I am thus loved it is not then I that am loved, but something in me, I know not what, and which is not me, is loved in my stead.[2] I say that I know not, but, to speak more truly, I know very well that it is nothing. For whatever is thought to exist, and does not, is nothing. The love and he who feels it is real enough, but the object of the love does not exist. That such should be capable of inspiring love is wonderful, but still more it is regrettable. It is from that we are able to feel whence and whither we go, what we have lost, what we find. By remaining united to Him, who is the real Being, and who is always happy, we also shall attain a continued and happy existence. By remaining united to Him, I said; that is, not only by knowledge, but by love. For certain of the sons of Adam *when they had known God, glorified Him not as God, nor were thankful, but became vain in their imagina-*

1 The title of this Letter is not the same in all the manuscripts. Colbertinus n. 1410, and that of the library of Compiègne have *to the same Haimeric* ; three other Colbertine MSS. *to the same*, that is to say to Peter the Deacon, which, as Mabillon thinks, is to be preferred.

This resembles a passage in S. Augustine, Ep. 143, n. 3.

tions (Rom. i. 21). Rightly, then, were *their foolish hearts darkened*, because since they recognized the truth and despised it, they were justly punished for their fault by losing the power to recognize it. Alas! in thus adhering to the truth by the mind, but with the heart departing from it, and loving vanity in its place, man became himself a vain thing. And what is more vain than to love vanity, and what is more repugnant to justice than to despise the truth? What is more just than that the power to recognize the truth should be withdrawn from those who have despised it, and that those who did not glorify the truth when they recognized it should lose the power of boasting of the knowledge? Thus the love of vanity is the contempt of truth, and the contempt of truth the cause of our blindness. *And because they did not like*, he says, *to retain God in their knowledge, He gave them over unto a reprobate mind* (Rom. i. 28).

2. From this blindness, then, it follows that we frequently love and approve that which is not for that which is; since while we are in this body we are wandering from Him who is the Fulness of Existence. And what is man, O God, except that Thou hast taken knowledge of Him? If the knowledge of God is the cause that man is anything, the want of this makes him nothing. But He who calls those things which are not as though they were, pitying those reduced in a manner to nothing, and not yet able to contemplate in its reality, and to embrace by love that hidden manna, concerning which the Apostle says: *Your life is hidden with Christ in God* (Cor. iii. 3). But in the meantime He has given us to taste it by faith and to seek for by strong desire. By these two we are brought for the second time from not being, to begin to be that His (new) creature, which one day shall pass into a perfect man, into the measure of the stature of the fulness of Christ. That, without doubt, shall take place, when righteousness shall be turned into judgment, that is, faith into knowledge, the righteousness which is of faith into the righteousness of full knowledge, and also the hope of this state of exile shall

be changed into the fulness of love. For if faith and love begin during the exile, knowledge and love render perfect those in the Presence of God. For as faith leads to full ✓ knowledge, so hope leads to perfect love, and, as it is said, *If ye will not believe ye shall not understand* (Is. vii. 9, acc. to lxx.), so it may equally be said with fitness, if you have not hoped, you will not perfectly love. Knowledge then is the fruit of faith, perfect charity of hope. In the meantime the just lives by faith (Hab. ii. 4), but he is not happy except by knowledge; and he aspires towards God as the hart desires the water-brooks; but the blessed drinks with joy from the fountain of the Saviour, that is, he delights in the fulness of love.

3. Thus understanding and love, that is, the knowledge of and delight in the truth, are, perhaps, as it were, the two arms of the soul, with which it embraces and comprehends with all saints the length and breadth, the height and depth, that is the eternity, the love, the goodness, and the wisdom of God. And what are all these but Christ? He is eternity, because "this is life eternal to know Thee the true God and Jesus Christ whom Thou hast sent" (S. John xvii. 3). He is Love, because He is God, and *God is Love* (1 S. John iv. 16). He is both the Goodness of God and the Wisdom of God (1 Cor. i. 24), but when shall these things be? When shall we see Him as He is? For *the expectation of the creature waiteth for the revelation of the sons of God. For the creature was subjected unto vanity, not willingly* (Rom. viii. 19, 20). It is that vanity diffused through all which makes us desire to be praised even when we are blameable, and not to be willing to praise those whom we know to be worthy of it. But this too is vain, that we, in our ignorance, frequently praise what is not, and are silent about what is. What shall we say to this, but that *the children of men are vain, the children of men are deceitful upon the weights, so that they deceive each other by vanity* (Ps. lxi. 9, lxx.). We praise falsely, and are foolishly pleased, so that they are vain who are praised, and they false who praise. Some flatter and are

deceptive, others praise what they think deserving, and are
deceived; others pride themselves in the commendations
which are addressed to them, and are vain. The only wise
man is he who says with the Apostle: *I forbear, lest any
man should think of me above that which he seeth me to be
or that he heareth of me* (2 Cor. xii. 6).

4. For the present I have noted down these things too
hastily (because of this in not so finished a way), rather
than dictated them for you, perhaps also at greater length
than I should, but to the best of my poor ability. But that
my letter may finish at the point whence it began, I beg
you not to be too credulous of uncertain rumour about me,
which, as you know well, is accustomed to be wrong both
in giving praise and in attaching blame. Be so kind, if you
please, as to weigh your praises, and examine with care
how far your friendship for me and your favour are well-
founded, thus they will be the more acceptable from my
friend as they are fitted to my humble merit. Thus when
praise shall have proceeded from grave judgment, and not
from the error of the vulgar, if it is more moderate it will
be at the same time more easy to bear. I assure you that
what attaches me (humble person as I am), to you is the
zeal, industry, and sincerity with which you employ yourself, as they say, in the accomplishment of your charge in
holy things. May it be always thus with you that this may
be said of you always with truth. I send you the book
which you desire to have in order to copy; as for the other
treatises of mine which you wish that I should send, they
are but few, and contain nothing which I should think
worthy of your attention, yet because I should prefer that
my want of intelligence should be blamed rather than my
goodwill, and I would rather endanger my inexperience
than my obedience in your sight, be so good as to let me
know by the present messenger which of my treatises you
wish that I should send you, so that I may ask for them
again from those persons to whom they have been lent, and
send them wherever you shall direct. That you may know
what you wish for, I may say that I have written a little

book *on Humility*, four Homilies on the *Praises of the Virgin Mother* (for the little book has this title), upon that passage of S. Luke where it is said *the Angel Gabriel was sent* (S. Luke i. 26). Also an *Apology* dedicated to a certain friend[1] of mine, in which I have treated of some of our observances, that is to say, those of Cîteaux, and those of Cluny. I have also written a few Letters to various persons, and finally, there are some of my discourses which the brethren who heard them have reproduced in their own words and keep them in their hands. Would that any of the simple productions of my humble powers might be of any service to you, but I do not dare to expect it.

LETTER XIX. (*Circa* A.D. 1127.)

To the Same.

He commends the deputies[2] from Rheims.

It is the time for me to ask the fulfilment of your promise, so as to prove that I have not been wrong in putting all my confidence in you, since I have had the honour to make your acquaintance and obtain your friendship. Be assured that I shall regard as done to myself whatever assistance you are able to give to these deputies from Rheims. I venture to make this request, not because I think myself of so great importance, but because you have made me the promise. Whether you have done well, it is for you to see.

[1] This was William, Abbot of Saint Thierry, and the Apology will be found in a subsequent volume.

[2] Mabillon says: I find nothing in Marlot about this deputation. Perhaps it was sent to Honorius to obtain of him the Pallium for Raynald de Martini, who had been translated from the See of Angers to that of Rheims, in 1124. But the following Letter speaks of another matter.

LETTER XX. (*Circa* A.D. 1127.)

TO HAIMERIC, THE CHANCELLOR, ON THE SAME SUBJECT.

To the illustrious Lord HAIMERIC, Chancellor of the Holy Roman See, Brother BERNARD, of Clairvaux, health and prayers.

Since I have once begun, permit me to speak to you, even though I shall make myself importunate; but importunate for charity, truth, and justice. For although I am not of sufficient importance to have at Rome business of my own, yet I do not regard any of the affairs of God as things in which I have no concern. Wherefore, if I have with you still the favour which many people suppose, permit me to beg you to forward the deputies of the Lord Archbishop of Rheims in their present business. I am sure that they neither resist for themselves nor ask from another anything but what is just.

LETTER XXI. (*Towards the end of* A.D. 1127.)

TO MATTHEW, THE LEGATE.[1]

He excuses himself very skilfully for not having obeyed the summons to take part in settling certain affairs.

1. My heart was, indeed, prepared to obey; not so my body. It was burned up by the heats of an acute and violent fever, and exhausted by sweats, so that it was too weak to carry out the impulse of the spirit. I wished, then, to go, but my good will was hindered by the obstacle which I have mentioned. Whether this was truly so, let my friends themselves judge, who, disregarding every

---

[1] He was born of noble parents in the province of Rheims. He became a canon of Rheims, then a monk of the Order of Cluny in the Monastery of S. Martin des Champs, Paris; at length Bishop of Albano, and was created Cardinal by Honorius II. in 1125, and being sent into France as Legate presided over the Council at Troyes in 1128, which was assembled by his authority; and Bernard was obliged to attend, notwithstanding his unwillingness.

excuse that I can make, avail themselves of the bonds of
obedience to my superiors to draw me out of my cloister
into cities. I beg them to remark that this reason is not a
pretext of my own invention, but a cause of much suffering
to me ; that they may thus learn that no project can prevail against the will of God. If I should reply to them.
*I have put off my coat, how shall I put it on? I
have washed my feet, how shall I defile them?* (Cant. v.
3), they would at once be indignant. But now let them
either object to or acquiesce in the ruling of Providence,
for it is that which has brought about, that even if I wish to
go forth, I am not in health to do so.

2. But the cause is great, they say, the necessity weighty.
They must, then, have recourse to some one suitable to
settle great matters. If they think me such an one, I not
only think, but know, that I am not. Furthermore, whether
the matters are great or small, to which they so earnestly
invite me, they are not my concern. Now, I inquire, Are
the matters easy or difficult which you are so anxious to lay
upon your friend, to the troubling of his peace? If easy,
they can be settled without me ; if difficult, they cannot
be dealt with by me, unless, perhaps, I am so estimated as
to be thought capable of doing what no one else can do,
and for whom great and impossible affairs are to be
reserved. But if it be so, O, Lord my God, how are Thy
designs so frustrated in me only? Why hast Thou put
under a bushel the lamp, which could shine upon a candle-
stick ; or, to speak more plainly, why hast Thou made me
a monk and hidden me in Thy sanctuary during the day of
evil, if I were a man necessary to the world, without whom
bishops are not able to transact their business? But this,
again, is a service that my friends have done me, that now
I seem to speak with discomposure to a man whom I am
accustomed to think of with serenity, and with the utmost
pleasure. But you know (I say it to you, my father) that so
far from feeling anger, I am prepared to keep your commands. But it will be a mark of your indulgence to spare
me whenever you find it possible to do so.

LETTER XXII. (*Before* A.D. 1128.)

TO HUMBALD,[1] ARCHBISHOP OF LYONS AND LEGATE.

He commends the cause of the Bishop of Meaux.

To the most Reverend Lord and Father HUMBALD, Archbishop of Lyons and Legate of the Roman See, Brother BERNARD, Abbot of Clairvaux, health and all that the prayers of a sinner can avail on his behalf.

The Lord Bishop of Meaux[2] was on his road to visit us, as it happened, when he received your letter. Since he wished to reply before leaving us, he begged me to join in a letter with him, in the hope that as I have the honour to be known to you, it might help to forward his business. I could not deny what he wished, and have thought it well to make this known to your Reverence in a few friendly words : because if you shall listen to the complaints of men who love only their own selves, and seek those things that are their own, against a Bishop who regards only those that are of Jesus Christ, it will be agreeable neither to your duty nor to your office.

LETTER XXIII. (*Circa* A.D. 1128.)

TO ATTO, BISHOP OF TROYES.

Bishop Atto had, in a sickness which he believed mortal, distributed all his goods to the poor. When he was restored to health, Bernard writes to console him, and praises what he had done.[3]

To a poor Bishop, a poor abbot, wishes health and that he may attain the reward of poverty, which is the kingdom of heaven.

---

[1] Ordericus calls him Humbert, and others Humbaud. From Archdeacon of Autun he became Archbishop of Lyons, and at the beginning of the Pontificate of Honorius II. was joined in the function of Legate with Cardinal Peter de Fontaines.

[2] This was without doubt Burchard, not Manasses II., his successor.

[3] Hato, or Atto, is thought to have been a Cluniac monk. But this was apparently not so. He seems to have lived long after the incident here referred to, and died at length at Cluny in A.D. 1145.

1. I should praise you, and rightly, did not that saying restrain me, *Praise no man before his death* (Ecclus. xi. 28). It is certain that you have done a thing worthy of praise : but the praise is to be ascribed to Him, from whom you have received both to will and to do what is praiseworthy. We glorify God, therefore, by you and working in you ; who also has willed to be glorified in you, only that He may render you glorious also. Who, since He is glorious in His Majesty, deigns to appear glorious in His Saints also, that He may not have glory alone. For although He Himself is sufficient unto Himself in an infinity of glory, yet He seeks glory also in His Saints, not that His own may be increased, but that He may partake it with them. For He knows them that are His : but we do not easily know them except He shall deign to reveal them to us. I know, indeed, of what kind of men it was written: *They are not in the trouble of men, and shall not be plagued with men* (Ps. lxxiii. 5). I know without doubt that those words do not concern you. I know also that it is written again, *Whom the Lord loveth He chasteneth, and scourgeth every son whom He receiveth* (Prov. iii. 12, and Hebrews xii. 6), and when I see you stricken and thereby amended, can I infer anything else than that you are of the number of His children ? I do not wish for a clearer proof that He has corrected you than your very poverty itself. A noble title is that of poverty, which God Himself commands by the mouth of the Prophet, saying, *I am a man who sees my poverty* (Lam. iii. 1, VULG.).[1] This title ennobles you more, and renders you more illustrious, than all the treasures of the kings of the earth.

2. I know that I have set down out of Scripture just now that a man is not to be praised during his life. But how can I refrain from the praise of him who no longer runs after gold, and who disdains to put his confidence in the treasures of the world ? Of such a man Scripture thus speaks : *Who is he and we will call him blessed ? For he*

---

[1] The A.V. more literally, affliction. S. Bernard enlarges on this subject in Ser. 2 de Cœnâ Domini.—[E.]

has done wonderful things in his life (Ecclus. xxxi. 8, 9). Perhaps man, indeed, is not to be praised during his life, inasmuch as it is a struggle upon the earth; yet ought he not to be praised when he is dead unto sin and lives unto God? That praise is indeed vain and seductive which is addressed to a sinner in his passions; whosoever calls him happy leads him into error, but will not the life of him who is able to say, *I live, yet not I, but Christ liveth in me* (Gal. ii. 20) be praiseworthy and much to be commended? When, then, a man is praised in whom not himself, but Christ, lives, he is praised, not in his own life, but in the life of Christ, and because of this he is not praised against the Scripture which forbids a man to be praised in his life.

Why, then, shall he not be worthy of my praises of whom God deigns to accept the praises to His Name? As David says, the poor and needy shall give praise unto Thy Name (Ps. lxxiv. 21).

3. Job is praised because he bore the loss of his goods patiently, and shall a Bishop not be praised who has both parted with them of his own accord, and distributed them liberally? He has not waited until death came, when he would have it in his power neither to give nor to retain anything: which many do, whose testament has no force until they have ceased to live, but while still placed between the hope of life and fear of death, it was then that in life, and with goodwill, he shared his goods among the poor, that his righteousness might remain for ever and ever (Ps. cxii. 9). Would the money itself have remained similarly for ever and ever? Good is the recompense of righteousness for money when in exchange for that which could not be held fast. A price is given which remains happily for ever, for righteousness is incomparably better than money, because the one enriches and fills only the chest, but the other the soul. Then the priests of God are clothed with righteousness, and thus far more richly and becomingly than in robes of gold or silk.

4. But render thanks to God who has inspired in you

a glorious contempt of the transitory glory belonging to these things, and at the same time stricken you with a salutary fear of the peril to your soul.   O, wonderful goodness of God towards you!   He has made you have trial of death so that you might not die; and made you fear it, to preserve you from its stroke.   This He has done, so that your goods might not be dearer to you than yourself.   A devouring fear was raging in the very marrow of your bones, and hindering the relief of perspiration, the disease grew graver day by day.   And now the limbs without grow cold, while within burned a devouring fire which wasted the viscera, already exhausted by long deprivation of nourishment.   Speedily the pale and doleful image of death was before your eyes.   But behold a voice, as it were from heaven, was heard: *I am He who destroys* (not thee, but) *thy iniquities* (Is. xliii. 25); and speedily when the priest of God had distributed all his goods to the poor, that as a poor man he might die, suddenly the sweat long unhoped-for burst forth from all its fountains; health came back equally both to body and soul, and clearly showed that what God promises in Scripture had been fulfilled in you: *I kill and I make alive; I wound and I heal; neither is there any that can deliver out of My hand* (Deut. xxxii. 39).   He has stricken the flesh to save the soul; He has slain avarice that you might live unto righteousness.   Now that you are restored to life and health, we hope that none will be able to snatch you from the hands of God, provided that you do not lose sight of that counsel in the Gospel: *Behold thou art made whole; sin no more lest a worse thing come unto thee* (S. John v. 14).   And if thy kind Father forewarns thee of this, it is because He does not desire it to happen; because he willeth not the death of a sinner, but rather that he should be converted and live.   And rightly.   For what advantage would there be in the death of a sinner?   The grave will not confess God, nor will death praise Him; but you who are living, do you bless the Lord and say: *I shall not die, but live and declare the works of the Lord; thou hast thrust sore at me that I might fall, but the Lord helped me* (Ps. cxviii. 17, 13).

LETTER XXIV. (*Circa* A.D. 1130.)

TO GILBERT, BISHOP OF LONDON, UNIVERSAL DOCTOR.[1]

He praises Gilbert, who practised poverty in the station of Bishop.

The report of your conduct has spread far and wide, and has given to those whom it has reached an odour of great sweetness. The love of riches is extinct ; what sweetness results ! charity reigns ; what a delight to all ! All recognize you for a truly wise man, who has trodden under foot the great enemy with true wisdom ; and this is most worthy of your name and of your priesthood. It was fitting that your special[2] philosophy should shine forth by such a proof, and that you should crown all your distinguished learning by such a completion. That is the true and unquestionable wisdom which contemns filthy lucre and judges it a thing unworthy [that philosophy should] dwell under the same roof as the service of idols. That the Magister Gilbert should become a bishop was not a great thing; but that a Bishop of London should embrace a life of poverty,[3] that is, indeed, grand. For the greatness of the dignity could not add glory to your name; but the humility of poverty has highly exalted it. To bear

[1] He was so called because he was acquainted with and excelled in all branches of the learning of that time, as Bernard writes in this place. Before becoming bishop he had been Canon of Autun, and the Necrology of that Church records that "on the 4th August there died Magister Gilbert, of venerable memory, a distinguished commentator on the Old and New Testament, canon of this Church, and afterwards Bishop of London. Besides other ornaments for this Church which he sent out of England, he presented to the same Church 82 pounds," etc. He was Bishop of London from A.D. 1128 to A.D. 1133.

[2] Otherwise, *spiritual.*

[3] Henry of Huntingdon, however, in a Letter on the Contempt of the World, preserved in the *Spicilegium*, Book viii., attributes this to a feeling of avarice on the part of Gilbert.

poverty with an equal mind, that is the virtue of patience; to seek it of one's own accord is the height of wisdom. He is praised and regarded as admirable who does not go out of his way after money; and shall he who renounces it have no higher praise ? Unless that clear reason sees nothing to be wondered at in the fact that a wise man acts wisely; and he is wise who having acquired all the science of the learned of this world, and having great enjoyment in acquiring them, has studied all the Scriptures so as to make their meaning new again. What then? You have dispersed, you have given to the poor, but money. But what is money to that righteousness which you have gained for it? *His righteousness,* it is said, *endureth for ever* (Ps. cxii. 9). Is it so with money? Then it is a desirable and honourable exchange to give that which passes away for that which endures. May it be granted to you always so to purchase, O, admirable and praiseworthy Magister! It remains that your noble beginning should attain an ending worthy of it; and the tail of the victim be joined to the head.[1] I have gladly received your benediction, which the perfectness of your virtue renders the more precious to me. The bearer of this letter, though exceedingly respectable for his own sake, I desire to commend for my sake also, to your Greatness. He is exceedingly dear to me for his goodness and piety.

_____

LETTER XXV. (A.D. 1130.)

To Hugo, Archbishop of Rouen.[2]

He exhorts Hugo to strive to be patient and peaceable among his Rouennais, and at the same time to temper his zeal with discretion.

1. If malice grows every day, yet let it not prevail; if it is boisterous, let it not trouble your peace. The waves of the

_____

[1] A familiar phrase with Bernard to signify perseverance; from Levit. iii. 7. See the notes to Letter 78. Peter Cellensis, Book v. 1, Letter 8, says: Beware of the *tail;* it is only in the tail, that is in the end of things, that praise or blame can be awarded.

[2] Respecting his election, which took place in A.D. 1130, there is extant a Letter of the Clergy of Rouen to Pope Honorius II. (*Spicileg.* B. iii. p.

sea are mighty, but the Lord in heaven is mightier, and the
mercy from on high has dwelt with you, illustrious father,
as you know, with extreme goodness even until now.   For
by a kindly Providence you are no sooner set to preside
over sinners than you are associated with the good and
pious, by whose example and company you may become
good, and so may be able to dwell in the midst of sinners
without ceasing to be righteous.   And, indeed, to be
righteous among the righteous assures salvation, but to be
so among sinners assures also praise.   The one is easy and
sure, the other as meritorious as difficult.   For the task is
as it were to touch pitch and not to be defiled therewith, to
walk in fire without being injured, and in the shadows
without being dark.   The Egyptians formerly were in darkness that might be felt, while of the people of God the
Scripture says *Wheresoever Israel was it was light* (Exod.
x. 23).   David was a true Israelite, and, therefore, spoke
with preciseness that he dwelt not "in Cedar," but *with the
dwellers in Cedar* (Ps. cxx. 5), and as one who habitually
dwelt in the light, although his bodily abode was with the
dwellers in Cedar [Kedar].   Wherefore also he blames
certain persons as not being true Israelites, because *they
were mingled among the heathen and learned their works,
and it became a snare unto them* (Ps. cvi. 35, 36).

2. I say, then, that it was sufficient when you were at
Cluny to keep yourself innocent, as it is written, *With an
innocent man Thou shalt be innocent* (Ps. xvii. 26, VULG.).
But now that you are among the Rouennais (otherwise, *at
Rouen*) you have need of patience, as the Apostle teaches :
*The servant of the Lord must not strive, but be patient
towards all* (2 Tim. ii. 24).   Nor must he be only patient, so

151) in which these words occur :—" We have chosen with one voice for
Bishop our [your?] son Hugo, Abbot of Reading. He was first a monk at
Cluny, then first Abbot of Reading, in England, in the Diocese of Salisbury."
In the same Letter is added :—" Upon which we have sought and obtained the
consent of our Lord Henry, King of the English, from the Bishop of Salisbury,
also under whose charge he discharged his office of abbot, we requested his
return to us free and discharged from obligation," etc. Ordericus mentions his
election B. 12 *ad finem.*

as not to be overcome of evil, but also pacific, to overcome evil with good. The one that you may bear with evil persons, the other that you may do good to those whom you thus bear with. *In your patience possess your soul* (S. Luke xxi. 19), but be also pacific, that you may have control also over the souls committed to you. What so great glory as to be able to say, *With those who hated peace I was pacific* (Ps. cxx. 7). Be, then, patient, because you are among evil men; be pacific, because you have such to govern. Let your charity be zealous, but moderate your severity for a time. Censure should, indeed, never be altogether foregone, but it may often be profitably intermitted. The vigour of justice should be always keen, but never precipitate. As not everything that is pleasing is permissible, so not everything permissible is expedient. You know all this better than I, and, therefore, I do not insist farther. I beg you to pray for me earnestly, because I do not cease to fall into sin.

LETTER XXVI. (*Circa* A.D. 1130.)

To Guy, Bishop of Lausanne.

You have undertaken great things; you have need of courage. You have become a watcher for the house of Israel; you have need of prudence. You are a debtor both to the wise and unwise; you have need of righteousness.

Lastly, you have, above all, need of temperance and self-control, so that one who has preached to others may not become (which may God forbid!) a reprobate.

LETTER XXVII. (*Circa* A.D. 1135.)

To Ardutio (or Ardutius), Bishop Elect of Geneva.

He warns him that he must attribute his election to the grace of God, and strive thenceforth faithfully to co-operate with it.

I am glad to believe that your election, which I have heard was effected with so complete an assent both of the clergy and people, was from God. I congratulate you on His grace, and I do not speak of your merits, since we ought not to render to you excessive praise, but to recognize that, not because of works of righteousness which you have done, but according to His mercy He has done this for you. If you (which may God forbid !) should think otherwise, your exaltation will be to your ruin. But if you acknowledge it to be of grace, see that you receive it not in vain. Make your actions and your desires good, and your ministry holy ; and if sanctity of life has not preceded, let it at least follow your elevation. Then I shall acknowledge that you have been prevented with the blessings of grace, and shall hope that after these you will receive still better graces. I shall be in joy and gladness that a good and faithful servant has been set over the family of the Lord, and you shall come to be as a son powerful and happy, meet to be set over all the good things of the Father. Otherwise, if it delights you to be in higher place rather in holier mind, I shall expect to see, not your reward, but your destruction. I hope, and pray God, that it may not be thus with you ; and am prepared, if there is need, to render my aid, as far as in me lies, to assist you in whatever you think proper and expedient.

LETTER XXVIII. (*In the Same Year.*)

TO THE SAME, WHEN BISHOP.

He exhorts him to adorn the dignity which he had obtained without preceding merits, by a holy life.

1. Charity gives me boldness, my very dear friend, to speak to you with great confidence. The episcopal seat which you have lately obtained requires a man of many merits ; and I see with grief none of these in you, or at least not sufficient, to have preceded your elevation. For your mode

of life and your past occupations seem in nowise to have been befitting the episcopal office. What then? Would you say, Is not God able of this stone to raise up a son of Abraham? Is not God able to bring about that the good works which ought to have gone before my episcopate may follow it? Certainly He is, and I desire nothing better than this, if it should be so. I know not why, but that sudden change wrought by the right hand of the Highest will please me more than if the merits of your former life pleaded for you. Then I could say, *This is the Lord's doing ; it is marvellous in our eyes* (Ps. cxviii. 23). So Paul, from a persecutor, became the Doctor of the Gentiles; so Matthew was called from the toll-booth, so Ambrose was taken from the palace, the one to the Episcopate, the other to the Apostolate. So I have known many others who have been usefully raised to the Episcopate, from the habits and pursuits of secular life. How many times it has been the case that where sin abounded, grace also did much more abound?

2. So then, my dear friend, encouraged by these examples and others like them, gird up your loins, and make your actions and pursuits henceforth good; let your latest actions make the old forgotten, and the correction of your mature life blot out the demerits of your youth. Take care to imitate Paul in honouring your ministry. You will render it honourable by gravity of manners, by wise plans, by honourable actions. It is these which most ennoble and adorn the Episcopal office. Do nothing without taking counsel, yet not of all, nor of the first comer, but of good men. Have good men in your confidence, in your service, dwelling in your house, who may be at once the guardians and the witnesses of your honourable life. For in this you will approve yourself a good man if you have the testimony of the good. I commend to your piety my poor brethren who are in your diocese, especially those of Bonnemont, in the Alps, and of Hautecombe. By your bounty towards these I shall see what degree of affection you have for me.

LETTER XXIX. (*Circa* A.D. 1126.)

To Stephen, Bishop of Metz.[1]

He congratulates Stephen on the restored peace of the Church, which he says is due only to the bounty of God.

To STEPHEN, by the Grace of God, the strenuous minister of the Church of Metz, his humble brethren in Christ from Clairvaux, wish health and assure him of their prayers.

From the day when, if you remember, you deigned to associate yourself with our community, and to commend yourself humbly to our prayers, I have always been anxious, as I ought, to know something of your state, and have frequently inquired as I was able respecting your welfare, from those who could inform me, earnestly desiring and praying that your work and all your undertakings might be prospered in God, and your steps directed in the path of His commandments. I bless God who has not rejected my prayer nor turned His mercy from you, who has made me glad by the coming of this venerable brother William, in whom I have not less confidence than in myself, and who has informed us of your good health and prosperity, and of the restoration of peace to your Church by your means. I congratulate you upon it, but I render glory to God, knowing that all you are able to do is of Him, and not of yourself. Which also I venture as a friend to warn you always to keep before your mind, that you may not fall into a kind of powerlessness either to be or to do anything, if you should think otherwise, and attribute to your own merits or powers (which God forbid) the least of your successes. Otherwise it is to be feared that your peace will be turned into trouble, your prosperity into adversity, by a just judgment of Him who is accustomed to resist the

---

[1] He succeeded to the See in A.D. 1120, on the deposition of Adalbero, the fourth Bishop of Metz of that name, as I find in the abridged annals of S. Vincent, at Metz, adjusted to the Paschal Cycle, in which Stephen is related to have died on 29th Dec., A.D. 1163. Bernard makes grave complaints of him in Letters 177 and 178.

proud, but give grace unto the humble ; who not only is
holy with the holy, but perverse with the perverse man, as
we read in the Psalm (Ps. xviii. 26), who not only makes
peace, but creates evil, as is described by the Prophet
(Is. xlv. 7).

LETTER XXX. (*Circa* A.D. 1126.)

To Albero, Primicerius of Metz.[1]

*He warns Albero to wait God's good time for the com-
pletion of a certain business which he was hurrying on,
and that He requires us rather to do good for a good
reason than from an interested motive.*

To the very honourable ALBERO, by the Grace of God
Primicerius of the Church of Metz, the brethren who serve
God to the best of their power at Clairvaux, health and
their prayers.

We have formerly heard and seen, and now have experienced for ourselves, your faithful zeal in the things of
God. But although you were favourable and your Bishop
gave prompt assent to the things proposed to him by the
brethren whom we last sent to you, after your counsel :
as our first duty is to know God's good pleasure in all things,

---

[1] Mabillon observes : " I find three persons of the same name who have borne
one after the other this title at this epoch. I believe that this Letter is addressed
to the *second* Albero, who became later on Archbishop of Treves." Bernard had
much affection for him, and it was on his behalf that the Letters 176-180 were
written.

The title *Primicerius* is generally derived from *qui in primâ cerâ hæres
scriptus*, and hence it denoted the chief in any department. It was used in
Italian Cathedrals especially. 1. In the abbey of Monte Casino it denoted the
chief over the *scriptorium* where MSS. were copied. 2. The chief of the
Cantorum Schola, founded by Pope Hilarius, and extended by Pope Gregory
the Great, for the improvement of singing. Similarly at Aberdeen Cathedral
the precentor was called by that title, and in other cathedrals it denoted the chief
chanter ; 3. A chief notary ; 4. The Chancellor of a Cathedral ; 5. In the
Church of S. Stephen, at Metz, the title was given to the first of the canons,
who was privileged (among other marks of honour) to wear a cross on the
breast, to use a purple vestment, and to take the chief place in choir and
chapter. [From Mabillon (and elsewhere).—E.]

especially in matters of religion, and to know what is His
good pleasure in that matter, we have thought it advisable,
as was agreed between our brethren and your Bishop, not
to abandon, but to defer until after the harvest (that time
being convenient in itself and for you), the execution of a
design of which your assistance prepares and facilitates
the progress, and your help will bring, as soon as possible,
to an honourable conclusion.   But now if your Bishop, and
you yourself, are still in the same mind as before, we have
still more confidence that it is the will of God, and that
there is nothing better to do than what you propose.   So
that we hope to satisfy your pious desire (which is shared
by us also) according as it was determined on.   I think
that to be accepted by God, we ought to study as much as
in us lies, to be burdensome to no one, that it may not
seem that we (which may God forbid) seek His glory less
than our own interests ; and especially that it would not be
pleasing to God, nor would be in accordance with our
manner of life, to make ourselves troublesome to you when
there is no need for an occasion of that kind ; nor to withdraw you from your other greater and more pressing occupations.

LETTER XXXI. (A.D. 1125.)

To Hugo,[1] Count of Champagne, who had become
a Knight of the Temple.

*He congratulates Hugo on having entered into a military
Order, and promises remembrance of his benefits.*

If for the cause of God you have, from being Count,
become a simple soldier, and from a rich man have become

---

[1] He was son of Theobald III., Count of Champagne. Hugo showed
extreme munificence towards religious houses in general, and especially towards
the monasteries of Moustier Ramey and Molesme.   He was at first Count of
Bar sur Aube, then of Troyes, after the death of his brother Eudes.   But having
suppressed the names of those counties when uniting them in his own person,
he was the cause that his successors took the title of Counts of Champagne in
lieu of that of Counts of Bar sur Aube and Troyes, which they had hitherto

a poor one, I congratulate you in the first place as is right, and in you I glorify God, knowing that this is the work of the Right Hand of the Most High. But I do not, I confess, anticipate without great regret being deprived, by the secret Providence of God, of your valued presence, and never more seeing you, in whose company I would wish always to be, were it possible. What then? Can I forget your friendship of old standing, and the benefits which you have so liberally bestowed upon our House?[1] May God

borne (François Chifflet). He went three times on pilgrimage to the Holy Land —the first time in A.D. 1113, the second in A.D. 1121, and the third when he joined the Order of the Templars, which was in A.D. 1125 (Alberic, *Chronicle*). When about to undertake this voyage beyond the sea, if Peter Pithon is to be believed (says Chifflet), he sold his county to Theobald, son of his brother Stephen, disinherited his son Eudes, and left *enceinte* his second wife, whom he had married after his marriage with Constance, daughter of Philip I., King of France, had been dissolved because of consanguinity in 1104. He died beyond the sea on the 14th June.

This Hugo is another person from Hugo, Master of the Knights of the Temple, to whom Bernard directed his exhortation *Ad Milites Templi*.

[1] It was Count Hugo who had given to Bernard and his monks the district of Clairvaux and its dependencies, and may merit to be called by the name of their Founder. As that fact has hitherto been noticed but by few, we give here the deed of donation itself, of which we owe the publication to Chifflet, whom we have already had often occasion to quote. He has copied it from the autograph at Clairvaux, and first published it in his Dissertation :—

"In Nomine Sanctæ et Individuæ Trinitatis incipit charta Comitis Hugonis. Notum sit omnibus præsentibus et futuris, quod ego Comes Trecensis, Do Deo, et beatæ Mariæ et fratribus Claræ Vallis, locum ipsum qui vocatur Clara-Vallis, cum pertinentiis agris, pratis, vineis, silvis et aquis, nihil omnino mihi aut hæredibus meis retinens. Unde testes Acardus Remensis et Petrus, et Robertus Aurelianensis milites mei. Et sciendum quod Gaufridus Felonia dat pasturas suas in finagio de Juvencourt, tam in bosco quam in plano, omni tempore: et si aliquod damnum intulerint animalia dictorum fratrum, solum capitale restituetur sine emenda. Hæc autem omnia dedi in præsentiâ supradictorum testium. Sciendum quoque est, quod dominus Josbertus de Firmitate, cognomine Rufus, et dominus Rainaudus de Perceris dederunt eisdem fratribus pasturam et usuarium per totam terram suam, et præcipue in aquis, silvis, pratis, in finagio de Perrecin. Hujus rei testes sunt Acardus Remensis et Robertus milites mei. Item sciendum quoque est, quod ego Hugo Comes Trecensis laudo et concedo eisdem fratribus libere et quiete possidere terram et silvam de Aretela. Has donationes confirmamus ego Joscerannus Lingonensis Episcopus, et ego Hugo Comes Trecensis de sigillo et annulo meo."

As to the year of foundation, which is not specified in this deed, Chifflet, following the *Chronograph* of S. Marianus, of Auxerre, refers it to June A.D. 1114.

Himself, for whose love you have done this, hold you in perpetual remembrance. Nor will we be ungrateful, but will keep in mind the recollection of your great kindness, and will show it, if possible, in our actions. O, how willingly would I have provided for the needs both of your body and of your soul, if it had been granted to us to pass our lives together! But as that is not possible, it only remains to assure you that though we cannot have you present with us, we shall always pray for you in your absence.

LETTER XXXII. (*Circa* A.D. 1120.)

To the Abbot of Saint Nicasius at Rheims.[1]

He consoles this abbot for the departure of the Monk Drogo and his transfer to another monastery, and exhorts him to patience.

1. How much I sympathize with your trouble only He knows who bore the griefs of all in His own body. How

All agree as to the month; as to the year, the documents, both domestic and from external sources, seem to negative it, and among others the *Exordium Cisterciense* (Dist. ii. cap 1), also the tablet attached to the tomb of S. Bernard, plainly say A.D. 1115. It seemed better, therefore, to adhere to the opinion long since received, considering that Bernard had scarcely made his profession in June, 1114, and Hugo himself, who made the grant, was still occupied in the East. Clairvaux was then founded by Hugo, Count of Champagne, and transferred in 1135 to a larger site with the aid of Count Theobald, his successor, and new buildings erected. Wherefore some have given him the name of the first founder, confounding the removal with the foundation.

1 Drogo, respecting whom Letters 32-34 were written, seems not to have persevered in the Cistercian Order, from whence he was recalled at length before making profession by the importunate complaints of his Abbot, Jorannus, to whom this Letter. He seems to have been the same who, when the monks were expelled from the convent of S. John, at Laon, led thither a company of monks, over whom from being Prior of S. Nicasius, at Rheims, he was set as their first abbot in 1128, as appears from Letter 48. Later on he was made Cardinal and Bishop of Ostia by Innocent II. in 1136 (as our Acherius proves in his notes to Guibert). He died in 1138.

As for the Abbot Jorannus, how the Convent of S. Nicasius flourished under his rule is shown by the number of distinguished men who went out from it to carry far and wide its rule and discipline. For, besides this Drogo, Geoffrey, willingly would I advise you if I knew what to say, or help you if I were able, as efficaciously as I would wish that He who knows and can do all things should advise and assist me in all my necessities. If brother Drogo had consulted me about leaving your house I should by no means have agreed with him; and now that he has left, if he were to apply to enter into mine I should not receive him. All that I was able to do in those circumstances I have done for you, and have written,[1] as you know, to the abbot who has received him. After this, reverend father, what is there more that I am able to do on your behalf? And as regards yourself, your Holiness knows well with me that men are accustomed to be perfected not only in hope, but also to glory in tribulation. The Scripture consoles them, saying: *The furnace proveth the potter's vessels, and temptation the righteous man* (Ecclus. xxvii. 6, VULG.); *The Lord is nigh unto them that are of a contrite heart* (Ps. xxxiv. 18); and *We must through much tribulation enter into the kingdom of God* (Acts xiv. 21); and *All who will live godly in Christ suffer persecution* (2 Tim. iii. 12). Yet none the less ought we to sympathize with our friends whom we see placed in care and grief; because we do not know what will be the issue of such, and fear lest it may be for ill; since whilst, indeed, to saints and the elect *tribulation worketh patience, patience experience, experience hope, and hope maketh not ashamed* (Rom. v. 3-5), to the condemnable and reprobate, on the contrary, tribulation causes discouragement, and discouragement confusion, and confusion despair, which destroys them.

and after him William, were chosen Abbots of S. Thierry, at Rheims. Simon was Abbot of S. Nicholas du Bois, in the Diocese of Laon, to whom Letters 83 and 84 were addressed; Arnulf at Gemblour, as the *Auctarium* of that monastery bears witness. As for Jorannus himself, induced by his love of solitude, he entered the Carthusian Order in the Monastery of Mons Dei A.D. 1138, where he so distinguished himself that Pope Innocent II. made him Cardinal, but since, when this Letter was written, Robert, the relative of S. Bernard, had not yet been restored to him, as the holy Doctor here asserts, it follows that its date should be about A.D. 1120.

1 This Letter is lost, as appears from the following, in which some parts of it are quoted.

204 LETTER XXXII.

2. In order, then, that this dreadful tempest may not submerge you, nor the frightful abyss swallow you up, and the unfathomable pit shut her mouth upon you, employ all the efforts of your prudence not to be overcome of evil, but to overcome evil with good. You will overcome if you fix solidly your hope in God, and wait patiently the issue of the affair. If that monk shall return to a sense of his duty, whether for fear of you, or because of his own painful condition, well and good; but if not, it is good for you to humble yourself under the mighty hand of God, nor to wish uselessly to resist His supreme ordering; because if it is of God it cannot be undone. You should rather endeavour to repress the sparkles of your indignation, however just, by a reflection which a certain saint is said in a similar case to have uttered. For when some of his monks were mixing demands with bitter reproaches because he did not require back again a fugitive who had fled to another monastery in defiance of his authority, " By no means," he said, " wheresoever he may be, if he is a good man, he is mine."

3. I should be wrong to counsel you thus, if I did not oblige myself to act thus. For when one of my brethren, not only a professed religious, but also nearly akin to me,[1] was received and retained at Cluny against my will I was afflicted, indeed, but endured it in silence, praying both for them that they might be willing to return the fugitive, and for him, that he might be willing of his own accord to return; but if not, leaving the charge of my vengeance to Him who shall render judgment to the patient and contend in equity for the meek of the earth. Please to warn Brother Hugo, of Lausanne, with your own mouth, and as from me, not to believe every spirit, and not to be induced rashly to desert the certain for the uncertain. Let him remember that perseverance alone is always attacked by the devil, because it is the only virtue which has the assurance of being crowned. It will be safer for him simply to persevere in the vocation wherein he is called than to

[1] This was Robert, to whom Letter I. was addressed.

renounce it under the pretext of a life more perfect, at the risk of not being found equal to that which he had the presumption to attempt.

LETTER XXXIII. (*Circa* A.D. 1120.)

To HUGO, ABBOT OF PONTIGNY.

He writes more plainly his views about the reception of Drogo, and removes unfavourable suspicion from himself.

To his very dear brother, Hugo, Lord Abbot, Brother Bernard, of Clairvaux, health and all that he desires for himself.

1. In my former letter I, as far as I can understand from yours, wrote less clearly than I wished, or you understood it otherwise than you ought. When I spoke of the consequences that might follow to you from the reception of that monk, I truly feared, and fear still, as I wrote. But in writing to you thus I had no intention of persuading you or giving you advice; nor certainly, as you write, did I think that he ought to be sent back, since I have long known his very strong desire, and I ought rather to congratulate him that he has now accomplished it. But as his abbot, my intimate friend, and the Archbishop of Rheims required of me a letter pressingly demanding him back, in order that I might take off every suspicion from myself, if it were possible, I took pains to dictate as well as I could such a letter, in terms which would both satisfy them and forewarn you of the reproaches which would be made against you by them, by not concealing them from you. I believed that your sagacity would be able to understand my intention in that letter at once, especially when reading the note which you remember I placed at the end of it, that it should be read by you in the same spirit it was written by me. For after having set out the evils which not unreasonably I feared for you, I went on: "It is for you to see whether

you prefer to endure all these things or to send him away;
the matter does not concern me." These very words were
used by me, or nearly these, and when I wrote thus at the
end, how else could I secretly intimate to you that all that
I had said previously was spoken by way of complaisance,
not to say of pretence?

2. But as for what you have written, that I should have
charged your messenger to say to the same monk, that if
he wished to enter our Order his absolution should be
privately obtained, I declare to you that it is not true. How
could I suppose or hope that I could receive a monk from a
monastery so well known to me, and whom I did not think
that even you could retain without great scandal? But let it
be so. Suppose that I envied you that monk, and desired to
attract him to me; and that I was hoping or fancying that I
might be able to do something towards obtaining his absolution. But is it for a moment to be believed that I should
be willing to lay open this plan of mine which I had con-
cocted against his own monastery to the very messenger
whom you had sent to me? But to convince you that what
you have believed hitherto concerning my affection towards
you is well founded, I feel myself obliged, for you even more
than for me, to redouble my efforts, as I have done up to the
present, so that our friendship may not altogether be dissolved, but be made more close and strong. What can I
say to you more? I, at least, could not believe you capable
of such an action, as you have without ground suspected me
of. Concerning another matter, your Blessedness knows
that Count Theobald has received my letter of recommendation for Humbert, but he has not as yet replied to me.
What you could do as to this your piety will best suggest,
if you will have the kindness to consider the miserable
state of a man unjustly stricken with exile.

LETTER XXXIV. (*Circa* A.D. 1120.)

To Drogo,[1] the Monk.

He congratulates Drogo on having embraced a more severe rule, and exhorts him to perseverance.

My Very Dear Drogo,

1. I find more than ever justified the great affection which I have long felt for you. You appeared to me before very lovable and accomplished in many things, but I had felt that there was something in you worthy of higher admiration than anything that I had seen or heard of you. Had you already heard the voice of the celestial Spouse, in whose arms your soul was closely clasped? Had you heard His voice saying to your soul, His modest turtle, *Thou art all fair, My love; there is no spot in thee?* (Cant. iv. 7). Who would believe that which you have done? The whole city is full of talk of your virtues and piety, so that it was not believed possible that anything could be added to all your good qualities, and then you, quitting your monastery as a secular might quit the world, were not ashamed to lay the burden of new observances and of a more severe Rule upon your neck, already worn with the yoke of Christ! In you now, brother, we verify that saying, *When a man hath arrived at perfection then he beginneth* (Ecclus. xviii. 7). The mark, then, of your perfectness is that you have now commenced, and in that you did not judge of that you had attained you prove that you have done so, for no one is perfect who does not desire to be more perfect, and a man shows himself more perfect, inasmuch as he aspires to greater perfection.

2. But behold, my dear friend, he by whose envy death entered into the world has bent his bow and prepared himself. Being driven from your heart, he has lost his power within, and therefore he will rage as much as is in his power

---

[1] In the Colbertine MS., 1410, and in that of Compiègne *ad Hug$\sim$Drogonem*, although *Drogo* is used in the body of the Letter. The name is compounded from that of Hugo, Abbot of Pontigny, with whom Drogo was in great favour.

without. And, to speak more plainly, do you not know that the Pharisees are scandalized at what you have done? But remember that there are scandals about which one ought not to be greatly troubled, according to the reply of the Lord, when He said, *Let them alone, they are blind and leaders of the blind* (S. Matt. xv. 14). For would it be better that a scandal should arise than that the truth should be abandoned? (Greg. Hom. 7 in Ezekiel). Remember who it was who was born for the fall and rising again of many (S. Luke ii. 34), and do not wonder if you, too, are to some as an odour of life unto life, and to others as an odour of death unto death. If they have directed maledictions against you, if they have launched at you darts of anathema, hear Isaac replying for you, *He who shall curse thee shall be himself cursed, and he who shall bless thee shall be loaded with blessings* (Gen. xxvii. 29). And you, fortified by the safe defence of your conscience, reply inwardly and say, *Though a host should encamp against me my heart shall not fear, although war should rise against me in this should I hope* (Ps. xxvii. 3). For you shall not be confounded when you speak thus with your enemies in the gate; but I trust in the Lord that if you stand firm against the first blows and do not yield either to their promises or threats, you will speedily bruise Satan under your feet. Then the righteous shall see and rejoice, and sinners shall be reduced to silence.

LETTER XXXV. (A.D. 1128.)

To Magister Hugo Farsit.[1]

He commends to him the cause of a certain Humbert, and warns him not to blush at retracting a certain erroneous opinion.

To his very dear brother and co-abbot, Brother BERNARD, health and assurance of the most sincere affection.

[1] I find many of this name about this period. Two monks : the one of Lagny, who is praised in the sixth book of the *Res Diplomatica* (p. 585), the other of S. Lucian of Beauvais, of whom the *Necrology* makes mention thus : " The

I commend to your protection, with the greatest confidence in your goodness, the poor man Humbert, who is said to have been unjustly disinherited. I have undertaken, for the love of God, to plead his cause with your Count, and I hope that you will help me, with the assistance of the Lord of Heaven, to reconcile him with his earthly prince, so that he may be restored to his country, his wife and children, his property and friends; for by taking the trouble to effect this you will both free from the hands of a sinner a man who is in distress, and will be labouring at the same time for the welfare of his oppressor. You will show yourself helpful to me in no small degree, without mentioning that by performing the office of a peacemaker you will prepare for yourself a high place among the children of God. Let us speak now of another matter. It has been reported to you, as I hear, that I have thrown into the fire the letter that your Holiness lately favoured me with. Be so kind as to believe that I preserve it carefully, for would it not have been the effect of envy, or rather of madness, rashly to condemn a work useful and praiseworthy, in which there was nothing but what was sound in faith, salutary in doctrine, and tending to spiritual edification? I ought, however, to except one passage, because between friends no timid and dangerous flattery ought to influence them against the truth. One passage, I confess, troubled and still troubles me, that in which you endeavoured to sustain

24th March died Hugo Farsit, a professed monk." It may be the same who is mentioned in the History of Louvet, p. 555. There was a third Hugo Farsit, who was Canon Regular of S. John des Vignes, who is praised in the *Necrology* of the Church of Soissons. Abaelard mentions a fourth of that name in his Sermon on S. John Baptist, p. 967, where he makes mention of S. Norbert and of Hugo Farsit, the companion of his Apostolate, perhaps Hugo, Abbot of Prémontré and successor over the Order, who was his first and most remarkable disciple, and to whom Letter 253 was addressed.

I think that he to whom the present Letter was addressed was the same to whom Hugo Metellus, at that time Canon Regular of Toul in Lorraine, inscribed Letter 34 of the MS., " To Hugo of Chartres, the venerable Magister." In fact, Hugo, of whom S. Bernard speaks, was abbot of a monastery situated on the lands of Theobald, Count of Champagne, at Blois or at Chartres, according to some writers.

and defend in beginning your work an opinion which you
had put forth already in an interview between us respecting
the Sacraments.   If you will reflect upon the doctrine that
you supported in that interview you will see whether it
agrees or no with the teaching of the Church.   It will be a
mark of your candour and humility not to be ashamed to be
corrected if you have ever held an opinion not conformable
to sound doctrine.   Farewell.

LETTER XXXVI. (A.D. 1128.)

To the Same.

*He replies to the letter of Hugo, and advises him to
desist from impugning the doctrine of a Bishop, then dead.*

To his very dear friend now as formerly, and by the
grace of God, holy Abbot HUGO, Brother BERNARD of
Clairvaux, health and the assurance of sincere and undi-
minished affection.

I intended to reply more at length, as it was my duty, to
the letter of your Worthiness, which was shorter than I
desired, though longer than I deserved, but the haste of
your messenger did not permit.   Nevertheless, that he may
not depart with his hands quite empty, I send in haste these
few lines in reply to the much longer letter, for which I
acknowledge myself the debtor.   I commence by saying, in
few but sincere words, as to an old and dear friend, to
whom I also am dear, that from the bottom of my heart I
hold you for a Catholic, a holy man, and one very dear to
me.   As to the purity of your faith, I trust your own confession ; your high reputation vouches for the holiness of
your life, and as for the affection which I have said that I
feel towards you, my own heart is a sufficient witness.

You protest that you do not retain the least vestige of
that opinion, which rightly, in my judgment, raised scruples
in my simple mind, and I receive the assurance as willingly
as I read with gladness in your last letter the concise state-

ment of most pure truth, so that I would rather believe that
it is I who have wrongly understood you than that you had
put forth any proposition contrary to the faith.   Now, permit me to advise you, with brotherly boldness, not to attack,
now that he is dead, the doctrine of a Bishop,[1] as holy as
learned, whom you have left unmolested while he lived, lest
in blaming one not now able to answer for himself you may
hear the whole Church replying for him, and seem to have
acted more from a want of charity than from love of the
truth.   For Humbert, as I have begged you, so I repeat my
request, that you will afford him, as far as you are able,
your advice and protection.   Farewell.

LETTER XXXVII. (A.D. 1128.)

TO THEOBALD, COUNT OF CHAMPAGNE.[2]

*He expresses astonishment at having been refused, in
the cause of Humbert, though he asked nothing but what
was right and just; he warns the Count, by the remembrance of the Supreme Judge, not to deny help and mercy
to an unfortunate man.*

To the noble Prince THEOBALD, BERNARD, the unprofitable servant of the servants of God who are in Clairvaux,
health and peace.

[1] If I do not mistake, this was William of Champeaux, Bishop of Chalons-
sur-Marne, a man for whom Bernard had the greatest affection.

[2] Many and high encomiums upon him are read in the writers of his age.
Anselm of Gembloux speaks thus of him in the year 1134: "Count Theobald
of Blois, or Chartres, was distinguished among all the princes of France by his
scrupulous justice.   He was a pious man, a familiar associate of good monks
and clergy, a defender of the Church, a helper of the poor, and consoler of the
afflicted; prudent and discreet in the conduct of affairs, justly severe to offenders."
A monk of Autun, named Hugo, renders to him the same praise A.D. 1136.
As regards his zeal for justice, which Anselm specially commends, a striking
example is found in Letter 39, and others, from which we learn with what vigour
he dared, first of all, or among the first, to repress the single combats which
were tolerated elsewhere by all other princes.   The Canons had long forbidden
them to Clerks, as Bishop Ivo, of Chartres, declares in his Letter 247.   Ernald
of Bonnevaux, like Geoffrey, speaks with admiration of the works of charity and

1. I am very grateful that you have been so good, as I have heard, as to be anxious about my poor health; and while I see in this a proof of your worthiness towards me, I cannot doubt of the love that you have towards God; for unless for that reason, when would one of your high rank deign to know so humble a person as myself? Since, then, it is certain that you love God, and me because of Him, I wonder the more that a small petition, preferred through confidence in God, and neither unjust, as I think, nor unreasonable, should have been refused to me by you. If I had asked of you gold or silver, or something of that kind[1] [either I am much deceived as to your goodness, or I should certainly have received it]. But what, I say, had I asked? Already, without asking, I have received very many gifts of your generosity. But this one thing which I requested from you,[2] not for my own sake, but in the name of God, much more in your interest than my own. What cause was there that I did not merit the granting of it? Did you think it an unworthy thing of me to ask, or of you to grant, that you should have mercy upon a Christian man, whatever might be the crime of which he was accused before you, after clearing himself of it? If you do not believe that he has fully cleared himself because he did not do this in your court, at least permit him to present himself there to establish his innocence, and thus obtain indulgence.

2. Are you ignorant of the threatenings of Him who has said, *When my time shall be come I shall judge the judgments themselves* (Ps. lxv. 2, VULG.)? And if He judges the judgments much more the injustices. Do you not fear what is written again, *With what measure ye have*

---

mercy of Theobald (*Life of S. Bernard*, B. ii. c. 8). Also the (new) Letter 416. He was buried in the Benedictine monastery at Lagny-sur-Marne, of which he was patron and protector, as we see from Bernard's Letter 230. This abbey was founded by Heribert, Count of Champagne, in A.D. 990, and there the porphyry tomb of Count Theobald may still be seen.

[1] So the S. Germanus MS. Others omit these words.

[2] Hence it appears that this was not the first Letter written on behalf of Humbert, but that Letter 39 was prior in time, and from this we learn the country of Humbert, and the punishment inflicted upon him.

measured it shall be again measured to you (S. Matt. vii. 2)? Do you not know that if it is easy for you to deprive Humbert of his heritage, it is as easy—it is even incomparably more easy—for God to deprive Count Theobald (which may God forbid) of his? And even in such cases where the fault appears so open and inexcusable as that there is no opportunity left for mercy except at the cost of justice, even then it is only with fear and regret that you ought to punish, more because obliged by the duty of your office than from a desire to inflict punishment. But when the crime charged is either not certainly known, or is capable of excusa, not only ought you not to deny, but ought most willingly to embrace an opportunity for pardoning, and be glad that when justice is secured your mercy and indulgence have found place.

I supplicate your Highness, then, for the second time to have pity upon Humbert, as you would that God should have pity upon you; and to lend an ear either to that gentle promise of the Lord, *Blessed are the merciful for they shall obtain mercy* (S. Matt. v. 7), or to that terrible threat, *He shall have judgment without mercy that hath showed no mercy* (S. James ii. 13). Farewell.

LETTER XXXVIII. (A.D. 1128.)

To the Same, on the Same Subject.

To the very pious Prince THEOBALD, BERNARD, Abbot of Clairvaux, health and prayers.

1. I am greatly afraid lest I should at length become troublesome by too presumptuously pouring my frequent appeals into your much-occupied ears. But what can I do? If I fear to offend you by writing to you too often, how much more ought I to fear to offend God, to whom still greater fear is due, by not interceding for an unfortunate man? Besides, pardon me for saying that I am unable to see without pitying the misery of that unfortunate, on whose

behalf I return again to weary you with my prayers. It is still about Humbert that I speak. His lot is the more unhappy that from having been rich he has become poor and a beggar for daily bread. I cannot but compassionate his widow and orphans, who are the more unhappy because deprived of their father while he is yet alive. I render you thanks for the favour that you have been so gracious as to accord me in this matter, in deigning to permit that Humbert should come himself to make his defence before you, and in doing him the justice not to listen to his slanderers. To perfect your work of charity, you had arranged most kindly that his patrimony should be restored to his wife and children; and I cannot but wonder that your charitable orders in this respect were not at once carried out.

2. When we receive, perhaps, from other princes words untrue or untrustworthy, it is something neither new nor wonderful to us. But in the case of Count Theobald it is a matter of great surprise that his Yes and No should be without weight, since a word from him is for us equivalent to an oath, and a slight untruth is regarded as a grave perjury; since of all the virtues which dignify your high rank and render your name celebrated throughout the whole world, the chief and the most extolled is your steadfast truthfulness. Who, then, has tried to weaken, either by artifice or counsel, the intrepid firmness of your soul ? who, I say, has endeavoured to enfeeble by his fraud your purpose so holy, so noble, so exemplary for all princes ? Falsely, not truly, does he love you, perfidiously, not faithfully, does he counsel you, who tries to obscure because of his cupidity your glorious reputation for truth, and endeavours by some malicious motive to render vain a word that your mouth has spoken—a word not less pleasing to God that it is worthy of you ; as just as it is pious, and pious as just. I entreat you, then, by the mercy of God, that you pursue your good purpose, and not permit the wicked to boast that the poor man is ruined ; rather take means for the full carrying out of the promise you have made, to

Dom. Norbert and to me, that you would restore the patrimony of Humbert to his wife and children.   Farewell.

LETTER XXXIX. (A.D. 1127.)

To the Same.[1]

He commends the causes of various people to Theobald ; then he urges him to treat with honour and reverence the Bishops assembled at Troyes to be present at a Council.

1. Among the many signs of condescension which you are pleased to display towards me, which arouse my grateful affection, that which I feel most is that, although I know I have ventured to address your Highness on behalf of many people, I never remember to have experienced a repulse from you. Having naturally become more confident, therefore, I approach you without hesitation to recommend to you the Canons of Larzicourt.[2]

I do not ask any favour for them, because I have so much trust in your justice and observance of law that I think if your enemy came to plead a cause in your Court he need not fear that he would not receive justice; but this is the supplication which I from a distance unite with them, and for them, to make : both that you would accord to them a speedy and favourable access to the presence of your Serenity, which I know they greatly need, in order that

[1] After having addressed other requests in this Letter to Count Theobald, Bernard intercedes for an unfortunate man named Humbert, who has been vanquished in a duel, and in consequence deprived by order of the prince, not only of his property, but also of sight, so that he had no means of sustaining his miserable existence. The penalty of his fault was cruel, and the charitable heart of Bernard was profoundly distressed; but so severe a remedy was called for by the great and inveterate evil of these single combats. Sirmund speaks of the great frequency and mischievous consequences of these in his notes to Geoffrey of Vendôme, B. iii. ep. 38 ; Duchesne *ad Bibli-thecam Cluniacensem*, and others. Compare Letter 376 of S. Bernard.

[2] These were Regular Canons of S. Augustine. Larzicourt is in the Deanery of Pertois, Diocese of Chalons-sur-Marne; the Jesuit Fathers possessed a Priory there in the time of Mabillon.

their neighbours may render them the respect which their piety deserves, and which they will do when they learn your good disposition towards them; and that if any of your soldiers or officials have acted unjustly towards them, they may understand that they must not henceforth trouble their Godly peace without incurring your displeasure.

2. I have another request respectfully to make. I met lately, when passing through Bar, a woman very much to be pitied; she was in great trouble, and my heart was moved on hearing her sufferings. She begged with tears and prayers that I would intercede for her with you. She is the wife of that man of yours, Belin, whom you were obliged to punish some time since for an offence which he had committed. Have mercy upon her, that God may have mercy also upon you.

3. Since I have once begun, I will continue to speak with my lord. In a duel which has lately been fought in the presence of the Prêvôt of Bar, the vanquished[1] was condemned by your order to lose his eyes on the spot; but, besides this, as if it were not enough to be vanquished and to lose his sight, he was deprived of all his goods, as he complains, by your people. Your benevolence will find it just that they should restore to him sufficient to sustain his miserable life; and, besides, the offence of the father ought not to be imputed to his innocent children. Let them, then, at least succeed to the father's possessions if he has any.

4. In conclusion, I would beg you to treat with all the honour, of which they are well worthy, those holy Bishops who have assembled in your capital to consider together matters of religion. Deign also to show yourself devoted and obedient as far as you can in all things to the Legate himself, who has chosen to honour you and your capital by the holding of so important a Council.[2] And be so kind as

[1] This was Humbert, on whose behalf Bernard wrote this Letter before Letter 37.

[2] This was the Council of Troyes in 1128, which is referred to in Letter 21 to the Legate Matthew.

to give your support and assent to the measures and the resolutions which he shall judge advisable for the promotion of
good ; but especially I beg you to receive with honour the
Bishop of Langres, who is your Bishop as well as mine, and
for the fief [1] which you hold of his Church you ought to
render the due homage.[2]   With humble respect, farewell.

LETTER XL. (*Circa* A.D. 1127.)

TO THE SAME.

He commends a poor religious to Theobald.

I commend unto you two things in this man whom you
see: poverty and piety, that if you do not compassionate the
one in him you may reverence the other, and may not deny
to him what he has come so far, and at the price of so many
fatigues, to ask of you.   Give him, then, some help, if not
for his sake, at least for your own ; for if he has need of you
because he is poor, you have as much and, indeed, more
need of him because he is a religious.   Finally, of all those
many people whom I have sent unto you for the same
cause, I do not know if there has been one other on whom
you might bestow a benefit with greater certainty that it
would be pleasing to God.   Farewell.

LETTER XLI. (*In the same year.*)

TO THE SAME.

He recommends to him an aged religious.

I fear that you are troubled by my frequent scribblings,
but the law of Christ and the necessity of friends drives me
to this opportunity.   I entreat you not to send away empty
this aged man whom I have recommended to you.   He is

[1] *Casamentum.* That is, a property dependent from the house (*Casa*) of the
Lord.
[2] *Hominium* or *homagium.*

aged as you see, and of a good and religious house, as I know. Besides this, I would ask you to be so good as to give him a letter to the King, your uncle,[1] whom he is going to seek. I would wish that all the servants of God might become, if it were possible, your debtors, so that they may receive you one day into the everlasting habitations in return for the mammon of iniquity which you share with them. Farewell.

LETTER XLII.

TO HENRY, ARCHBISHOP OF SENS.

This Letter deserved a place among the Treatises, and we have removed it thither under this title: *De Moribus et Officio Episcoporum Tractatus*, or Letter 42 to Henry, Archbishop of Sens.

LETTER XLIII. (*Circa* A.D. 1128.)

TO THE SAME HENRY.

He writes on behalf of the Abbey of Molesme.

The kind reception which you gave to my last request gives me room to hope to obtain what I now ask. I would first express my most earnest thanks for your previous kindness, and then venture to beg that you would make me a second time your debtor, namely, by permitting the Abbey of Molesme to possess freely the Church,[2] on account of which they are grieved to have lost the favour of your

---

[1] Henry I., King of England, uncle of Theobald (*Ernoldus Vit. Bernard* B. ii. *sub finem*, and Robert du Mont under A.D. 1151), by Adela, daughter of William the Conqueror, sister of Henry I., and mother of Theobald.

[2] A house of the Benedictines, in the Diocese of Langres, founded by Abbot Robert, who was also Abbot of Cîteaux; it was that reason which caused Bernard to care always for the interests of that Abbey. See Letters 44, 60, and 80. Peter de Celles speaks of it thus in his fourteenth Letter to the monks of Molesme, B. vii.: "Molesme is a hen full of plumes and furnished with wings. How many and great offspring has it produced? From it has emerged the original germ of Cîteaux." The reference in this Letter, as in the following, is to the Church of Senan, which was formerly a Priory in the Diocese of Sens and Deanery of Courtenay.

Serenity, and which it is certain that they possessed in the time of your predecessors.   Farewell.

LETTER   XLIV.   (*Circa*   A.D.   1128.)

To the Same, on the Same Subject.

You see how often I count on your bounty, so that I do not fear, although I have received so much from you, to make myself again an importunate suppliant and to weary you with new demands.   My presumption, indeed, is great, but it does not merit indignation, since it is caused by affection and not by want of consideration.   Your Paternity remembers, I doubt not, that when I was lately at Troyes you were so good as to relinquish for the love of God, and at my entreaty, all the claims which you had made against the monks of Molesme on the Church at Senan.   Now, the same monks complain that I know not what new, and, as they say, undue prærogatives are asserted over the forenamed Church. I beseech you that these also may be remitted, and trust that in this even you will not refuse me, so that, as you have granted me the greater favours, so I may be successful in obtaining the lesser.   Farewell.

LETTER   XLV.   (A.D.   1127.)

To Louis, King of France.[1]

The monks of Cîteaux take the liberty to address grave reproaches to King Louis for his hostility to and injuries inflicted upon the Bishop of Paris, and declare that they will bring the cause before the Pope if the King does not desist.

To Louis, the glorious King of France, Stephen, Abbot of Cîteaux, and the whole assembly of the abbots and brethren of Cîteaux, wish health, prosperity, and peace in Christ Jesus.

1. The King of heaven and earth has given you a kingdom

[1] Louis VI., "the Fat."

on earth, and will bestow upon you one in heaven if you study to govern with justice and wisdom that which you have received. This is what we wish for you, and ;pray for on your behalf, that you may reign here faithfully, and there in happiness. But why do you of late put so many obstacles in the way of our prayers for you, which, if you recollect, you formerly with such humility requested? With what confidence can we now presume to lift up our hands for you to the Spouse of the Church, while you so inconsiderately, and without the slightest cause (as we think), afflict the Church? Grave indeed is the complaint she lays against you before her Spouse and Lord, that she finds you an opposer whom she accepted as a protector. Have you reflected whom you are thus attacking? Not really the Bishop of Paris,[1] but the Lord of Paradise, *a terrible God who cuts off the spirit of Princes* (Ps. lxx. 12), and who has said to Bishops, *He who despiseth you despiseth me* (S. Luke x. 16).

2. That is what we have to say to you. Perhaps we have to say it with boldness, but at the same time in love; and for your sake we pray you heartily, in the name of the friendship with which you have honoured us, and of the brotherhood with which you deigned to associate yourself, but which you have now so grievously wounded, quickly to desist from so great a wrong; otherwise, if you do not deign to listen to us, nor take any account of us whom you called brethren, who are your friends, and who pray daily for you and your children and realm, we are forced to say to you that, humble as we are, there is nothing which we are not prepared to do within the limits of our weakness

---

[1] Stephen, who was Bishop of Paris from 1124 to 1144. The cause of these persecutions was the withdrawal of Stephen from the Court, and the liberty of the Church which he demanded. Henry, Archbishop of Sens, had a similar difficulty, and for causes not unlike (Letter 49). The mind of the King was not induced to yield by this Letter, and the death of his son Philip, who was already associated with him as King, passed for a punishment from Heaven for his obstinacy. It is astonishing that after his death the nobles and bishops should have had thoughts of hindering the succession of Louis the Younger (*Ordericus*, Book xiii. p. 895 sqq.)

for the Church of God, and for her minister, the venerable
Bishop of Paris, our father and our friend. He implores
the help of poor religious against you, and begs us by the
right of brotherhood[1] to write in his favour to the Lord
Pope. But we judge that we ought first to commence by
this letter to your royal Excellence, especially as the same
Bishop pledges himself by the hand of all our Congregation to give every satisfaction provided that his goods,
which have been unjustly taken away from him, be restored,
which it seems to us justice itself requires; in the meantime, we put off the sending of his petition. And if God
inspires you to lend an ear to our prayers, to follow our
counsels, and to restore peace with your Bishop, or rather
with God, which we earnestly desire, we are prepared to
come to you wherever you shall be pleased to fix for the
sake of arranging this affair; but if it be otherwise, we
shall be obliged to listen to the voice of our friend, and to
render obedience to the priest of God. Farewell.

LETTER XLVI. (A.D. 1127.)

To the Lord Pope Honorius II., on the Same Subject.

*They complain to the Pope that by the raising surrep-
titiously of the interdict, the King of France, before disposed to peace, was rendered more obstinate.*

To the supreme Pontiff HONORIUS, the abbots of the poor
of Christ, HUGO of Pontigny, and BERNARD of Clairvaux,
health and all that the prayer of sinners can effect.
We are not able to conceal the tears and complaints of
the Bishops, and, indeed, of the whole Church, of which we
have the honour, however unworthy, to be sons. We speak
of what we have seen. A great necessity has drawn us
from our cloisters into public, and what we have seen there

1 All those who in a Society had the right of suffrage were regarded as
brothers. So the monks of Chaise-Dieu call Louis Le Jeune by the name of
brother (*Duchesne*, Vol. iv. Letter 308).

we report to you. We have seen and repeat sad things.
In the time of Honorius the honour of the Church has been
deeply wounded. Already the humility, or rather the
constancy, of the bishops had bent down the anger of the
King, when the supreme authority of the supreme pontiff
intervening,[1] alas ! threw down constancy and set up pride !
We know, indeed, that that mandate must have been
obtained from you by falsehood, as is quite evident from
your letter, or you would not have ordered an interdict so
just and so necessary to be put an end to. But should not
the falsehood be at length detected—should not iniquity be
made to feel that it has lied against itself, and not against
dignity such as yours ? For it is that which astonishes us,
that judgment should have been given without hearing the
two parties, and that the absent should have been condemned, which, indeed, we do not blame with rash presumption, but with the love of sons we suggest to the heart
of our Father how greatly from this act the wicked triumphs
and the poor is cast down; but how long he ought to
suffer thus, and in what degree you ought to suffer with
him, it is not for us, most holy Father, to prescribe to you ;
it is for you to consult your own heart. Farewell.

LETTER XLVII. (A.D. 1127.)

TO THE SAME POPE, IN THE NAME OF GEOFFREY,
BISHOP OF CHARTRES.

*He explains to the Pontiff the cause why the Bishop of
Paris was unjustly oppressed by King Louis. The interdict of the bishops of France had put pressure upon him,
and he had promised to make restitution, when the absolution of Honorius rendered him contumacious, and prevented his fulfilling his promise.*

It is superfluous to recall to you, very holy Father, the
cause and order of a very afflicting history, and to linger

---

[1] Viz., by relaxing the interdict which by the bishops of the province had been
laid upon the Royal domain, because of the persecution of which the Bishop of
Paris was the object. See the following Letter.

over what you have already heard from the pious Bishop of
Paris, and which must have profoundly affected your
paternal heart. Yet my testimony also ought not to be
wanting to my brother and co-bishop; what I have seen
and heard respecting this matter, this I have undertaken to
make you acquainted with in few words. When the
before-mentioned Bishop had brought forward his complaint,
which he did with great moderation, in our provincial
assembly, where had gathered with our venerable metropolitan the Archbishop of Sens, all the bishops of the province, and certain religious also whom we had summoned,
we determined to represent to the King, with all becoming
humility, his unjust proceeding, and to beg that he would
restore to the Bishop unjustly maltreated what had been
taken from him; but we obtained no satisfaction from him.
Understanding, at length, that in order to defend the
Church we had decided to have recourse to the weapons of
the Church, he was afraid, and promised the restitution
demanded. But almost in the same hour arrived your
letter, ordering that the interdict over the royal domains
should be raised, thus, unfortunately, strengthening the
King in his evil doings, so that he did not perform at all
what he had promised. Nevertheless, as he had given a
fresh promise that he would do what we required, we
presented ourselves on the day appointed. We laboured
for peace, and it did not come; but instead of it worse
confusion. Thus the effect of your letter has been that the
goods unjustly seized are more unjustly retained, and those
which remain are seized day by day, and that so much
more securely, as he is assured of entire impunity in retaining them. The just (as we consider) interdict of the
Bishop has been raised by your order, and as the fear
of displeasing you has made us suspend that which we
proposed to send forth by our own authority, and by which
we hoped to obtain peace, we are made in the meantime
the derision of our neighbours. How long is this to be?
Let the compassion of your piety be exercised on our
behalf.

LETTER XLVIII. (*Circa* A.D. 1130.)

To Haimeric, the Chancellor, on the Same Subject, and against Detractors.

He justifies himself against attacks made upon him, and begs to be allowed to enjoy solitude and silence.

To the illustrious HAIMERIC, Chancellor of the holy Roman See, Brother BERNARD, called Abbot of Clairvaux, health eternal.

1. Does truth bring hatred even to the poor and indigent, and does not even their misery secure them against envy? Ought I to complain or to glory because I am made an enemy for speaking the truth or for doing right? That is what I leave to be considered by your brethren, who, against the law, speak evil of one deaf (Lev. xix. 14), and not fearing the malediction of the Prophet, *call evil good and good evil* (Is. v. 20). I ask of you, O good men, what in me has displeased your brotherhood?[1] Is it because at Chalons was deposed the Bishop of Verdun,[2] a man everywhere decried, because he had dissipated in management the goods of his Lord committed to him in the Church over which he presided? Or was it because at Cambray,

---

[1] *Fraternitati.* So all, or almost all, write constantly, and rightly so; for Cardinals formerly used to be called simply *Brothers* (*Life of S. Bernard*, B. ii. n. 42), and in *Chron. Andreæ. Spicilegii*, Vol. ix. p. 481, the Abbot Peter is brought forward as having visited "not only the lord Pope, but also the *Brothers* according to the custom." Some wrongly read "*our* brethren," instead of "*your* brethren," at the beginning of this Letter. See also *William of Tyre*, B. iii. c. 15: "The Cardinals are Brothers whether bishops, priests, or deacons."

[2] Henry, the same to whom Letters 62 and 63 are addressed. Laurence of Liége, speaks of his deposition in his "History of Verdun" (*Spicilegium*, Vol. xii. p. 311), saying that this affair had been confided by Pope Honorius to the care of his Legate in France, Matthew, Bishop of Albano, who assembled a Council at Chalons-sur-Marne to deal with it. "Henry at first consulted Bernard, Abbot of Clairvaux, of holy memory, whose counsels are at this day," says Laurence, "the support of the realms and churches of France. He advised Henry that it was a very grave thing to retain an episcopal charge over unwilling people. Therefore, before a very ignominious charge should come against him in the public hearing of so many great men, he, being

Fulbert, who conducted his monastery manifestly to its destruction, was obliged to yield his place to Parvin,[1] a prudent and faithful servant, according to the testimony of all? Or, again, was it because, at Laon, a sanctuary[2] of God was restored to him after having been made a shrine of Venus? For which of these things do you, I do not say stone me, so that I may not borrow the language of my Lord (S. John x. 32), but tear me to pieces? And this I should be right to reply to you with pride, if any of the credit of these things belong to me. But, now, why am I judged for what others have done? Or if for my actions, why am I accused as if I had done something wrong, when no one can be so silly as to doubt, or so shameless as to deny that all these things were done justly and well? Choose now which alternative you please; either deny or assert that I am the author of these things. If I have done them, it is a thing worthy of praise to have brought about praiseworthy actions, and I am wrongly blamed for that which renders me worthy of praise. If I have not done them, as I have deserved no praise, I deserve no blame. It is a new kind of detraction that is employed against me, and has some resemblance to the work of Balaam, who, being brought and paid to curse the people, heaped them with blessings instead (Num. xxii. and xxiv.). What more just and more consoling for him whom the design was to blame than to see that, though willing to blame him, you unwillingly praise, and unknowingly employ the language of laudation for that of insult? Could you not find enough of real

alone, should yield to all and resign the See. He followed this counsel, gave up the pastoral staff, and retired from the See in the thirteenth year after he had received it from the hand of Cæsar," *i.e.*, in A.D. 1129.

[1] Parvin was a monk of S. Vincent at Laon when he was made abbot of S. Sepulchre of Cambray, after Fulbert had been displaced by Rainauld des Prés, Archbishop of Rheims, on account of his bad administration. The monastery of S. Sepulchre, of the Order of S. Benedict, was formerly beyond the walls of Cambray, and was founded A.D. 1064 by Bishop Lietbert.

[2] This refers to the convent of S. John Baptist at Laon, from which the nuns who had previously occupied it were driven out because of the irregular lives of some of them. They were replaced in 1128 by monks who had at their head as abbot, Drogo, a monk of S. Nicasius at Rheims.

defaults in me that you reproach me for a good action as
if it were evil, or rather that you impute to me what I have
not done ?

2. But I am not distressed by undeserved reproaches, nor
do I accept unmerited praises ; nothing concerns me which
I have not done. Let them praise if they will or blame if
they dare his lordship of Albano for the first matter,
for the second his lordship of Rheims, and for the third the
same archbishop, with the Bishop of Laon, with the King
in the same degree, and with many other reverend persons,
who will by no means disown that they have taken a
principal part in them. If they have done well, or if
otherwise, what is it to me ? My sole and only fault is
that I have been present at these assemblies, being a man
deserving only of solitude, who ought to judge only myself,
to be the accuser and arbiter of my own conscience only, if
I wish that my life should display what my profession
declares, and my name of monk describe truly my solitary
habit of life. For I was present, I avow it; but it was
because I had been summoned, and, as it were, forced to
come. If this has been displeasing to my friends, I confess
it has displeased me also. Would that I had not gone to
these assemblies, would that I may not go to any similar to
them ! Would that I had never gone where I had the
sorrow to see (as lately) a violent tyrant armed against the
Church by the authority of the Holy See, as if he had not
been already by himself sufficiently powerful ! Then at
length I felt as the Prophet says, my tongue cleave to my
mouth (Ps. cxxxvii. 6), when I saw that unquestionable
authority bear us down with its weight, and when the
Pope's letter was brought forward. Alas ! I was mute, *I
was humbled, I was silent even from the good : and my
sorrow was renewed* (Ps. xxxix. 3, VULG.), when suddenly
I saw the letter of the Pope cover the faces of the innocent
with confusion, make the impious and sinners to rejoice
and triumph in their wickedness. The indulgence which
was shown to the wicked, as says the Prophet, did not
teach him to do righteousness ; and he who dealt unjustly

in the land of the righteous (Is. xxvi. 10) was freed from the most just interdict under which his domain was held.[1]

3. For reasons of this kind, even if there were no others, I am vexed to have meddled in the transaction of business, especially as I know that in it there is nothing that concerns me. I am vexed, yet I am forced to go. But by whom could I better hope to be relieved from this necessity than by you, O best of men ! to whom in such a matter neither is power wanting nor, as I know well, the will. I rejoice, therefore, to know that my occupation in such matters is displeasing to your wisdom; you are entirely right, and I recognize in it your friendship for me. Since, then, such is your desire, or rather since you perceive and determine that it is better for your friend and more becoming to a Religious, take means, I pray you, to ensure that both your will at once and mine may be accomplished as soon as possible, that justice may be satisfied, and the safety of my soul cared for. Forbid, if you please, those clamorous and importunate frogs to come forth from their hiding-places, but let them stay contentedly in their marshes. Let them not be heard in Councils, nor enter into palaces; let no necessity, no authority draw them to mingle in the settlement of disputes or of any business. So, perhaps, your friend may be able to escape from the charge of presumption. I do not know, indeed, how there can be any occasion for it, for my resolution is fixed not to set foot out of my monastery unless summoned by the Legate of the Apostolic See, or, at least, by my own Bishop, since, as you well know, it would be altogether wrong for a humble person like myself to resist these unless by privilege of some higher authority. If ever you shall succeed in effecting this, as I sincerely hope, then, without doubt, I shall have peace myself and leave others in peace. Yet, even although I shut myself up and keep silence, I do not suppose that the murmurs of the Churches will cease, if the Roman Curia continues to do injury to the absent in order to be complaisant to those who are near at hand. Farewell.

[1] See Letters 46, 47.

LETTER XLIX. (A.D. 1128.)

TO THE LORD POPE HONORIUS, ON BEHALF OF HENRY, ARCHBISHOP OF SENS.

To the Supreme Pontiff, HONORIUS, his servants and sons (if we are worthy to be so called), STEPHEN of Cîteaux, HUGO of Pontigny, BERNARD of Clairvaux, health and their best prayers for their most reverend lord and kind father.

Though dwelling in monasteries, to the shelter of which our sins have driven us, we do not cease to pray for you and for the Church of God committed to your charge, and share the rejoicing both of the Spouse of the Lord over so faithful a guardian, and of the friend of the Bridegroom over labouring so abundantly for her. In faith and truth we make known to you, holy Father, the evils to which we see with grief our Mother, the Church, exposed in this realm. As far as we, being on the spot, are able to judge, King Louis is hostile not so much to Bishops, as to any zeal for justice, practice of piety, and even religious living in the Bishops. That this is the fact the penetration of your Holiness will easily infer from this, that the very men who previously in secular life were highly honoured by him, judged faithful, regarded as familiar friends, are now treated as enemies, because they behave worthily in the priesthood and honour their ministry in all things. This is the cause of the insults and injuries with which the Bishop of Paris, though innocent, has been attacked, yet he has not been crushed, because the Lord arrested the King's hand when he opposed yours. Hence, also now he endeavours to weary and break down the constancy of the Archbishop of Sens, so that when the Metropolitan is vanquished (which may God forbid) he may easily, as he supposes, prevail over all th suffragans. Finally, who doubts that what he really wis'·y to attack is religion, which he looks upon openly as ¹t destruction of his realm and the enemy of his crow·e Another Herod holds Christ in suspicion, but it is Christ꞉h longer in the cradle, but triumphant in the Churches, whᵒt obnoxious to him. Nor do we think that his hostility to tʸ archbishop has any other object than this, that he strives to extinguish [1] in him, as in others, the spirit with which he is animated. Finally, if we are thought to be deceiving you, or to be ourselves deceived about these matters to which we bear witness, we desire that you will examine into them yourself as quickly as possible, so that (which we vehemently desire and suppliantly entreat) judgment may come forth from your presence, most holy Father, and in it we have no doubt that you will seek equity and protect innocence. But that the cause should be brought back into the presence and under the power of the King is plainly nothing else than that the just should be delivered into the hands of his enemies.

LETTER L. (A.D. 1128.)

TO THE SAME, ON THE SAME SUBJECT.

He demands that it should be allowed to the Archbishop to appeal to the Apostolic See.

It would be desirable, if it seems good to your authority, that the cause of the Archbishop of Sens should be discussed in your own presence, so that being, as he is, obnoxious to the King, he may not seem to be a man delivered to the will of his enemies by having to answer for himself to his adversaries in the presence and power of the King; but as whatever you direct must be inviolably adhered to, so it may be firmly hoped that whatever course you decree may issue in some good. This only we demand very humbly of your bounty, with all our Religious, viz., that if it shall happen that this Prelate should be crushed by the sovereign power (as it has happened only too often) he may be permitted to seek refuge in your fatherly bosom, because hitherto we se 'ave never heard that you have refused this refuge to a m ierson oppressed. Otherwise let Joseph, the just man, see

m
co [1] This expression must not be taken too absolutely, since it is evident that Louis was far from being a bad prince; but is used because he seemed to pl persecute in them the *zeal for righteousness* in wishing to stop the first motions)f the Bishops of Sens and Paris towards a new manner of life.

to it, what he must do now to save the Child and his Mother, because even now in the province of Sens Christ is sought for destruction. For, to say more plainly that which is the fact, it is clear that the King persecutes in the Archbishop of Sens his new piety, because he advanced him by all possible means and dismissed him into his Diocese with the assurance of freedom from every disturbance, as long as he lived in his former worldly life and conversation.

LETTER LI. (A.D. 1128.)

To Haimeric, the Chancellor, on the Same Subject.

To the very illustrious Haimeric, Chancellor of the Holy Roman See, Bernard, Abbot of Clairvaux, health and all that the prayer of a sinner can avail.

How long will it be true to say, *All who will live piously in Christ suffer persecution* (2 Tim. iii. 12)? How long shall the rod of sinners be extended over the heritage of the just? Who shall enable the just to stand[1] against those who have oppressed them?

Who can bear to see so great a degree of discord between heaven and earth, that while the Angels rejoice at the amendment of the evil, the sons of Adam rage and are envious? Has not Jesus by His sufferings and His blood purified the things which are in heaven and those on earth; and was not God in Him reconciling the world unto Himself? Formerly the Archbishop had nothing but praise, when he was ruled only by the desires of his heart—nothing but approval as long as his life and conversation were worldly. But now simony is sought for under the swaddling clothes of the infancy of Jesus, and a malign curiosity searches among the rising virtues (of the prelate) for even the ashes of dead vices. You see clearly that it is Jesus Himself who is the mark for the hostility of these men. In His name I beseech you; for His sake I am a

---

[1] Some read *in great constancy* here, but the words are wanting in MSS.

suppliant to you. He is well worthy both of your reverence and of your pity. Stand fast for Him in the defence of the Archbishop, and remember that you yourself must one day stand before Him to be judged. Farewell.

LETTER LII. (*Circa* A.D. 1128.)

To the Same.

He declares that the Bishop of Chartres has not projected a journey to Jerusalem. He begs to be released from the weight of public affairs.

Your friend and mine, the Lord Bishop of Chartres, wished the assurance to be conveyed to you by me that he has not had either the intention or the wish to be allowed to go to Jerusalem, as we know the Pope has been made to believe. For although he would greatly have wished to make the journey, yet he was not able to leave without great scandal here to all good people, who fear that his absence would do more harm to his own flock than his presence would do good to foreigners. This is what I have to say on behalf of that Bishop.

But that I may say something also on my own behalf, according to what Scripture admonishes, saying: *Have pity on your own soul if you wish to please God* (Ecclus. xxx. 23, VULG.). Does it please you that I should be loaded with burdens and occupied with business, so that I have no leisure to attend to my own duties, being entirely immersed in those which belong to others? If I have found favour in your eyes, be so good as to relieve me of all these affairs, so that I may be able to pray God for your sins and my own. It is true that I consider nothing could be safer for me than to follow the will of my lord the Pope; but if he would be so kind as to consider the limit of my powers, he would realize that I am not able to do these things, or with how much difficulty I can do them. And upon that matter sufficient is said to an intelligent person like yourself.

The Bishop of Chartres asked of me some of my little treatises to send to you; but I have nothing at hand which seems to me worthy of your attention. There is, indeed, a little book concerning Grace and Free Will which I have lately put forth. This I will gladly send to you, if you wish it. Farewell.

LETTER LIII. (*Circa* A.D. 1128.)

To the Same.

He presents to Haimeric two religious, and in them himself.

I remember that I have written to you on behalf of many people, and by the medium of many; but now I, who have often corresponded with you, am present before you in person. Represent to yourself *three* persons in the two whom you behold, since without me these are not able to exist, in whose hearts I rest in close companionship, and even more safely and sweetly than in my own. I seem to exaggerate, but only to one who has never felt the power of friendship, who is ignorant of the force of affection, who does not believe that *the multitude of believers were of one heart and of one soul* (Acts iv. 32). He, then, who sees them sees me also, though not in my own body, and what they say I say also with their tongues. I am absent in body, I confess; but the body is the least part of me. And if it is true that he who sees my face may assert with truth that he sees me and not a part of me only, when notwithstanding he sees only a part of me, and that the least considerable, how much more truly may I say that I am present, even without bodily presence, where I feel my will, my spirit, and affection, which is the greater and more worthy part of me, to be? Know, then, that we are one person in three bodies, not of equal holiness, for in this I am inferior to each of these two, but having the same will, and perfect union of souls. For why should not the bond of affection bring about the unity of several persons in one spirit, if the bond of marriage makes two to be one flesh? I could wish that you would make yourself the fourth with us, if you do not consider that unity of affection unworthy of you. This you will easily obtain, if you do not disdain it; only if you do not desire it, I beg you not to let them perceive this. Farewell.

LETTER LIV. (*Circa* A.D. 1136.)

To the Same.

He recommends the Abbot Vivian, and warns Haimeric to think seriously of the salvation of his soul.

I desire and entreat that you will assist in his business, for the love of God and for my sake, the bearer of this letter, the venerable Vivian, Abbot of Haute Combe,[1] for whom I have a most intimate friendship, on account of his piety. This is what I have to say on his behalf; the remainder of the letter is for yourself. *What shall it profit ·a man if he shall gain the whole world and lose his own soul; or what shall a man give in exchange for his soul?* (S. Matt. xvi. 26). Not the whole world would be sufficient. A soul, which has been redeemed with the blood of Christ, is a valuable thing. Great was the loss of the soul, which could not be repaired except by the Cross of Christ. If, again, it shall perish by sin even unto death, whence, then, shall it be restored? Is there either another Christ, or will He be crucified again for it? Upon this subject I would wish that you would never forget the counsel of the wise man: *My son, remember thy latter end, and thou shalt not ever sin* (Ecclus. vii. 36, 40, VULG.).

[1] This monastery was founded in 1135, in the Alps; its first abbot was Vivian, a monk of the Cistercian Order. He was succeeded by Amadeus in 1139.

LETTER LV. (*Circa* A.D. 1128.)

To Geoffrey, Bishop of Chartres.

He begs that Geoffrey would receive and assist a certain religious recluse who had deserted his calling, but was repentant.

To the most faithful and prudent servant of God, Geoffrey, Bishop of Chartres,[1] Bernard, of Clairvaux, servant of the poor of Christ, health and the fulness of the glory of the everlasting hills.

The more fame and honour the holiness of your life procures for you, the more labour it brings you. Thus the person who brings you this letter, and.on whose behalf it is written, has felt himself, like so many others, drawn to you from far, by the fragrance of your pity, and by the hope of finding in you not only counsel what he ought to do, but also aid to accomplish it. This is his case. He had for the love of God shut himself in a certain cell, intending to live as a recluse. He himself will explain to you the causes why he quitted his cell and broke his vow.[2] Now he desires to return to his purpose; but intends to ask your help for so doing, if you will accord it to him at my request by this letter, with which he was desirous to strengthen his application. Act, therefore, in your accustomed way; give help to this unhappy man, and the more since I know you hold yourself a debtor both to the wise and to the unwise; quickly draw this wandering lamb of Christ from the jaws of the wolf, bring him back to his former pasture, and order him to be reclosed in some little

[1] Bernard was a great admirer and publisher of the virtues of this great prelate, of which he was an eye-witness, inasmuch as he was frequently associated with him by the Pope in transacting business of the Church (*Life of S. Bernard*, B. ii. ch. 1, 2, 6, etc.). He was a man truly apostolic, whose character, disposition, and ability were closely allied to those of Bernard, as is shown by the affectionate memory in which the latter testifies that he held him. In the life of William, Duke of Aquitaine, he is called "a man full of the spirit of power and wisdom." He died 24th Jan., 1138.

[2] Grimlac, in his *Rule for Solitories*, shows that it was not permitted to those who had been with solemn ceremony enclosed in their cell to quit it again.

cell near one of your houses; unless, perhaps, you see that some other course is the better for the man to take, and you succeed in convincing him that he ought to take it.

LETTER LVI. (*Circa* A.D. 1128.)

TO THE SAME.

He is uncertain respecting the pilgrimage of Norbert to Jerusalem. He does not share his opinion about Antichrist. He also recommends Humbert.

I am quite ignorant respecting the matter of which you inquire of me, namely, whether the Lord Norbert is about to go to Jerusalem. For when I saw him last, a few days ago, he said nothing of it to me, though I was honoured in being able to drink in many words from his mouth, as it were a sweet-toned flute.[1] But when I asked what he thought concerning Antichrist, he declared himself quite convinced that Antichrist was to be revealed during this generation that is now.[2]

[1] High praise to Norbert (says Mabillon) from such a man; but not less remarkable is the discernment of Bernard in divine things, since he did not easily yield faith to any kind of pious imaginativeness, as we see from Letter 174, n. 6. Norbert (whom we have already praised in Letters 35 and 38) was the founder of the Præmonstratensian Order, which counted already almost seventy abbeys in its first twenty years of existence (Laurence of Liége, *Spicilegium*, Vol. xii., p. 32). See Letter 253.

[2] Not Norbert only, but many of the older Fathers (not to speak of the more recent) were persuaded that Antichrist was on the point of appearing, and that the last day of the world was drawing near—as may be seen in S. Jerome, Pope Leo, S. Gregory the Great, and even S. Augustine. They were led to believe this by the iniquity of the times, and the appearance of very many of the signs foretold by Christ by which the end of the world should be preceded. But we may go even further back. Even from the time of the Apostles there were many judgments, conjectures, opinions, predictions upon Antichrist and upon the end of the world. Very many philosophers and astronomers, a great number also of impostors, stage players, and scandal-mongers, [1] certain heretics also and fanatics wished to be prophets on this subject, and to appear to know more about it than other mortals; but the event has already shown that the greater number of these predictions were vain, and has convicted their

[1] Lit., dealers in female finery, *nugivenduli*.

I begged him to tell me on what he rested his conviction,

authors of vanity and falsehood. The remainder will receive, without doubt, from the present and from the future a similar confutation, and the truth will be shown of that saying in Acts i. 7 : *It is not for you to know the times and the seasons ;* and of that also in S. Matt. xxiv. 36 : *But of that day and hour knoweth no one.* It will not be tedious to the reader if we give here a few examples of these out of a great many.

The first who thought that the end of the world was imminent were the Thessalonians, who wrongly understood those words of the Apostle (1 Thess. iv. 17) : *Then we which are alive and remain shall be caught up together with them in the clouds to meet the Lord in the air, and so shall we ever be with the Lord.* It was to recall these from this opinion that S. Paul judged it necessary to write a second Epistle to the Thessalonians (S. Jerome, *Epist. ad Miner. et Alex.*).

Lactantius thought that the destruction of the world would take place in the five hundredth year after Christ (*Div. Inst.* B. i. c. 25).

Others, called Chiliasts, assigned to the world a duration of a thousand years after Christ, founding that on the words of S. John Apoc. xx. 7 : *After a thousand years shall have passed, Satan shall be unbound and shall come out of prison.*

A certain Florentine Bishop asserted that Antichrist was born in A.D. 1105 (See *Plat. in Paschale* ii.).

Peter John, Chief of the Beguines and Beghards, used to say that the reign of Antichrist would finish in 1335 (Joseph a Costa *de Temp. novis.*).

A certain Spaniard, named Arnold, indicated (according to Florimund) the year 1345 as that in which Antichrist would appear, and fixed on the day of Pentecost in that year as the time when his disciples would spread themselves through the world.

Abbot Joachim thought that Antichrist would appear within 60 years from his own time ; he lived about A.D. 1200.

Peter d'Ailly, Bishop of Cambray and Cardinal, predicted from astronomical observations and calculations that Antichrist would be born in 1789.

Nicholas of Cusa did not hesitate to assert that the coming of Antichrist would be in A.D. 1700 or 1734.

The illustrious John Picus Mirandola conjectured in his *Assertions* (Concl. 9) that Antichrist would appear in 1994.

Jerome Cardan (*de Variet.* B. ii. c. 2) and James Naclant (*in Prælud. Medullæ* c. 4) thought that Antichrist would come in A.D. 1800.

In a former age, by I know not what itch of prophesying, many, both astrologers and heretics, occupied themselves with predicting the end of the world, which continued to exist all the same, and made them its laughing stock.

John of Konigsberg, a very distinguished mathematician, assigned A.D. 1588 as that which would see the destruction of the world. John Stoffler, an astronomer not less famous, was of the same opinion ; also Henry de Rantzan, a Danish nobleman, in his book on fatal years and on the periods of empires. κ.τ.λ.

but his reply did not convince me that he was right. But at length he asserted this, that before his own death he would see a general persecution in the Church.

Concerning another matter, permit me to recall to the remembrance of your Piety a poor exile named Humbert. He begged you lately when you were at Troyes to intercede for him with Count Theobald, who had deprived him of his goods. I also by this letter entreat for him, and with him, the same thing of your Piety. I have written[1] on that subject to intercede with the Prince himself, but have not succeeded in obtaining the favour which I asked.

One thing I ought to tell you, which I know you will gladly hear. Stephen, your former disciple, so runs not as uncertainly, so fights not as one that beateth the air. Pray for him that he may so run that he may obtain, may so fight that he may overcome.

LETTER LVII. (*Circa* A.D. 1128.)

To the Same.

Lesser vows ought not to be a motive to hinder greater spiritual progress. This seems to be written, if I do not mistake, in the cause of the monk who is the subject of Letter 55.

As this man has reported to me from you, you have declined up to the present to accede to his desire and petition, because it seems to you to make void his first vow of proceeding to Jerusalem. Upon which, if you ask my opinion, I consider that more important vows ought not to be hindered by less important; and that God will not require the fulfilment of a good vow if it has been discharged by the performance of one still better. For would you be right to complain of a debtor who owed you twelve pence if on the appointed day he paid you a silver mark?

_____

[1] Letters 37-39.

and if it is from his Bishop that you fear some objection, you may be sure that not only will you not displease him by rendering help to this man, but that he will be very grateful to you. Farewell.

LETTER LVIII. (*Circa* A.D. 1126.)

To Ebal, Bishop of Chalons-sur-Marne.

He begs Ebal to take means for the choosing of a fit man to preside over the Abbey of All Saints.

To the venerable EBAL, by the grace of God, Lord Bishop of Chalons, Brother BERNARD, Abbot of Clairvaux, health and all that the prayers of a sinner can avail.

1. It is not good that you should neglect or disregard the danger of that little vessel (I speak of the Church of All Saints')[1] which is drifting under your eyes, being deprived of its ruler. It is a matter which belongs to your charge ; therefore I wonder what motive hinders you in conscience from requiring the acceptance of the post by that ecclesiastic, a pious man, as it is said, who has been elected by religious persons to the same, even although some of the monks of that abbey show themselves unworthy of your interest by their carelessness and indifference. I have understood that they have nothing to object to him who has been chosen except that he is religious, and that they have dared to desire your Greatness to permit them to choose another who appears to them more agreeable and more affable, because he is not a stranger to them, but is as agreeable as he is well known to the citizens, and being well acquainted with the customs of the country is gratified for transacting the business of the Church. In reality that which you ask (I should reply to those very cautious advisers) is someone who will not object to your faults, and who will either consent or will

---

[1] This was the Abbey of regular Canons of the Order of S. Augustine at Chalons-sur-Marne. Hugo Metellus, regular Canon of S. Leo at Toul, in Lorraine, wrote a Letter (unedited) to Peter, the abbot of this Church, perhaps the first after the reform.

not dare to oppose himself to your objectionable way of life. These are not to be listened to, but rather, whether they wish it or no, action ought to be taken by you, so as to put at the head of that unfortunate Church this man, whose reputation is unquestioned, since, if he is such as he is reported to be, God will, without doubt, be with him, will pour His grace upon him, that he may be acceptable to all and successful in all his enterprises.

2. If those people are altogether unworthy of him and he cannot by any means be obtained for the post, let another be sought out who shall seem fit, from some other religious house ; not such a person as those people desire, who desire nothing but what flatters their carnal tastes, but one who, as he knows how to manage the temporal administration, so also is able to prefer the care of souls in all things. Under the Lord William, your predecessor of holy memory, the two monasteries of S. Peter and S. Urban [1] were similarly deprived of pastoral care ; he was not deterred by the length of the journey, nor by the severity of the winter, but came in person twice to Cluny, and, if I do not mistake, once to Dijon. Thence he obtained a good man, Lord Hugo, who afterwards died, and from Cluny Lord Radulf, whom he had sought with many prayers, and who still survives. These he placed one over each monastery, not judging it safe to commit that charge to any one of the monks on the spot; which I have adduced as an example, for this reason that I may impress upon your charity how it becomes you to act with no less caution and care in this matter which is now in your hands.

[1] These were two monasteries of Benedictines, afterwards under the Congregation of S. Vito, the first in the town itself, the second in the Diocese of Chalons-sur-Marne, which William of Champeaux reformed.

LETTER LIX. (A.D. 1129.)

To Guilencus,[1] Bishop of Langres.

He counsels him, in order to take away any occasion for scandal and calumny, to abandon to the Church of S. Stephen at Dijon, certain articles which Garnier had left there on dying.

To his lord and father GUILENCUS, by the Grace of God, Bishop of Langres, Brother BERNARD, Abbot of Clairvaux, health and his entire devotion.

On hearing of the death of the Archdeacon Dom Garnier[2] I have thought it necessary to address a prayer to your Paternity and even to press upon you my advice, if you will deign to attend to the suggestions of one so humble. As relates to the goods which the late Abbot possessed in the Church of S. Stephen at Dijon, have the generosity to renounce the rights that you have over these things. I know well that they ought to return to you as I remember was arranged and settled in writing in the Chapter of Langres, when your son Harbert was constituted the first regular abbot of that house. But because I know that for you on any account to assert your rights over these properties which that Church has so long held would be an occasion of grave scandal to the Canons and of great reproach to the Abbot, whom they would accuse of having by coming among them established a bad precedent, since it was because of him and at his coming that their Church sustained so great a loss, I beg you, therefore, and at the same time advise and entreat you, to spare so great a

[1] Wilencus or, as others write, Guillermus. He had been Archdeacon of Langres. Perard, *Burgund. Monum.*, p. 87.

[2] He had been Abbot of S. Stephen at Dijon, before regular canons were introduced there, which was done in 1113, in which year the four canons retired to Quincy to lead there the life of regulars. In 1116, then numbering twelve, they returned to their former house. That house was governed up to 1125 by the Priors Arnulf and afterwards Galo; and that year Dom Erbert or Harbert was instituted as abbot in the presence of Hubaud, Archbishop of Lyons; Stephen, Bishop of Autun; Goceran, or Josceran, Bishop of Langres, and other persons (Perard).

scandal to so many feeble servants of Christ, and at the
same time to free this vicar of Christ from such a reproach
by conceding to this Church what has been theirs so long.[1]

LETTER LX. (*Circa* A.D. 1128.)

TO THE SAME.

He intercedes for the Abbey of Molesme.

I hope that you will not think me an importunate meddler
if I approach you to intercede on behalf of the Abbey of
Molesme. There are many motives which encourage me
to believe that I need not fear a refusal from you. First,
because the house for which I make request is not a foreign
one; it depends upon you. Next, that it asks only its
right from your justice, and is not usurping that which
belongs to another; and, thirdly, that our request is joined
in by such a person as would be sufficient to obtain even
a greater thing from your kindness. I mean Count
Theobald. If I presume to add a fourth, it is with diffi-
dence that I do so. For neither have I such distrust in my
humility but that I would venture, if need were, to commit
myself to your long-tried kindness in making any request
that might be reasonable. Farewell.

[1] That was, in fact, done by Guilencus in 1129, as we learn from a charter
published by Perard (p. 97) and subscribed by many other persons, among
others by the Abbots of Cîteaux and Clairvaux, assembled at Langres. In the
same year a controversy, which was between the same Church and the monks
of S. Seine, was settled by the same Josceran at the advice and with the counsel
of Gautier, Bishop of Chalons-sur-Saone, and the abbots of Cîteaux, Busay, and
Clairvaux (*Ib.*, p. 102). The matter was afterwards submitted to Pope
Innocent, who remitted the decision to Stephen, Abbot of Cistell, and Bernard of
Clairvaux (p. 103). See how Bernard alone exercised influence over all things,
and alone was in the habit of closing all lawsuits and controversies (Mabillon's
note).

LETTER LXI. (*Circa* A.D. 1125.)

TO RICUIN, BISHOP OF TOUL, IN LORRAINE.

He sends back to the Bishop a man who had been sent to him for the purpose of undergoing penitence, and charges him with his restoration.

To the Reverend Lord and Father RICUIN,[1] by the grace of God, Bishop of Toul, Brother BERNARD, Abbot of Clairvaux, health and prayers.

For this sinner whom your Worthiness has thought fit to send to me, who am myself a sinner, for spiritual advice, as he says, I have no wiser counsel at the present than that he should return to the bosom of your fatherly goodness, and should learn his duty from the mouth of the priest; for I, in order to remain within the narrow limits of my powers and my office, which I ought not to transgress, am not at all accustomed to impose penance, especially for great faults, on anyone but those alone who are under my jurisdiction. For what rashness would it be in me, a sinner, and inexperienced as I am, to undertake episcopal functions and matters so important? Ought I not also, just as other men, to have recourse, as is proper, to the opinion of the bishop, as often as there presents itself among us some affair more weighty than usual, which either I know not, or dare not, or am unable to settle by myself; and am I not far from secure until I have been fortified by the opinion and advice of my bishop? Let this poor diseased sheep be provided for, then, by his own pastor, who is one who well knows the canons, with a suitable medicine of penance, that a soul for which Christ died may not (which God forbid) die in sin, and the Chief Pastor require his blood at your hand. But I have persuaded him to leave the world since God has given him a thought of so doing; if by your intercession he may obtain the favour of being received,

[1] Ricuin died in 1126, from whence it follows that this Letter cannot be later than that year. On the other hand, it appears certain that it cannot have been written before 1124, since the Letter implies that Bernard already had a certain celebrity for his teaching. Letter 396 is addressed to the same Ricuin.

though an old man and poor, into some monastery of holy men within your diocese. May God one day receive you, holy and venerable father, full of days and good works, into the sacred habitations in which one day is better than a thousand passed elsewhere.

LETTER LXII. (*Before* A.D. 1129.)

To HENRY,[1] BISHOP OF VERDUN.

He recommends to the bishop a woman laden with many sins, but now penitent.

To the Lord HENRY, by the grace of God, Bishop of Verdun, Brother BERNARD, Abbot of Clairvaux, health and prayers.

This poor woman, whom already Satan has bound, lo! these many years, with many and tangled knots of sin, has sought counsel respecting her salvation from me, though unworthy, and has been advised by me; but after many and daily wanderings this poor lost sheep should return with confidence to the fold of her own pastor. You will succour her with the more care and speed in her distress inasmuch as you know perfectly well that you will render a strict account of her safety to the Lamb who has died for her and has committed her to your care. It was our duty to correct her when wandering, it is yours not to despise her as a sinner, but to receive her as a penitent; and if her unhappy history which she has told me be true, to reconcile her to her former husband, if he still lives, or if he is unwilling to receive her, to oblige both the one and the other to live in single life. Farewell.

[1] Concerning him, see Letter 48, where we have noted that he resigned his see in 1129, at the advice of Bernard.

LETTER LXIII. (*Circa* A.D. 1128.)

TO THE SAME.

He justifies himself respecting an imprudence of which he had been accused; he seeks his friendship, and commends to him the Abbot Guy.

Respecting those matters about which it has pleased your Excellency to make inquiry of me, either I am deceived or he who has reported them to you misinforms you. If there is any foundation of truth in those reports (for I distrust my memory, which, I know, is defective, and I would not suspect such great falseness in the brother who has spoken to you about them), at least I am quite sure, and you may believe without doubt this, that I have never used a word of blame against you at any time or to any person, nor made any accusation. May such rashness be far from a humble person like myself as to dare to speak against bishops, especially in their absence, about matters which do not concern me, and of which, besides, I have no correct knowledge. I gratefully accept the honour which you have done me in deigning to wish for my acquaintance, and I desire both that I should be better known to you and that you should know me better. It is with the same confidence in the goodness of your Highness that I address to you a request, or rather a recommendation, in favour of that monastery which my reverend brother and co-abbot Dom Guy, of Trois-Fontaines, has undertaken to erect under your protection, and, as they say, at your request. I shall see in that which you do for him what is your regard for me, and I shall hold as done for myself all that you are so good as to do in his favour. Farewell.

LETTER LXIV. (*Circa* A.D. 1129.)

To Alexander,[1] Bishop of Lincoln.

A certain canon named Philip, on his way to Jerusalem, happening to turn aside to Clairvaux, wished to remain there as a monk. He solicits the consent of Alexander, his bishop, to this, and begs him to sanction arrangements with the creditors of Philip. He finishes by exhorting Alexander not to trust too much in the glory of the world.

To the very honourable lord, ALEXANDER, by the Grace of God, Bishop of Lincoln, BERNARD, Abbot of Clairvaux, wishes honour more in Christ than in the world.

1. Your Philip, wishing to go to Jerusalem, has found his journey shortened, and has quickly reached the end that he desired. He has crossed speedily this great and wide sea, and after a prosperous voyage has now reached the desired shore, and anchored at length in the harbour of salvation. His feet stand already in the Courts of Jerusalem, and Him whom he had heard of in Ephrata he has found in the broad woods, and willingly worships in the place where his feet have stayed. He has entered into the Holy City, and has obtained an heritage with those of whom it is rightly said : *Now ye are no longer strangers and foreigners, but fellow-citizens with the saints and of the household of God* (Ephesians ii. 19). He goes in and out with the saints, and is become as one of them, praising God and saying as they : *Our conversation is in heaven* (Philip. iii. 20). He is become, therefore, not a curious spectator only, but a devoted inhabitant and an enrolled citizen of Jerusalem ; but not the Jerusalem of this world with which is joined Mount Sinai, in Arabia, which is in bondage with her children, but of her who is above, who is free, and the mother of us all (Gal. iv. 25-26).

2. And this, if you are willing to perceive it, is Clairvaux. This is Jerusalem, and is associated by a certain

[1] This Alexander was Bishop of Lincoln in England from 1123 to 1147.

intuition of the spirit, by the entire devotion of the heart, and by conformity of daily life, with her which is in heaven. This shall be, as he promises himself, his rest for ever. He has chosen her for his habitation, because with her is, although not yet the realization, at least the expectation, of true peace of which it is said : *The peace of God which passes all understanding* (Philip. iv. 17). But this is true happiness ; although he has received it from above, he desires to embrace it with your good permission, or rather he trusts that he has done this according to your wish, knowing that you are not ignorant of that sentence of the wise man, that a wise son is the glory of his father.[1] He makes request, therefore, of your Paternity, and we also make request with him and for him, to be so kind as to allow the payments which he has assigned to his creditors[2] from his prebend to remain unaltered, so that he may not be found (which God forbid) a defaulter and breaker of his covenant, and so that the offering of a contrite heart, which he makes daily, may not be rejected by God, inasmuch as any brother has a claim against him. And lastly, he entreats that the house which he has built for his mother upon Church land, with the ground which he has assigned there, may be preserved to his mother during her life. Thus much with regard to Philip.

3. I have thought well to add these few words for yourself, of my own accord, or rather at the inspiration of God, and venture to exhort you in all charity, not to look to the glory of the world which passeth away, and to lose that which abides eternally ; not to love your riches more than yourself, nor for yourself, lest you lose yourself and them also. Do not, while present prosperity smiles upon you, forget its certain end, lest adversity without end succeed it. Let not the joy of this present life hide from you the sorrow

---

[1] Prov. x. 1. Bernard always quotes this passage thus. In the VULGATE it is, *Filius sapiens lætificat patrem.*

[2] Letter 18 from the Abbot Philip to Alexander the Third is on a very similar subject, and begs that the property of the Archdeacon of Orleans, who had become a monk, should be given up to his creditors (*Biblioth. Cisterc.* Vol. i. p. 246).

which it brings about, and brings about while it hides. Do not think death far off, so that it come upon you unprepared, and while in expectation of long life it suddenly leaves you when ill-prepared, as it is written : *When they say Peace and safety, then sudden destruction cometh upon them, as travail upon a woman with child, and they shall not escape* (1 Thess. v. 3). Farewell.

LETTER LXV. (*Circa* A.D. 1129.)

To Alvisus, Abbot of Anchin.

He praises the fatherly gentleness of Alvisus towards Godwin. He excuses himself, and asks pardon for having admitted him.

To Alvisus, Abbot of Anchin.[1]

1. May God render to you the same mercy which you have shown towards your holy son Godwin. I know that at the news of his death you showed yourself unmindful of old complaints, and remembering only your friendship for him, behaved with kindness, not resentment, and putting aside the character of judge, showed yourself a father in circumstances that required it. Therefore, you strove to render to him all the duties of charity and piety which a father ought to render to a son. What better, what more praiseworthy, what more worthy of yourself could you have done ? But who believed this ? Truly no one knows what is in man, except the spirit of man which is in him

---

[1] A monastery of the Benedictine Order on the river Scarpe two miles from Douai. It dates from 1029, and was at first named S. Saviour. It was situated on an island named Anchin, and was founded by two illustrious persons, Sicher and Gautier, under the episcopate of Gerard II., Bishop of Cambray, to whose diocese that place then belonged. The monks of Anchin were associated with the congregation of Cluny, whose reform they accepted in 1110. The name and glory of Anchin were greatly increased by the College in the Academy of Douai, which John Lentailler, the very worthy abbot of that place, gave with remarkable and praiseworthy generosity to the Fathers of the Society of Jesus. Alvisus, who is mentioned in Letter 66, became Bishop of Arras, on which Anchin depended, in 1131. Letter 395 is addressed to him.

(1 Cor. ii. 11). Where is now that austerity, that severity, that indignation which tongue, eyes, and countenance were accustomed to display and terribly to pour upon him? Scarcely is the death of your son named to you than your fatherly bosom is moved. Suddenly all these sentiments which were adopted for a purpose, and therefore only for a time, disappeared, and those which were truly yours, but were concealed — charity, piety, benignity — appeared. Therefore in your pious mind mercy and truth have met together, and because mercy has certainly prevailed over judgment, *righteousness and peace have kissed each other* (Ps. lxxxv. 10). For as far as I seem to be able to form an idea, I think I see what passed in your mind then, when truth, fired with zeal for justice, prepared to avenge the injury which it seemed to you had been done. The sentiment of mercy which, after the example of Joseph, prudently dissimulated at first, yet not enduring longer to be concealed, and in this also like to Joseph (Gen. xlv. 1), burst forth from the hidden fount of piety, and making common cause with truth, repressed agitation, calmed wrath, made peace with justice.

2. Then from the pure and peaceful fountain of your heart poured forth like limpid streams such thoughts as these: What need have I to be angry? Would it not be better to pity him, and not to forget what is written, *I will have mercy and not sacrifice* (Hos. vi. 6), and to fulfil what is ordered, *Study to keep the unity of the Spirit in the bond of peace* (Eph. iv. 3), so as to be able to count on what is promised, *Blessed are the merciful, for they shall obtain mercy* (S. Matt. v. 7)? After all, was not that man my son? And who can rage against his son?— unless, perhaps, he was only then my son when he was with me, and not also when he deserted me. In withdrawing from me in body for a time, has he withdrawn equally from my heart, or can even death take him away from me? Must the necessity of the body and of place so hamper the freedom of souls which love each other? I am quite sure that neither distance of places, nor the absence, or even the

death, of our bodies would be able to disjoin those whom one spirit animates, one affection binds together. Finally, if *the souls of the righteous are in the hand of God* (Wisd. iii. 1), we, both those who are already at rest, having laid down the burden of the flesh, and those who, being still in the flesh, do not war according to the flesh, beyond a doubt are still together. Mine he was when living, mine he will be dead, and I shall recognize him as mine in the common fatherland. If there is any who is able to tear him from the Hands of God, then he may be able to separate him from me also.

3. Thus your affection, father, has enabled you to make excuses for your son. But what has it said of me, or what satisfaction from me will be worthy of you, which you could impose for the great injury inflicted upon you, because when your son left you he was received by me? What can I say? If I should plead I have not received him (would I were able to say so without sin) it would be a falsehood. If I should plead I received him, indeed, but with good reason, I should seem to wish to excuse myself. The safer way will be to answer, I did wrong. But how far did I do wrong? I do not say it by way of defence, but by whom would he not be received? Who, I say, would repel that good man from his door when he knocked, or expel him when once received? But who knows if God did not wish to supply our need out of your abundance, so that He directed to us one of the many holy men who were then in great number in your house, for our consolation, indeed, but none the less for a glory to you? For a wise son is the glory of his father (Prov. x. 1). Moreover, I did not make any solicitation to him beforehand. I did not gain him over by promises to desert you or to come to us. Quite on the contrary, God is my witness. I did not consent to receive him until he begged me to do so, until he knocked at my door and entreated to have it opened, until I had tried to send him back to you, but as he would not agree to that I at length yielded to his importunity. But if it is a fault that I received him, a monk, a stranger, alone, and

received him in the way I did, it will not be unworthy of
you to pardon such a fault, which was committed once only,
for it is not lawful for you to deny forgiveness even to those
who sin against you seventy times seven.

4. But yet I wish that you should know that I do not
treat this matter lightly or negligently, and on the contrary
that I cannot pardon myself for ever having offended your
Reverence in any manner. I call God to witness that often
I have in mind (since I was not able to do it in body) thrown
myself at your feet as a suppliant, and I often see myself
before you making apology on my knees. Would that the
Holy Spirit who perhaps inspired me with these feelings
make you also feel with what tears and regrets worthy
of pity I humble myself at this moment before your knees
as if you were present. How many times with bare
shoulders, and bearing the rods in my hands, prepared, as it
were, to strike at your bidding; I seek your pardon, and
trembling wait for your forgiveness! I earnestly desire,
my father, to learn from you, if it is not too painful for you
to write to me, that you receive my excuses, so that if they
are sufficient I may be consoled by your indulgence, but if
on the contrary I must be more humiliated (as it is just)
that I may endeavour, whatever else I can do, to give you
fuller satisfaction. Farewell.

LETTER LXVI. (*Circa* A.D. 1129.)

TO GEOFFREY, ABBOT OF S. MEDARD.[1]

*He begs Geoffrey's help in reconciling him with Abbot
Alvisus, and consoles him in his tribulations.*

To Dom GEOFFREY, Abbot of S. Medard, Brother
BERNARD, unworthy superior of Clairvaux, health everlasting.

[1] All the printed copies, and MSS., which I have seen, except one, have *S. Thierry*,
but it should be read *S. Medard*, as in the Corbey copy, from which I restore the
following inscription, which is wanting in others, except in *Spicilegium*, Vol. iii.,
Domno, etc. But although Geoffrey was successively Abbot of St. Medard at
Soissons, and S. Thierry at Rheims, he was then Abbot of S. Medard, when this

In the first place, I beg that you would be so good as to forward the enclosed letter to the lord Abbot of Anchin, and that you would not fail to do what you can in favour of your absent friend, as opportunity shall serve, that he obtain that which it asks. For I ought not to conceal the cause of offence, whether just or unjust, which anyone, and especially so venerable a father has against me ; which that I may not do, I should perhaps have been better able to explain my meaning better by speech than by writing, for in such matters word of mouth is wont to be more acceptable than written words, and the tongue than the pen. The expression of the eye gives confidence in the words. Nor is the hand able to express our sentiments as is the countenance. But now not being able in my absence to do as I would, I have recourse to you to give satisfaction as far as I can. I entreat you, then, again and again to take away, as far as in you lies, this offence from the kingdom of God, which is on our account, lest if this resentment endure (which may God forbid) until the day when the Angels shall be charged themselves to take away that offence, we may both be left without excuse. Concerning the tribulations of which you complained to me some time since, you know that it is said, *The Lord is nigh unto them who are of a troubled spirit* (Ps. xxxiv. 18). Trust in Him because He hath overcome the world. He knows among what people you are dwelling, and those who trouble you are in His sight. He who now tries you by the waters of persecution, He will grant you a refuge from the tempest. Farewell.

Letter was written. For it was written, as can be gathered from the order of the Letters, before the year 1131, in which Geoffrey was raised to the Bishopric of Chalons-sur-Marne from the Abbacy of S. Medard, which he had held since 1119. He had been previously Abbot of S. Thierry for eight years.

LETTER LXVII. (*Circa* A.D. 1125.)

TO THE MONKS OF FLAY.[1]

He justifies his reception of B., a monk, as being from a monastery entirely unknown to him, and having just causes for his departure.

To Dom H., Superior of the Convent of Flay, and to the brethren who are with him, the brethren in Clairvaux wish health.

1. We learn by your letter that your Reverence is aggrieved because we have received one of your monks among us. I also am much grieved, fearing that this grief of yours be not that whereof the Apostle said : *Ye were made sorry according to God* (2 Cor. vii. 9). For if it had been according to God it would not have so provoked you, and you would not have shown so much bitterness and violence in the reproaches which you make to us, the first time that you write to us, since although we are un-

---

[1] Thus, after the best MSS., and not *of Flavigny* (*Flaviniacenses*), as Horstius and some others affirm. The context furnishes three convincing proofs of this. For, first, Bernard asserts in this Letter to the monks, to whom he writes : "We have had no knowledge of nor have we ever heard the least mention of your house, nor of the sanctity of your life, up to the present time." Then he adds : "We are separated from each other by a long distance, by different provinces, and by difference of language." And, lastly : "Not only are we not resident in the same diocese, but we do not belong to the same archbishopric." And it is too evident to need proof that these expressions do not at all apply to the Abbey of Flavigny. For Flavigny is a town in the Duchy of Burgundy, not far from Fontaines, where Bernard was born, nor a very great distance from Clairvaux, having an Abbey of Benedictines, which was in the Diocese of Autun, the Archbishopric of Lyons, just as Clairvaux was, and which possessed the relics of a holy queen. We must, therefore, restore "of Flay" (*Flaviacenses*), a little village of the Diocese of Beauvais, on the Epte, where S. Germer founded, in 650, a famous monastery of Benedictines ; whence it was sometimes called Flay, sometimes S. Germer of Flay.

· As for the name of the abbot, whom Bernard indicates by his first Letter to Dom H., Abbot of Flay, I think that it is no other than Hildegaire I., who was Abbot of Flay from 1106 to 1123, as is stated in the Catalogue of Acherius, following Guibert. But I collect from the order of these Letters that he was still abbot in 1126. Some think (but wrongly) that Hugo is meant in this place.

known to you, and we have never yet held communication by speech or by letter, we are none the less your brethren, and if you permit me to say so, even your friends. You wonder, as you write us, that we have received Brother Benedict[1] among us, and you address threats to us unless we immediately send him back. You remind us that the Rule forbids a monk to be received from a known monastery, and you are no doubt persuaded that yours is not unknown. But what if it is known to others, provided that it is not known to us? Even although, as you tell me, the reputation of your community has so spread that the history of your church is known even at Rome; yet it has, I know not how, so passed over us, who are a long way this side of Rome, that we have never heard speak of you the least in the world, neither of your abbot nor of your monks, nor of the very name of your house, nor have we the least knowledge of the sanctity of your life up to the present time. Nor is that wonderful, considering that we are separated from each other by a long distance, by different provinces, and by difference of language. Not only are we not residing in the same diocese, but we do not belong to the same archbishopric. We think, then, that we are prohibited from receiving monks only from monasteries which are known to us, and not from those which others know; otherwise, since there is no monastery which is not known to somebody, not one would be left from which monks might properly be received. How, then, would that be fulfilled which was permitted and even ordered by the blessed Benedict, that a stranger monk ought not only to be received as a guest, as long as he pleases to remain, but also to be urged to remain permanently, if he is found useful to the community?

2. We, nevertheless, took another course with regard to the brother before mentioned. For when he came humbly praying to be received by us he was at first repulsed, and

---

[1] In the printed copies the initial G. is found, in not a few MSS. B. That of Corbey, which is most highly estimated, has the full name *Benedict*, and following it we have restored the name in several places.

then bidden to return to his own monastery. But he not being willing to do this, betook himself to a hermitage near us, and there dwelt quietly almost seven months, without any evil report of him arising. But not thinking it safe for himself to live alone, he was not ashamed, after this first repulse, to ask of us again what he had asked before. We a second time admonished him about his return, and when we inquired the cause of his departure he said : " My abbot treated me not as a monk but as a physician.[1] He obliged me to serve, or rather he himself served by means of me, not God, but the world ; since, in order not to incur the ill-will of secular princes, he used to compel me to give medical care to tyrants, robbers, and excommunicate. I declared to him both in public and in private the peril which my soul incurred ; but as this was to no purpose, I at length, relying on the advice of certain wise men, fled from the destruction of my soul, not from religion or from my community. Do not reject one who seeks salvation, open the door to one who knocks." At the sight of his perseverance, having heard his reason, and knowing no ill of him, we granted him admission ; we approved him after his time of probation, we admitted him to make profession, and now we consider him as one of us. We did not compel him to enter, and now we will not oblige him to depart. And if we should drive him out he would not (as he asserts) return to you, but would fly still farther from you. Cease then, brethren, to persecute unoffending people with unmerited reproaches, and to trouble them with useless letters, because we will not be provoked even by reiterated insults to reply to you otherwise than with respect ; nor will we be terrified into not keeping among us a monk whom we believe that we have received according to the Rule.

[1] Formerly clerks and monks used to act as physicians. As to clerks, Christianus Lupus shows that in notes upon various Letters, both of the Ephesine and Chalcedonian Council (p. 100, *et seqq.*) As to monks, various examples are cited, of which a remarkable one is in Lupus Ferrariensis Ep. 72, respecting Dido, Abbot of Sens. Modern law forbids the practice of medicine to monks as well as to clergy. (Mabillon's note.)

LETTER LXVIII.

To the Same, upon the Same Subject.

To the Reverend the Abbot of Flay, to the brethren of that convent, and to certain others, Brother BERNARD wishes health.

MY GOOD BRETHREN,—

1. It would have been a proof of moderation on your part had you shown yourselves satisfied with my former explanation in answer to your complaint, and refrained from harassing those who do not deserve it. But as to your former attacks you have added greater ones, and have thrown among us new germs of discord (which, we trust, will no more be fruitful than the former were), and as by not replying I may seem to acknowledge fault where there is none, I reply truthfully a second time to what you angrily object. This is the whole of my fault, which you consider so great; this the vast injustice that I have done to you; that a monk, alone, a wanderer, poor, miserable, flying from peril to his soul, seeking earnestly his own salvation, at his earnest application and request we have received; or that having thus received him, we do not eject him without cause, and so make ourselves prevaricators, destroyers of what we have built. For this we are considered transgressors of the Rule, of the canons, of the law of nature itself! You demand with indignation, why we have presumed to admit among us a monk of yours, excommunicated by you, which we would not suffer ourselves. But as to the excommunication, why need we reply, when you give a sufficient reply yourselves for us, since you know without doubt that he was received by us, before he was excommunicated by you? But if he was regularly received, it is a monk under our jurisdiction and not under yours, that you have excommunicated: and you will see, whether that was rightly done.

2. It remains therefore to be ascertained, whether he was rightly received; and this is the sole question between

us. You indeed, since you cannot deny that a monk may regularly be received from a monastery that is unknown, contend that yours was known to us. We deny it, and you do not believe us. But if you do not believe us in a simple denial, do so when we affirm by oath. I take God to witness that I did not know you, and do not know you; I have received the writings of unknown persons and I have replied to unknown persons. I feel indeed your violence and your attacks, but yet I am not acquainted with the assailants themselves. But you for the purpose of convincing me of pretended ignorance, employ the crushing argument that those cannot be unknown to me whose name, that of the abbot and of the monastery itself I have placed in my letters; as if when you know the names of things you know the things themselves also. Since in that case I have the pleasure to know the names of Michael and Gabriel and Raphael, by the mere hearing of these words, I am already blessed by the knowledge of those blessed spirits themselves. It is no small profit to me, I say, if because I have learned from the Apostle to call by their names Paradise and the third Heaven, I have therefore, though not rapt thither with the Apostle, learned the secrets of Heaven from their names alone, and heard unspeakable words which it is not lawful for man to utter. Foolish am I who, already knowing the name of my God, yet still groan superfluously every day, I know not why; uselessly sighing with the Prophet, and saying, *Thy face O Lord will I seek* (Ps. xxvii. 8). And *When shall I come to appear before God* (Ps. xlii. 2). And: *Show us Thy Face, and we shall be saved* (Ps. lxxx. 3).

3. But what is it we do towards you which we are unwilling to be done towards us ? Do you suppose that we are unwilling that any monk departing from our monastery should be received in any other ? Would that you might be able to save without us all those committed to us. If any monk of ours should have passed over to you for the sake of greater perfection, or from the desire of a severer life, not only are we not offended if you assist him in so good a wish, but we

earnestly entreat you to do so: nor should we complain as persons offended, but confess ourselves to have received a great service. Then you deny what we had heard of you, that Brother B. as long as he was with you, practised the medical art by your consent or even by your order upon secular persons, and you accuse of falsehood him who has said this. Whether he has told the truth I know not; let him see to it; but this I know, that if he practised medicine, whether of his own accord, as you declare, or to obey you, as he testifies, he exposed his soul to great dangers. Who, then, could be so inhuman as not to help a person in such peril if he were able, or to counsel him if he were not able? And if, as you assert, that it was not compelled by obedience but by the desire of gain for himself, or a taste for wandering, that he used to travel about here and there making merchandise of his art; what cause existed for his leaving you? Was it because by the tightening of pastoral discipline, that was no longer permitted to him which had been permitted before? But in that case why did you, when he was with us, wishing to recall him, promise him that he should remain quiet in the convent, for the purpose of persuading him to return; unless that you knew that the man wished for this, and remembered that he had asked for it? but he, having already obtained among strangers what he could not obtain among his own, nor desiring to quit the certain for the uncertain, has held fast what he already enjoyed, despising what was offered to him too late.

4. Cease, then, my brethren, cease, from being careful for a brother for whom it is not at all needful that you should take care: unless, perhaps, which I hope is not the case, you seek your own interests and not those of Jesus Christ, and love more the advantage which you derive from him than his salvation. For since he was always when among you a rolling stone,[1] and, as you write, expending for his own purposes what he acquired by his art, against the obligations of his condition and the command of his abbot; let those who love him rejoice, because by the pity of God he

[1] Gyro vagus.

has, while among us, been entirely cured. For we give our testimony to him that never now does he wander abroad on any pretence, but remains quietly in the monastery; he lives without complaint as a poor man among poor men. Far from regarding, as you say, the first engagements which he made as null and void, he now considers them valid, and accomplishes them all without exception, which, when with you, he failed to do ; and this with a regularity and perfect obedience without which he deceives himself who trusts in his stability of place. I entreat you, then, brethren, that your indignation may now be calmed and your inquietude cease. But if otherwise, do what you please, write as you please, persecute me as much as you please; charity endures all things, suffers all things. For I am quite re-solved not to abandon on account of this matter the purest affection, the deepest respect, and a brotherly consideration towards you.

LETTER LXIX.

To Guy,[1] Abbot of Trois Fontaines.[2]

He instructs Guy what to do. The latter had conse-crated by mistake a Chalice, in which, by oversight of the servers, there was no wine.

1. I know, my dear friend, that you are distressed, and I praise you for being so, if your distress be not excessive ; for you are, I believe, distressed, as the Apostle says,

[1] He was the second abbot of Trois Fontaines, and has been already praised in Letter 63 ; he had succeeded Roger, the first abbot, in 1129. See, respecting his death, Letter 71.

[2] The Abbey of Trois Fontaines, first daughter house of Clairvaux, was founded, as William, Abbot of S. Thierry, states (*Life of S. Bernard*, B. i. c. 13), in 1118, in the Diocese of Châlons-sur-Marne, with the assistance of William of Champeaux, then Bishop of that see.

It was by the Abbey of Trois Fontaines that was created that of Haute Fon-taine, in the same Diocese of Châlons-sur-Marne.

It was another abbey of Trois Fontaines, or of SS. Vincent and Anastasius, at Tres Fontes, near Rome, to which abbey the election of Abbot Turold refers, of which mention is made in Letter 306.

according to God (2 Cor. vii. 9); nor is it doubtful that sorrow of this kind will be one day changed into joy. Therefore, be angry and sin not, for you will sin not less by too much anger than by no anger at all. For not to be angry when where is cause for anger is to be unwilling to correct what is wrong; but to be more angry than there is cause for being is to add sin to sin; and if it is wrong not to correct what is wrong, how much more would it not be to increase it? If judgment depended on the issue of actions inculpated, your sorrow, however great, could not be blamed, since, unquestionably, it rests on the fact that the fault had been great. For a fault would appear the graver the more sacred is the matter which it is concerned with. But as it is the motive and not the matter, the intention and not the result of actions which distinguishes between praise and blame, according to the word of the Lord, *If thine eye be single, thy whole body shall be full of light : but if thine eye be evil, thy whole body shall be full of darkness* (S. Matt. vi. 22, 23); therefore, in the examination of your act, I consider the dignity of holy things is not so much the point to be regarded as your own intention. Furthermore, our Prior and I, after thinking over the whole matter privately and consulting together about it, decided that in it there was ignorance on your part, and negligence on the part of the servers ; but evidently no ill intention in either. And you know well that no work is good unless it be founded in good will. How then can an act not done with consent of the will be a great sin? Otherwise, if it were the case that without the assent of the will, a good action indeed obtains no approval, but a bad one severe punishment ; that would be as much as to say, that for one and the same cause both evil is reckoned and good not credited ; and whosoever thinks thus let him assert, if he will, that good does not prevail over evil, but that evil prevails over good.

2. Nevertheless, in order to set at rest your troubled conscience, and lest perhaps this lamentable occurrence should be a warning of some secret sin lurking still in the monas-

tery, I enjoin upon you by way of penance to recite[1] the Seven Penitential Psalms daily until Easter, seven times prostrating yourself, and to receive the discipline seven times. In this manner also let him who ministered to you at that Mass make satisfaction. But as for him who had made the preparations[2] beforehand and had forgotten to put wine into the chalice, his fault I consider greater than that of others, and, if you agree with me, I leave him to your judgment. If a report of this has gone forth among the brethren, I think that they also should severally receive the discipline, that that may be fulfilled which is written, *Bear ye one another's burdens* (Gal. vi. 2). Afterwards, I greatly approve of your having poured some wine into the chalice, upon a particle of the consecrated Host, when the negligence had been found out, though it was found out too late ; and I consider that the liquid, though not changed by a proper and solemn consecration into the Body and Blood of Christ, yet became hallowed by the contact with the Sacred Body.[3] It is said, nevertheless, that some other writer, I know not whom, was of another opinion, and thought that the Sacrifice could not be without the three—bread, wine, and water ; so that if either of the three should be in any case wanting, the other two were not consecrated. But on this point every-one must be satisfied in his own mind.

3. For myself, if the same thing had happened to me, I should (according to my poor opinion) proceed to repair the omission in one out of two ways : either that which you did, or I would rather have iterated the sacred words from that place where it is said, " Likewise after supper He took the cup " (simili modo postquam cœnatum est), and

---

[1] *Decantare, i.e.,* to recite, in which sense the word is used everywhere among old writers. " The holy Bishop Ambrose," says the Ven. Bede, speaking concerning the Faith, directs the faithful to recite (*decantent*) the words of the Creed in matins.

[2] Some MSS. have *apparaverat.*

[3] This was also the opinion of James de Vitry, besides the scholastics (*Hist. Occident,* p. 427). He proposes the present case (*Ibid.* 444). See my *Comm. in Ordinem Rom.* and our Edmund Martene, *de Ritibus monasticis* (B. ii. c. 7).

so have supplied what remained to do of the sacrifice.[1]
For I could not possibly doubt that the Body was already
consecrated, according to the Rite of the Church, since I
have learned from the Church, what she also has learned
from her Lord, to present Bread and Wine together; yet (I
have not learned) to be confident that the Mystery is con-
summated in these together. Since, then, according to the
custom of the Church, the Body is perfected from bread,
before the Blood from wine: if by forgetfulness, that
which is to be consecrated the later, is presented too late,
I do not see why that lateness of the latter should annul
the preceding consecration. For I think that if it had
pleased the Lord, after His Body made from bread, to
intermit for a little while the consecration of the wine, or
even altogether to omit it, none the less His Body which
He had made[2] would have remained, nor would things not
yet done affect those done. It is not that I deny that bread
and wine mixed with water ought to be presented together,
on the contrary, I assert that it ought to be thus done and
not otherwise; but it is one thing to blame negligence,
and another to deny efficacy (as a result of it); in the
one case we assert that all things are not done as they
should be, in the other we deny that they are done at all.
In the meantime, you have here what I think and feel
about this matter, without the least unwillingness to consider either your opinion, if it be wiser than mine, or that
of any other better qualified person.

LETTER LXX.

To the Same.

*Bernard reminds him what feelings of mercy a pastor
ought to have, and advises him to withdraw a sentence
which he had passed upon an offending monk.*

[1] See *General Rubrics of the Mass*: chap., "Concerning Defects in Matter;"
art., "Concerning Defect of Wine."

[2] *Fecerat*, otherwise *fuerat*.

To the Lord Abbot GUY, Brother BERNARD, health, with
the spirit of wisdom and piety.[1]

Considering the miserable condition of this unhappy
man, I feel myself touched with pity, but I fear lest it be
in vain.   Yet even though he should remain in his unhappy
state I do not think that my pity would be altogether
wasted, but would be of advantage, at least to me.   The
pity which I feel is not, however, prompted by any advantage to myself, but a brotherly sympathy is produced in
my inmost heart by the misery of a brother.   Pity is a
feeling which is not governed by the will, nor subjected to
the reason, nor is anyone drawn to it by deliberate purpose ;
but it necessarily imposes itself of its own accord on compassionate hearts at the sight of the suffering of others, so
that even if it were a sin to be moved with compassion I
could not help pitying, even if I wished.   The reason and
the will would, indeed, be able to prevent our acting upon
the feeling; but could they eradicate the feeling itself?
Far from me be those who would console me by saying
that my prayer shall return unto my own bosom, although
he for whom it is offered is not yet converted.   Nor do I
listen to those who flatter me by quoting: *The righteousness of the righteous shall be upon him* (Ezek. xviii. 20)
while the wicked still remains in his impiety.   No, I say, I
cannot be consoled while I see the desolation of a brother.
If, then, my dear son, your pious mind is similarly affected,
or rather because it is similarly affected, although that unhappy man seems to have practised shameful and repeated
flight from the monastery after having returned, yet
because he thinks otherwise, you ought to listen, not only
patiently but also willingly to what he humbly urges (however ill-founded), if perchance any reasonable opportunity
may be found for saving a man whose safety is despaired
of; which (as your experience, equally with my own,
teaches) is difficult to find even in congregation, but is
much more difficult when he is without in the world.   Do
not disdain, therefore, having called an assembly of all the

---

[1] This inscription has been restored from the Corbey MS., No. 553.

brethren, to recall all the censures that you have launched against him, insomuch that his contumacy shall be healed by your humility, and perhaps some means may be found, without violating the Rule, for receiving him once more. Nor need you fear that by this retractation you will displease our just and merciful God, if mercy shall be exalted above justice.[1]   Farewell.

[1] Out of eight MS. copies of this Letter which I have seen, there are five in which the following addition is found after these words, viz., two of Cîteaux, one of Vauluisant, one of Corbey, and five of Foucarmont; but in three Colbertine MSS. it is wanting :—

"*A similar case, which I remember to have happened to me. I adduce as an example to you. A certain brother (otherwise Bartholomew) I one day, carried away by anger because he had vexed me, bade with threatening voice and look to go out of the monastery ; he immediately went out, and proceeding to one of our farmhouses there remained. Which being known, I wished to recall him ; but he replied that he would only return if he might take his previous order and standing, instead of being last of all; and not as a fugitive, but as one rashly and without reasonable judgment driven forth ; because, he said, he ought not to submit to the ordinary judgment of the Rule in returning, as that had not been waited for in expelling him. Not wishing to decide on his answer and my action myself, since I distrusted my own judgment on account of a feeling of carnal resentment, I committed the matter to the judgment of all the brethren. Therefore in my absence it was decided that his recall ought not to be subject to the precept of the Rule, as it appeared that his expulsion had not been regularly made. If, then, so great and pious consideration was shown in the case of one who had once only gone out of his monastery, what ought not to be shown for your monk in the situation of peril in which he is?*"

This entire addition appears to me entirely alien as well to the character of Bernard as to his conduct. That transport of rage, and headlong ejection of a monk from the convent could never have been found in so good a man. He had without doubt ardent zeal, but founded on gentleness and clemency, as appears even in this Letter, where he urges the showing of so much lenity to a deserter. Besides, if our Saint had fallen into this fault he would rather have buried it in silence, and striven to efface it by penitence ; nor would he have committed such an imprudence, as to adduce to Abbot Guy for an example, what would have been so contrary to the object of Bernard himself, and an occasion of scandal to Guy. I think, then, that this story was cited at first by some abbot, perhaps on the margin of a Codex, it may be one of the Cistercian MSS., and then removed from the margin to the text, and that from this Codex others received it ; but by no means any of those at Clairvaux, which in this matter are of the greatest weight.

LETTER LXXI. (A.D. 1127.)

To the Monks of the Same Place.

*He excuses himself for having hitherto put off making a
visit to them, not from negligence on his part, but from
waiting for a suitable opportunity ; he consoles them for
the death of their Abbot, Roger.*

Do not impute it to negligence that I have not come to
you yet. I care for you indeed as for my own bowels. If
a mother is able to neglect the care of her own child, then
can I be suspected of neglecting you. I have been waiting,
and I am waiting now, only for an opportunity, so that when
I come my visit may not be without profit. In the meantime, let not your heart be troubled for the departure of
your father. God, we hope, will provide him a worthy successor. Nor, indeed, is he lost to you ; the Lord has translated him, not taken him entirely away. Only he, who was
your own peculiar property, now belongs to us all as well.
Until I come to you, work bravely, let your hearts be comforted, and let all your actions be done in charity. Farewell.

LETTER LXXII.

To Rainald, Abbot of Foigny.[1]

*Bernard declares to him how little he loves praise ; that
the yoke of Christ is light ; that he declines the name of
father, and is content with that of brother.*

1. In the first place, do not wonder if titles of honour[2]
affright me, when I feel myself so unworthy of the honours

---

[1] Foigny, in the Diocese of Laon, one of the daughter houses of Clairvaux,
was founded by Bishop Bartholomew in 1131. Rainald was the first abbot of
that house, and to him this Letter was written. Concerning Foigny, see Letter
5 and *Life of S. Bernard*, n. 25.

[2] Bernard refers to the titles of *Dom* (*Domnus*, for it is written thus) and
Father. Truly a wonderful example of modesty in Bernard to show himself
afraid of titles of dignity, in which others rejoice more than in the dignities them-

themselves; and if it is fitting that you should give them to me, it is not expedient for me to accept them. For if you think that you ought to observe that saying, *In honour preferring one another* (Rom. xii. 10), and: *Submit yourselves one to another in the fear of God* (Eph. v. 21), yet the terms *one another, one to another,* are not used at random, and concern me as well as you. Again, if you think that the declaration of the Rule is to be observed, "Let the younger honour their elders,"[1] I remember what the Truth has ruled: *The last shall be first, and the first last* (S. Matt. xx. 16), and, *He that is the greater among you, let him be as the younger* (S. Luke xxii. 26), and *The greater thou art, the more humble thyself* (Ecclus. iii. 18), and *Not because we have dominion over your faith, but are helpers of your joy* (2 Cor. i. 24), and, *Have they made thee the master? Be then among them as one of them* (Ecclus. xxxii. 1), and *Be ye not called Rabbi; and Call no man your father upon the earth* (S. Matt. xxiii. 8, 9). As much, then,

selves. We find a similar example (besides those which I have collected above, in notes on Letter 11) in the *Life of the Blessed Mechthildis,* c. 10. " Sister Mechthildis," says the author, " desired that she should not be called *Dame* [*Domna*], and refused every appellative of rank; but the custom of the house and the Rule of the convent required that she should be called *Dame* and *Abbess.*" Augustus (Suetonius, August. Vit. c. 53) always disliked the title of Lord (Dominus) as an opprobrium and a sort of curse. Tiberius himself regarded it as a kind of outrage. Thence it came about that writers in later times, wishing to employ an expression less ambitious, cut off a syllable from the word, and gave the title of *dom* to holy personages, Bishops, and others, up to the time of Bernard. So Severus Sulpicius Ep. 2, "They announce that Dom Martin was dead." So Gregory the Great, B. i. Ep. 6, and B. vii. Ep. 127; so everywhere in the Epistles of Didier of Cahors and in Gregory of Tours, *Hist.* B. ix. cap 42, from whom the custom was derived to the Spaniards and Italians. We see also among the modern Greeks the word κύριος changed into κύρος, as our Hugh Menard has very learnedly observed in his *notes ad Concord. Regul.* cap. 70. Our holy father Benedict makes mention of this word *Domnus* in the Rule, c. 63, where we read : " Let the Abbot, who seems to act in the place of Christ, be called Domnus and Abbas, not as arrogating it to himself, but for the honour and love of Christ." And although this name was by the Rule granted to the Abbot only, yet in process of time it was given, like that of Father, to all monks who were Priests. (See on this subject Menard *l.c.*; Häften B. iii. *Dissert.* 4 and 5; Jul. Nigron. in Reg. comm. Soc. Jesu Reg. 22).

[1] Rule of S. Benedict cap. 63.

as I am carried away by your compliments, so much am I
restrained by the weight of these texts. Wherefore I
rightly, I do not say sing, but mourn; *While I suffer Thy
terrors I am distracted* (Ps. lxxxviii. 15), and *Thou hast
lifted me up and cast me down* (Ps. cii. 10). But I should,
perhaps, represent more truly what I feel if I say that he who
exalts me really humiliates me ; and he who humiliates me,
exalts. You, therefore, rather depress me in heaping me
with terms of honour, and exalt me by humbling. But that
you may not humble so as to crush me, these and similar
testimonies of the Truth console me, which wonderfully
raise up those whom they make humble, instruct while they
humiliate. Thus this same Hand that casts me down
raises me up again and makes me sing with joy. *It
was good for me, O Lord, that I was afflicted, that I
might learn Thy statutes ; the law of Thy mouth is good
unto me, above thousands of gold and silver* (Ps. cxix. 71,
72). This marvel the word of God, living and efficacious,
produces. This, that Word by which all things are done,
gently and powerfully brings to pass ; this, in short, is the
work of the easy yoke and light burden of Christ (S. Matt.
xi. 30).

2. We cannot but wonder how light is the burden of
Truth. Is not that truly light which does not burden, but
relieves him who bears it ? What lighter than that weight,
which not only does not burden, but even bears everyone upon whom it is laid to bear? This weight was
able to render fruitful the Virgin's womb, but not
to burden it.[1] This weight sustained the very arms
of the aged Simeon, in which He was received. This
caught up Paul, though with weighty and corruptible
body, into the third heaven. I seek in all things to find if
possible something like to this weight which bears them who
bear it, and I find nothing but the wings of birds which in
any degree resembles it, for these in a certain singular
manner render the body of birds at once more weighty and
more easily moved. Wonderful work of nature! that at

---

[1] *Gravidare ; gravare.*—[E.]

the same time increases the material and lightens the burden, and while the mass is greater the burden is in the same degree less. Thus plainly in the wings is expressed the likeness of the burden of Christ, because they themselves bear that by which they are borne. What shall I say of a chariot? This, too, increases the load of the horse by which it is drawn, but at the same time renders capable of being drawn a load which without it could not be moved. Load is added to load, yet the whole is lighter. See also how the Chariot of the Gospel comes to the weighty load of the Law, and helps to carry it on to perfection, while decreasing the difficulty. *His word,* it is said, *runneth very swiftly* (Ps. cxlvii. 15). His word, before known only in Judea, and not able, because of its weightiness, to extend beyond, which burdened and weighed down the hands of Moses himself, when lightened by Grace, and placed upon the wheels of the Gospel, ran swiftly over the whole earth, and reached in its rapid flight the confines of the world.

3. Do you, therefore, my very dear friend, cease from overwhelming me rather than raising with undeserved honours; otherwise you range yourself, though with a friendly intention, in the company of my enemies. These are they of whom I am in the habit of thus complaining to God alone in my prayers. Those who praised me were sworn against me (Ps. cii. 8, Vulg.). To this, my complaint, I hear God soon replying, and bearing witness to the truth of my words: *Truly they which bless thee lead thee into error* (Is. ix. 16, *cited from memory*). Then I reply, *Let them be soon brought to shame who say unto me, There, There!* (Ps. lxx. 3). But I ought to explain in what manner I understand these words, that it may not be thought I launch maledictions or imprecations against any of my adversaries. I pray, then, that whosoever think of me above that which they see in me or hear respecting me may be turned back, that is, return from the excessive praises which they have given me without knowing me. In what way? When they shall know better him whom they

praise without measure, and consequently shall blush for
their error, and for the ill service that they have rendered
to their friend. And in this way it is that I say, Turn
back ! and blush ! to both kinds of my enemies ; those who
wish me evil and commend me in order to flatter, and those
who innocently, and even kindly, but yet to my injury,
praise me to excess.   I would wish to appear to them so
vile and abject that they would be ashamed to have praised
such a person, and should cease to bestow praises so
indiscreetly.   Therefore, against panegyrists of each kind I
am accustomed to strengthen myself with those two verses :
against the hostile with the former, *Let them be turned back
and soon brought to shame who wish me evil,* but against the
well-meaning, *Let them be turned backward and made to
blush who say over me, There, There !*

4. But as (to return to you) I ought, according to the
example of the Apostle, to rejoice with you only, and not to
have dominion over your piety, and according to the word
of God we have one Father only who is in heaven, and all
we are brethren, I find myself obliged to repel from me with
a shield of truth the lofty name of Lord and Father with
which you have intended, I know well, to honour me, not to
burden ; and in place of these I think it fitter that you
should name me brother and fellow-servant, both because
we have the same heritage, and because we are in the same
condition, lest perchance if I should usurp to myself a title
which belongs to God, I shall hear from Him : *If I be a
Father where is my honour, and I be a Lord where is my
fear ?* (Mal. i. 6).   It is very true, however, that if I do not
wish to attribute to myself over you the authority of a
father, I have all the feelings of one, nor is the love with
which I embrace you less, I think, than that of a father or of
a son.   Sufficient, then, on the subject of the titles which
you give me.

5. I wish to reply now to the rest of your letter.   You
complain that I do not come to see you.   I could complain
equally of you for the same reason, unless, indeed (which
you yourself do not deny) the will of God must be pre-

ferred to our feelings and our needs. If it were otherwise, if it were not the work of Christ that was in question, would I suffer to be so far away from me a companion so dear and necessary to me, so obedient in labour, so persevering in studies, so useful in conference, so prompt in recollection? Blessed are we if we still remain thus until the end always and in everything, seeking not our own interests, but those of Jesus Christ.

--- · -

LETTER LXXIII.

To the Same.

He instructs Rainald, who was too anxious and distrustful, respecting the duty of superior which had been conferred upon him ; and warns him that he must bestow help and solace upon his brethren rather than require it from them.

To his very dear son RAINALD, Abbot of Foigny, BERNARD, that God may give him the spirit of strength.

1. You complain, my very dear son, of your many tribulations, and by your pious complaints you excite me also to complain, for I am not able to feel that you are sorrowing without sharing your sorrow, nor can I be otherwise than troubled and anxious when I hear of your troubles and anxieties. But since I foresaw these very difficulties which you say have happened to you, and predicted them to you, if you remember—it seems to me that you ought to be better prepared to endure them, and to spare me vexation when you can. For am I not sufficiently tried, and more than sufficiently, to lose you, not to see you, nor to enjoy your society, which was so pleasant to me ; so that I have almost regretted that I should have sent you away from me. And although charity obliged me to send you, yet not being able to see you where you have been sent, I mourn you as if lost to me. When then, besides this, you who ought to be the staff of my support, belabour me as it were with the rod of

your faint-heartedness, you heap sorrow upon sorrow, and torment upon torment; and if it is a mark of your filial affection towards me that you do not hide any of your difficulties from me, yet it is hard to add fresh trouble to one already burdened. Why is it needful to occupy with fresh anxieties one already more than anxious enough, and to torture with sharper pains the bosom of a father, already wounded by the absence of his son? I have shared with you my weight of cares, as a son, as an intimate friend, as a trusty assistant; but how do you help to bear your father's burden, if, instead of relieving me, you burden me still more? You, indeed, are loaded, but I am not lightened of my load.

2. For this burden is that of sick and weak souls. Those who are in health do not need to be carried, and are not, therefore, a burden. Whomsoever, then, of your brethren you shall find sad, mean-spirited, discontented, remember well that it is of these and for their sakes, you are father and abbot. In consoling, in exhorting, in reproving, you do your duty, you bear your burden; and those whom you bear in order to cure, you will cure by bearing. But if anyone is in such spiritual health that he rather helps you than is helped by you, recognize that to him you are not father and abbot, but equal and friend. Do not complain if you find more trials than consolations from those among whom you are. You were sent to sustain and console others, because you are spiritually stronger and better able to bear than they, and because with the grace of God you are able to aid and sustain all without needing yourself to be aided and sustained by any. Finally, if the burden is great, so also is the reward; but, on the other hand, the more assistance you receive, the more your own reward is diminished. Choose, therefore; if you prefer those who are for you a burden, your merit will be the greater; but if, on the contrary, you prefer those who console you, you have no merit at all. The former are the source whence it arises for you; the second as the abyss in which it is swallowed up; for it is not doubtful that those who are partakers of the labour, will be also sharers of the reward. Knowing, then, that you

were sent to help, not to be helped, bear in mind that you
are the vicar of Him who came not to be ministered unto,
but to minister. I could have wished to write at greater
length, in order to comfort you, but that it was not necessary; for what need is there of filling a dead leaf with
superfluous words, while the living voice is speaking? I
think that when you have seen our prior, these words will
be sufficient for you, and your spirit will revive at his
presence, so that you will not require the consolation of
written words, in the delight and help which his discourse
will give you. Do not doubt that I have communicated to
him, as far as was possible, my inmost mind, which you
begged in your letters might be sent to you. For you
know well that he and I are of one mind and one will.

LETTER LXXIV.

To the Same.

*He had desired Rainald to refrain from querulous com-
plaints; now he directs Rainald to keep him informed of
all his affairs.*

I had hoped, my dear friend, to find a remedy for
my care about you, if I were not informed by you of your
little vexations. And I remember that I said to you,
amongst other things, in my last letter, " if it is a mark of
your filial affection towards me that you do not hide any of
your difficulties from me, yet it is hard to add trouble to
one already burdened." But the remedy which I thought
would lighten my cares has increased them, and I feel
more burdened than before. For then I, indeed, felt vexation and fear, but only on account of the troubles named
by you, but now I fear that some evil, I know not what, is
happening to you, and like your favourite Ovid—

> When have I not made the perils which I feared
> Greater than they really were? [1]

I fear all things because I am uncertain of all things, and

[1] *Heroid.* Ep. I. v. 11.

feel often real sorrow for imaginary evils. The mind which affection dominates is hardly master of itself. It fears what it knows not; it grieves when there is no need; it is troubled more than it wished, and even when it does not wish; unable to rule its sensibility, it pities or sympathizes against its will. And because you see, my son, that neither my timid industry nor your pious prudence in this respect are of service to me, do not, I pray you, conceal from me henceforth anything that concerns you, that you may not increase my uneasiness by seeking to spare me. The little books of mine which you have, please return to me when you can.

LETTER LXXV.   (A.D. 1127.)

To Artaud, Abbot of Prully.[1]

To his very dear friend and colleague, Abbot ARTAUD, Brother BERNARD wishes health.[2]

Whatever affection and heartfelt kindliness absent friends are able to bestow upon one another I feel is due both from me to you and from you to me, not only because we share the same vows and method of life, but also because we have neither of us forgotten our ancient friendship. And we are in no way better able to show to each other or to recognize how acceptable this is to each of us, and how warmly it exists in the heart of each of us, than not to conceal from each other if either should hear of anything unbecoming or unsuitable concerning his friend. Now, I have heard that you have the intention of founding an abbey in Spain to be dependent on your holy convent. The plan occasioned great surprise to me, nor could I conjecture for what end, with what design or hope of usefulness, you should wish to send some of

---

1 Of *Prully*, not of *Poitiers*. See notes to Letter 80. Prully was a monastery of Cistercians, situated in the Diocese of Sens, founded in 1118, by Theobald, Count of Champagne, and Adèle, his mother, as William de Nangis reports in his *Chronicle*, cited by Manrique in his *Annals* under that year. But Theobald was not then Count, as may be gathered from the notes to Letter 31.

2 This inscription is restored from the Corbey MS.

your monks into exile to a place so distant, and which will cost you so much both in trouble and in money to reach and to build upon, when you have quite near you a house already built and well-fitted up, where you may settle any of them.   For you cannot, I suppose, excuse yourself by saying that the place I refer to is not yours, when I know quite well that it may easily be yours if you wish.   Do you suppose that the Lord Abbot of Pontigny,[1] to whom it belongs, would refuse it to you if you asked him for it? On the contrary, it would be most agreeable to him if you were willing to accept it; not because it is not a good house, but because, as you know, he has no need of it. We ought both of us to take great care in our conduct, of the advice which the Apostle gives: *Let no man despise thy youth* (1 Tim. iv. 12), because we are remarked the sooner for levity, as we are young men.   But I trust that you will act with more consideration, and choose this place, as it is nearer to you and already built; which, while it will perfectly meet your wants, is only a burden to our friend the abbot, who at present holds it.   Farewell.

LETTER   LXXVI.

To the Abbot of The Regular Canons of S. Pierremont.[2]

He considers what is to be done in the case of a man who, after a long time spent in a monastery and in the habit of a religious, has returned to the world and contracted a second marriage.

[1] Thus in the Corbey MS. In others, the *Abbot P.* The place here referred to is Vauluisant, in which Artaud, at the advice of Bernard, founded a monastery in 1127 (the date of this Letter), sending twelve monks thither under Norpald as abbot.

[2] In all editions there has been up to the present *To the Same;* we have replaced the correct subscription and title of the Letter from the Corbey MS. Pierremont is an abbey of the Augustine Order, in the diocese of Toul, not far from the little river Mortagne, an affluent of the Meurthe. This Letter explains the doubt which Bernard proposes to himself in the fourth division of *Concerning Precept and Dispensation*, ch. xvii.

To the most Reverend the Father of the Canons of S. Pierre-mont, Brother BERNARD, health and the affection which is due to him.

Since it pleased your worship that this brother should consult my unworthy self, I have let him know my opinion without at all pretending that he ought to follow it, that I may not stand in the way of better advice.   Not to weary you by repeating circumstances which you already know, this is the sum of my advice.   It is very dangerous, perhaps unlawful, that a man who has so long dwelt in a convent and worn the religious habit, should have returned to the world; also that he who with the consent of his former wife, while she was living, had long observed absolute continence should contract a second marriage is indecent and dishonourable.   Yet since the marriage was publicly and solemnly performed as others are, and without protest or opposition, it does not seem to me safe that the man should dismiss his wife against her will, unless he shall have had recourse to episcopal authority or advice, or at all events to an ecclesiastical and canonical judgment.[1] But since, in my opinion, the great danger in which the man now is, is due, in no small degree, to you (in that you deferred too long his taking the vow, though he wished and desired to do so, and thus gave opportunity to the tempter to precipitate him into those unhappy courses), I counsel and advise you in the name of charity to employ all your efforts to rescue the unfortunate man, even at any cost.   Address yourself, for instance, to the wife herself, and obtain from her a promise to dismiss her husband and live in continence, or procure that the bishop should summon them both before him and separate them, which I believe may justly be done.

[1] It is not clear by what vow (if any) the man was bound.   Consult the passage already referred to De Præcepto et Dispensatione, ch. xvii, and the notes upon it.

LETTER LXXVII.

To Magister Hugo, of S. Victor.

This Letter also, on account of its importance, has been placed among the Treatises.

LETTER LXXVIII. (A.D. 1127.)

To Suger, Abbot of S. Denis.[1]

He praises Suger, who had unexpectedly renounced the pride and luxury of the world to give himself to the modest habits of the religious life. He blames severely the clerk who devotes himself rather to the service of princes than that of God.

1. A piece of good news has reached our district; it cannot fail to do great good to whomsoever it shall have come. For who that fear God, hearing what great things He has done for your soul, do not rejoice and wonder at the great and sudden change wrought by the Right Hand of the Most High. Everywhere your courage is praised in the Lord; the gentle hear of it and are glad, and even those who do not

---

[1] The Benedictine Abbey of S. Dionysius the Areopagite, the apostle of France, one of the most celebrated foundations of the country, is about two leagues from Paris, and was founded by Dagobert I., King of the Franks. Suger succeeded Abbot Adam, whom Abaelard wrongly accused as a man disreputable by his vices (*Hist. Calam.* p. 19. See the notes of Duchesne on the same passage). He was chosen Abbot in 1123 in his absence, while he was fulfilling a mission from Louis le Gros, King of France, to Pope Calixtus II. He died in 1152, at the age of seventy years, and was buried in the Abbey Church, which he had himself erected, such as we see it at the present time. It is a magnificent edifice in the form of a cross, 390 feet long, 100 feet broad, 80 feet high from the pavement to the vault, and upheld by 60 columns or pillars. Its windows are incomparably beautiful, its choir laid with marbles of various colours and ornamented with sixty high stalls, and it is enriched with very many tombs of kings and princes. The Annals of this Abbey declare that " [Suger] by his zeal restored the order of our holy Religion. For before, by the negligence of the Abbots who preceded him, and of certain monks of that house, obedience to the Rule had been so broken through that there was scarcely an appearance of the Religious life left," as also Bernard says here. See notes to Letter 266.

know you,[1] but have only heard of you, what you were and what you are now, wonder and glorify God in you. But what adds still more to their admiration and joy is that you have been able to make your brethren partake of the counsel of salvation poured upon you from above, and so to fulfil what we read, *Let him that heareth say, Come* (Rev. xxii. 17), and that *What I tell you in darkness that speak ye in light, and what ye hear in the ear that preach ye upon the house tops* (S. Matt. x. 27). So a soldier intrepid in war, or rather a general full of bravery and devotedness, when he sees almost all his soldiers turned to flight and falling everywhere under the hostile blades, although he may see that he would be able to escape alone, yet he prefers to die with those, without whom he would think it shame to live. He holds firm on the field of battle and combats bravely; he ranges, sword in hand, along the ranks, through the bloody blades which seek him; he terrifies his adversaries and reanimates his followers with all his powers of voice and gesture. Wherever the enemy press on more boldly and there is danger of his friends giving ground, there he is present; the enemy who strikes he opposes, the friend who sinks exhausted he succours; and he is the more prepared to die for each one, that he despairs to save them all. But while he makes heroic efforts to hinder and to stop the pursuers who press upon his followers, he raises as best he can those who are fallen and recalls those who have taken flight. Nor is it rare that his splendid valour procures a safety as welcome as unhoped for, throws into confusion the hostile ranks, forces them to fly from those whom they were pursuing, and overcomes those who bore themselves almost as victors, so that they who a little before were struggling for life are now rejoicing in victory.

2. But why do I compare an event so profoundly religious to things secular, as if examples were wanting to us from religion itself ? Was not Moses quite certain of what God had promised him, that if, indeed, the people over whom he ruled should have perished, he himself should not only

---

[1] Otherwise *viderunt*, have seen.

not perish with them, but should be besides the chief of a
great nation ? Nevertheless, with what affection, with
what zeal, with what bowels of piety did he strive to save
his people from the wrath of God ? And, finally, inter-
posing himself on behalf of the offenders, he cries : *If Thou
wilt forgive their sin*— ; *and if not, blot me, I pray
Thee, out of Thy book which Thou hast written* (Exod.
xxxii. 32). What a devoted advocate ! who, because he
does not seek his own interests, easily obtains everything
which he seeks. What a benign chief, who, binding
together his people with bonds of charity as the head is
united with the members, will either save them with
himself or else encounter the same danger as they !
Jeremiah, also bound[1] inseparably to his people, but by the
bond of compassion, not by sympathy for their revolt,
quitted voluntarily his native soil and his own liberty[2] to
embrace in preference the common lot of exile and slavery.
He was free to remain in his own country had he chosen,
while others must remove, but he preferred to be carried
away captive with his people, to whom he knew that he
could render service even in captivity. Paul, animated beyond doubt by the same spirit, desired that he might be
anathema even from Christ Himself for his brethren
(Romans ix. 3). He experienced in his own heart how
true is that saying, *Love is as strong as death, jealousy is
cruel as the grave* (Cant. viii. 6). Do you see of whose
great examples you have shown yourself an imitator ? But
I add one more whom I had almost passed over, that of the
holy king David, who, perceiving and lamenting the
slaughter of his people, wished to devote himself for them,
and desired that the Divine vengeance should be transferred
to himself and to his father's house (2 Sam. xxiv. 17).

    3. But who made you aspire to this degree of perfection ?
I confess that though I earnestly desired to hear such things
of you, I never hoped to see it come to pass. Who would
have believed that you would reach, so to speak, by one
sudden bound, the practice of the highest virtues, and

---

[1] *Vinctus*, otherwise *junctus*.					[2] Otherwise *voluntatem*.

approach the most exalted merit? Thus we learn not to measure by the narrow proportions of our faith and hope the infinite pity of God, which does what It will and works upon whom It will, lightening the burden which It imposes upon us, and hastening the work of our salvation. What then? the zeal of good people blamed your errors at least, if not those of your brethren : it was against your excesses more than theirs that they were moved with indignation; and if your brothers in religion groaned in secret, it was less against your entire community than against you ; it was only against you that they brought their accusation. You corrected your faults, and their criticisms had no longer an object; your conversion at once stilled the tumult of accusation. The one and only thing with which we were scandalized was the luxury, the pride, the pomp, which followed you everywhere.[1] At length you laid down your pride, you put off your splendid dress, and the universal indignation ceased at once. Thus you had at the same time satisfied those who complained of you, and even merited our praises. For what in human doings is deserving of praise, if this is not considered most worthy of admiration and approval? It is true that a change so sudden and so complete is not the work of man, but of God. If in heaven the conversion of one sinner arouses great joy, what gladness will the conversion of an entire community cause, and of such a community as yours?

4. That spot so noble by its antiquity and the royal favour, was made to serve the convenience of worldly business, and to be a meeting-place for the royal troops. They used to render to Cæsar the things which were Cæsar's promptly and fully; but not with equal fidelity did they render the things of God to God. I speak what I have heard, not what I have seen : the very cloister itself of your monastery was frequently, they say, crowded with soldiers, occupied with the transaction of business, resounding with

[1] It is, perhaps, of this man that Bernard speaks in his *Apology* c. 10: "I have seen, I do not exaggerate, an abbot going forth escorted by 60 horses and more . . . etc."

noise and quarrels, and sometimes accessible even to
women. How, in the midst of all that, could place be
found for thoughts of heaven, for the service of God, for
the interests of the spiritual life? But now there is leisure
for God's service, for practising self-restraint and obedience,
for attention to sacred reading. Consider that silence and
constant quiet from all stir of secular things disposes the
soul to meditation on things above. And the laborious
exercise of the religious life and the rigour of abstinence
are lightened by the sweetness of psalms and hymns.
Penitence for the past renders lighter the austerity of the
new manner of life. He who in the present gathers the fruits
of a good conscience, feels in himself a desire for future
good works, which shall not be frustrated, and a well-
founded hope. The fear of the judgment to come gives
way to the pious exercise of brotherly charity, for *love
casteth out fear* (1 S. John iv. 18). The variety of holy
services drives far away weariness and sourness of temper,
and I repeat these things to the praise and glory of God,
who is the Author of all; yet not without praise to yourself
as being His co-worker in all things. He was able, indeed,
to do them without you, but He has preferred to have you
for the sharer of His works, that He might have you for
the sharer of His glory also. The Saviour once reproached
certain persons because they made the *house of prayer a
den of thieves* (S. Matt. xxi. 13). He will doubtless then
have in commendation the man who has accomplished the
task of freeing His holy place from the dogs, of rescuing
His pearl from the swine; by whose ardour and zeal the
workshop of Vulcan is restored to holy studies, or rather
the house of God is restored to Him from being a synagogue
of Satan to be that which it was before.

5. If I recall the remembrance of past evils it is not in
order to cast confusion or reproach on anyone, but from
the comparison with the old state of things to make the
beauty of the new appear more sharply and strikingly; because there is nothing which makes the present good shine
forth more clearly than a comparison with the evils which

preceded it.   As we recognize similar things from similar,
so things which are unlike either please or displease more
when compared with their opposites.   Place that which
is black beside that which is white, and the juxtaposition
of the two colours makes each appear more marked. So,
if beautiful things are put beside ugly, the former are
rendered more beautiful, the ugliness of the latter is more
apparent. That there may be no occasion of offence or
confusion, I am content to repeat with the Apostle : *Such,
indeed, ye were, but ye are washed, ye are sanctified*
(1 Cor. vi. 11).   Now, the house of God ceases to open to
people of the world, there is no access to sacred precincts
for the curious ; no gossip about trifling things with the
idle ; the chatter of boys and girls is no longer heard.   The
holy place is open and accessible only to the children of
Christ, of whom it is said : *Behold I and the children
whom the Lord hath given me* (Isaiah viii. 18).   It is reserved for the praises of God and the performance of sacred
vows with due care and reverence.   How gladly do the
martyrs, of whom so great a number ennoble that place,
listen to the loud songs of these children, to whom they in
turn reply no less with a voice of charity : *Praise, O ye
servants of the Lord, praise the name of the Lord* (Ps.
cxiii. 1), and again, *Sing praises to our God, sing praises,
sing praises to our King, sing praises* (Ps. xlvii. 6).

6. When your breasts are beaten with penitent hands,
and your pavements worn with your knees, your altars
heaped with vows and devout prayers, your cheeks fur-
rowed with tears ; when groans and sighs resound on all
sides and the sacred roofs echo with spiritual songs instead
of worldly pleadings, there is nothing which the citizens of
heaven more love to look upon, nothing is more agreeable
to the eyes of the Heavenly King.   For is not this what is
said : *The sacrifice of praise shall honour me* (Ps. l. 23) ?
O, if anyone had his eyes opened, as were those of the
prophet's servant at his prayer ! He would doubtless see
(2 Kings vi. 17) *The princes go before, joined with the
minstrels in the midst of the players on timbrels* (Ps.

lxvii. 26, VULG.). We should see, I say, with what care
and ardour they assist at the chants, and at the prayers
how they unite themselves with those who meditate, they
watch over those who repose, they preside over those who
order and care for all. The powers of heaven fully recognize their fellow-citizens; they earnestly rejoice, comfort,
instruct, protect, and provide for all those who take the
heritage of salvation, at all times. How happy I esteem
myself while I am still in this world to hear of these things,
although I am absent and do not see them! But your
felicity, my brethren, to whom it is given to bear part
in them, far surpasses mine, and blessed above all is he
whom the Author of all good has deigned to make the
chief worker of so good a work; it is you, my dear friend,
whom with justice I congratulate for this, that you have
brought about all which I so greatly admire.

7. You are wearied, perhaps, with my praises, but you
ought not to be so; they are far different from the flatteries
of those *who call evil good and good evil* (Isaiah v. 20), and
so please a person to lead him into error. Sweet but
perilous is the praise *when the wicked is praised in the
desire of his heart, and the unjust is blessed* (Ps. ix. 3,
VULG.). The warmth of my praises comes from charity,
and does not once pass, as I believe, the limits of truth.
He is safely praised, who is praised in the Lord, that is, in
the truth. I have not called evil good, but have pointed out
as evil what was evil. But if I boldly raise my voice
against that which is evil, ought I to be silent in presence of
good, and not give my testimony to it? That would be to
show myself an envious critic, not a corrector; and to
prefer to mangle rather than to mend, if I am silent as to
good and raise my voice only about evil. The just reproves
in mercy, the wicked flatters in impiety; the one that he
may cure, the other in order to hide that which needs to be
cured. Do not be afraid that those among us who in the
fear of the Lord praise you will pour upon your head that
ointment of the sinner with which they were wont to
anoint you. I praise you because you are doing right.

But I do not flatter you ; I only accomplish in your case,
by the gift of God, those words of the Psalmist : *Those who
fear Thee shall see me and shall rejoice, because I have
hoped in Thy word* (Ps. cxix. 74) ; and again : *Many shall
show forth his wisdom* (Ecclus. xxxix. 10).   It is, then, your
wisdom which more praised than blamed the former folly.

8. I would that you should take pleasure in the praises
of such as fear just as much to flatter vice as to depreciate
virtue.   That is the true praise, which, as it is wont to
extol nothing but what is good, so it knows not how to
caress what is evil.   All other is pretended praise, but
really blame, which Scripture refers to : *The sons of men
are vain ; they are deceitful upon the weights, so that they
deceive even more than vanity* (Ps. lxii. 10).   Such are
altogether to be avoided according to the counsel of the
wise man : *My son, if sinners entice thee consent thou not*
(Prov. i. 10), since their milk and their oil, though they be
sweet, are poisonous and deadly.   *Their words,* he says
(that is, those of flatterers), *are softer than oil, and yet are
they very swords* (Ps. lv. 21).   The righteous has oil, too, but
of mercy, of sanctification, of spiritual joy.   He has wine,
which he pours into the wounds of the haughty soul.   But⁻ -
for the soul of him that mourns, and for him of contrite
heart, he has the oil of mercy, with which he is wont to
soften its sorrow.   Where he corrects, he pours in wine ;
when he soothes, oil ; but wine without bitterness, and oil
without guile.   Thus, not every praise is flattery, nor every
blame mixed with rancour.   Blessed is he who can say :
*Let the righteous smite me in mercy, and reprove me :
but let not the oil of the sinner break my head* (Ps. cxli. 5),
which when you have put far from you, you have shown
yourself worthy of the oil and wine of the saints.

9. Let the children of Babylon seek for themselves
pleasant mothers, but pitiless, who will feed them with
poisoned milk, and soothe them with caresses which
will make them fit for everlasting flames; but those of
the Church, fed at the breasts of her wisdom, having
tasted the sweetness of a better milk, already begin

to grow up in it unto salvation, and being fully satiated with it they cry: *Thy fulness is better than wine, Thy fragrance than the sweetest ointments* (Cant. i. 1, 2). This to their mother. But, then, having tasted and known how sweet the Lord is, how truly the best of fathers, they say to Him: *How great is Thy goodness, O Lord, which Thou hast laid up for them that fear Thee* (Ps. xxxi. 19). Now my whole desire is accomplished. Formerly when I saw with regret with what avidity you sucked in[1] from the lips of flatterers their mortal poison, the seed of sin, I used, with grief, to desire better things for you, saying: *Who shall give thee to me, my brother, who sucked the breasts of my mother* (Cant. viii. 1)? Far from thee henceforth be those men with caresses and dishonest praises, who bless you before your face and expose you at the same time to the reproach and derision of all men, whose applause in your presence is the world's by-word, or rather makes you a by-word to the world. If they murmur even now, say to them: *If I yet pleased you, I should not be the servant of Christ* (Gal. i. 10). Those whom we please in evil things we cannot please in good things, unless they are themselves changed, and begin to hate what we were, and so at length to love what we are.

10. In our time two new and detestable abuses have arisen in the Church, of which one (permit me to say it) was no stranger to you when you lived in forgetfulness of the duties of your profession; but this, thanks to God, has been amended to His glory, to your everlasting gain, to our joy and an example to all. God is able to bring about that we may soon be consoled for the second of these evils, the odious novelty of which I do not dare to speak of in public, and yet am afraid to pass over in silence. My grief urges my tongue to speak, but fear restrains the words; fear only lest I may offend someone if I speak openly of what troubles me, since truth sometimes makes enemies. But for enmity of this kind thus incurred I hear the truth consoling me. *It is needful,* he says, *that offences should come.*

---

[1] *Sugere.* Bernard is playing upon the name of his correspondent Suger.

And I do not think that those words which follow, *Woe to that man by whom the offence cometh* (S. Matt. xviii. 7) concern me. For when vices are attacked and a scandal results thence, it is not he who makes the accusation who is to answer for the scandal, but he who renders it necessary. In short, I am neither more cautious in word nor circumspect in action than he who says, " It is better that a scandal should arise than the truth be compromised " (S. Greg. Magn. Hom. 7 in Ezech. near the beginning, and S. Aug. de Lib. Arbitr. et de Prædest. sanctor.). Although I know not what advantage it would be were I to hold my tongue about that which all the world proclaims with a loud voice, nor can I alone pretend to overlook the pest whose ill odour is in all nostrils, and not dare to guard my own nose from its ill effect.

11. For whose heart is not indignant, and whose tongue does not murmur either openly or secretly to see a deacon equally serving God and Mammon,[1] against the precept of

---

[1] This deacon was Stephen de Garlande, seneschal or officer of the table to the King of France. Many have wrongly confounded him with the Chancellor Stephen, who became later on Bishop of Paris, as Duchesne rightly remarks in his notes on Abaélard. Teulf says of him, in his *Annals of Maurigny*, B. ii.: " At the death of William, brother german of Anselle, officer of the King's table, Stephen, the brother of both, became Mayor of the King's palace. It was a thing unheard of up to that time, that one who occupied the position of a deacon should perform the military functions of a Court. He was an enterprising man, and endowed with rare worldly ability. His ecclesiastical revenues were considerable. The King had such a friendship for him that he seemed rather to obey him than command. He enjoyed greater temporal prosperity than any other man in our times. He married his niece to Almaric de Montfort, who received the title of Rochefort on his marriage. Swollen by prosperity, and forgetful of what he was, he rendered himself odious to the Queen Adela by many slights towards her, and having become disliked by all, he lost his favour with the King, was removed from his place and obliged to quit the Court. Then, as if he were seized with a kind of insanity, he did all in his power to throw the realm into confusion, and, with the aid of Almaric, who was a man of remarkable bravery, he took up arms against his country. It was of the same Stephen, if I do not mistake, for he was surnamed de Garlande, that Ivo, Bishop of Chartres, speaks in terms not at all flattering in his eighty-seventh Letter, where, addressing the cardinals, he accuses the people of Beauvais of taking him for a Bishop. ' Violating all the canons,' he says, ' they have taken for Bishop a clerk ignorant, a gambler, addicted to a crowd of vices, completely wanting in

the Gospel heaping up ecclesiastical dignities, so that he
seems not to be inferior to Bishops, yet so mixed up in
military offices that he is preferred even to Dukes. What
monster is this, that being a clerk, and wishing at the same
time to appear a soldier, is neither? It is equally an abuse
that a deacon should serve at the table of the King, and that
the server of the King should minister at the altar during the
holy mysteries. Is it not a wonder, or rather a scandal, to
see the same person clothed in armour march at the head
of armed soldiery, and vested in alb and stole read the
Gospel in the midst of the Church; at one time give the
signal for battle with the trumpet, and at another convey
the orders of the Bishop to the people? Unless, perhaps,
that man (which would be scandalous) is ashamed of the
Gospel of which S. Paul, that Vessel of election, was so
proud? Perhaps he is ashamed to appear a cleric, and
thinks it more honourable to be supposed a soldier,
preferring the Court to the Church, the table of the
King to the Altar of Christ, and the cup of demons to the
chalice of Christ. This seems the more probable, because
he is prouder (they say) to be called by the name of that
one post which he has obtained at the palace than by any of
those titles of ecclesiastical dignities which, in defiance of
the canons, he has heaped upon himself, and instead of
delighting to be called Archdeacon, Dean, or Provost to his
various Churches, he prefers to be styled *Dapifer* to H.M.
the King. O, unheard of and hateful perversity! thus to
prefer the title of servant of a man to that of the servant of
God, and to consider the position of an official of an earthly
king one of higher dignity than that of an heavenly! He
who prefers military warfare to the work of the ministry

all that Holy Orders require, a man, in short, who was formerly driven from the
Church by the Archbishop of Lyons, Legate of the Holy See, because of a public
adultery, and that by the order of the King and Queen. This man, who was
intruded, is Stephen de Garlande. If ever the Apostolic authority shall permit
him to ascend into the Episcopal chair, a fatal silence will be manifestly imposed
on the canons. For how shall we drink at the spring of knowledge if by those
who hold the keys we are not permitted to enter?'" So Ivo. Even this Stephen
Bernard won over to God.

places the world before the Church, is convicted of preferring human things to Divine, earthly to heavenly. Is it
then more honourable to be called the King's *Dapifer* than
Dean or Archdeacon? It may be to a layman, not to a
cleric; to a soldier, not to a deacon.

12. It is a strange but blind ambition to delight more in
the lowest things than in the highest, and that the man
whose lines had fallen to him in pleasant places should re-
create himself upon a dunghill with eager desire, and count
his precious lands as nothing worth. This man mingles the
two orders and cunningly abuses each. Military pomps
delight him, but not the risks and labours of warfare; the
revenues of religion, but not its duties. Who does not see
how great is the disgrace, as much to the State as to the
Church? for just as it is no part of clerical duty to bear arms
at the pay of the King, so it is no part of the royal duties to
administer lay affairs by means of clerics.[1] What king has
ever put at the head of his army an unwarlike clerk instead
of some brave soldier? What clerk, again, has ever thought
it otherwise than unworthy of him to be bound to obey any
lay person whatsoever? The very sign which he bears upon
his head[2] is rather the mark of royalty than of servitude; on

---

[1] Bernard here blames equally clerics who bear arms for the King's pay and
kings who impose military service upon clerks. Each is wrong: the one because he loses sight of the dignity of his status, the others because they confide
without choice or discrimination functions of the Court or of the Army upon
clerks instead of giving them to laymen, as they ought. A similar practice was
renewed under Louis XI., King of France. For when Cardinal Balue, Bishop of
Evreux, was sent by the King to Paris to review the troops, he performed that
duty unworthy of a prelate, riding a mule and wearing a linen rochet. Chabanne, who commanded the cavalry, was indignant, and, seeking the King, he
begged of him a commission to visit the Chapter of Evreux, or to examine the
candidates for orders. "Your demand astonishes me," said the King. "Do
you not know that those functions belong to others, and require a character
which you have not?" "Why," retorted Chabanne, "should I be less fit to
bring clerks to orders than a Bishop to review soldiers?" which reply confounded the King and aroused the mirth of the bystanders. Guaguin, *Hist. of
the Clergy*, B. x.; Claud Espence, a man famed in France for learning and
sanctity, B. ii. c. 6; *Digress. in i. Ep. ad Timoth.*; Bosquier, in *Plutarch. Christ.*;
Corozetus, *Apophtheg. Gall.*

[2] The tonsure, or clerical crown.

the other hand, the throne finds a better support in the
force of arms than in chanting of Psalms. Still, if the
abasement of the one contributes to the greatness of the
other, as is sometimes the case ; if, for example, the humiliation of the King raised higher the dignity of the priest, or
the abasement of the clerk added something to the royal
honour ; as it happens, for instance, if a woman of noble
rank marries a man of the people, she indeed loses in grade
by him, but he gains by her; if, then, I say, either the King
had advantage from the clerk, or the clerk from the King, it
would be an evil only in part, and perhaps ought to be
borne with ; but, on the contrary, since there is no gain to
either from the humiliation of the other, but there is loss to
each; since neither does it become a cleric, as has been
said, to be or to be called the server of the King; nor is it
for the King's advantage to put the reins of government into
any but strong and brave hands. Truly then it is strange
that either power endures such a man as this; that the
Church does not repulse the deacon-soldier, or the State
the prince-ecclesiastic.

13. I had wished to inculcate these principles by still
stronger and more detailed arguments, and perhaps ought
to do so, did not the necessary limits of a letter oblige me
to defer this for the present; and because, most of all, I
fear to offend you, I have spared a man for whom, it is
said, you had formerly a great regard. I would not that
you should have a friend at the expense of the truth.   But
you have still a friendship for him; show yourself a true
friend, and exert yourself to make him, too, a friend of the
Truth.   Then at length there will be a true friendship between you, if it is bound together by a common love of
truth.   And if he will not yield to you in this, hold fast what
you have ; join the tail to the head of the sacrifice.[1] You

---

[1] That is, join the end to the beginning of your work. He exhorts to perseverance, alluding to that precept of the Law which prescribed the offering at
the same time of the head and the tail of the victim (Exod. xxix.; Lev. iii.).
Radulfus gives the mystical sense of the precept thus : "The tail, which is the
end of the body, is the symbol of perseverance in, and the perfecting of, good
works." The same writer says, in Homil. 25 in Evang. : " In the precept of the

have received by the grace of God a robe of many colours; take pains to make it reach even to the feet, for what will it profit you to have put your hand to the work if (which, God forbid) you do not attain finally to persevere? I end my letter by warning you to make a good ending of your good work.

_____

LETTER LXXIX. (*Circa* A.D. 1130.)

To Abbot Luke.[1]

Bernard warns him that familiarity with women is to be shunned, and indicates what is to be done in regard to a brother who has fallen into sin.

1. My very dear friend, you have singularly edified me, and have shown an example only too rare of goodness, because not only have you not despised the warnings of one of less importance than yourself, but have besides this returned thanks to your adviser, wisely looking not to who or what he might be, but to what was his advice. I thank God for it, and that my presumption in advising has met with gratitude rather than indignation. Encouraged, therefore, by this striking proof of your humility I feel myself bolder in repeating my former advice. I pray you, therefore, by that Blood which was poured out for souls not to regard as a matter of small importance the peril that is incurred by souls of so great value by the meeting of persons of different sexes in familiar intercourse. This cannot be doubted by those who have long struggled against the temptations of the

Law the tail of the victim is ordered to be offered in sacrifice; and that since the tail is the actual ending of the body, and he offers a complete sacrifice who carries out his offering of a good work to its due end and perfection."

[1] Abbot of Cuissy, of the Premonstratensian Order in the Diocese of Laon, as is evident from the *Biblioth. Premonstrat.*, and, as Bernard himself sufficiently indicates when he expresses his surprise that William, Abbot of S. Thierry, as being very near, or some brother at Prémontré, since that was in his immediate neighbourhood, had not been consulted instead of himself. Of Luke and of the monastery of Cuissy you have the following from the monk Hermann: Bartholomew Bishop of Laon, " built also in a place named Cuissy another monastery of clerks, and there ordained as abbot Dom Luke, a religious man " (Miraculis B. Mariæ Laudunens, B. iii. c. 16).

devil, and have learned by their own experience to say with the Apostle, *We are not ignorant of his devices* (2 Cor. ii. 11). And if there is anything that should induce you to take into serious consideration, not my advice indeed, but that of the Apostle himself, or rather his precept about this matter, when he cries aloud *Flee from fornication* (1 Cor. vi. 18), it is the proof of peril given by the shameful fall of the brother, about whom you have deigned to consult me. But, indeed, I wonder that it should have seemed to you expedient to seek me for an adviser, although at such a distance, when you have beside you a wise man of our Order and a special lover of your house, namely, William, Abbot of S. Thierry. And I do not doubt that there are in the Abbey of Prémontré also men of sense, who have prudence and faithfulness to show you the way out of your difficulties.

2. But since it has pleased you rather to have recourse to me, for which, no doubt, you have some good reason, the best advice I can give is at your disposal. If that brother has come of himself to confess his fault, however grave and shameful it may have been, endeavour should be made to bring about his amendment, and he should not be expelled. But as the ill odour of such a crime betrays it to others, it is needful to proceed with care, if it is possible, and in a different way from heretofore. For it is, perhaps, not expedient that he should be allowed to remain longer among you, lest, perhaps, as you have with great reason written, this sick sheep should infect your young and tender flock with his disease. On the other hand, a father ought not to close his heart entirely against his son, though a sinner; I should consider it, therefore, a course kindly in the father and salutary for the son that you should endeavour to remove him into another of the houses of Dom Norbert, but a distant one, where he may do penance under a stricter discipline, changing his abode but not his purpose, until the time when it shall seem good to you to recall him to his own monastery. As for his passing into our Order, that, perhaps, would not be of advantage to you. You wrote to me, it is true, that he

had often said that he had my promise to receive him if he should come with your licence; but in my presence he denied having said any such thing. Perhaps you may not be disposed to send him to any of those places to abide which I have mentioned, or he may not be willing to go, or if both are willing, perhaps a place ready to receive him may not be found : then one of two things will be advisable in the necessity of the case; one, to dismiss him with letters of licence to travel whither he will for the good of his soul; the other to keep him among you, by special grace of forgiveness, if, that is to say, you are able to take away every occasion of his repenting or disseminating his former wickedness. But sufficient on this subject.

3. There is still one point on which with my usual presumption I will make bold to tell you what I think. I speak of that mill at which the lay brothers [1] who are in charge are obliged to permit the resort of women. If you will follow my advice do one of three things ; either forbid entirely any entrance of women to the mill; or let the mill be put into the charge of some outside person, and not left to the lay brothers ; or let it be altogether given up.

LETTER LXXX. (*Circa* A.D. 1130.)

TO GUY, ABBOT OF MOLÊSMES.[2]

Bernard consoles him under a great injustice which he had suffered, and recommends him to temper his vengeance with mercy.

God who knows the hearts of all men, and is the inspirer of all good dispositions, knows with what sympathy I condole with you in this your adversity, of which I have heard. But, again, when I consider rather the person who has caused you this trial than Him who permits it, just as much

---

[1] Conversi. Respecting these see Letter 143 and note. Letter 404 similarly recommends the avoidance of relations with women.

[2] Guy was the second Abbot of Molêsmes, after S. Robert. See on this subject Letters 43, 44, and 60.

as I feel with you in the present misfortune, so much I hope
soon to rejoice with you in the prosperity which must
speedily come. But only do not let yourself be at all crushed
by discouragement; think with me how, by the example of
holy Job,[1] you ought to receive with the same cheerfulness
troubles from the hand of the Lord as you do blessings.
Indeed, you ought, after the example of holy David,[2] not so
much to be angry with those people who have caused you
such great sufferings, although they are your own servants,
as to know that you ought to humble yourself under the
mighty hand of God, who doubtless has sent them to bring
about this misfortune to you. But since it appears that
their correction devolves upon you, as they are serfs of the
Church committed to your government, it is proper that
these unfaithful serfs should be punished for their very
wicked presumption, and that the loss of the monastery
should be recompensed in some degree out of their goods.
But that you may not seem rather to be avenging your own
injury in this than punishing their fault, I beg you and also
advise you not to think so much of what they deserve as
what is fitting for you to do, so that mercy may be exalted
above strict justice, and that in your moderation God may
be glorified. For the rest, I beg you to press upon that
your son, who is dear to me as well for your sake as in a
great degree for his own, with your own lips, as with my
spirit, not to show in his accusations a bitterness and a
violence such as prove that he forgets that precept of our
Lord—Whosoever shall smite thee on thy right cheek turn
to him the other also (S. Matt. v. 39).

[1] Job. ii. 10.   [2] 2 Sam. xvi. 10.

LETTER LXXXI. (*Circa* A.D. 1130.)

TO GERARD,[1] ABBOT OF POTTIÈRES.

*He defends himself against a false accusation which had
been made against him.*

I do not remember that I ever wrote anything to the
Count of Nevers, to accuse you personally, nor is it
true to say that I have. But if I have written a letter
to that prince it is on behalf of your Church, and I
consider that in this I have acted not against you, but on
your behalf. I had heard that on your advice, and with
your consent, he proposed to come to you on a visit
of inspection, in order to ascertain whether there was any
truth in the many evil reports which were going abroad
concerning your house, and, if so, to whom the blame was
to be laid, so that he might correct with zeal and care anything that he might find to be wrong.[2] I do not see that
you have any right to feel yourself injured or to complain
because I took pains to strengthen the prince by my
encouragement in a resolution so just and so pious. On the
contrary, I think I did rightly and in the interests of the
House of God in rousing the zeal of the man who was able
to apply a remedy to the evil from which it suffered. You
quote the Holy Scripture to convince me that I have done
wrong because I did not begin by warning you; but know
that I have absolutely no complaint against you personally,
and in all that I have done for the sake of charity I have had
in view only the restoration of peace in your Church.
Finally, you shall be fully convinced of the truth of what I
say if, as you announce to me, you come to show me the
whole business. You will be sure to find me here on whatever day of the coming week you please.

[1] Pottières was an Abbey of Benedictines in the Diocese of Langres, founded
by Gerard, Count of Nevers, and not far from his Chateau. He was buried
there with his wife Bertha. *Acherius Opera Guiberti de Novigentum*, p. 653,
notes.

[2] Because he had succeeded to the rights of Count Gerard, founder of the
monastery of Pottières.

LETTER LXXXII. (*Circa* A.D. 1128.)

TO THE ABBOT OF S. JOHN AT CHARTRES.[1]

Bernard dissuades him from resigning his charge, and undertaking a Pilgrimage to Jerusalem.

1. As regards the matters about which you were so good as to consult so humble a person as myself, I had at first determined not to reply. Not because I had any doubt what to say, but because it seemed to me unnecessary or even presumptuous to give counsel to a man of sense and wisdom. But considering that it usually happens that the greater number of persons of sense—or I might say that all such—trust the judgment of another person rather than their own in doubtful cases, and that those who have a clear judgment in the affairs of others, however obscure, frequently hesitate and are undecided about their own, I depart from my first resolution, not, I hope, without reason, and without prejudice to any wiser opinion explain to you simply how the matter appears to me. You have signified to me, if I do not mistake, by the pious Abbot Ursus of S. Denis,[2] that you have it in contemplation to desert your country and the monastery over which, by the Providence of God, you are head, to undertake a pilgrimage to Jerusalem, to occupy yourself henceforth only with God and the salvation of your own soul. Perhaps, if you aspire unto perfection, it may be expedient for you to leave your country, when God says, *Go forth from thy country and from thy kindred*

---

[1] Doubtless Stephen, who from being Abbot of S. John at Chartres, of the Augustinian Order, was made Patriarch of Jerusalem at the beginning of 1128 after Germundus (Orderic. Vit. B. 12, towards the end). It was he who sent a letter, it is said, to Fulk, Count of Anjou, by means of William de Bury. (Analect. B. iii. p. 335, Lett. 35 and 36, and the Preface by Papebroch, *On the Patriarchs of Jerusalem*, Vol. iii. of May.)

[2] Ursus, or Ursio, fifth Abbot of the Regular Canons of S. Denis of Rheims, of the Order of S. Augustine, and afterwards Bishop of Verdun, is mentioned in *Spicilegium*, Vol. xii. p. 312. He was promoted to the See of Verdun in 1129, and had Gilbert for successor at S. Denis, but at length laying down his dignity he resumed after a time his rule as Abbot. (Marlot, *Metrop. Remens.* Vol. ii. p. 152.)

(Gen. xii. 1). But I do not see at all on what ground you ought to risk, by your departure, the safety of the souls entrusted to you. For is it pleasant to enjoy liberty after having laid down your burden? But charity does not seek her own interests. Perhaps the wish for quiet and rest attracts you? But it is obtained at the price of the peace of others. Freely will I do without the enjoyment of any desire, even a spiritual one, which cannot be obtained except at the price of a scandal. For where there is scandal, there, without doubt, is loss of charity: and where there is loss of charity, surely no spiritual advantage can be hoped for. Finally, if it is permitted to any one to prefer his own quiet to the common good, who is there that can say with truth: *For me to live is Christ, and to die is gain* (Phil. i. 21)? And where will that principle be which the Apostle declares: *No one lives to himself, and no one dies to himself* (Rom. xiv. 7); and, *Not seeking mine own profit, but the profit of many* (1 Cor. x. 33); and, *That he who lives should not any longer live unto himself, but unto Him who died for all* (2 Cor. v. 15)?

2. But you will say: Whence comes my great desire, if it is not from God? With your permission I will say what I think. *Stolen waters are sweet* (Prov. ix. 17); and for whosoever knows the devices of the devil, it is not doubtful that the angel of darkness is able to change himself into an angel of light, and to pour upon the thirsting soul those waters of which the sweetness is more bitter than worm-wood. In truth, what other can be the suggester of scandals, the author of dissension, the troubler of unity and peace, except the devil, the adversary of truth, the envier of charity, the ancient foe of the human race, and the enemy of the Cross of Christ? If death entered into the world through his envy, even so now he is jealous of whatever good he sees you doing; and since he is a liar from the beginning, he falsely promises now better things which he does not see. For when did the Truth oppose that most faithful saying, *Art thou bound unto a wife? seek not to be loosed* (1 Cor. vii. 27)? Or when did charity urge to

scandal, who at the scandals of all shows herself burning with regret? He, then, the most wicked one, opposed to charity by envy, and to truth by falsehood, mixing falsehood and gall with the true honey, promises doubtful things as certain, and gives out that true things are false, not that he may give you what you vainly hope for, but that he may take away what you are profitably holding now. He prowls around and seeks how he may take away from the flock the care of the pastor, to make a prey of it when there is none to defend it from his attacks; and, besides this, to bring down upon the pastor that terrible rebuke, *Woe to him by whom scandal cometh* (S. Matt. xviii. 7). But I have full confidence in the wisdom given to you by God, that by no cunning devices of the wicked one you will be seduced or made to renounce certain good, and for the hope of uncertain advantage to incur certain evil.

LETTER LXXXIII. (*Circa* A.D. 1129.)

To Simon, Abbot of S. Nicholas.[1]

Bernard consoles him under the persecution of which he is the object. The most pious endeavours do not always have the desired success. What line of conduct ought to be followed towards his inferiors by a prelate who is desirous of stricter discipline.

1. I have learned with much pain by your letter the persecution[2] that you are enduring for the sake of righteous-

---

[1] He was Abbot of S. Nicholas, at Rheims, and was made Abbot of S. Nicholas aux Bois, in the diocese of Laon. Hermann, a monk of Laon, speaks of him in B. iii. of *Miracles of Mary*, c. 18. He was brother of William, Abbot of S. Thierry, who is mentioned in Letters 85 and 86. See also the Admonition to the Brothers of Mont Dieu.

[2] This refers to the persecution which Simon endured from his monks because he had resigned into the hands of the Bishop of Arras certain altars (that is the name which used to be given to the cures of parishes), because the possession of them was stained by simony. We find on this subject a Letter of Samson, Bishop of Rheims, and of Joscelin, Bishop of Soissons, to Pope Innocent II., who had named them as judges of that cause. We read also a Letter of Eugenius III.

ness, and although the consolation given you by Christ in the promise of His kingdom may suffice amply for you, none the less is it my duty to render you both all the consolation that is in my power, and sound and faithful advice as far as I am able. For who can see without anxiety Peter stretching his arms in the midst of the billows?—or hear without grief the dove of Christ not singing, but groaning as if she said, *How shall we sing the Lord's song in a strange land?* (Ps. cxxxvii. 4). Who, I say, can without tears look upon the tears of Christ Himself, who from the bottom of the abyss lifts now His eyes unto the hills to see from whence cometh His help? But we to whom in your humility you say that you are looking, are not mountains of help, but are ourselves struggling with laborious endeavours in this vale of tears against the snares of a resisting enemy, and the violence of worldly malice, and with you we cry out, *Our help is from the Lord, who made Heaven and earth* (Ps. cxxi. 2).

2. All those, indeed, who wish to live piously in Christ suffer persecution (2 Tim. iii. 12). The intention to live piously is never wanting to them, but it is not always possible to carry it perfectly out, for just as it is the mark of the wicked constantly to struggle against the pious designs of the good; so it is not a reproach to the piety [of the latter], even although they are frequently unable to perfect their just and holy desires, because they are few against many opposers. Thus Aaron yielded against his will to the impious clamours of the riotous people (Exod. xxxii.). So Samuel unwillingly anointed Saul, constrained by the too

to Bartholomew, Bishop of Laon, in which he informs him that he wishes to know the ground of the dispute between Alvisus, Bishop of Arras, and G., Abbot of S. Nicholas. In the Letter from Samson to Pope Innocent it is said that Abbot Simon, "because his monks did not agree with him to resign those altars, laid down the abbacy for a while, and retired into a distant region;" but at length he was recalled by his monks, "who preferred to be without those altars than without their abbot." From this may be understood the integrity and disinterestedness of Simon, under whom the monastery flourished (says Hermann), "both in religion and in material prosperity." The time, then, of the writing of this Letter may be, without doubt, placed before the accession of Innocent, *i.e.*, before 1130. As to Gilbert, the successor of Simon, see Letter 399.

eager desires of the same people for a king (1 Sam. x.). So David, when he wished to build a Temple, yet because of the numerous wars which that valorous man had constantly to sustain against enemies who molested him, he was forbidden to do what he piously proposed (2 Sam. vii.). Similarly, venerable father, I counsel you, without prejudice to the better advice of wiser persons, so to soften, for the present only, the rigour of your purpose of reform, and that of those who share it with you, that you may not be unmindful of the salvation of the weaker brethren. Those, indeed, over whom you have consented to preside in that Order of Cluny ought to be invited to a stricter life, but they ought not to be obliged to embrace it against their will. I believe that those who do desire to live more strictly ought to be persuaded either to bear with the weaker out of charity as far as they can without sin, or permitted to preserve the customs which they desire in the monastery itself, if that may be done without scandal to either party; or at least that they should be set free from the Order to associate themselves where it may seem good with other brothers who live according to their proposal.

LETTER LXXXIV.

To the Same.

He sends back an erring monk, but advises that he should be treated more gently and kindly after his return.

In the first place, please to notice that your wandering sheep[1] has been detained by us against our custom, not for ourselves, but for his own sake, and for you; not without a good result, as you see, since we have succeeded by such treatment, and by salutary counsels, in satisfying his desire for a stricter life, and in giving you at the same time full satisfaction, by his return to you with his own assent.

I say this to you not to show you our kindly feeling towards you, which I could never sufficiently show, but to

[1] Bernard himself calls him Nicholas in his Apology to William, par. 4.

convince you of the truth of what I have already said to you, if I remember rightly, that the trial of a Rule somewhat more strict often suffices to calm unquiet spirits who are not content with the kind of life that they are living. You have written to say that you wish to have my advice on the subject of this very brother who is now reconciled to you; but I have thought it now unnecessary to give it, now that he has returned to you with the intention not of extorting his own will from you, but of doing yours, as it is right he should. I beg you on his behalf, and with him, kindly to soften the difficulty of his first return, which he greatly fears, and to treat him with greater kindness and condescension than is usual with other fugitives, because, although the circumstances are similar[1] to these, yet the cause of his conduct was different, and should justify different treatment. It is evident that there is a great distinction between one who quits his monastery from fear and dislike of the religious state, and one who quits it to go to another from love of his vocation and desire to practise it better.

———

To William, Abbot of S. Thierry.

Here is inserted in some editions a Letter of S. BERNARD, which we have prefixed as a preface to the Apology of Bernard, addressed to the same WILLIAM.

[1] But the actions were not really similar: because, according to philosophers, it is the final and determining causes which make the difference between actions. Thus they are similar only in class (*in genere entis*) to borrow their language, not in moral quality (*in genere moris*). S. Augustine draws out this difference excellently in his 93rd Letter, notes 6 and 7.

LETTER LXXXV. (*Circa* A.D. 1125.)

To the same William.[1]

Bernard gently reproaches him for complaining that a sufficient return was not made to him by Bernard in offices of friendship.

To Dom Abbot WILLIAM, Brother BERNARD wishes health and the charity which comes of a pure heart and a good conscience and faith unfeigned.[2]

1. If no one knoweth the things of a man, save the spirit of man which is in him (1 Cor. ii. 11), if man sees only the

---

[1] The venerable William, whose friendship was a great delight to Bernard, was of a noble family of Liège, and was sent to Rheims to study there with another young man of good family, named Simon, whom a MS. of Marmoutiers, containing many Letters of Bernard, says was his own brother. William, despising the delights of the world, entered with his companion into the monastery of S. Nicasius, of Rheims, where he was celebrated for strict observance of the rule. After having happily passed through his noviciate, as each of them was exemplary in virtues, the one became Abbot of S. Nicholas aux Bois and the other, William, succeeded, in 1120, as Abbot of the monastery of S. Thierry, of Rheims, to Geoffrey, who had been named Abbot of S. Medard, of Soissons. However, the reputation of Bernard for sanctity spread everywhere, and inspired many persons with the desire to see and admire him. This William, then a simple monk of S. Nicasius, having heard of the sickness with which the holy man was seized soon after he became Abbot of Clairvaux, went to see him with a certain abbot; and from the interviews they then had commenced that close friendship with which they were afterwards bound. It is that which explains the grief which he felt on hearing the calumnies of which Bernard was the object; and not being able to bear them longer, he occupied himself in justifying him against all the accusations made against him by the monks of Cluny, which he did in the elegant Apology written by him, and which will be found in a later volume. These were not the only vexations which the love of William for Bernard caused him to endure. Weary of the weight of his pastoral charge, and desirous of the society of Bernard, when he had been often refused entrance into Clairvaux, as will be understood after this Letter, he at length laid down his charge and betook himself to the monastery of Signy, of the Cistercian Order, in the Diocese of Rheims, about 1135, after having been fourteen years and five months Abbot of S. Thierry. He was professed at Signy in 1135, and after having passed many years there in great humility and exemplary modesty, as in the contemplation of heavenly things (which a MS. Chronicle of Signy calls "his daily occupation"), he quitted the world about 1150, or at all events after 1144.

[2] Inscription from the Corbey MS.

face, while God reads the heart, I wonder, I cannot sufficiently wonder how and by what means you have been
able to measure and distinguish between your affection for
me and mine for you, so that you can judge, not only of
the feelings of your own heart, but also of that of another
person. It seems to be the error of the human mind, not only
to think good evil and evil good, or true things false and
conversely, but also to regard sure things as doubtful and
doubtful things as sure. Perhaps it is true what you say,
that you are loved less by me than you love me ; but I am
quite sure of this, that you can have no certainty about it.
How, then, do you affirm as certain what you cannot
possibly have any certainty of ? Wonderful ! Paul did
not trust himself to his own judgment, saying, *I judge not
my own self* (1 Cor. iv. 3). Peter mourned for the presumption with which he had deceived himself, when he
said of himself, *Though I should die with Thee I will not
deny Thee* (S. Matt. xxvi. 35). The disciples, not trusting
their own consciences, replied one after the other concerning
the denial of the Lord, *Is it I, Lord ?* (S. Matt. xxvi. 22).
David confesses his own ignorance of himself in his prayer,
Remember not my sins of ignorance (Ps. xxv. 7, VULG.).
But you, with marvellous confidence, declare so positively,
not only about your own heart, but mine, " Though I love
more, I am loved less."

2. These were, in fact, your words. I could wish they
had not been, because I do not know whether they are
true. But if you know, how do you know? How, I
repeat, have you made proof that I am more loved by you
than you by me ? Is it from what you have added in your
letters, that those who go and come between our houses
never bring you a pledge of regard and affection from me ?
But what pledge, what proof of love do you require from
me ? Is this the trouble that disturbs you, that to none of
your many letters to me have I ever replied?[1] But how
could I think that the ripeness of your wisdom could take
any pleasure in the scribblings of my inexperience ? For

[1] This was the first Letter of Bernard to William.

I knew who said, *My little children, let us not love in word nor by tongue, but in deed and in truth* (1 S. John iii. 18). When have you ever had need of my help and it has failed you? O, Thou who searchest the hearts and the reins! who alone, as the Sun of Righteousness, lightenest the hearts of Thy servants with the differing rays of Thy grace; Thou knowest I feel that I love him by Thy gift, and because he merits it; but how much I love him Thou knowest and I do not. Thou, O Lord, who hast given the love that we have, I for him or he for me, knowest how much Thou hast given. And by what right does any of us, to whom Thou hast not revealed it, dare to say, "I love more, I am loved less," unless he already sees his light in Thy light; that is, he recognizes in the light of Thy truth how bright the fire of charity may be?

3. In the meantime I am content, O Lord, to see my own darkness in Thy light, until Thou shalt visit me sitting in the darkness and the shadow of death; and by Thee the thoughts of men's hearts shall be revealed and the secret things of darkness made manifest, and the shadows being dissipated, nothing but light shall remain in Thy light. I feel, indeed, that, by Thy gift, I love him; but I do not yet see in Thy light whether I love him sufficiently. Nor do I yet know if I have reached that degree of affection, than which there can be none greater, that one should lay down his life for his friends. For who will boast that his heart is pure, or that it is perfect? O, Lord, who hast lighted in my soul a lamp by whose light I see and shudder at my own darkness, my God! enlighten also that very darkness, that I may see and rejoice in my affections perfectly regulated within me, that I may know and love what ought to be loved, and to the right degree and for the right reason. May I not desire to be loved except in Thee, and no more than I ought to be loved. Woe to me also if (which I greatly fear) either I was more loved by him than I deserved, or he less loved by me than he was worthy to be. Nevertheless, if those who are the better ought to be loved the more (for those are the better who love the

more), what else shall I say than that I do not doubt that I love him more than myself, whom I know to be better than myself; but I confess at the same time that I love him less than I ought to do, because I have less capability of doing so.

4. But, my father, the greater is your love, the less ought you to despise the imperfection of mine, because although you love more, having greater capability, yet you do not love more than your capacity enables you. It is thus with me, although I love you less than I ought, yet I love you as much as my capacity permits, and I can only do what I have received the capacity of doing. Draw me, then, in your train that I may reach unto you, and with you, receiving capacity more fully, may love more abundantly. Why, then, do you endeavour that I should attain and complain that I am not able to do so, since you have succeeded as you see and may dispose of me as you please, but such as I am, not such as you hoped to find me? Indeed, you see in me something, I know not what, which I have not, and pursue as me what is not me. Therefore you do not attain it, because I am insufficient for this, and, as you rightly complain in your letter, it is not I that fail you, but God in me. Now, if all this verbiage pleases you that I have ventured upon here, tell me, and I will repeat it, since in obeying you I shall not fear the reproach of presumption. The little Preface[1] which you have ordered to be sent to you I have not now at hand, nor did I think it necessary as yet to draw it up. I pray that He who has given you to will may in His good pleasure accomplish to you and to your friends whatsoever you will rightly, my pious and most reverend father, who art fully worthy of all my regard.

[1] This is the Letter which is placed at the head of his Apology, addressed to William, and was written about 1125.

LETTER LXXXVI. (*Circa* A.D. 1130.)

TO THE SAME.

Bernard sends back to him to be severely reprimanded a fugitive monk. He persuades William, who was meditating a change of state or retiring into private life, to persevere.

To his friend, Brother BERNARD, of Clairvaux, all that a friend can wish for a friend.

1. You have given me this formula of salutation when you wrote, "to his friend all that a friend can wish."[1] Receive what is thine own, and perceive that the assumption of it is a proof that we are of one mind, for my heart is not distant from him with whom I have language in common. I must now reply briefly to your letter, because of the time : for when it arrived the festival of the Nativity of our Lady[2] had dawned; and being obliged to devote myself entirely to its solemnities, I had no leisure to think of anything else. Your messenger also was anxious to be gone; scarcely would he stay even until to-morrow morning that I might write to you these few words after all the Offices of the festival. I send back to you a fugitive brother after having subjected him to severe reprimand suited to his hard heart. It seemed to me that there was nothing better to do than to send him back to the place whence he had fled, since I ought not, according to our rules, to detain any monk in the house without the consent of his abbot. You ought to reprove him very severely also, and press him to make humble satisfaction and then comfort him a little by a letter from yourself addressed to his abbot on his behalf.

2. Concerning my state of health, I am not able to reply very precisely to your inquiry except that I continue, as in

---

[1] *Suus ille quod suus.*

[2] It was by the example of the Cistercians, as, I think, all of whose monasteries were dedicated to the Blessed Virgin, that she began to be called Our Lady. Hence, Peter Cellensis says of Bernard : "He was a most devoted child of Our Lady, to whom he dedicated not one church only, but the churches of the whole Cistercian Order" (B. vi. Ep. 23).

the past, to be weak and ailing, neither much better nor much worse. If I have not sent the person whom I had thought of sending, it is only because I feel much more the scandal to many souls than the danger of one body. Not to pass over any of the matters of which you speak to me, I come to yourself. You wrote that you wished to know what I desired you to do (as if I were aware of all that concerned you). But this plan, if I should say what I think, is one that neither I could counsel nor you carry out. I wish, indeed, for you what, as I have long known, you wish for yourself.[1] But putting on one side, as is right, both your will and mine, I think more of what God wills for you, and, to my mind, it is both safer for me to advise you to that, and much more advantageous for you to do it. My advice is, then, that you continue to hold your present charge, to remain where you are, and study to profit those over whom you are set, nor flee from the cares of office while you are able to be of use, because woe to you if you are over the flock and do not profit them; but deeper woe still if, because you fear the cares of office, you abandon the opportunity of usefulness.

LETTER LXXXVII. (*Circa* A.D. 1126.)

To Oger, Regular Canon.[2]

Bernard blames him for his resignation of his pastoral charge, although made from the love of a calm and pious life. None the less, he instructs him how, after becoming a private person, he ought to live in community.

To Brother OGER, the Canon, Brother BERNARD, monk but sinner, wishes that he may walk worthily of God even to the end, and embraces him with the fullest affection.

---

1 See note to Letter 85.

2 Some blame and some ridicule such a title as this, as being a vicious pleonasm, since these two words differ only in the language from which each is borrowed, and mean exactly the same thing; as if canons were something different from regulars, or as if there were some canons who were regulars and others who were not. But it may be seen in John Bapt. Signy *Lib. de Ord.*

1. If I seem to have been too slow in replying to your letter, ascribe it to my not having had an opportunity to send to you. For what you now read was written long since, but, as I have said, though written without delay, was delayed for want of a bearer. I have read in your letter that you have laid down with regret the burden of your pastoral charge, permission having been obtained with great difficulty, or rather, extorted by your importunity, from your Bishop; and only on the condition that you should remain under his authority, though fixing yourself elsewhere. But this not being satisfactory to you, you appealed to the Archbishop, and, obtaining the relaxation of this condition, you have returned to your former house and put yourself under your original abbot. Now you ask to be advised by me as to how you ought to live hence-forth. An able teacher, indeed, and incomparable master am I! And when I shall have begun to teach what I do not know myself, it will soon be discovered that I know nothing. You act, in consulting me, as a sheep who seeks wool from a goat, a mill expecting water from an oven, a wise man expecting sound counsel from a fool. Besides this, you heap upon me, from one end of your letter to the other, complimentary speeches, and attribute to me excellences of which I am not conscious; and as I ascribe them to your kind feelings, so I forgive them to your ignorance. For you look upon the countenance, but God upon the heart; and if I examine myself with attention under His awful gaze, I find that I know myself much better than you know me, since I am much less far from myself than you are. Therefore I give greater credence to that which I see in myself than to what you suppose, without seeing, to be

Canon, B. ii., and Navarre, *Com. I. de Regul.* ad c. 12, *Cui portio Deus,* q. 1, where he shows that every pleonasm is not necessarily a battology. For in legal documents certain expressions or clauses are often repeated to give them more force. It is the same in Hebrew (Ps. lxxxvii. 5, Ps. lxviii. 12 VULG. and lxx.).

Oger was the first Dean of the Regular Canons of S. Nicholas des Pres, near Tournay. Picard states this upon the authority of Denis Viller, Canon and Chancellor of Tournay.

in me.   Nevertheless, if you may have heard from me anything that is profitable to you, give thanks to God, in whose
hand I am and all my words.

2. You explain to me also for what reason you have not
followed my advice, not only not to allow yourself to be
discouraged or overcome by despondency, but to bear
patiently the burden laid upon you, which once undertaken'
you were not at liberty to lay down; and I accept your
explanations.   I am well aware, indeed, of the infertility of
my wisdom, and I always hold myself in suspicion for rashness and inexperience, so that I ought not to take it ill, nor
do I, when the course which I approve is not taken; and I
wish, on the contrary, that action should be taken on better
advice than mine.   As often as my opinion is chosen and
followed I feel myself weighed down, I confess it, with
responsibility, and await with inquietude, never with confidence, the issue of the matter.   Yet it is for you to see
if you have acted wisely in not following my advice about
this thing ;[1] it must be decided also by those wiser persons
than I, on whose authority you have relied, whether you

[1] Bernard had counselled him not to resign his abbacy, and this advice he
had not followed.   Hence is suggested the serious question : Is it lawful to lay
down the pastoral charge, to withdraw one's self from cares and business, for the
purpose of serving God in peace and quiet, and caring for one's own soul ?
The examples of so many holy men whom we know to have done this add to
the difficulty of the question.   Many might be cited among prelates of lower
rank, not a few Bishops, Cardinals, and even some Popes.   Bruno III., Count of
Altena, and afterwards Bishop of Cologne, quitted his see, in 1119, and retired to
the Cistercian monastery of Aldenberg.   Eskilus, Archbishop of Lunden, in
Denmark, came to live at Clairvaux as a simple monk ; Peter Damian, who,
from a Benedictine monk, became Cardinal and Bishop of Ostia, after he had
rendered signal service to the Church for a number of years, with wonderful constancy, in the high office to which he had been raised, returned into his cell
from love of solitude and quiet, and passed the rest of his days in profound
peace, in the midst of his brethren ; but was blamed by the Pope because he,
a useful and able man, postponed public usefulness to his private safety.   One
remarkable fact is recorded of him, that the Pope imposed upon him a penance
of a hundred years for quitting his' Bishopric : he was to recite Ps. l. [li.] and
give himself the discipline every day for a hundred years ; and this he completed
entirely in the space of one year.   This I remember to have read somewhere
(*Works*, Vol. i. ep. 10, new ed., Vol. iii. opusc. 20).   To Pope Alexander and
Cardinal Hildebrand, who became Pope later under the name of Gregory VII.,

have done according to reason. They will tell you, I say, whether it is lawful for a Christian man to lay down the burden of obedience before his death, when Christ was made obedient to the Father even unto death. You will reply, "I have acted by license, asked and received from the Bishop." True, you have, indeed, asked for license, but in a manner you ought not to have done, and, therefore, have rather extorted than asked it. But an extorted or compelled license should rather be called violence. What, therefore, the Bishop did unwillingly, when overcome by your importunity, was not to release you from your obligations, but violently to break them.

3. You may indeed be congratulated, since you are thus exonerated; but I fear lest you have, as much as lieth in you, taken from the glory[1] of God, whose will you, beyond doubt, resist in casting yourself down from the post to which He had advanced you. Perhaps you excuse yourself by pleading the necessity of religious poverty; but it is necessity that brings the crown, in rendering achievements difficult and almost impossible; for all things are possible to him who has faith. But answer to me what is most true, that you have consulted your own quiet, rather than the ad-

---

he tries to justify his quitting his see, and opposes numerous examples of conduct similar to his, to the blame of the Pope and the cardinals.

But it is necessary to hold to what the law prescribes rather than to the examples of other persons. The Angelical Doctor says: "Every pastor is obliged by his function to labour for the salvation of others, and it is not permitted to him to cease to do so, not even to have leisure for peaceful meditation upon spiritual things. For the Apostle regards the obligation to occupy himself with the salvation of others who depend upon him as being of such importance that it must not be postponed even to heavenly meditation: *I know not what to choose*, he says, *for I am in a strait betwixt two, having a desire to depart and to be with Christ, which is far better; nevertheless, to abide in the flesh is more needful for you* (Phil. i. 22-23). It may be added that the Episcopate being a state more perfect than that of the monk, it follows that just as it is not permitted to quit the second to re-enter the world, so it is not allowable to renounce the first in order to embrace the second, considering that the latter is less perfect than the former. That would precisely be to look back after having put one's hand to the plough, and to show one's self unfit for the kingdom of God (S. Luke ix. 62).

[1] *Exoneratus ; exhonoratus.*

vantage of others. Nor is this strange. I confess that I, too, am pleased that quiet should delight you, if only it does not delight you too much. For that, even although a great thing, which pleases us to such a degree that we wish to bring it about, even although by wrong means, pleases us too much; and because it cannot be brought about by right means, it ceases to be good. For *if you offer rightly, but do not divide rightly, you have sinned* (Gen. iv. 7, lxx). Either, therefore, you ought not to have accepted the cure of the Lord's flock, or, having accepted it, ought not to have relinquished it, according to those words: *Art thou bound unto a wife? seek not to be loosed* (1 Cor. vii. 27).

4. But to what end do I strive in these arguments? To persuade you to take your charge again? You cannot, since it is no longer vacant. Or to drive you to despair by fixing upon you the blame of a fault which you are no longer able to repair? By no means; I wish only that you should not neglect the fault you have committed, as if it were nothing or nothing much, but that you should rather repent of it with fear and trembling, as it is written: *Happy is the man that feareth alway* (Prov. xxviii. 14). But the fear which I wish to inspire is not that which falls into the nets of desperation, but which brings to us the hope of blessedness. There is, indeed, a fear, useless, gloomy, and cruel, which does not seek pardon, and, therefore, does not obtain it. There is also a fear, pious, humble, and fruitful, which easily obtains mercy for a sinner, however great be his offence. Such a fear produces, nourishes, and preserves not only humility, but also sweetness, patience, and forbearance. Whom does not so blameless an offspring delight? But of the other fear the miserable progeny is obstinacy, excessive sorrow, rancour, horror, contempt, and desperation. I have wished to recall you to the remembrance of your fault, but only in order to awaken in you, not the fear which produces desperation, but that which produces hope; being afraid lest you should not have any fear at all, or should have too little.

5. There is something, however, which I fear still more

for you, namely, that which is written of certain sinners, that they *rejoice in having done evil and delight in wicked actions* (Prov. ii. 14) ; that you should be deceived, and not only think that what you have done is not wrong, but also (which, God forbid) glory in your heart, thinking that you have done something great, and which is usually done by few, in renouncing voluntarily the power to command others, and, despising rule, have preferred to be subjected again to a ruler.   That would be a false humility, causing real pride in the heart of him that should think such thoughts.   For what can be more proud than to ascribe to spontaneous and, as it were, free choice that which the force of necessity or faint-hearted weakness obliges us to do ?   But if you have not been forced by necessity or exhausted by labour, but have done it willingly, there is nothing more proud than this ; for you have put your own will before that of God, you have chosen to taste the sweetness of repose rather than serve diligently in the work to which He has set you. If, then, you have not only despised God, but glory in utterly contemning Him, your glorying is not good.   Beware of boastfulness and self-satisfaction ; more useful for you were it to be always in care, always humbly trembling, not, as I have said, with the fear that provokes wrath, but with that which softens it.

6. If that horrible fear ever knocks at the door of your soul to terrify it, and to suggest that your service to God cannot be accepted, and that your penitence is unfruitful because that in which God has been offended by you cannot be amended ; do not receive it even for a moment, but reply with confidence : I have done wrong indeed, but it is done and cannot be undone.   Who knows if God has foreseen that good should come to me out of it, and that He who is good has willed to do me good even from my evil ?   Let Him then punish the evil which I have done, but let the good which He had provided for remain.   The goodness of God knew how to use our ill-governed wills and actions to the beauty of the order which He established, and oft en, in His goodness, even to our benefit.   O indulgent bounty

of Divine love towards the sons of Adam! which does not cease to load us with benefits, not only where no merit was found, but often even where entire demerit was seen. But let us return to you. According to the two kinds of fear which are distinguished above, I wish you to fear, and yet not to fear ; to presume, and yet not to presume. To feel that you may repent, not to feel that you may have confidence ; and again, to have confidence that you may not distrust, and not to be confident that you may not grow inactive.

7. You perceive, brother, how much confidence I have in you, since I permit myself to blame you so sharply, to judge and disapprove so freely what you have done, when perhaps you have had better reasons for doing it than have hitherto been made known to me. For you have not perhaps wished to state those reasons in your letters, by which your action might well be excused, either through your humility or through want of space. Leaving, then, undecided for the present my opinion about any part of the matter with which I may not be fully acquainted, one thing that you have done I unreservedly praise, namely, that when you had laid down the yoke of ruling, yet without a yoke you were not willing to continue, but took up again a discipline to which you were attached, without being ashamed to become a simple disciple when you had borne the title of master. For you were able, when freed from your pastoral charge, to remain under your own authority, since in becoming abbot you were released from the obedience owed to your former abbot.[1] But you did not wish to be under no authority but your own, and as you had declined to rule over others, so you shrunk from rule over yourself ; and inasmuch as you thought yourself not fit to be the master of others, so also you did not trust yourself to be your own master, and in your distrust of yourself, even for your own guidance, would not be your own disciple. And rightly. For he who makes himself his own master,

[1] Because a monk, when he became an abbot, was freed from the control of his own abbot.

subjects himself to a fool as master. I know not what others may think of this ; as for me, I have had experience of what ·I say, that it is far more easy and safe to govern many others than my own single self. It was, therefore, a proof of prudent humility and of humble prudence that, by no means believing that you were sufficient for your own salvation, you proposed to live henceforth by the judgment of another person.

8. I praise you also that you did not seek out another master nor another place, but returned to the cloister whence you had gone forth, and to the master under whom you had made progress in good. It was very right that the house which had nurtured you, but had sent you forth through brotherly charity, should receive you when freed from your charge, rather than that another house should have in its place the joy of possessing you. As, however, you have not obtained the sanction of the Bishop for what you have done, do not be negligent in seeking it, but either yourself, or through some third person, be prompt to give him satisfaction as far as is in your power. After this, study to lead a simple life among your brethren, devoted to God, submissive to your superior, respectful towards the older monks, and obliging towards the younger. Be profitable in word, humble in heart, pleasing to the Angels, courteous to all. But beware of thinking that you have a right to be honoured more than others because you were once placed in a position of dignity, but show yourself as one among the rest, only more humble than all. For it is not becoming that you should be honoured on account of a post, the labour of which you have shunned.

9. Another danger also may arise from this of which I wish to forewarn you and strengthen you against it. For as we are very changeable, and it frequently happens that what we wished for yesterday to-day we refuse, and what we shrink from to-day to-morrow we desire, so it may happen sometime by the temptation of the devil that, from the remembrance of the honour you have resigned, a selfish desire may knock at the door of your heart, and you may

begin weakly to covet what you bravely resigned. The
recollection of things which before were bitter to you will
then be sweet; the dignity of the position, the care of the
house, and the administration of its property, the respectful
obedience of domestics, the freedom of your own actions,
the power over others; it may be as much a source of
regret to you that you have given up these things, as it was
before of weariness to bear them.   If you yield even for an
hour (which may God forbid) to this most injurious temptation you will suffer great loss to your spiritual life.

    10. This is the whole of the wisdom of that most accom-
plished and eloquent Doctor, by whom you have wished to
be taught from such a distance.   This is the eulogy, desired
and waited for, which you have been so eager to hear.
This is the sum of all my wisdom.   Do not look for any
other great thing from me ; you have heard all.   What
can you require more ?   The fountain is drained, and would
you seek water from the dry sand ?   I have sent you,
according to the example of that widow in the Gospel,[1] out
of my poverty all that I had.   Why art thou ashamed, and
why does thy countenance fall ?   You have obliged me.
You have asked for a discourse ; a discourse you have.   A
discourse, I say, long enough, indeed, but saying nothing ;
full of words, empty of meaning.   Such is the discourse
which ought to be received by you with charity, as you
have requested it, but which only seems to reveal my lack
of knowledge.   Perhaps it would not be impossible for me to
find excuses for it.   Thus I might say that I have dictated
it while labouring under a tertian fever, as also while occupied with the cares of my office, while yet it is written,
Write at leisure of wisdom (founded on Ecclus. xxxviii.
25).   I should rightly put these reasons forward if I had
adventured upon some great and laborious work.   But now,
in such a brief treatise that my engagements afford me no
excuse, I can allege nothing, as I have often said already,
but the insufficiency of my knowledge.

    11. But I console myself in my mortification by consider-

[1] S. Luke xxi. 1-4.

ing that if I had not done as you requested, if I had not sent what you hoped for, you would not have been quite sure of my goodwill to-day. I hope that my good intention will content you when you see that the power to do more was wanting to me. And although my Letter be without utility to you, it will profit me in promoting humility. *Even a fool when he holdeth his peace is counted wise* (Prov. xvii. 28), for that he holds his peace is counted to him as the reserve of humility, not as want of sense. If, then, I had still kept silence, I should have had the benefit of a similar judgment, and have been called wise without being so. But now some will ridicule me as a man of little wisdom, some laugh at me as ignorant, and others indignantly accuse me of presumption. Do not think that all this serves little to the profit of religion, since humility, which humiliation teaches us to practise, is the foundation of the entire spiritual fabric. Thus humiliation is the way to humility, as patience to peace, as reading is to knowledge. If you long for the virtue of humility, you must not flee from the way of humiliation. For if you do not allow yourself to be humiliated, you cannot attain to humility. It is a benefit to me, therefore, that my ignorance should be made known, and that I should be rightly put to confusion by those who are instructed, since I have often been undeservedly praised by those who could not form a correct opinion. The fear of the Apostle makes me fear when he says, *I forbear, lest any man should think of me above that which he seeth me to be, or that he heareth of me* (2 Cor. xii. 6). How finely he has said *I spare* [restrain] you. The arrogant, the proud, the desirous of vain glory, the boaster of his own deeds, who either takes merit to himself for what he has done, or even claims what he has not done, he does not restrain himself. He alone who is truly humble, he restrains his own soul, who is even afraid to let the excellency that is in him be known, that he may not be thought to be what he is not.

12. Great in truth is the danger, that anyone should speak of us above what we feel our desert to be. Who

shall give me to be as deservedly humiliated among men for
well-founded reasons as I have been undeservedly praised
for ill-founded ones? I should, then, be able to take to
myself the word of the Prophet: *After having been exalted
I have been cast down and filled with confusion* (Ps.
lxxxviii. 15, VULG.), and this, *I will play and will be yet
more vile* (2 Sam. vi. 21, 22). Yes, I will play this foolish
game that I may be ridiculed. It is a good folly, at which
Michal is angry and God is pleased. A good folly which
affords a ridiculous spectacle, indeed, to men, but to
angels an admirable one. Yes, I repeat; an excellent folly,
by which we are exposed to disgrace from the rich and
disdain from the proud. For, in truth, what do we appear
to people of the world to do except indulge in folly, since
what they seek with eagerness in this world we, on the
contrary, shun, and what they avoid we eagerly seek?
Upon the eyes of all we produce the effect of jugglers and
tumblers, who stand or walk on their hands, contrary to
human nature, with their heads downward and feet in the
air. But our foolish game has nothing boyish in it, nothing
of the spectacle at the theatre, which represents low actions,
and with effeminate and corrupt gestures and bendings
provoke the passions, but it is cheerful, honourable, grave,
decent, and capable of delighting even the celestial beings
who gaze upon it. This it was he was engaged in, who
said, *We are made a spectacle to Angels and to men* (1 Cor.
iv. 9). May it be ours also in this meantime, that we may
be ridiculed, confounded, humiliated, until He shall come
who puts down the powerful and exalts the humble, to fill us
with joy and glory, and to raise us up for ever and ever.

LETTER LXXXVIII. (*Circa* A.D. 1127.)

TO THE SAME.

*Bernard, being hindered by many occupations, has not
yet been able to find time to satisfy his wishes, and is*

obliged even to write to him very briefly. He forbids a
certain one of his treatises to be made public unless it
were read over and corrected.

1. I pass over now my want of experience, my humble
profession, or rather my profession of humility, nor do I
shelter myself behind (I do not say my lowness, but, at
least) my mediocrity of position or name, since whatever
I should allege of that kind you would declare to be rather
a pretext for delay than a reasonable excuse. It seems to
me that you interpret my shyness and modesty at your will,
now as indiscretion, now as false humility, and now as real
pride. Of these reasons, therefore, since they would appear
doubtful to you, I say nothing. Only I wish that your
friendship should be fully convinced of one thing, that since
the departure of your messenger (not the one who carries
this letter, but the other) left me I have not had a single
instant of leisure to do what you asked, so busy are my
days and so short my nights. Even now your latest letter
has found me so engrossed that it would take me too long
to write to you the mere occupations, which would be my
excuse with you. I have scarcely been able even to read
your letter through, except during my dinner, for at that
hour it was delivered to me, and scarcely have I been able
to write back to you these few words hastily and, as it
were, furtively. You will see that you must not complain
of the brevity of my letter.

2. To speak the truth, my dear Oger, I am forced to be
angry with all these cares, and that on your account,
although in them, as my conscience bears witness, I desire
to serve only charity, by the requirements of which, as I am
debtor both to the wise and to the unwise, I have been
made unable as yet to satisfy your wishes. What, then?
Does Charity deny to you what you ask in the name of
Charity? You have requested and begged, you have
knocked at the door, and Charity has rendered your requests
unavailing. Why are you angry with me? It is Charity
whom you must be angry with, if you will and dare to be

so, since it is she who is the cause that you have not
obtained what you expected to have by her means. Already
she is displeased at my long discourse, and is angry with
you who have imposed it. Not that the ardour with which
you do this is displeasing to her, since it is she which has
inspired you with it, but she wishes that your zeal should
be ruled according to knowledge, and that you should be
careful not to hinder greater things for the sake of lesser.
You see how unwillingly I am torn away from writing to you
at greater length, since the pleasure of conversing with you,
and the wish to satisfy you, make me troublesome to my
mistress, Charity, who has long since been bidding me to
make an end, and I am not yet silent. How wide is the
matter for reply in your letter, if it were permissible to do
as you would wish, and as I, too, should, perhaps, be well
enough pleased to do ! But she who requires otherwise of
me is mistress, or rather is the Master. For *God is charity*
(1 S. John iv. 16), and it is very evident that such is her
authority, that I ought to obey her rather than either
myself or you. And since it is incumbent on Charity to obey
God rather than men, I unwillingly, and with grief, put off
for a time the doing what you ask, not refuse altogether
to do it, and I fear in endeavouring humbly to respond to
your desires to appear to wish, under the pretext of a
pretended humility, which is only pure pride, to revolt here
below, I, who am only a miserable worm of the earth, against
the strength of that power which, as you truly declare, rules
even the Angels in heaven.

3. As for the little treatise which you ask for, I had
asked for it back again from the person to whom I had lent
it, even before your messenger came to me, but I have not
yet received it ; but I will take care that at all events when
you come here, if you are ever coming, you shall find it
here, see and read it, but not transcribe it. For that other
treatise which you mention that you have transcribed I had
sent to you to be read, indeed, but not to be copied ; and I
do not know to what good purpose or for whose good you
can have done it. In sending it to you I did not intend

that the Abbot of S. Thierry should have it,[1] and I had not bidden you to send it; but I am not displeased that you have done so. For why should I be afraid that my little book should pass under his eyes, under whose gaze I would willingly spread my whole soul if I were able? But, alas! why does the mention of so good a man present itself at such a time of hurried discourse, when it is not permitted to me to linger, as would be fitting, and converse with you about that excellent man, when I ought already to have come to the end of my letter? I entreat you to make an opportunity of going to see him, and do not give out my book to be read or copied until you shall have gone over the whole of it with him; read it then together and correct what in it needs correction, that every word in it may have the support of two witnesses. After that, I commit to the judgment of each of you whether it be expedient that it should be shown publicly, or only to a few persons, or to some particular person only, or not at all to anyone. And I make you judge equally if that little preface[2] which you have fitted to the same out of fragments from other letters of mine should stand as it is, or whether another fitter one should be composed.

4. But I had almost forgotten that you complained at the beginning of your letter that I had accused you of falsehood. I do not clearly recollect whether I ever said that; but if I said anything like it (for I should prefer to think that I had forgotten rather than that your messenger had falsely reported) do not doubt that it was spoken in joke, and not seriously. Can I have even thought that you had used levity and were capable of trifling with your word?

---

1 He is here, without doubt, speaking of the Apology to the Abbot William. Oger was at Clairvaux while Bernard was writing it, as appears from the last words of that work. But as he left before the final touches were put to it, Bernard afterwards sent it to him for perusal; and he, without direction, communicated it to Abbot William, to whom it was inscribed, and to whom Bernard intended to send it.

2 This little preface is the Letter addressed to the same William, and counted the 85th among the Letters of S. Bernard; it is placed at the head of the Apology.

Far from me be such a suspicion of you, who have from
your youth been happy in bearing the yoke of truth, and
when I find in you a gravity of character beyond your years.
Nor am I so simple as to see a falsehood in a word artlessly
spoken without duplicity of heart; nor so indifferent as to
have forgotten either the project which you have long since
formed or the obstacle which hinders its realization.

LETTER LXXXIX. (*Circa* A.D. 1127.)

To the Same.

*He excuses the brevity of his letter on the ground that
Lent is a time of silence; and also that on account of his
profession and his ignorance he does not dare to assume
the function of teaching.*

1. You will, perhaps be angry, or, to speak more gently,
will wonder that in place of a longer letter which you had
hoped for from me you receive this brief note. But remember what says the wise man, that there is a time for all
things under the heaven; both a time to speak and a time
to keep silence (Eccles. iii. 1-7). But when shall silence
have its time, if our chatter shall occupy even these sacred
days of Lent? Correspondence is more absorbing than
conversation, inasmuch as it is more laborious; since when
in each other's presence we may say with little labour what
we will, but when absent we require diligently to dictate in
turn the words which we mutually seek, or which are sought
from us. But while being absent from you I meditate,
dictate or write down what you are in time to read, where,
I pray you, is the silence and quiet of my retreat?[1]   But

[1] In this Letter the Saint expresses in forcible words how little he felt himself
inclined to write to his friends Letters without necessity or usefulness, and to
take time and leisure for doing so which belonged to more important and
sacred employments. Also, he felt that the labour of literary composition
interfered with the silence to which monks were bound, as also with inward
quiet and peace. Bernard speaks of the function and calling of a monk like
himself. For the monk, as such, is not called to preach and to teach, but to
devote himself in solitude to God and to his own salvation, through meditation

all these things, you say, you can do in silence; yet, if you think, you will not answer thus. For what a tumult there is in the mind of those who dictate, what a crowd of sentiments, variety of expressions, diversity of senses jostle; how frequently one rejects that word which presents itself and seeks another which still escapes; what close attention one gives to the consecutiveness of the line of thought and the elegance of the expression! How it can be made most plain to the intellect, how it can be made most useful to the conscience, what, in short, shall be put before and what after for a particular reader, and many other things do those who are careful in their style, attend to most closely. And will you say that in this I shall have quiet; will you call this silence, even though the tongue be still?

2. Besides, it is not only the time, but also my profession and my insufficiency which prevent my undertaking what you desire, or being able to fulfil it. For it is not the profession of a monk, which I seem to be, or of a sinner, which I am, to teach, but to mourn for sin. An unlearned person (as I truly confess myself to be) never acts more unlearnedly than when he presumes to teach what he knows not. Therefore, to teach is the business neither of the unlearned in his rashness, nor of the monk in his boldness, nor of the penitent in his distress. It is for this reason I have fled from the world and abide in solitude, and propose to myself with the prophet, *to take heed to my ways that I offend not with my tongue* (Ps. xxxix. 2) since, according to the same prophet, *A man full of words shall not prosper upon the earth* (Ps. cxl. 11), and to another Scripture, *Death and*

and the practice of virtues. Wherefore he says, in ep. 42 : " Labour and retirement and voluntary poverty, these are the signs of the monk; these render excellent the monastic life." But if there should be anywhere lurking slothful monks who are so imprudent and rash as to abuse the authority of the Saint to the excuse of their own indolence, let such hear him accusing them in plain words : " I may seem, perhaps, to say too much in disparagement of learning, as if I wished to blame the learned and prohibit the study of literature. By no means. I do not overlook how greatly her learned sons have profited and do profit the Church, whether in combating her enemies or in instructing the simple," etc. (Sermon 36 on the *Canticles*).

life are in the power of the tongue (Prov. xviii. 21). But silence, says Isaiah, *is the work of righteousness* (Is. xxxii. 17), and Jeremiah teaches us *to wait in silence for the salvation of the Lord* (Lam. iii. 26). Thus to this pursuit and desire of righteousness, since righteousness is the mother, the nurse, and the guardian of all virtues, I would not seem entirely to deny what you have asked, and I invite and entreat you and all those who, like you, desire to make progress in virtue, if not by the teaching of my words, at least by the example of my silence, to learn from me to be silent, you who press me in your words to teach what I do not know.

3. But what am I doing? It will be wonderful if you do not smile, seeing with what a flood of words I condemn those who are too full of words, and while I desire to commend silence to you, I plead against silence by my loquacity. Our dear Guerric,[1] concerning whose penitence and whose manner of life you wished to be assured, as far as I can judge from his actions, is walking worthy of the grace of God, and bringing forth works worthy of penitence. The little book which you ask of me I have not beside me just now. A certain friend of ours, with the same desire to read it as you, has kept it a long time, but not to frustrate altogether the desire of your piety,[2] I send you another which I have just completed on the *Glories of the Virgin Mother,* which, as I have no other copy of it, I beg that you will return to me as soon as possible, or bring it with you if you will be coming here soon.

LETTER XC. (*Circa* A.D. 1127.)

To the Same.

A sincere love has no need of lengthy letters, or of many words. Bernard has been in a state of health almost despaired of, but is now recovering.

---

[1] This Guerric was made Abbot of Igny in 1138. He is mentioned again in the following Letter.

[2] Or *benignity.*

1. I have sent you a short letter in reply to a short one from you. You have given me an example of brevity, and I willingly follow it. And truly what need have true and lasting friendships, as you truly say, of exchanging empty and fugitive words? However great be the variety of quotations and verses, and the multiplicity of the phrases by which you have endeavoured to display or to prove your friendship for me, I feel more certain of your affection than I do that you have succeeded in expressing it, and you will not be wrong if you think the same in respect to me. When your letter came into my hands you were present in my heart, and I am quite convinced that it will be the same for me when you receive my letter, and that when you read it I shall not be absent. It is a labour for each of us to scribble to the other, and for our messengers a fatigue to carry our letters from the one to the other, but the heart feels neither labour nor fatigue in loving. Let those things cease, then, which without labour cannot be carried on, and let us practise only that which, the more earnestly it is done, seems to cost the less labour. Let our minds, I say, rest from dictating, our lips from conversing, our fingers from writing, our messengers from running to and fro.[1] But let not our hearts rest from meditating day and night on the law of the Lord, which is the law of love. The more we cease to be occupied in doing this the less quiet shall we enjoy, and the more engrossed we are in it, so much the more calm and repose we shall feel from it. Let us love and be loved, striving to benefit ourselves in the other, and the other in ourselves. For those whom we love, on those do we rely, as those who love us rely in turn on us. Thus to love in God is to ~~love~~ charity, and therefore it is to labour for charity, to strive to be loved for the sake of God.

2. But what am I doing? I promised brevity, and I am sliding into prolixity. If you desire news of Brother Guerric, or rather since you do so, he so runs not as uncer-

---

[1] This kind of correspondence is a hindrance to devotion and the spirit of prayer, as he says in the Letter placed at the head of his Apology addressed to Abbot William, and also in Letter 89.

tainly, so fights not as one that beateth the air. But since
he knows that salvation depends not on him who fights, nor
on him who runs, but on God, who shows mercy, he begs
that he may have the help of your prayers for him, so that
He who has already granted to him both to fight and to run,
may grant also to overcome and to attain. Salute for me
with my heart and by your mouth your abbot, who is most
dear to me, not only on your account, but also because of his
high character. It will be most agreeable to me to see him
at the time and place which you have promised. I do not
wish to leave you ignorant that the hand of God has for a
little while been laid heavily upon me. It seemed that I
had been stricken to the fall, that the axe had been laid to
the root of the barren tree of my body, and I feared that I
might be instantly cut down ; but lo ! by your prayers and
those of my other friends, the good Lord has spared me
this time also, yet in the hope that I shall bear good fruits
in the future.

LETTER XCI. (*Circa* A.D. 1130.)

To the Abbots assembled at Soissons.[1]

*Bernard urges the abbots zealously to perform the duty
for which they had met. He recommends to them a great
desire of spiritual progress, and begs them not to be delayed in their work if lukewarm and lax persons should
perhaps murmur.*

[1] This was one of the first general Chapters held by the Black Monks (as they
are called) in the province of Rheims. It seems that its cause and occasion was
the Apology addressed by Bernard to Abbot William, who was the prime mover
in calling together this assembly, after the example of the Cluniacs and Cistercians, that they might re-establish the observance of the Rule which was being
let slip. It was held without doubt at S. Medard under the Abbot Geoffrey, to
whom Letter 66 was addressed. He was Bishop of Châlons-sur-Marne when
Peter the Venerable spoke of him thus (B. ii. Ep. 43) : " It is he who first spread
the divine Order of Cluny through the whole of France, who was its author and
propagator ; and, far more, it was he who expelled ' the old dragon ' from his
resting-places in so many monasteries, and who roused monks from their
torpor." Innocent II. determined that these general Chapters should be held
every year in future.

To the Reverend Abbots met in the name of the Lord in Chapter at Soissons, brother BERNARD, Abbot of Clairvaux, the servant of their Holiness, health and prayer that they may see, establish, and observe the things which are right.

1. I greatly regret that my occupations prevent me from being present at your meeting—at least, in body. For neither distance nor a crowd of cares are able to banish my spirit, which prays for you, feels with you, and rests among you. No, I repeat, I cannot be wanting in the assembly of the saints, nor can distance of place nor absence of body altogether separate me from the congregation and the counsels of the righteous, in which, not the traditions of men are obstinately upheld or superstitiously observed; but diligent and humble inquiry is made what is the good and acceptable and perfect will of God (Rom. xii. 2). All my desires carry me where you are; I am with you by devotion, by friendship, by similarity of sentiment, and partaking of your zeal.

2. That those who now applaud you may not hereafter ridicule you as having assembled to no purpose (which God forbid !), strive, I beseech you, to make your conduct holy and your resolutions good, for too good they cannot be. Grant that you may be too just or even too wise, yet it is plain that you cannot be good beyond measure. And indeed I read: *Do not carry justice to excess* (Eccles. vii. 17, VULG.). I read : *Be not wiser than is befitting* (Rom. xii. 3, VULG.). But is it ever said : Do not carry goodness to excess ? or, Take care not to be too good ? No one can be more good than it behoves him to be. Paul was a good man, and yet he was not at all content with his state ; he reached forward gladly to the things that were before, forgetting those that were behind (Phil. iii. 13), and striving to become continually better than himself. It is only God who does not desire to become better than He is, because that is not possible.

3. Let those depart both from me and from you who say : We do not desire to be better than our fathers ; declaring themselves to be the sons of lukewarm and lax persons,

whose memory is in execration, since they have eaten sour grapes, and their children's teeth are set on edge. Or if they pretend that their fathers were holy men, whose memory is blessed, let them imitate their sanctity, and not defend, as laws instituted by them, the indulgences and dispensations which they have merely endured. Although holy Elias says, *I am not better than my fathers* (1 Kings xix. 4), yet he has not said that he did not wish to be. Jacob saw upon the ladder Angels ascending and descending (Gen. xxviii. 12); but was any one of them either sitting, or standing still? It was not for angels to stand still on the uncertain rounds of a frail ladder ; nor can anything remain fixed in the same condition during the uncertain period of this mortal life. Here have we no continuing city; nor do we yet possess, but always seek for, that which is to come. Of necessity you either ascend or descend, and if you try to stand still you cannot but fall. It may be held as certain that the man is not good at all who does not wish to be better ; and where you begin not to care to make advance in goodness there also you leave off being good.

4. Let those depart both from me and from you who call good evil and evil good. If they call the pursuit of righteousness evil, what good thing will be good in their eyes ? The Lord once spoke a single word, and the Pharisees were scandalized (S. Matt. xv. 12). But now these new Pharisees are scandalized not even at a word, but at silence. You plainly see then that they seek only the occasion to attack you. But leave them alone ; they be blind leaders of the blind. Take thought for the salvation of the little ones, not of the murmurs of the evil-disposed. Why do you so much fear to give scandal to those who are not to be cured unless you become sick with them ? It is not even desirable to wait to see whether your resolutions are pleasing to all of you in all respects, otherwise you will determine upon little or no good. You ought to consult not the views, but the needs of all ; and faithfully to draw them towards God, even although they be unwilling, rather

than abandon them to the desires of their heart. I commend myself to your holy prayers.

LETTER XCII. (A.D. 1132.)

To HENRY, KING OF ENGLAND.

He asks the King's favour to the monks sent by him to
construct a monastery.

To the illustrious HENRY, King of England, BERNARD,
Abbot of Clairvaux, that he may faithfully serve and
humbly obey the King of Heaven in his earthly kingdom.
There is in your land a property[1] belonging to your Lord
and mine, for which He preferred to die rather than it
should be lost.   This I have formed a plan for recovering,
and am sending a party of my brave followers to seek,
recover, and hold it with strong hand, if this does not
displease you. And these scouts whom you see before
you I have sent beforehand on this business to investigate
wisely the state[2] of things, and bring me faithful word
again.   Be so kind as to assist them as messengers of your

[1] The history of the Abbey of Wells, in England, explains to us what is
meant by these words of Bernard. "The Abbot of Clairvaux, Bernard, had
sent detachments of his army of invasion to take possession of the most distant regions; they won brilliant triumphs over the ancient enemy of salvation,
bearing from him his prey and restoring it to its true Sovereign.   God had
inspired him with the thought of sending some hopeful slips from his noble vine
of Clairvaux into the English land that he might have fruit among that
nation, as in the rest of the world. The very letter is yet extant which he
wrote for these Religious to the King, in which he said that there was a property of the Lord in that land of the King, and that he had sent brave men out
of his army to seek it, seize it, and bring it back to its owner.   He persuades
the King to render assistance to his messengers, and not to fail to fulfil in this
his duty to his suzerain; which was done.   The Religious from Clairvaux were
received with honour by the King and by the realm, and they laid new foundations in the province of York, founding the Abbey of Rievaulx.   And this was
the first planting of the Cistercian Order in the province of York."   (*Monast.*
Anglican. Vol. i. p. 733.)   Further mention of Henry I. is made in the notes to
Letter 138.

[2] *Esse.* This word is a common one with Bernard to signify the state of a
man or a business. See Letters 118, 304.

Lord, and in their persons fulfil your feudal[1] duty to Him. I pray Him to render you, in return, happy and illustrious, to His honour, and to the salvation of your soul, to the safety and peace of your country, and to continue to you happiness and contentment to the end of your days.

LETTER XCIII. (*Circa* A.D. 1132.)

To Henry,[2] Bishop of Winchester.

Bernard salutes· him very respectfully.

To the very illustrious Lord HENRY, by the Grace of God Bishop of Winchester, BERNARD, Abbot of Clairvaux, health in our Lord.

[1] Since kings and princes are, as it were, vassals to God.

[2] He was nephew, by his mother, of Henry I., King of England, brother of King Stephen, and son of Stephen, Count of Blois. "His mother, Adela," says William of Newburgh, "not wishing to appear to have borne children only for the world, had him tonsured." In 1126, *The History of the Abbey of Glastonbury* counts him among the number of the abbots of that monastery, and says, "he was a man extremely versed in letters, and of remarkable regularity of character. By his excellent administration the Abbey of Glastonbury profited so much that his name will be held in everlasting memory there" (*Monast. Anglican.* Vol. ii., p. 18). Henry was elevated later on to the see of Winchester, and Bernard complains of him in writing to Pope Eugenius. "What shall I say of his Lordship of Winchester? The works which he does show sufficiently what he is." Harpsfield reports that he extorted castles from nobles whom he had invited to a feast, and Roger that he had consecrated the intruder William to the See of York (*Annal.* under year 1140). The latter calls him legate of the Roman See. Brito and Henriquez must, therefore, be wrong in counting him among the Cistercians, and the latter in particular, in speaking of him as a man of eminent sanctity, taking occasion from the testimony of Wion (*Ligno ritæ*), who calls him a man gifted with prophecy, because when on his death-bed, in receiving the visit of his nephew, Henry, he predicted to him that he would be punished by God on account of the death of S. Thomas of Canterbury, whom he had himself consecrated; as if that saying may not have been inspired by fear rather than prophecy, as Manrique rightly says in his *Annals*. Peter the Venerable wrote many letters to him, which are still extant, among others Letters 24 and 25 in Book iv., in which he requests that he may return to Cluny to die and be buried there. Being invited to do so at the request of Louis, the King of France, and of the chief nobles of Burgundy, and also at the letters of Pope Hadrian IV., he sent on his treasures to Peter the Venerable, and, leaving England without the permission of the King, arrived at Cluny in 1155. He discharged from his

It is with great joy that I have learned from the report
of many persons that so humble a person as myself has
found favour with your Highness. I am not worthy of it,
but I am not ungrateful for it. I return you, therefore,
thanks for your goodness; a very unworthy return, but all
that I am able to make. I do not fear but that you will
receive the humble return that I make, since you have been
so kind as to forestall me by your affection and the honour
that you have done to me; but I defer writing more until I
shall know by some token from your hand, if you think fit
to send one, how you receive these few words. You may
easily confide your reply, in writing, or by word of mouth
if it shall so please you, to Abbot Oger, who is charged to
convey to you this note. I beg your Excellency also to be
so good as to honour that Religious with your esteem and
confidence, inasmuch as he is a man commendable for his
honour, knowledge, and piety.

LETTER XCIV. (A.D. 1132.)

To the Abbot of a certain Monastery at York, from which the Prior had departed, taking several Religious with him.[1]

1. You write to me from beyond the sea to ask of me
advice which I should have preferred that you had sought

own means the debts of the abbey, which were then enormous; he expended
for the support of the monks who lived at Cluny, more than four hundred in
number, 7,000 marks of silver, which are equal to 40,000 livres. He gave forty
chalices for celebrating mass, and a silk *pannus* (which may have been an
altar vestment, or more probably a hanging—[E.]) of great price; he buried with
his own hands Peter the Venerable, who died January 1st, 1157. Having
returned at length to his see, he died, to the great grief of the Religious of Cluny,
on August the 9th, 1171.

[1] Letter 318 clearly shows what monastery these had left, namely, the
Benedictine Abbey of S. Mary, at York, and this the *Monasticon Anglicanum*
confirms.

The Abbey of S. Mary, at York, was founded in 1088 by Count Alan, son of
Guy, Count of Brittany, in the Church of S. Olave, near York, to which King
William Rufus afterwards gave the name of S. Mary. Hither were brought
from the monastery of Whitby the Abbot Stephen and Benedictine monks,

from some other. I am held between two difficulties, for if I do not reply to you, you may take my silence for a sign of contempt ; but if I do reply I cannot avoid danger, since whatever I reply I must of necessity either give scandal to some one or give to some other a security which they ought not to have, or at all events more than they ought to have. That your brethren have departed from you was not with the knowledge nor by the advice or persuasion of me or of my brethren. But I incline to believe that it was of God, since their purpose could not be shaken by all your efforts ; and that the brethren themselves thought this also who so earnestly sought my advice about themselves ; their conscience troubling them, as I suppose, because they

under whom monastic discipline was observed ; but about the year 1132, under Geoffrey, the third abbot, it began to be relaxed. It was at that time that the Cistercian order was everywhere renowned, and was introduced into England in the year 1128 (its first establishment being at Waverley, in Surrey). Induced by a pious emulation, twelve monks of S. Mary, who were not able to obtain from their abbot permission to transfer themselves to this Cistercian Order, begged the support of Thurstan, Archbishop of York, to put their project into execution. With his support they left their monastery on October 4th, 1132, notwithstanding the opposition of their abbot, to the number of twelve priests and one levite (deacon). Of these one was the Prior Richard, another Richard the sacristan, and others named in the *History* before mentioned, taking nothing from the monastery but their habit. Troubled by their desertion, Abbot Geoffrey complained to the king, to the bishops and abbots of the neighbourhood, as well as to S. Bernard himself, of the injury done by this to the rights of all religious houses, without distinction. Archbishop Thurstan wrote a letter of apology to William, Archbishop of Canterbury, and at the same time Bernard himself wrote to Thurstan and to the thirteen Religious to congratulate them, and another to Abbot Geoffrey to justify their action (Letters 94 to 96 and 313). In the meantime these monks were shut up in the Episcopal house of Thurstan ; and as they refused, notwithstanding the censures of their abbot, to return to their former monastery, Thurstan gave them in the neighbourhood of Ripon a spot of ground previously uncultivated, covered with thorn bushes and situated among rocks and mountains which surrounded it on all sides, that they might build themselves a house there. Their Prior Richard was given to them for abbot by Thurstan, who gave him the Benediction on Christmas Day. Having passed a whole winter in incredible austerity of life, they gave themselves and their dwelling-place, which they had called Fountains, to S. Bernard. He sent to them a Religious, named Geoffrey, of Amayo, from whose hands they received the Cistercian Rule with incredible willingness and piety (*Life of S. Bernard*, B. iv. c. 2).

⌐quitted you. Otherwise, if their conscience, like that of
the Apostle, did not reproach them, their peace would not
have been disturbed (Rom. xiv. 22). But what can I do
that I may be hurtful to no one neither by my silence nor
by my reply to the questions asked me ? Thus, perhaps, I
may relieve myself of the difficulty if I shall send those who
question me to a person more learned, and whose authority is
more reverend and sacred than mine. Pope S. Gregory says
in his book on the *Pastoral Rule*, "Whosoever has proposed to himself a greater good does an unlawful thing
in subordinating it to a lesser good." And he proves this
by a citation from the Gospel, saying, *No one putting his
hand to the plough and looking back is fit for the kingdom
of God* (S. Luke ix. 62) ; and he proceeds : "He who
renounces a more perfect state which he has embraced, to
follow another which is less so, is precisely the man who
looks back " (Part iii. c. 28). The same Pope, in his third
Homily on Ezekiel, adds: "There are people who taste
virtue, set themselves to practise it, and while doing so
contemplate undertaking actions still better; but afterwards
drawing back, abandon those better things which they had
proposed to themselves. They do not, it is true, leave off
the good practices they had begun, but they fail to realize
those better ones which they had meditated. To human
judgment these seem to stand fast in the good work, but to
the eyes of Almighty God they have fallen, and failed in
what they contemplated."

2. Here is a mirror. In it let your Religious consider,
not the features of their faces, but the fact of their turning
back. Here let them determine and distinguish their
motives, their thoughts, accusing or excusing them with
that sentence which the spiritual man passes who judges all
things, and is himself judged by no one. I, indeed, cannot
rashly determine whether the state which they have left or
that which they have embraced was the greater or less, the
higher or lower, the severer or the more lax. Let them
judge according to this rule of S. Gregory. But to you,
Reverend Father, I declare, with as much positive assurance

as plain truth, that it is not at all desirable that you should set yourself to quench the Spirit. *Hinder not him,* it is said, *who is able to do good, but if thou canst, do good also thyself* (Prov. iii. 27, VULG.). It more befits you to be proud of the good works of your sons, since *a wise son is the glory of his father* (Prov. x. 1). For the rest, let no one make it a cause of complaint against me that I have not hidden in my heart the righteousness of God, unless, perhaps, I have spoken less of it than I ought, for the sake of avoiding scandal.

LETTER XCV. (A.D. 1132.)

TO THURSTAN, ARCHBISHOP OF YORK.

Bernard praises his charity and beneficence towards the Religious.

To the very dear father and Reverend Lord THURSTAN, by the Grace of God Archbishop of York, BERNARD, Abbot of Clairvaux, wishes the fullest health.

The general good report of men, as I have experienced, has said nothing in your favour which the splendour of your good works does not justify. Your actions, in fact, show that your high reputation, which fame had previously spread everywhere, was neither false nor ill-founded, but manifest and certain. Especially of late how brilliantly has your zeal for righteousness and your sacerdotal energy shone forth in the defence of the poor Religious who had no other helper.[1] Once, indeed, the whole assembly of the saints used to venerate your works of mercy and alms deeds; but in doing so it narrated always what is common to you with very many, since whosoever possesses the goods of this world is bound to share them with the poor. But this is your episcopal task, this the noble proof of your paternal affection, this your truly divine fervour, the zeal

---

[1] What Thurstan did for the protection of these monks, who 'had taken refuge with him in the desire to embrace a more austere life, may be seen in a Letter from him which we have taken from the *Monasticon Anglicanum* and placed after those of S. Bernard.

which no doubt has inspired and aroused in you who
makes His angels spirits and His ministers a flaming fire.
This, I say, belongs entirely to you. It is the ornament of
your dignity, the badge of your office, the adornment of your
crown. It is one thing to fill the belly of the hungry, and
quite another thing to have a zeal for holy poverty. The
one serves nature, the other grace. *Thou shalt visit thy
kind, He says, and thou shalt not sin* (Job. v. 24, VULG.).
Therefore he who nourishes the flesh of another sins not in
so doing, but he who honours the sanctity of another does
good to his own soul ; therefore he says again, Keep your
alms in your own hand until you shall find a righteous man
to whom to give it. For what advantage ? Because *He
who receives a righteous man in the name of a righteous
man shall receive a righteous man's reward* (S. Matt.
x. 41). Let us, then, discharge the debt that nature
requires of us, that we may avoid sin ; but let us be
co-workers with grace, that we may merit to become
sharers of it. It is this that I so admire in you, as
I acknowledge that it was given to you from above. O,
Father, truly reverend and to be regarded with the sincerest
affection ; the praise for what you have laid out of your
temporal means to the relief of our necessities, will be
blended with the praises of God for ever.

LETTER XCVI. (A.D. 1132.)

To RICHARD,[1] ABBOT OF FOUNTAINS,[2] AND HIS COM-
PANIONS, WHO HAD PASSED OVER TO THE CISTERCIAN
ORDER FROM ANOTHER.

He praises them for the renewal of holy discipline.

How marvellous are those things which I have heard and

[1] He had been Prior of the monastery of S. Mary, at York, which he quitted,
followed by twelve other Religious, as we have seen above. He died at Rome,
as may be seen in *Mon. Anglic.* p. 744. He had for successor another Richard,
formerly sacristan of the same monastery of S. Mary, who died at Clairvaux
(*Ibid.*, p. 745). He is mentioned in the 320th Letter of S. Bernard.

[2] The monastery of Fountains, in the Diocese of York, passed over to the

learned, and which the two Geoffries have announced to me, that you have become newly fervent with the fire from on high, that from weakness you have become strong, that you have flourished again with new sanctity.

This is the finger of God secretly working, softly renewing, healthfully changing not, indeed, bad men into good, but making good men better. Who will grant unto me to cross over to you and see this great sight? For that progress in holiness is not less wonderful or less delightful than that conversion. It is much more easy, in fact, to find many men of the world converted to good than one Religious who is good becoming better than he is. The rarest bird in the world is the monk who ascends ever so little from the point which he has once reached in the religious life. Thus the spectacle which you present, dearest brethren, is the more rare and salutary, not only to men who desire greatly to be the helper of your sanctity, but it rightly rejoices the whole Church of God as well; since the rarer it is the more glorious it is also. For prudence made it a duty to you to pass beyond that mediocrity so dangerously near to defect, and to escape from that luke-warmness which provokes God to reject you; it was even a duty of conscience for you to do so, since you know that it is not safe for men who have embraced the holy Rule to halt before having attained the goal to which it leads. I am exceedingly grieved that I am obliged by the pressing obligations of the day and the haste of the messenger to express the fulness of my affection with a pen so brief, and to comprise the breadth of my kindness for you within the narrow limits of this billet. But if anything is wanting, brother Geoffrey [1] will supply it by word of mouth.

Cistercian Rule in 1132. It is astonishing to read of the fervour of these monks in *Monast. Anglican.* Vol. i. p. 733 and onwards. Compare also Letters 313 and 320 for what relates to the death of Abbot Richard, the second of that name and Order.

[1] This Geoffrey, "a holy and religious man," who founded or reformed numerous monasteries, had been sent by Bernard to Fountains to train them according to the Rule of the Cistercian Order (*Monast. Anglican.* Vol. i. p. 741). Concerning the same Geoffrey see *The Life of S. Bernard,* B. iv. c. 2.

LETTER XCVII. (A.D. 1132.)

To Duke Conrad.[1]

Bernard urges upon him not to make war upon the Count of Geneva, lest he should draw upon himself the vengeance of God.

1. All power comes from Him, to whom the prophet says, *Thine is the power, Thine the kingdom, O, Lord ; Thou art over all nations* (1 Chron. xxix. 11). Therefore I have thought it fit, O illustrious Prince, to warn your Excellency how great reverence it behoves you to show to that terrible One, who takes away the life of princes themselves. The Count of Geneva, as I know from his own mouth, offers to do you justice with respect to all the causes of complaint which you declare you have against him. If, after this, you continue to invade the country of another, to destroy churches, to set houses on fire, to plunder the poor, to perpetrate homicides, and to pour out human blood, it is certain that you will arouse against you the stern anger of Him who is the Father of orphans and the judge of widows. And if He is angry with you, neither the number nor the bravery of your soldiers will profit you at all. The Almighty Lord of Sabaoth will give the victory to whom He pleases, whether it be by many or by few. He has made, when He saw fit, one soldier put to flight a thousand, and two ten thousand (Deut. xxxii. 30).

2. The cry of the poor which has come to me has inspired me, a poor man, to use this language to your Greatness, knowing that it is more honourable and worthy of you to yield to the entreaties of the humble than to the threats of your enemies; not that I think your enemies more

---

[1] Samuel Guichenon, in his *History of the Dukes of Savoy*, written in French, reports that Conrad, Duke of Zeringen, was at this time contemplating hostilities against Amadeus I., Count of Geneva. Zeringen, says Munster (*Cosmography*, B. iii.), was a certain castle, now destroyed, situated on the Brisgau, half a mile below Fribourg, from which the Dukes of Zeringen derived their title. These Dukes were descended from the Counts of Hapsburg by a certain Gebizo about the time of the Emperor Henry III.; and continued until 1357. The sixth and last inheritor of the title was named Egon.

powerful than you, but that I know Almighty God is far
more powerful than either, and that He resists the proud
while he gives grace unto the humble. If I had been able
I would have come unto your presence, noble Prince, to
treat of this matter, but now I have sent to you, in my place,
these of my brethren to obtain from your Highness, by
their prayers united with mine, either a solid peace, if that
be possible, or, at least, a truce while we endeavour to
settle the conditions of a definitive peace, according to the
will of God, and both to your honour and the safety of your
country. Otherwise, if you neither accept the satisfaction
offered you, nor deign to regard our entreaties, or rather
do not give ear to the salutary advice which God gives you
by me, let Him look upon it and judge. For I know, nor
can I reflect upon it without trembling, that such great
armies can hardly meet in battle without horrible carnage
and slaughter of each side.

LETTER XCVIII.

CONCERNING THE MACCABEES, BUT TO WHOM WRITTEN IS UNKNOWN.[1]

*He replies to the question why the Church has decreed a
festival to the Maccabees alone of all the righteous under
the ancient law.*

1. Fulk, Abbot of Epernay,[2] had already written to ask

[1] Such is the title in almost all the MSS. But in one at Cîteaux the Letter is
inscribed *To Bruno of Cologne, as is believed, on the martyrdom of the Maccabees.*
In an old edition *It is thought to have been written to Hugo of S. Victor.* What
seems to have occasioned the conjecture that it was addressed to that prelate
was that the relics of the Maccabees were preserved in Cologne, but it must be
noted that it was not until after the death of Bernard they were brought thither
from Milan by Bishop Reinold, who obtained them from the Emperor, Frederick
I. In many MSS. Letter 77, addressed to Hugo of S. Victor, immediately
precedes this.

[2] Fulk, Abbot of S. Martin, at Epernay, on the Marne, in the Diocese of
Rheims. It is he to whom is addressed Letter 13 of Hugo Metellus: "To the
Reverend Fulk, Abbot of Epernay, blessed in Our Lord," on the subject of a
certain canon of Epernay whom he reclaimed from Abbot William. Fulk was

me the same question as your charity has addressed to your
humble servant by Brother Hescelin. I have put off replying to him, being desirous to find, if possible, some statement
in the Fathers about this which was asked, which I might
send to him, rather than to reply by some new opinion of
my own. But as I do not come upon one, in the meantime
I reply to each of you with my thoughts upon the matter,
on condition that if you discover anything better and more
probable in your reading, conversation, or by your meditations, you will not omit to share it with me in turn. You
ask, then, why it seemed good to the Fathers to decree
that an annual commemoration, with veneration equal to
our martyrs, should be solemnly made in the Church, by a
certain peculiar privilege, to the Maccabees alone out of
all the ancient saints? If I should say that having made
proof of the same courage as those, they were worthy now
of the same honours, that would, perhaps, answer the
question why they were included, but not why they alone
were; while it is quite evident that there were others
amongst the ancients who suffered with equal zeal for
righteousness, but yet have not attained to be reverenced
with equal solemnities. If I reply that the latter have not
received the same honours as our martyrs because, although
their valour deserved it, the time when they lived deprived
them of it, why was not the same consideration applied
also to the Maccabees, if, indeed, they, too, on account of
the era when they lived, did not at once enter into the
light of Heaven, but descended into the darkness of Hades?
For the Firstbegotten from the dead, He who opened to
believers the kingdom of Heaven, the Lamb of the tribe of
Judah, who opens and no more shuts, at Whose entrance
with complete authority it was sung by the heavenly
powers: *Lift up your heads, O ye gates, and be ye lift up
ye everlasting doors, and the King of Glory shall come in*
(Ps. xxiv. 7),—He had not yet appeared. If on that

the first abbot of that monastery; after that, on the advice of Bernard and of
Guy, the order of Regular Canons was established there in 1128. He was
brought from the Abbey of S. Leo, at Toul.

account it appears unsuitable to commemorate with joy the passing away of those which was not a passage of glory and of joy, why was there an exception made for the Maccabees? Or if they obtained favour on account of the courage which they displayed, why was not the same favour extended to those others? Or ought it to be said, in order to explain this difference, that if the martyrs of the ancient law, as well as those of the new law, have suffered for the same cause of religion, yet they did not suffer in the same condition with those who have attained to the glory of martyrdom? It is agreed that all the martyrs, whether of the Old or the New Testament, equally suffered for the sake of religion; but there is a distinction, because the one class suffered because they held it, the other because they censured those who held it not; the one because they would not desert it, the other because they declared that those would perish who deserted it, and to sum up in a word, that in which the two differ, perseverance in the faith has done in our martyrs that which zeal for the faith has done in those of the ancient law. The Maccabees are alone among the ancient martyrs, because they possessed not only the same cause as the new martyrdom, but also, as I have said, the form of it; and rightly, therefore, they have attained the same glory and fame as the new martyrs of the Church. For like our martyrs, they were urged to pour libations to false gods, to renounce the law of their fathers, and even to transgress the commandments of God, and like them they resisted and died.

2. Not so did Isaiah or Zecharias, or even that great prophet, John the Baptist, die; of whom the first is said to have been sawn asunder, the second slain between the temple and the altar (S. Matt. xxiii. 25), and the third beheaded in prison. If you ask by whom? It was by the wicked and irreligious. For what cause? For justice and religion. In what manner? For confessing and openly upholding these. They openly upheld the truth before those who hated it, and thus drew upon themselves the hatred which caused their death. That which the un-

righteous and wicked persecuted was not so much religion
in itself as those who brought it before them, nor was
their object to attack the righteousness of others, but to
remain undisturbed in their own unrighteousness. It is
one thing to seize upon the good things of another, and
another to defend one's own goods; to persecute the truth,
and not to be willing to follow it one's self; to grudge at
believers, and to be angry at their reproofs; to stop the
mouth of those who confess their faith, and not to be able
to bear patiently the taunts of those who contradict. Thus
Herod sent and seized John. Wherefore! Because he
preached Christ, or because he was a good and just man?
On the contrary, he reverenced him the more on this
account, *and having heard him, did many things.* But it
was because John reproached Herod *because of Herodias,
his brother Philip's wife;* on that account he was bound
and beheaded; no doubt he suffered for the truth, but
because he urged its interests with zeal, not because he
was urged to deny it. This is why the suffering of so
great a martyr is observed with less solemnity than those
even of far less famous men.

3. It is certain that if the Maccabees had suffered in
such a matter, and for such a reason as S. John, there would
not have been any mention of them at all. But a confession of the truth, not unlike that of the Christian martyrs,
made them like those; and rightly, therefore, a similar
veneration follows. Let it not be objected that they did
not, like our martyrs, suffer for Christ expressly by name;
because it does not affect his status as a martyr whether
a person suffers under the Law, on behalf of the observances
of the Law, or under grace for the commandments of the
Gospel. For it is recognized that each of these equally
suffers for the truth, and, therefore, for Christ, who said: *I am
the Truth* (S. John xiv. 6). Therefore the Maccabees are
more deserving of the honours that have been conferred
upon them for the kind of their martyrdom than for the
valour displayed in it, since we do not see that the Church
has decreed such honour to the righteous of a former time,

although they have displayed equal courage on behalf of righteousness, for the time in which they lived. I suppose that it was thought unfit to appoint a day of festival for a death, however laudable, before the Death of Christ, especially since before that saving Passion those who died, instead of entering into joy and glory endured the darkness of the prison-house. The Church then, as I said above, considered that an exception should be made in favour of the Maccabees, since the nature of their martyrdom conferred upon them what the time of their suffering denied to others.

4. Nor them only, but those also who preceded in their death, the Death of Him who was the Life manifest in the flesh, either dying during His life, as Simeon and John the Baptist, or for Him, as the Innocents, we venerate with solemn rites, although they, too, descended into Hades; but for another reason. Thus, in the case of the Innocents, it would be unjust to deprive innocence dying on behalf of righteousness of fame even in the present. John also, knowing that from his day the kingdom of heaven suffered violence, therefore proclaimed, *Do penitence, for the kingdom of heaven is at hand* (S. Matt. iii. 2, VULG.); and, seeing that the Life would immediately follow him, endured death with joy. He, before his death, was careful to inquire from the Lord Himself respecting this, and had the happiness to be informed of it. For when he sent his disciples to ask of Jesus *Art Thou He that should come, or are we to look for another?* he received for answer, after the enumeration of very many miracles, *And blessed is he who shall not be offended in me* (S. Matt. xi. 3-6). In which answer the Lord intimated that He was about to die, and by such a death as might be to the Jews a stumbling block and to the Greeks foolishness. At this word the friend of the Bridegroom went onward rejoicing and with a willing mind, because he could not doubt that the Bridegroom also would speedily come. Therefore he who so joyfully could die merited also to be held in joyful remembrance. And that old man, too, as full of virtues as of days, who when death

was already so near said, holding in his arms Him who was the Life, *Now lettest Thou Thy servant depart in peace, for mine eyes have seen Thy salvation* (S. Luke ii. 29, 30), as if he had said, *I go down* without fear into Hades, because I feel that my redemption is so nigh; he, too, who died with such fearless joy and such joyful security rightly deserves to be commemorated with joy in the Church.

5. But on what principle shall a death be accounted joyful which is not accompanied by the joys of heaven? or from whence should a dying person derive joy who was sure that he was going down into the darkness of the prison-house, and yet did not bear with him any certitude, how soon the consolation of a deliverer thence should come to him? Thus it was that when one of the saints heard *Set thy house in order, for thou shalt die, and not live,* he turned himself to the wall and wept bitterly, and so asked and obtained some deferring of hateful death. Thus also he lamented miserably, saying, I shall go to the gates of the grave; I am deprived of the half of my days (Is. xxxviii. 10); and a little after added, *I shall not see the Lord in the land of the living: I shall behold man no more with the inhabitants of the world* (Is. xxxviii. 11). Hence also another says: *Who shall grant me that Thou wouldest protect me in the grave, that Thou wouldest keep me secret until Thy wrath be passed; that Thou wouldest appoint me a set time and remember me?* (Job xiv. 13). Israel also said to his sons, *Ye will bring down my grey hairs with sorrow to the grave* (Gen. xlii. 38). What appearance is there in these deaths, of solemn joy, of rejoicing and festival?

6. But our martyrs desire to be unclothed and be with Christ, knowing well that where the Body is there without delay will the eagles be gathered together. There will the righteous rejoice in the sight of God, and be in joy and felicity. There, there, O most blessed Jesus, shall every saint who is delivered from this wicked world be filled speedily with the joy of Thy countenance. There in the habitations of the just resounds for ever one song of joy

and salvation: *Our soul is delivered as a bird out of the net of the fowler : the net is broken and we are delivered* (Ps. cxxiv. 7). How could those sing this song of gladness who in Hades sat in darkness and the shadow of death, while as yet there was no Redeemer for them, no Saviour; while the Sun rising from on high, Christ the first fruits of them that slept, had not yet visited us? Rightly, then, does the Church, who has learnt to rejoice with them that rejoice and to weep with them that weep, distinguish, because of the time at which they lived, between those whom she judges equal in valour: and does not think the descent into Hades proper to be followed with equal honour as is the passage into life.

7. Therefore, though the motive makes martyrdom, yet the time and the nature of it determine the difference between martyrdoms. Thus the time in which they lived separates the Maccabees from the martyrs of the new law and joins them with those of the old; but the nature of their martyrdom associates them with the new and divides them from the old. From these causes come the differences of observance with which they are kept in memory in the Church. But that which is common to the whole company of the Saints before God is what the holy prophet declares: *Precious in the sight of the Lord is the death of His saints* (Ps. cxvi. 15). And why he calls it precious he explains to us: *When He has given sleep to His beloved, behold, children, the heritage of the Lord ; His reward, the fruit of the womb* (Ps. cxxvii. 3). Nor must we think that martyrs alone are beloved, since we remember that it was said of Lazarus, *Our friend Lazarus sleeps* (S. John xi. 11), and elsewhere, *Blessed are the dead who die in the Lord* (Apoc. xiv. 13). Not those alone who die for the Lord, like the martyrs, but without doubt those also who die in the Lord as confessors are blessed. There are two things, as it seems to me, which make death precious, the life which precedes it and the cause for which it is endured ; but more the cause than the life. But when both the cause and the life concur that is the most precious of all.

LETTER XCIX.

To a certain Monk.[1]

Bernard writes that he had been anxious because of the rumoured departure of this monk from his convent, and that he had been freed from such fear by his letter.

The messenger by whom you say that you have been disturbed was sent by Brother William in your interest, and not in his own. He, indeed, by the grace of God, acts bravely, as he is wont, and does not merit so far that that declaration should be applied to him: *A double-minded man is unstable in all his ways* (S. James i. 8). He walks simply and faithfully in the ways of the Lord, and does not fear that woe that is spoken: *Woe be to the sinner that goeth two ways* (Ecclus. ii. 12). For we had heard that you, being mixed up in a dispute, had left your convent, to the grave scandal of your abbot and your brethren, and were living alone in, I know not what unsuitable place. Being greatly distressed by this rumour, I ask myself, with anxiety, in what way I could be of service to you, and nothing occurred to me to do better than to beg you to come to see me so as to make me aware of what had passed about yourself, so that I might, without delay, counsel you by word of mouth. But since my letter and your reply have put to flight the fears and suspicions which were in the mind of each of us, let us say nothing more of the matter. It has been shown, at all events, by this false report, how true is the mutual affection between us; and I think that this affection has been not unfruitfully renewed by our mutual anxiety; I should hope that we might taste this fruit far more fully if leave and opportunity were given you to pay me a visit. Otherwise it were better that I should still be content without seeing you rather than enjoy your presence at a time when it is unsuitable or inconvenient to you.

[1] In many MSS. the four Letters which follow have no other title than this, *Concerning the same subject*, viz., the Maccabees, which is false. William, of whom mention is made at the beginning of the Letter, was that monk of Clairvaux who is referred to in Letter 103.

LETTER C.

To a certain Bishop.

Bernard praises his liberality and kindness towards poor Religious.

If I were less acquainted with your zeal for undertaking a work of such importance I should urge and entreat you to it. But now, since your piety has anticipated my intention, it only remains to me to give thanks to Him, from whom all good things proceed, for having put into your heart to wish this good, and to pray Him to add to it, that you may bring to perfection that which you have piously desired. Yet I cannot hide from you my joy, nor dissimulate the pleasure which your good intentions inspire in me. My soul will be delighted to the full if I could know that you are untiring in edifying and honourable pursuits. For I rejoice, not because I seek a gift, but because I require fruit. I willingly accept a benefit which profits the giver, otherwise I should not walk in that charity which seeketh not her own (1 Cor. xiii. 5). And, indeed, your gifts are profitable to me, but more to you, according to that declaration: *It is more blessed to give than to receive* (Acts xx. 35). This liberality is befitting a Bishop; it is the glory of your priesthood, it adorns your crown, and ennobles your dignity. If the charge he holds forbids a person to be poor let his conduct show that he is a lover of the poor. For it is not poverty, but the love of poverty, which is counted a virtue; and it is said, *Blessed are the poor,* not in worldly wealth, but *in spirit* (S. Matt. v. 3).

LETTER CI.

To certain Monks.

Bernard asks that a monk who had departed without permission should be received with kindness.

I send back to you Brother Lambert, whom I received, in some respects wavering in mind, but to whom your prayers have restored calm, so that he is not, as I think, labouring any more under his former scrupulosity. I have carefully questioned him about the cause of his coming, and also about the reason and manner of his departure. He does not seem to me to have had any bad intention in acting as he has done; but his reason for leaving in such a manner, that is, without permission, was plainly insufficient. I took occasion from this to blame him as he deserved, to chide him sharply, to remove his hesitations and doubts, and to persuade him to return to you. Now that he is returning, I entreat you, my very dear brethren, to receive him kindly, and to be indulgent to the presumption of a brother in which there is more simplicity than malice, since he turned neither to the right nor left, but came straight to me, whom he knew for certain to be the devoted servant of your Holiness, a very sincere lover and faithful imitator of your piety. Receive him, therefore, you who are spiritual men, in a spirit of gentleness; let your charity be confirmed towards him, and let his good intention excuse his bad action. Therefore, receive him back with joy, whom, when lost, you grieved for; and let gladness at the return of your brother speedily chase away the grief caused by his transgression and departure. I trust that, by the mercy of God, all the bitterness which his irregular departure occasioned will be soon softened by this improvement in his life.

LETTER CII.

To a certain Abbot.

Bernard advises that all possible means should be tried to correct a refractory monk, but that, if incorrigible, he should be expelled, lest he should infect others by his company.

1. Respecting the brother who is disorderly and disorders others, nor respects the authority of his superior, I give you brief but faithful advice. It is the occupation of the devil to go about in the House of God and seek whom he

may devour; on the other hand, it is the task committed to your watchfulness, never as far as you are able, to give place to the devil. The more efforts he makes then to separate from the flock a poor little sheep that he may draw it away the more easily whither there will be none to deliver it from him, the more strenuously, as far as in you lies, ought you to resist, that the enemy may not be able to snatch it from your arms, and say I have prevailed against him. Have recourse, then, in order to save that brother, to every office of charity; spare neither kindnesses, good advice, private reprimands, nor public remonstrances, even the sharp correction of words and, if necessary, blows, but, above all, what is usually more efficacious, the pious intercessions of yourself and your brethren to God for him.

2. But if, when you have done all these things you have no success, you are bound to follow the counsel of the Apostle when he says, *Put away from among yourselves that wicked person* (1 Cor. v. 13). Let the wicked man be taken away, that he may not make others wicked, for an evil tree can bear only evil fruit. I say that he should be taken away, but not in the manner that he himself wishes; nor should he suppose that he can be permitted to live with your license away from the community, against his profession avoiding obedience, under his own authority, and that according to the law[1] and with conscience wrongly at ease; but he should be cut off, as a diseased sheep is parted from the flock, as a gangrened limb from the body; and in going forth he should be made to know for certain that he will be held by you as a heathen man and a publican. And do not fear that you will act against charity if you provide for the peace of many by the expulsion of one—of one whose

---

[1] The discipline for refractory monks differed in various times and places. The Rule of S. Benedict (capp. 28 and 29) ordered that they should be expelled. The Council of Cloveshoo, A.D. 747, in Can. 24, decided that this should not be done except by the decree of a synod. Another method was pursued towards nuns. One was expelled from the convent of S. Peter, at Metz, her veil having been taken from her. By Can. 9 of a Synod at Metz such a person was to be brought back and "placed in a dungeon within the monastery." In the twelfth century regular canons were expelled. (See Stephen of Tournay, Let. 38).

malice may easily destroy the peace of many brethren who dwell together. Let that declaration of Solomon console you, *No one can correct that person whom God leaves alone* (Eccles. vii. 13), and that of the Saviour, *Every plantation which My Father hath not planted shall be rooted up* (S. Matt. xv. 13), and that of S. John the Evangelist concerning schismatics, *They went out from us, because they were not of us* (1 S. John ii. 19), and that from the Apostle, *If the unbelieving depart, let him depart* (1 Cor. vii. 15). Otherwise the rod of the wicked ought not to be left over the lot of the righteous, lest the righteous put forth their hand unto wickedness. For it is better that one member should perish than the whole community.[1]

LETTER CIII.

TO THE BROTHER OF WILLIAM, A MONK OF CLAIRVAUX.[2]

Bernard, after having made a striking commendation of religious poverty, reproaches in him an affection too great for worldly things, to the detriment of the poor and of his own soul, so that he preferred to yield them up only to death, rather than for the love of Christ.

1. Although you are unknown to me by face, and although distant from me in body, yet you are my friend, and this friendship between us makes you to be present and familiar to me. It is not flesh and blood, but the Spirit of God which has prepared for you, though without your knowledge, this friendship, which has united your brother William and me with a lasting bond of spiritual affection, which includes you, too, through him, if you think it worth acceptance. And if you are wise you will not despise the friendship of

---

[1] On the question whether a monastery has the right of expelling an incorrigible monk, consult Haeften in *Disquisitionibus Monasticis*, Menard, and Edmund Martene in his Commentaries upon the Rule.

[2] Such of the title of the Letter in two Vatican MSS. and in certain others. In those of Citeaux it is inscribed *Letter of exhortation to a friend*. But at the end of Letter 106 I conjecture the reference to be to Ivo, who signs it with William.

those whom the Truth declares blessed, and calls kings of
heaven ; which blessedness we would not envy to you, nor
if communicated to you would it be diminished to us, nor
would our boundaries be at all narrowed if you should reign
over them too. For what cause can there be for envy where
the multitude of those who share a blessing takes nothing
from the greatness of the share which each enjoys ? I wish
you to be the friend of the poor, but especially their imitator. The one is the grade of beginner, the other of the
perfect, for the friendship of the poor makes us the friend
of kings, but the love of poverty makes us kings ourselves.
The kingdom of heaven is the kingdom of the poor, and
one of the marks of royal power is to do good to friends
according to our will. *Make to yourselves friends*, it is
said, *of the mammon of unrighteousness, that when ye
fail they may receive you into everlasting habitations* (S.
Luke xvi. 9). You see what a high dignity sacred poverty
is, so that not only does it not seek protection for itself, but
extends it to those who need. What a power is this, to
approach by one's self to the Throne of God without the
intervention of any, whether angels or men, with simple
confidence in the Divine favour, thus reaching the summit
of existence, the height of all glory !

2. But would that you, without pretence, would consider
how you hinder your own attainment of these advantages.
Alas ! that a vapour which appears but for a moment should
block up the entrance to eternal glory, hide from you the
clearness of the unbounded and everlasting light, prevent
you from recognizing the true nature of things, and deprive
you of the highest degree of glory ! How long will you
prefer to such glory the grass of the field, which to day is,
and to-morrow is cast into the oven ? I mean carnal and
worldly glory.   For *all flesh is grass, and its glory as the
flower of the field* (Is. xl. 6). If you are wise, if you have
a heart to feel and eyes to see, cease to pursue those
things which it is misery to attain. Happy is he who
does not toil at all after those things, which when
possessed are a burden, when loved a defilement, and

when lost a torment. Will it not be better to have
the honour to renounce them than the vexation to lose
them ? Or will it be more prudent to yield them up for the
love of Christ than to have them taken away by death ?—
death, which is a robber lying in wait for you, into whose
hands you cannot help falling, with all that belongs to you.
When he shall do so you cannot foresee, because he will
come as a thief in the night. *You brought nothing into
this world, and it is certain you can carry nothing out* (1
Tim. vi. 7). You shall sleep your sleep, and find nothing
in your hands. But these things you know well, and it
would be superfluous laboriously to teach them to you.
Rather I will pray God that you may have the grace to
fulfil in practice what it has been given you already to
know.

LETTER CIV.

To Magister [1] Walter de Chaumont.

*He exhorts him to flee from the world, advising him to
prefer the cause and the interests of his soul to those of
parents.*

My Dear Walter,
           I often grieve my heart about you whenever the
most pleasant remembrance of you comes back to me,
seeing how you consume in vain occupations the flower of
your youth, the sharpness of your intellect, the store of your
learning and skill, and also, what is more excellent in a
Christian than all of these gifts, the pure and innocent
character which distinguishes you ; since you use so great
endowments to serve not Christ their giver, but things
transitory. What if (which God forbid !) a sudden death
should seize and shatter at a stroke all those gifts of yours,

---

[1] S. Bernard usually designates thus Doctors and Professors of Belles
Lettres. See Letters 77, 106, and others. It is thus that in the *Spicilegium* iii. pp.
137, 140, Thomas d'Etampes is called sometimes *Magister*, sometimes *Doctor*.
In a MS. at the Vatican we read, "To *Magister* Gaucher."

as it were with the rush of a burning and raging wind, just
like the winds whirl about and dry grass or as the leaves of
herbs quickly fall.   What, then, will you carry with you of all
your labour which you have wrought upon the earth ?   What
return will you render unto the Lord for all the benefits
that He hath done unto you?   What gain will you bring
unto your creditor for those many talents committed to you ?
If He shall find your hand empty, who, though a liberal
bestower of His gifts, exacts a strict account of their use !
" For he that shall come will come and will not tarry, and
will require that which is His own with usury."   For He
claims all as His own, which seems to ennoble you in your
land, with favours full at once of dignity and of danger.
Noble parentage, sound health, elegance of person, quick
apprehension, useful knowledge, uprightness of life, are
glorious things, indeed, but they are His from whom they
are.   If you use them for yourself "there is One who
seeketh and judgeth."

   2. But be it so ; suppose that you may for a while call these
things yours, and boast in the praise they bring you, and be
called of men Rabbi and make for yourself a great name,
though only upon the earth ; what shall be left to you after
death of all these things ?   Scarcely a remembrance alone—
and that, too, only upon earth.   For it is written, *They have
slept their sleep, and all the men whose hands were mighty
have found nothing.* (Ps. lxxvi. 5).   If this be the end of all
your labours—allow me to say so—what have you more
than a beast of burden ?   Indeed, it will be said even of
your palfrey when he is dead that he was good.   Look to
it, then, how you must answer it before that terrible judgment throne if you have received your soul in vain, and
such a soul ! if you are found to have done nothing more with
your immortal and reasonable soul than some beast with
his.   For the soul of a brute lives no longer than the body
which it animates, and at one and the same moment it both
ceases to give life and to live.   Of what will you deem
yourself worthy, who, being made in the image of your
Creator, do not guard the dignity of so great a majesty ?

And being a man,[1] but not understanding your honour, art compared unto the foolish beasts and made like unto them, seeing that forsooth, you labour at nothing of a spiritual or eternal nature, but, like the spirit of a beast which as soon as it is loosed from the body is dissolved with the body, have been content to think of nothing but material and temporal goods, turning a deaf ear to the Gospel precept: *Labour not for the meat that perisheth, but for that meat which endureth unto everlasting life* (S. John vi. 27). But you know well that it is written that only he ascends into the hill of the Lord who hath not Lift up his mind unto vanity (Ps. xxiv. 3).[2] And not even he except he hath clean hands and a pure heart. I leave you to decide if you dare to claim this of your deeds and thoughts at the present. But if you are not able to do so, judge what is the reward of iniquity, if mere unfruitfulness is enough for damnation. And, indeed, the thorn or thistle will not be safe when the axe shall be seen laid to the root of the fruit tree, nor will He spare the thorn which stings, who threatens even the barren plant. Woe, then; aye! double woe to him of whom it shall be said, *I looked that he should bring forth grapes, and he hath brought forth wild grapes* (Is. v. 4).

3. But I know how freely and fully you can nourish these thoughts, though I be silent, but yet I know that, constrained by love of your mother, you are not as yet able to abandon what you have long known how to despise. What answer shall I make to you in this matter? That you should leave your mother? That seems inhuman. That you should remain with her? But what a misery for her to be a cause of ruin to her son! That you should fight at once for the world and for Christ? But no man can serve two masters. Your mother's wish being contrary to your salvation is equally so to her own. Choose, therefore, of these two alternatives which you will; either, that is, to secure the wish of one or the salvation of both. But if you

---

[1] Some add "in honour" from Ps. xlviii., but it is wanting in the MSS., and certainly is redundant here.

[2] *Hath not received it in vain*, VULG.

love her much, have the courage to leave her for her sake, lest if you leave Christ to remain with her she also perish on your account. Else you have ill-served her who bare you if she perish on your account. For how doth she escape destruction who hath ruined him whom she bare? And I have spoken this in order in some way to stoop to assist your somewhat worldly affection. Moreover, it is a faithful saying and worthy of all acceptation, although it is impious to despise a mother, yet to despise her for Christ's sake is most pious. For He who said, *Honour thy father and mother* (S. Matt. xv. 4), Himself also said, *He who loveth father or mother more than Me is not worthy of Me* (S. Matt. x. 37).

LETTER CV.

To Romanus, Sub-Deacon of the Roman Curia.

He urges upon him the proposal of the religious life, recalling the thought of death.

Bernard, Abbot of Clairvaux, to his dear Romanus, as to his friend.

My Dearest Friend,

How good you are to me in renewing by a letter the sweet recollection of yourself and in excusing my tiresome delay. It is not possible that any forgetfulness of your affection could ever invade the hearts of those who love you ; but, I confess, I thought you had almost forgotten yourself until I saw your letter. So now no more delays; fulfil quickly the promise that you have written; and if your pen truly expresses your purpose, let your acts correspond to it. Why do you delay to give birth to that spirit of salvation which you have so long conceived? Nothing is more certain to mortals than death, nothing more uncertain than the hour of death, since it is to come upon us as a thief in the night. Woe unto them who are still with child [of that good intention] in that day! If it shall anticipate and prevent this birth of salvation, alas! it will pierce through the house and destroy the holy seed: *For when they shall say Peace and safety, then sudden destruction shall come upon them as travail upon a woman with child, and they shall not escape* (1 Thess. v. 3). I wish you not to flee from death, but only to fear it. For the just, though he avoids it not, because he knows that it is inevitable, yet does not fear it. Moreover, he awaits it as a rest (Wisdom iv. 7) and receives it in perfect security; for as it is the exit from the present life, so it is the entrance into a better. Death is good if by it thou die to sin, that thou mayest live unto righteousness. It is necessary that this death should go before, in order that the other which follows after may be safe. In this life, so long as it lasts, prepare for yourself that life which lasts for ever. While you live in the flesh, die unto the world, that after the death of the flesh you may begin to live unto God. For what if death rend asunder the coarse envelope[1] of your body so long as from that moment it clothes you with a garment of joy? O, how *blessed are the dead which die in the Lord* (Apoc. xiv. 13), for they hear from the Spirit, that "they may rest from their labours." And not only so, but also from new life comes pleasure, and from eternity safety. Happy, therefore, is the death of the just because of its rest; better because of its new life, best because of its safety (Ps. xxxiv. 21). On the other hand, worst of all is the death of sinners. And hear why worse. It is bad, indeed, through loss of the world; it is worse through separation from the flesh; worst of all through double pain of worm and fire. Up, then, hasten; go forth out of the world, and renounce it entirely; let your soul die the death of the righteous, that your last end also may be like His: *Oh, how dear in the sight of the Lord is the death of His saints* (Ps. cxvi. 13). Flee, I pray you, lest you stand in the way of sinners. How canst thou live where thou durst not die?[2]

---

[1] *Saccus.*

[2] A familiar figure of speech with Bernard. See Letter 107, § 13; 124, § 2, etc.

LETTER CVI.

To MAGISTER HENRY MURDACH.[1]

He urges him to embrace the religious life, briefly describing its delights.

To his beloved HENRY MURDACH, BERNARD, called Abbot of Clairvaux, wishes eternal life.

1. What wonder if you are tossed to and fro by the waves of prosperity and adversity, since you have not yet set your feet upon the rock ? But if you are quite resolved to keep the righteous judgments of the Lord, can anything sever you from the love of Christ ? O, if you only knew, and if I were able to convey to you ! but *Eye hath not seen, without Thee, O God, the things that Thou hast prepared for them that love Thee* (Is. lxiv. 4). But you, my brother, who, as I hear, read the prophets, and no doubt suppose that you understand the sense of their writings, is it not clear to you if you understand that the meaning of the prophetic declaration refers to Christ ? And if you desire to lay hold on Him, I assure you that you can attain to Him sooner by following Him than by reading, merely reading óf Him. Why do you seek in the Word written, the Word who is already here before your eyes, the Word made flesh ? He has long quitted his hiding-place among the prophets to come forth before the eyes of Fishermen ; already He has left the deep, shady hills of the ancient Law, as a bridegroom leaves his chamber, and has leapt forth to the plain of the Gospel. Now let him who hath ears to hear, hear Him crying in the Temple, *If any man thirst, let him come unto Me and drink* (S. John vii. 37), and

[1] This Henry was by birth an Englishman, and master of a school in England. Among His disciples were William and Ivo, as appears from the end of the epistle. He yielded at length to the exhortations of Bernard, and became a monk of Clairvaux ; afterwards he was Abbot of Vauclaire, and then third Abbot of Fountains, in England (see Letters 320 and 331); and, lastly, after the deposition of the Treasurer, William, by Eugenius III., Archbishop of York, on which subject several letters occur below. See also William of Newburgh, B. i. c. 17 ; Roger Hoveden, under the year 1140; Robert du Mont, Appendix to Sigebert.

Come unto Me all ye that labour and are heavy laden and I will refresh you (S. Matt. xi. 28). Do you, then, fear to fail where Truth promises to sustain you? Surely if the storm-rain from the clouds of heaven so delights you, how much sweeter will be the draught that you may draw from the pure fountains of the Saviour?

2. If you could once for a moment taste of that bread with which Jerusalem is satisfied, how gladly you would leave your dry crusts for Jewish scholars to gnaw! How happy should I be to have you for my companion in the school of piety under the Master, Jesus! Would that it were mine first to purge the vessel of your heart that it might be filled with the unction that makes wise about all things! How willingly would I break with you those loaves, still warm and steaming, and, as it were, freshly drawn from the oven, which Christ of His heavenly bounty often breaks unto His poor! Would that, if God deigned of His sweetness to shed at any time on my poor soul some drop of the free rain which He keeps for His inheritance, ah! would that then I could pour it out upon you, and again receive from you in turn that which you had felt! Believe one who has tried: you shall find a fuller satisfaction in the woods than in books. The trees and the rocks will teach you that which you cannot hear from masters. Do you think that you cannot draw honey from the rock and oil from the hardest flint? Do not our mountains drop sweetness? the hills flow with milk and honey? and the valleys stand thick with corn? When so much occurs to me to say to you I scarce restrain myself. But inasmuch as you ask not for a lecture, but for prayers, may God open your heart in His law and in His statutes. Farewell.

3. Let William and Ivo, too, have share in this my prayer. What more shall I say to you? You know that I long to see you, and why; but how much I long neither I can tell nor you can know. So I pray God that He may grant you even to follow whither you ought to have preceded me, since in this matter I hold you to be master

of so great humility as not to disdain, though a master, to
follow your disciples.

LETTER CVII.

To Thomas, Prior of Beverley.[1]

*This Thomas had taken the vows of the Cistercian
Order at Clairvaux. As he showed hesitation, Bernard
urges his tardy spirit to fulfil them. But the following
letter will prove that it was a warning to deaf ears, where
it relates the unhappy end of Thomas. In this letter
Bernard sketches with a master's hand the whole scheme
of salvation.*

BERNARD to his beloved son THOMAS, as being his son.
1. What is the good of words? An ardent spirit and a
strong desire cannot express themselves simply by the
tongue. We want your sympathy and your bodily presence
to speak to us; for if you come you will know us better,
and we shall better appreciate each other. We have long
been held in a mutual bond as debtors one to another; for
I owe you faithful care and you owe me submissive
obedience. Let our actions and not our pens, if you
please, prove each of us. I wish you would apply to
yourself henceforth and carry out towards me those words
of the Only Begotten : *The works which the Father hath
given Me to finish, the same works bear witness of Me*
(S. John v. 36). For, indeed, only thus does the spirit of
the Only Son bear witness with our spirit that we also are
the sons of God, when, quickening us from dead works, He
causes us to bring forth the works of life. A good or bad
tree is distinguished, not by its leaves or flowers, but by its
fruit. So *By their fruits*, He saith, *ye shall know them*
(S. Matt. vii. 16). Works, then, and not words, make the
difference between sons of God and sons of unbelief. By
works, accordingly, do you display your sincere desire and
make proof of mine.

[1] See Letter 411.

2. I long for your presence; my heart has long wished for you, and expected the fulfilment of your promises. Why am I so pressing? Certainly not from any personal or earthly feeling. I desire either to be profited by you or to be of service to you. Noble birth, bodily strength and beauty, the glow of youth, estates, palaces, and sumptuous furniture, external badges of dignity, and, I may also add, the world's wisdom—all these are of the world, and the world loves its own. But for how long will they endure? For ever? Assuredly not; for the world itself will not last for ever; but these will not last even for long. In fact, the world will not be able long to keep these gifts for you, nor will you dwell long in the world to enjoy them, for the days of man are short. The world passes away with its lusts, but it dismisses you before it quite passes away itself. How can you take unlimited pleasure in a love that soon must end? But I ever love you, not your possessions; let them go whence they were derived. I only require of you one thing: that you would be mindful of your promise, and not deny us any longer the satisfaction of your presence among us, who love you sincerely, and will love you for ever. In fact, if we love purely in our life, we shall also not be divided in death. For those gifts which I wish for in your case, or rather for you, belong not to the body or to time only; and so they fail not with the body, nor pass away with time; nay, when the body is laid aside they delight still more, and last when time is gone. They have nothing in common with the gifts above-mentioned, or such as they with which, I imagine, not the Father, but the world has endowed you. For which of these does not vanish before death, or at last fall a victim to it?

3. But, indeed, that is the best part, which shall not be taken away for ever. What is that? *Eye hath not seen it, nor ear heard, neither hath it entered into the heart of man* (1 Cor. ii. 9). He who is a man and walks simply according to man's nature only, he who, to speak more plainly, is still content with flesh and blood, is wholly ignorant what that is, because flesh and blood will not

reveal the things which God alone reveals through His Spirit. So the natural man is in no way admitted to the secret; in fact, *he receiveth not the things of the Spirit of God* (1 Cor. ii. 14). Blessed are they who hear His words. *I have called you friends, for all things that I have heard of My Father I have made known to you* (S. John xv. 15). O, wicked world, which wilt not bless thy friends except thou make them enemies of God, and consequently unworthy of the council of the blessed. For clearly he who is willing to be thy friend makes himself the enemy of God. And if the servant knoweth not what his Lord doeth, how much less the enemy? Moreover, the friend of the Bridegroom standeth, and rejoiceth with joy because of the Bridegroom's voice; whence also it says, *My soul failed when [my beloved] spake* (Cant. v. 6). And so the friend of the world is shut out from the council of the friends of God, who have received not the spirit of this world but the spirit which is of God, that they may know the things which are given to them of God. *I thank Thee, O Father, because Thou hast hid these things from the wise and prudent, and hast revealed them unto babes : even so, Father, for so it seemed good in Thy sight* (S. Matt. xi. 25, 26), not because they of themselves deserved it. For all have sinned, and come short of Thy glory, that Thou mayest freely send the Spirit of Thy Son, crying in the hearts of the sons of adoption : Abba, Father. For those who are led by this Spirit, they are sons, and cannot be kept from their Father's council. Indeed, they have the Spirit dwelling within them, who searches even the deep things of God. In short, of what can they be ignorant whom grace teaches everything?

4. Woe unto you, ye sons of this world, because of your wisdom, which is foolishness! Ye know not the spirit of salvation, nor have share in the counsel, which the Father alone discloses alone to the Son, and *to him to whom the Son will reveal Him. For who hath known the mind of the Lord? Or who hath been His counsellor?* (Rom. xi. 34). Not, indeed, no one ; but only a few, only those who

can truly say: *The only begotten Son, which is in the bosom of the Father, He hath declared Him.* Woe to the world for its clamour! That same Only Begotten, like as the Angel of a great revelation, proclaims among the people: *He who hath ears to hear let him hear.* And since he finds not ears worthy to receive His words, and to whom He may commit the secret of the Father, he weaves parables for the crowd, that hearing they might not hear, and seeing they might not understand. But for His friends how different! With them He speaks apart: *To you it is given to know the mysteries of the kingdom of God* (S. Luke viii. 8-10); to whom also He says: *Fear not, little flock, for it is your Father's good pleasure to give you the kingdom* (S. Luke xii. 32). Who are these? These are they whom He foreknew and foreordained *to be conformed to the image of His Son, that He might be the first born among many brethren.* The Lord knows who are His. Here is His great secret and the counsel which He has made known unto men. But He judges no others worthy of a share in so great mystery, except those whom He has foreknown and foreordained as His own. For those whom He foreordained, them also He called. Who, except he be called, may approach God's counsel? Those whom he called, them also He justified. Over them a Sun arises, though not that sun which may daily be seen arising over good and bad alike, but He of whom the Prophet speaks when addressing himself to those alone who have been called to the counsel, he says: *Unto you that fear My name shall the Sun of Righteousness arise* (Malachi iv. 2).[1] So while the sons of unbelief remain in darkness, the child of light leaves the power of darkness and comes into this new light, if once he can with faith say to God: *I am a companion of all them that fear Thee* (Ps. cxix. 63). Do you

---

[1] So all texts, except a few, in which the reading is: "Indeed, that Sun is promised to those who have been called," etc. In the first edition, and many subsequent ones: "For the Sun which arises is not that which is daily to be seen rising over good and bad, but one promised by the prophetic warning to such as fear God, to those only who have been called," etc.

see how faith precedes, in order that justification may follow? Perchance, then, we are called through fear, and justified by love. Finally, *the just shall live by faith* (Rom. i. 17), that *faith,* doubtless, *which works by love* (Gal. v. 6).

5. So at his call let the sinner hear what he has to fear; and thus coming to the Sun of Righteousness, let him, now enlightened, see what he must love. For what is that saying: *The merciful goodness of the Lord endureth from everlasting to everlasting upon them that fear Him* (Ps. ciii. 17). *From everlasting,* because of predestination, to *everlasting,* because of glorification. The one process is without beginning, the other knows no ending. Indeed, those whom He predestines from everlasting, He glorifies to everlasting, with an interval, at least, in the case of adults, of calling and justification between. So at the rising of the Sun of Righteousness, the mystery, hidden from eternity, concerning souls that have been predestinated and are to be glorified, begins in some degree to emerge from the depths of eternity, as each soul, called by fear and justified by love, becomes assured that it, too, is of the number of the blessed, knowing well that *whom He justified, them also He glorified* (Rom. viii. 30). What then? The soul hears that it is called when it is stricken with fear. It feels also that it is justified when it is surrounded with love. Can it do otherwise than be confident that it will be glorified? There is a beginning; there is continuation. Can it despair only of the consummation? Indeed, if the fear of the Lord, in which our calling is said to consist, is the beginning of wisdom, surely the love of God—that love, I mean, which springs from faith, and is the source of our justification—is progress in wisdom. And so what but the consummation of wisdom is that glorification which we hope for at the last from the vision of God that will make us like Him? And so *one deep calleth another because of the noise of the water-pipes* (Ps. xlii. 9), when, with terrible judgments, that unmeasured Eternity and Eternal Immensity, whose wisdom cannot be

told, leads the corrupt and inscrutable heart of man by Its own power and goodness forth into Its own marvellous light.

6. For instance, let us suppose a man in the world, held fast as yet in the love of this world and of his flesh ; and, inasmuch as he bears the image of the earthly man, occupied with earthly things, without a thought of things heavenly, can anyone fail to see that this man is surrounded with horrible darkness, unless he also is sitting in the same fatal gloom ? For no sign of his salvation has yet shone upon him ; no inner inspiration bears its witness in his heart as to whether an eternal predestination destines him to good. But, then, suppose the heavenly compassion vouchsafes sometime to have regard to him, and to shed upon him a spirit of compunction to make him bemoan himself and learn wisdom, change his life, subdue his flesh, love his neighbour, cry to God, and resolve hereafter to live to God and not to the world ; and suppose that thenceforward, by the gracious visitation of heavenly light and the sudden change accomplished by the Right Hand of the Most High, he sees clearly that he is no longer a child of wrath, but of grace, for he is now experiencing the fatherly love and divine goodness towards him—a love which hitherto had been concealed from him so completely as not only to leave him in ignorance whether he deserved love or hate, but also as to make his own life indicate hatred rather than love, for darkness was still on the face of the deep—would it not seem to you that such an one is lifted directly out of the profoundest and darkest deep of horrible ignorance into the pleasant and serene deep of eternal brightness ?

7. And then at length God, as it were, divides the light from the darkness, when a sinner, enlightened by the first rays of the Sun of Righteousness, casts off the works of darkness and puts on the armour of light. His own conscience and the sins of his former life alike doom him as a true child of Hell to eternal fires ; but under the looks with which the Dayspring from on high deigns to visit him, he breathes again, and even begins to hope beyond hope

that he shall enjoy the glory of the sons of God. For
rejoicing at the near prospect with unveiled face, he sees it
in the new light, and says : *Lord, lift Thou up the light of
Thy countenance upon us ; Thou hast put gladness in my
heart* (Ps. iv. 7) ; *Lord, what is man that Thou hast such
respect unto him, or the son of man that Thou so regardest
him ?* (Ps. cxliv. 3). Now, O good Father, vile worm and
worthy of eternal hatred as he is, he yet trusts that he is
loved, because he feels that he loves ; nay, because he has
a foretaste of Thy love he does not blush to make return of
love. Now in Thy brightness it becomes clear, Oh ! Light
that no man can approach unto, what good things Thou
hast in store for so poor a thing as man, even though he be
evil ! He loves not undeservedly, because he was loved
without his deserving it ; and his love is for everlasting,
because he knows that he has been loved from everlasting.
He brings to light for the comfort of the sorrowful the
great design which from eternity had lain in the bosom of
eternity, namely, that God wills not the death of a sinner,
but rather that he should be converted and live. As a
witness of this secret, Oh ! man, thou hast the justifying
Spirit bearing witness herein with thy spirit that thou
thyself also art the son of God. Acknowledge the counsel
of God in thy justification ; confess it and say, *Thy testimonies are my delight and my counsellors* (Ps. cxix. 24).
For thy present justification is the revelation of the Divine
counsel, and a preparation for future glory. Or rather,
perhaps, predestination itself is the preparation for it, and
justification is more the gradual drawing near unto it.
Indeed, it is said, *Repent ye, for the kingdom of heaven is
at hand* (S. Matt. iii. 2). And hear also of predestination
that it is the preparation : *Come, inherit,* He says, *the
kingdom prepared for you from the foundation of the
world* (S. Matt. xxv. 34).

8. Let none, therefore, doubt that he is loved who already
loves. The love of God freely follows our love which it
preceded. For how can He grow weary of returning their
love to those whom He loved even while they yet loved

Him not? /He loved them, I say; yes, He loved. For as a ·
pledge of His love thou hast the Spirit; thou hast also ˎ
Jesus, the faithful witness, and Him crucified. Oh! double
proof, and that most sure, of God's love towards us. Christ
dies, and deserves to be loved by us. The Spirit works,
and makes Him to be loved.ˑ The One shows the reason
why He is loved: the Other how He is to be loved. The
One commends His own great love to us; the Other makes
it ours. In the One we see the object of love; from the
Other we draw the power to love. With the One, therefore, is the cause; with the Other the gift of charity. What
shame to watch, with thankless eyes, the Son of God dying
—and yet this may easily happen, if the Spirit be not with
us. But now, since *The love of God is shed abroad in our
hearts by the Holy Ghost which is given unto us* (Rom. v.
5), having been loved we love; and as we love, we deserve
to be loved yet more. *For if,* says the Apostle, *while we
were yet enemies, we have been reconciled to God through
the death of His Son; much more, being reconciled, shall
we be saved through His life* (Rom. viii. 32). For *He
that spared not His own Son, but delivered Him up for
us all, how shall He not with Him also freely give us all
things?*

9. Since, then, the token of our salvation is twofold,
namely, a twofold outpouring, of the Blood and of the
Spirit, neither can profit without the other. For the Spirit
is not given except to such as believe in the Crucified; and
faith avails not unless it works by love. But love is the
gift of the Spirit. If the second Adam (I speak of Christ)
not only became a living soul, but also a quickening spirit,
dying as being the one, and raising the dead as being the
other, how can that which dies in Him profit me, apart
from that which quickens? Indeed, He Himself says: *It
is the spirit that quickeneth, the flesh profiteth nothing*
(S. John vi. 63). Now, what does "quickeneth" mean
except "justifieth?" For as sin is the death of the soul
(*The soul that sinneth it shall die,* Ezek. xviii. 4), without
doubt righteousness is its life; for *The just shall live by*

faith (Rom. i. 17). Who, then, is righteous, except he who returns to God, who loves him, His meed of love? And this never happens unless the Spirit by faith reveal to the man the eternal purpose of God concerning his future salvation. Such a revelation is simply the infusion of spiritual grace, by which, with the mortification of the deeds of the flesh, man is made ready for the kingdom which flesh and blood cannot inherit. And he receives by one and the same Spirit both the reason for thinking that he is loved and the power of returning love, lest the love of God for us should be left without return.

10. This, then, is that holy and secret counsel which the Son has received from the Father by the Holy Spirit. This by the same Spirit He imparts to His own whom He knows, in their justification, and by the imparting He justifies. Thus in his justification each of the faithful receives the power to begin to know himself even as he is known: when, for instance, there is given to him some foretaste of his own future happiness, as he sees how it lay hid from eternity in God, who foreordains it, but will appear more fully in God, who is effecting it. But concerning the knowledge that he has now, for his part, attained, let a man glory at present in the hope, not in the secure possession of it. How must we pity those who possess as yet no token of their own calling to this glad assembly of the righteous. *Lord, who hath believed our report?* (Is. liii. 1). Oh! that they would be wise and understand. But except they believe they shall not understand.

11. But you, too, ye unhappy and heedless lovers of the world, have your purpose far from that of the just. Scale sticks close to scale, and there is no air-hole between you. You, too, oh! sons of impiety, have your purpose communicated one to another, but openly *against the Lord and against His Christ* (Ps. ii. 2). For if, as the Scripture says, *The fear of God, that is piety* (Job xxviii. 28),[1] of course anyone who loves the world

---

[1] The lxx. has ἰδοὺ θεοσέβεια ἐστι σοφία. The VULGATE reads " Ecce timor Domini ipsa est sapientia," with which the A. V. coincides, " Behold the fear of the Lord, that is wisdom." Does Bernard quote from memory?

more than God is convicted of impiety and idolatry, of
worshipping and serving the creature rather than the
Creator. But if, as has been said, the holy and impious
have each their purpose kept for themselves, doubtless there
is a great gulf fixed between the two. *For as the just
keeps himself aloof from the purpose and council of evil
men* (*cf.* Ps. i. 6), so the impious never rise in the judgment, nor sinners in the purpose[1] for the just. For there
is a purpose for the just, a gracious rain which God hath set
apart for His heritage. There is a purpose really secret,
descending like rain into a fleece of wool—a sealed fount
whereof no stranger may partake—a Sun of Righteousness
rising only for such as fear God.

12. Moreover, the prophet, noting that the rest remain in
their own dryness and darkness, being ignorant of the rain
and of the light of the just, mocks and brands their unfruitful gloom and confused perversity. *This is a nation,*
he says, *that obeyeth not the voice of the Lord their God*
(Jer. vii. 28). You are not ready, oh! miserable men, to
say with David, *I will hearken what the Lord God will
say with regard to me* (Ps. lxxxv. 8), for being exhausted
abroad upon [the quest of] vanity and false folly, you seek
not for the deepest and best hearing of the truth. *Oh! ye
sons of men, how long will ye blaspheme mine honour, and
have such pleasure in vanity and seek after leasing* (Ps. iv.
2). You are deaf to the voice of truth, and you know not
the purpose of Him who thinks thoughts of peace, who also
speaks peace to His people, and to His saints, and to such
as are converted in heart. *Now,* he says, *ye are clean
through the word which I have spoken to you* (S. John xv.
3). Therefore, they who hear not this word are unclean.

13. But do you, dearly beloved, if you are making ready
your inward ear for this Voice of God that is sweeter than
honey and the honey-comb, flee from outward cares, that
with your inmost heart clear and free you also may say
with Samuel, *Speak, Lord, for thy servant heareth* (1 Sam.

---

[1] This must be the reading, not "congregation," [*concilio*] as in Ps. i, for
the sense demands "purpose," [*consilio*] and the MSS. so read.

iii. 9). This Voice sounds not in the market-place, and is not heard in public. It is a secret purpose, and seeks to be heard in secret. It will of a surety give you joy and gladness in hearing it, if you listen with attentive ear. Once it ordered Abraham (Gen. xii. 1) to get him out of his country and from his kindred, that he might see and possess the land of the living. Jacob (Gen. xxxii. 10) left his brother and his home, and passed over Jordan with his staff, and was received in Rachel's embrace (Gen. xxix. 11). Joseph was lord in Egypt (Gen. xxxvii. and xli.), having been torn by a fraudful purchase from his father and his home. Thus the Church is bidden, in order that the King may have pleasure in her beauty, to forget her own people and her father's house (Ps. xlv. 11, 12). The boy Jesus was sought by His parents among their kinsfolk and acquaintance, and was not found (S. Luke ii. 44, 45). Do you also flee from your brethren, if you wish to find the way of salvation. Flee, I say, from the midst of Babylon, flee from before the sword of the northwind. A bare sustenance I am ready to offer for the help of everyone that flees. You call me your abbot; I refuse not the title for obedience' sake—obedience, I say, not that I demand it, but that I render it in service to others, even as *The Son of Man came not to be ministered unto, but to minister and to give His life a ransom for many* (S. Matt. xx. 28). But if you deem me worthy, receive as your fellow-disciple him whom you choose for your master. For we both have one Master, Christ. And so let Him be the end of this Letter, who is *The end of the law for righteousness to every one that believeth* (Rom. x. 4).

LETTER CVIII.

To Thomas of St. Omer,[1] after he had Broken his Promise of Adopting a Change of Life.

He urges him to leave his studies and enter religion, and sets before him the miserable end of Thomas of Beverley.

[1] See Letter 382.

To his dearly beloved son, THOMAS, Brother BERNARD, called Abbot of Clairvaux, that he may walk in the fear of the Lord.

1. You do well in acknowledging the debt of your promise, and in not denying your guilt in deferring its performance. But I beg you not to think simply of what you promised, but to whom you promised it. For I do not claim for myself any part of that promise which you made, in my presence, indeed, but not to me. Do not fear that I am going to reprove you on account of that deceptive delay: for I was summoned as the witness, not as the lord of your vow.[1] I saw it and rejoiced; and my prayer is that my joy may be full—which it will not be until your promise is fulfilled. You have fixed a time which you ought not to have transgressed. You have transgressed it. What is that to me? To your own lord you shall stand or fall. I have determined, because the danger is so imminent, to deal with you neither by reproofs nor threats, but only by advice—and that only so far as you take it kindly. . If you shall hear me, well. If not, I judge no man ; there is One who seeketh and judgeth ; for *He who judgeth us is the Lord* (1 Cor. iv. 4). And I think for this cause you ought to fear and grieve the more, inasmuch as you have not lied unto men, but unto God. And though, as you wish, I spare your shame before men, is that shamelessness to go unpunished before God? For what reason, pray, is there in feeling shame before the judgment of man and not fearing the face of God? *For the face of the Lord is against them that do evil* (Ps. xxxiv. 16). Do you, then, fear reproaches more than torments ; and do you, who tremble at the tongue of flesh, despise the sword which devours the flesh? Are these the fine moral principles with which, as you write, you are being stored in the acquisition of knowledge, the ardour and love for which

---

[1] Bernard regards as a vow that kind of promise by which a man had determined in his presence to enter the religious state. See Letter 395, and *Sermons on Canticles*, 63, n. 6, in which he mourns the lapse and fall of novices.

so heats and excites you that you do not fear to slight your sacred vow?

2. But, I pray you, what proof of virtue is it, what instance of self-control, what advance in knowledge, or artistic skill, to tremble with fear where no fear is needful, and to lay aside even the fear of the Lord. How much more wholesome the knowledge of Jesus and Him crucified —a knowledge,·of course, not easy to acquire except for Him who is crucified to the world. You are mistaken, my son, quite mistaken, if you think that you can learn in the school of the teachers of this world that knowledge which only the disciples of Christ, that is, such as despise the world, attain; and that by the gift of God. This knowledge is taught, not by the reading of books, but by grace; not by the letter, but by the spirit; not by learning, but by the practice of the commandments of God : *Sow*, says the Prophet, *to yourselves in righteousness, reap the hope of life, kindle for yourselves the light of knowledge* (*cf.* Hos. x. 12). You see that the light of knowledge cannot be duly attained, except the seed of righteousness [first] enter the soul, so that from it may grow the grain of life, and not the mere husk of vain glory. What then? You have not yet sown to yourself in righteousness, and therefore you have not yet reaped the sheaves of hope; and do you pretend that you are acquiring the true knowledge? Perchance for the true there is being substituted that which puffeth up. You err foolishly, *Spending thy money for that which is not bread, and thy labour for that which satisfieth not* (Is. lv. 2). ·I entreat you, return to the former wish of your heart, and realize that this year of delay which you have allowed to yourself has been a wrong to God; is not a year pleasing to the Lord, but a seedplot of discord, an incentive to wrath, a food of apostasy, such as must quench the Spirit, shut off grace, and produce that lukewarmness which is wont to provoke God to spue men out of His mouth (*cf.* Rev. iii. 16).

3. Alas ! I think that, as you are called by the same name, so you walk in the same spirit as that other Thomas,

once, I mean, Provost of Beverley. For after devoting himself, like you, to our Order and House with all his heart, he began to beg for delay, and then by degrees to grow cold, until he openly ended by being a Secular, an apostate, and, twofold more, a child of hell, and was cut off prematurely by a sudden and terrible death (S. Matt. xxiii. 15)—a fate which, if it may be, let the pitiful and clement Lord avert. The letter[1] which I wrote to him in vain still survives. I simply freed my own mind, by warning him, so far as I could, how it must soon end. How happy would he have been if he had taken my advice! He cloked his sin. I am clean from his blood. But that is not enough for me. For though in so acting I am quite at ease on my own account, yet that charity which *seeketh not her own* (1 Cor. xiii. 5) urges me to mourn for him who died not in safety, because he lived so carelessly. Oh! the great depth of the judgments of God! Oh! my God, terrible in Thy counsels over the sons of men! He bestowed the Spirit, whom he was soon again to withdraw, so that a man sinned a sin beyond measure, and grace found entrance that sin might abound; though this was the fault, not of the Giver, but of him who added the transgression. For it was the act of the man's own freewill (whereby, using badly his freedom, he had the power to grieve the free Spirit) to despise the grace instead of bringing to good effect the inspiration of God, so as to be able to say: *His grace which was bestowed on me was not in vain* (1 Cor. xv. 10).

4. If you are wise, you will let his folly profit you as a warning; you will wash your hands in the blood of the sinner, and take care to release yourself at once from the snare of perdition, and me from horrible fear on your account. For, I confess, I feel your erring steps as the rending of my heart, because you have become very dear to me, and I feel a father's affection for you. Therefore, at every remembrance of you that sword of fear pierces through my heart the more sharply, as I consider that you have too little fear and uneasiness. I know where I have

[1] No. 107.

read of such : *For when they shall say peace and safety, then sudden destruction cometh upon them, as travail upon a woman with child, and they shall not escape* (1 Thess. v. 3). Yea, I foresee that many fearful consequences threaten you if you still delay to be wise. For I have had much experience ; and Oh ! that you would share and profit by it. So believe one who has had experience ; believe one who loves you. For if you know for the one reason that I am not deceived, for the other you know also that I am not capable of deceiving you.

LETTER CIX.

To the Illustrious Youth, Geoffrey de Perrone,[1] and his Comrades.

He pronounces the youths noble because they purpose to lead the religious life, and exhorts them to perseverance.

To his beloved sons, GEOFFREY and his companions, BERNARD, called Abbot of Clairvaux, wishes the spirit of counsel and strength.

[1] A very ancient edition reads *Geoffrey de Parrone*, which is a well-fortified town on the Somme. So it is from that place that Godfrey derives his name and lineage. He was one of those whom S. Bernard is said to have converted to religion in Belgium (See *Life*, Bk. iv. Chap. 3). A companion in his conversion was the other Geoffrey, afterwards Prior of Clairvaux. The authority for this is Herman, a monk of Tournay (*Spicilegium*, Vol. xii. p. 479), where he speaks of S. Bernard, and says that " from the Church of S. Mary, of Tournay, as well as from the diocese itself, many famous clerks followed Dom Bernard, Abbot of Clairvaux, by whom they had attained to the grace of conversion." Herman relates this fact, p. 476, after the twenty-fourth year of the Episcopate of Simon, Bishop of Noyon, who acceded to that See 1122. This Letter, therefore, cannot, as Manrique thinks, be referred to 1131. Peter de Roya, a novice of Clairvaux (see Letter 479, 2, 9) gives praise to Geoffrey de Perrone. This is Mabillon's view, but Horst does not agree, because he believes this same Geoffrey to have been Prior of Clairvaux, of whom he has this account :—" This man S. Bernard converted to religion in Flanders, with twenty-nine other noble and cultured youths. But now that he is hesitating and delaying, Bernard urges him forward in this Letter. Afterwards he became Prior of Clairvaux, the fifth in order, and at length being elected Bishop of Tournay (others say of Nantes), he declined the honour. Peter of Blois records the story thus." We read that Geoffrey de Perrone, Prior of Clairvaux, being elected Bishop of Tournay, entirely refused

1. The news of your conversion that has got abroad is edifying many, nay, is making glad the whole Church of God, so that *The heavens rejoice and the earth is glad* (Ps. xcvi. 11), and every tongue glorifies God. *The earth shook and the heavens dropped at the presence of the God of Sinai* (*cf.* Ps. lxviii. 8, 9), raining on those days more abundantly than usual a gracious rain which God keeps for His inheritance (Ps. lxvii. 9, 10, VULG.). Never more will the cross of Christ appear void of effect in you, as in many sons of disobedience, who, delaying from day to day to turn to God, are seized by sudden death, and go down straightway to hell. We see flourish again under our eyes the wood whereon the Lord of Glory hung, who died not for His own nation only, *But also that He should gather together in one the children of God that were scattered abroad* (S. John xi. 52)," He, yes, He Himself draws you, who loves you as His own flesh, as the most precious fruit of His cross, as the most worthy recompense of the blood He shed. If, then, the Angels *Rejoice over one sinner that repenteth* (S. Luke xv. 10), how great must be their joy over so many, and those, too, sinners. The more illustrious they seemed for rank, for learning, for birth, for youth, the wider was their influence as examples of perdition. I had read, *Not many noble, not many wise, not many mighty hath God chosen* (1 Cor. i. 26, 27). But to-day, through a miracle of Divine power, a multitude of such is converted. They hold present glory cheap, they spurn the charm of youth, they take no account of high birth, they regard the wisdom of the world as foolishness, they rest not

the election. Afterwards, when he was dead, he appeared to a certain brother, who asked how it was with him, and in reply he said, " The Holy Trinity has revealed to me that if I had undertaken the Episcopate I should have been of the number of the lost." So by this instance he struck the hearts of certain other prelates, saying, " What, then, will become of those unhappy beings who, of their own will and pleasure, drown themselves in the flood of worldly cares, who pass their life among vanities, dining luxuriously, sleeping, drinking, sitting at the receipt of custom, paying out cash, seeking the things that are their own, or rather the things that are Cæsar's, and not God's ? " So Peter of Blois, Letter 102. To the same effect *Cæsarius*, Bk. ii. c. 29. See on the matter Henriquez, *Menologium*, Feb. 15.

in flesh and blood, they renounce the love of parents and friends, they reckon favours and honours and dignities as dung that they may gain Christ. I should praise you if I knew that this, your lot, were your own doing. But it is the finger of God, clearly a change due to the right hand of the Most High (*cf.* Ps. lxxvii. 10 VULG., lxxvi. 11). Your conversion is a good gift and a perfect gift, without doubt descending from the Father of lights (S. James i. 17). And so to Him we rightly bring every voice of praise who only doeth marvellous things, who hath caused that plenteous redemption that is in Him to be no longer without effect in you.

2. What, then, dearly beloved, remains for you to do, except to make sure that your praiseworthy purpose attain the end it deserves? Strive, therefore, for perseverance. the only virtue that receives the crown. Let there not be found among you *Yea and Nay* (2 Cor. i. 18, *sq.*), that ye may be the sons of your Father which is in Heaven, with whom, you know, there is *no variableness, neither shadow of turning* (S. James i. 17). You also, brethren, are *changed into the same image from glory to glory, even as by the Spirit of the Lord* (2 Cor. iii. 18). Take heed with all watchfulness not to be yourselves found light, inconstant, or wavering. For it is written, *A double-minded man is unstable in all his ways* (S. James i. 8), and again, *Woe be . . . to the sinner that goeth two ways* (Ecclus.·ii. 12). And for myself, dearly beloved, I congratulate you, and myself not less, for, as I hear, I have been reckoned worthy of being chosen to have a part in this, your good purpose. I both give you my counsel and promise my help. If I am thought necessary, or, rather, if I be deemed worthy, I do not decline the task, and so far as in me lies will not fail you. With eager devotion I submit my shoulders to this burden,[1] old though they be, since it is laid on me from heaven. With a glad heart and open arms, as they say, I welcome the fellow-citizens of the saints and servants of

---

[1] Hence it is clear that Bernard was already approaching old age when he wrote this Letter.

God. How gladly, according to the prophet's command, do I assist with my bread those that flee *from the face of the sword, and bring water to the thirsty* (*cf*. Is. xxi. 14). The rest I have left to the lips of my, or rather your, Geoffrey. Whatsoever he shall say to you in my stead, that, doubt not, is my counsel.

LETTER CX.

A Consolatory Letter to the Parents of Geoffrey.

There is no reason to mourn a son as lost who is a religious, still less to fear for his delicacy of constitution.

1. If God makes your son His son also, what do you lose or what does he himself lose? Being rich he becomes richer; being already high born, of still nobler lineage; being illustrious, he gains greater renown; and—what is more than all—once a sinner he is now a saint. He must be prepared for the Kingdom that has been prepared for him from the beginning of the world; and for this end, the short time that he has to live he must spend with us; until he has scraped off the filth of the worldly life, and wiped away the earthly dust, and at last is fit for the heavenly mansion. If you love your son, of course you will rejoice, because he goes to His Father and to such a Father as He. Yea, he goes to God. But you lose him not: nay, rather through him you gain many sons. For all of us who are in or of Clairvaux, acknowledge him as a brother and you as parents.

2. But perchance you fear the effect of a severe life upon his body, which you know to be frail and delicate. But of such fear it is said, "*There were they brought in great fear where no fear was*" (Ps. xiv. 9). Reassure yourselves, and be comforted. I will be to him a father, and he shall be to me a son, until *the Father of mercies and the God of all consolation* (*cf*. Rom. xv. 5) receive him from my hands. So do not mourn; do not weep. For your

Geoffrey is hastening to joy and not to grief. I will be to him father, mother, brother, and sister. I will make the crooked *straight for him and the rough ways smooth* (*cf.* S. Luke iii. 5). I will so order and arrange everything for him that his soul shall profit and his body not suffer loss. Moreover, he shall serve the Lord in joy and gladness, and shall *sing in the ways of the Lord that great is the glory of the Lord* (Ps. cxxxviii. 5).

LETTER CXI.

IN THE PERSON OF ELIAS, A MONK, TO HIS PARENTS.

He exhorts them not to try to hinder him in or draw him back from his wish to serve God. Such attempt would be unworthy and useless.

ELIAS, a monk, but a sinner withal, to his dear parents INGORRAN and IVETTE, with his daily prayers.[1]

1. There is only one circumstance in which it would be wrong to obey parents, and that is when God forbids it. For He Himself says: "*He that loveth father or mother more than me is not worthy of me*" (S. Matt. x. 37). If you love me in truth like good and affectionate parents: if you have a true and faithful affection towards your son, why are you restless at my hastening to please God, the Father of all? and why do you try to withdraw me from His service, whom to serve is to reign? Truly now I see how *a man's enemies are the men of his own house* (Micah

[1] This heading is now for the first time restored from the Corbey MS., which is much valued. Is this Letter one of those which the Saint sometimes entrusted to the composition of scribes? (see Ep. 389). Of it Horst speaks as follows:— "Bernard wrote this Letter in the name of Elias, his novice, to his parents, that he might restrain them in their attempt to dissuade their son from his purpose." "Its contents," says Lessius, "might have seemed rather severe, had they not proceeded from so great wisdom and piety. For who would dare reprove that chosen instrument of the Holy Spirit? He knew how important the question was. Yet it is not his way to write in such sharp tones, unless it is clear that their importunity must throw a man into great danger, or that his friends do not cease pressing him." See that most useful treatise on "The choice of a position in life," quest. 4, 36; compare Letter 104.

vii. 6). Herein I must not obey you; herein I own you not as parents, but as foes. If you loved me, surely you would rejoice because I go to my Father and your Father, nay, to the Father of all. Besides, what is there common between me and you? What have I from you but sin and misery? It is only this corruptible body which I wear that I confess and own to have from you. Is it not enough for you unhappy ones, to have brought me unhappy into the unhappiness of this world; for you sinners, to have given birth in your sin to me a sinner; to have reared in sin a son born in sin; but you must, by grudging me the compassion which I have gained from Him who willeth not the death of a sinner, make me besides all this, a child of Hell?

2. O, stern father! O, harsh mother! O, parents cruel and void of affection—nay, not parents at all, but murderers, whose only grief is the salvation of their offspring, whose only comfort the death of their son, who would rather I should perish with them than reign without them! They are trying to call me back again to the wreck from which I at last escaped, naked; back to the fire from which with much difficulty I have emerged, half-burnt; back to the robbers by whom I was left half-dead, but from whom, through the compassion of the Good Samaritan, I have now a little recovered. Aye, and in the moment of triumph, when the soldier of Christ has almost carried the citadel of heaven—I boast not in myself but in Him who has conquered the world—they strive to bring him back to the world from the very threshold of glory, as it were a dog to his vomit, a sow to her wallowing in the mire. What monstrous treatment! The house is in flames, the fire presses on from behind. He who would flee is prevented from going out; he who would escape is persuaded to return! And that by those who are set in the midst of the conflagration, and who, out of sheer obstinate infatuation and infatuated obstinacy, will not flee from the danger! What madness! If you think nothing of your own death, why do you also wish for mine? If, I say, you neglect your own salvation, what pleasure

is it to put hindrance in the way of mine? Why not rather follow me in my flight, that you may escape the flames? But, perhaps, it lightens your torment if you drag me also into your ruin; and your only fear is to perish by yourselves? What solace will the burning of one man be able to afford to others in like case? What comfort, I ask, is it to the damned to have partners in their damnation? What remedy is it to the dying to see others dying? That is not the belief that I learn from the rich man of Scripture, who, being in torments (*cf.* S. Luke xvi. 28) and despairing of freedom for himself, asked that a message might be sent to his brethren, lest they also should come to the same place of torment. Doubtless he feared that his own suffering would be increased by that of his kindred.

3. What then? Shall I go and console my sorrowing mother by a short visit in time, simply that in eternity I may sorrow both for myself and her without consolation? Shall I go, I say, and make amends to my angry father for my absence in time, and myself find comfort for a time in his presence, that afterwards each for himself and either for other we may be abandoned to an inconsolable grief? Were it not better to follow the example of the Apostle, and, *Conferring not with flesh and blood* (Gal. i. 16), to listen to the voice of the Lord, who commands, *Let the dead bury their dead?* (S. Matt. viii. 22). Shall I not sing with David, *My soul refused comfort* (Ps. lxxvii. 2), and with Jeremiah, *Neither have I desired the woeful day, thou knowest?* (Jer. xvii. 16). For why? *The lot is fallen unto me in a fair ground; yea, I have a goodly heritage* (Ps. xvi. 7). Am I, then, tricked by an earthly promise, or charmed by some fleshly comfort? When men have tasted of spiritual dainties, needs must that those of the flesh seem tasteless. Set your affections on things above, and things below are insipid; yearn after things eternal, and you scorn things transient. Cease, then, my dear parents, cease to trouble yourselves with vain laments and to disturb me to no purpose by calling me back; lest,

if you keep on sending messengers about me, you compel me to withdraw still more. But if you abandon [me], I shall never abandon Clairvaux : *This shall be my rest for ever ; here will I dwell, for I have a delight therein* (Ps. cxxxii. 15). Here will I pray instantly for your sins and mine ; here with constant prayers will I obtain, if I can, what you also desire, that we, who for love of Him are separated from each other for this short life, may in the happy and indissoluble fellowship of another world live in His love for ever and ever. Amen.

LETTER CXII.

To Geoffrey, of Lisieux.[1]

He grieves at his having abandoned his purpose to enter the religious life and returned to the world. He exhorts him to be wise again.

1. I am grieved for you, my son Geoffrey, I am grieved for you. And not without reason. For who would not grieve that the flower of your youth, which, amid the joy of angels, you offered unimpaired to God *for the odour of a sweet smell* (Phil. iv. 18), should now be trampled under the feet of devils, stained by the filthiness of vice and the uncleanness of the world ? How can you, who once wast called by God, follow the devil who calls you back ? How is it that you, whom Christ began to draw after Himself, have suddenly withdrawn your foot from the very threshold of glory ? In you I now have proof of the truth of the Lord's word, when He said: *A man's foes shall be they of his own household* (S. Matt. x. 36). Your friends and kinsfolk have approached and stood against you. They have called you back into the jaws of the lion, and have placed you once more in the gates of death. They have

---

1 Some have " Luxeuil." This word Ordericus also generally uses to designate Lisieux, in Neustria, so that there is no uniform distinction of names between Lisieux and Luxeuil, in the County of Burgundy, found among writers of this period.

placed you in dark places, like the dead of this world ; and now it is a matter for little surprise that you are descending into the belly of hell, which is hasting to swallow you up, and to give you over as a prey to be devoured by those who roar in their hunger.

2. Return, I pray you ; return before *the deep swallow thee up and the pit shut her mouth upon thee* (Ps. lxix. 16) ; before you sink whence you shall never more rise ; before you be *bound hand and foot and cast into outer darkness, where there is weeping and gnashing of teeth* (S. Matt. xxii. 13) ; ~~before you be~~ thrust down to the place of darkness, and covered with the gloom of death. Perhaps you blush to return, because you gave way for an hour. Blush, indeed, for your flight, but do not blush to return to the battle after your flight, and to fight again. The fight is not over yet. Not yet have the opposing lines drawn off from each other. Victory is still in your power. If you will, we are unwilling to conquer without you, and we do not grudge to you your share of glory. I will even gladly come to meet you and gladly welcome you with open arms, saying : *It is meet that we should make merry and be glad ; for this thy brother was dead and is alive again ; he was lost and is found* (S. Luke xv. 32).

LETTER CXIII.

To the Virgin Sophia.

He praises her for having despised the glory of the world : and, setting forth the praises, privileges, and rewards of Religious Virgins, exhorts her to persevere.

BERNARD, Abbot of Clairvaux, to the Virgin SOPHIA, that she may keep the title of virginity and attain its reward.

1. *Favour is deceitful and beauty is vain ; but a woman that feareth the Lord, she shall be praised* (Prov. xxxi. 31). I rejoice with you, my daughter, in the

glory of your virtue, whereby, as I hear, you have been
enabled to reject the deceitful glory of the world. That,
indeed, deserves rejection and disdain. But whereas
many who in other respects are wise, are in their estimation of worldly glory become foolish, you deserve to be
praised for not being deceived. It is *as the flower of the grass*
—(James i. 10)—*a vapour that appeareth for a little time*
(S. James iv. 14). And every degree of that glory is without
doubt more full of care than joy. At one time you have
claims to advance, at another, yourself to defend; you envy
others, or are suspicious of them; you are continually aim-
ing to acquire what you do not possess, and the passion for
acquiring is not satisfied even by success ; and as long as
this is the case, what rest is there in your glory ? But if
any there be, its enjoyment quickly passes, never to return;
while care remains, never to leave. Besides, see how
many fail to attain that enjoyment, and yet how few
despise it. Why so ? Just because though many of necessity endure it [*i.e.*, the deprivation of pleasure], yet but
few make of doing so a virtue. Few, I say, very few, and
particularly of the nobly-born. Indeed, *not many noble
are called ; but God hath chosen the base things of the
world* (1 Cor. i. 26-28). You are, then, blessed and privileged
among women of your rank in that, while others strive in
rivalry for worldly glory, you by your contempt of this
glory are raised to a greater height of glory, and are
elevated by glory of a higher kind. Certainly you are the
more renowned and illustrious for having made yourself
voluntarily humble than for your birth in a high rank.
For the one is your own achievement by the grace of God,
the other is the doing of your ancestors. And that which
is your own is the more precious, as it is the most rare.
For if among men virtue is rare—a " rare bird on the
earth "—how much rarer is it in the case of a weak woman
of high birth ? *Who can find a virtuous woman ?* (Prov.
xxxi. 10). Much more " a virtuous woman " of high birth
as well. Although God is not by any means an accepter
of persons, yet, I know not how, virtue is more pleasing in

those of noble birth. Perhaps that may be because it is more conspicuous. For if a man is of mean birth and is devoid of glory, it is not easily clear whether he lacks virtue because he does not wish for it or because he cannot attain it. I honour virtue won under stress of necessity. But I honour more the virtue which a free choice adopts than that which necessity imposes.

2. Let other women, then, who have not any other hope, contend for·the cheap, fleeting, and paltry glory of things that vanish and deceive. Do you cling to the hope that confounds not. Do you keep yourself, I say, *for that far more exceeding weight of glory, which our light affliction,. which is but for a moment, worketh* (2 Cor. iv. 17) for you on high. And if the daughters of Belial reproach you, those who walk with *stretched forth necks mincing as they go* (Isaiah iii. 16), decked out and adorned like the Temple, answer them : *My kingdom is not of this world* (S. John xviii. 36) ; answer them : *My time is not yet come, but your time is always ready* (S. John vii. 6) ; answer them : *My glory is hid with Christ in God* (Col. iii. 3) ; *When Christ, who is my life, shall appear, then shall I also appear with Him in glory* (Col. iii. 4). And yet if one needs must glory, you also may glory freely and fearlessly, only in the Lord. I omit the crown which the Lord hath prepared for you for ever. I say nothing of the promises which await you hereafter, that as a happy bride you are to be admitted to behold with open face the glory of your Bridegroom ; that He will *present you to Himself a glorious bride, not having spot or wrinkle or any such thing* (Eph. v. 27) ; that He will receive you in an ever-lasting embrace, will place *His left hand under your head and His right hand shall embrace you* (Cant. ii. 6). I pass over the appointed place, which being set apart by the prerogative of virginity, you shall without doubt gain among sons and daughters in the kingdom. I say nothing of that new song which you, a virgin among virgins, shall likewise sing in tones of unrivalled sweetness, rejoicing therein and making glad the city of God, singing and

running and *following the Lamb whithersoever he goeth.*
In fact, *eye hath not seen nor ear heard, neither have
entered into the heart of man the things which He hath
prepared* (1 Cor. ii. 9) for you, and for which it behoves you
to be prepared.

3. All this I omit, that is laid up for you hereafter. I
speak only of the present, of those things which you already
have, of *the first fruits of the Spirit* (Rom. viii. 23), the
gifts of the Bridegroom, the earnest money of the espousals,
the blessings of goodness (Ps. xxi. 3), wherewith he hath
prevented you, whom you may expect to follow after you,
and complete what still is lacking. Let Him, yea let Him,
come forth to be beheld in His great beauty, so adorned as
to be admired of the very angels, and if the daughters of
Babylon, *whose glory is in their shame* (Phil. iii. 19), have
aught like Him, let them bring it forth, *Though they be clothed
in purple and fine linen* (S. Luke xvi. 19). Yet their souls
are in rags; they have sparkling necklaces, but tarnished
minds. You, on the other hand, though ragged without,
are *all glorious within* (Ps. xlv. 14), though to Divine and not
human gaze. Within you have that which delights you, for
He is within whom it delights; for certainly you do not doubt
that you have *Christ dwelling in your heart by faith* (Eph.
iii. 17). In truth, *The King's daughter is all glorious
within* (Ps. xlv. 14). *Rejoice greatly, O daughter of Zion:
shout, O daughter of Jerusalem,* because the King hath
desired thy beauty; if *thou art clothed with confession
and honour* (Ps. civ. 1, VULG.), and *deckest thyself with
light as it were with a garment—For confession and
worship are before Him* (Ps. xcvi. 6, VULG.). Before
whom? Him who is *fairer than the sons of men* (Ps. xlv.
3), even Him whom the angels desire to look upon.

4. You hear, then, to whom you are pleasing. Love that
which enables you to please, love "confession," if you
desire "honour." "Confession" is the handmaid of
"honour," the handmaid of "worship." Both are for you.
"Thou art clothed with confession and honour," and
"Confession and worship are before Him." In truth,

where confession is, there is worship, and there is honour. If there are sins, they are washed away in confession; if there are good works, they are commended by confession. When you confess your faults, it is a sacrifice to God of a troubled spirit; when you confess the benefits of God, you offer to God the sacrifice of praise. Confession is a fair ornament of the soul, which both cleanses a sinner and makes the righteous more thoroughly cleansed. Without confession the righteous is deemed ungrateful, and the sinner accounted dead. *Confession perisheth from the dead as from one that is not* (Ecclus. xvii. 28). Confession, therefore, is the life of the sinner, the glory of the righteous. It is necessary to the sinner, it is equally proper to the righteous. *For it becometh well the just to be thankful* (Ps. xxxiii. 1). Silk and purple and rouge and paint have beauty, but impart it not. Every such thing that you apply to the body exhibits its own loveliness, but leaves it not behind. It takes the beauty with it, when the thing itself is taken away. For the beauty that is put on with a garment and is put off with the garment, belongs without doubt to the garment, and not to the wearer of it.

5. Do not you, therefore, emulate those evil disposed persons who, as mendicants, seek an extraneous beauty when they have lost their own. They only betray how destitute they are of any proper and native beauty, when at such great labour and cost they study to furnish themselves outside with the many and various graces of the fashion of the world which passeth away, just that they may appear graceful in the eyes of fools. Deem it a thing unworthy of you to borrow your attractiveness from the furs of animals and the toils of worms; let your own suffice you. For that is the true and proper beauty of anything, which it has in itself without the aid of any substance besides. Oh! how lovely the flush with which the jewel of inborn modesty colours a virgin's cheeks! Can the earrings of queens be compared to this? And self-discipline confers a mark of equal beauty. How self-discipline calms

the whole aspect of a maiden's bearing, her whole temper
of mind. It bows the neck, smooths the proud brows,
composes the countenance, restrains the eyes, represses
laughter, checks the tongue, tempers the appetite, assuages
wrath, and guides the deportment. With such pearls of
modesty should your robe be decked. When virginity is
girt with divers colours such as these, is there any glory to
which it is not rightly preferred? The Angelic? An angel
has virginity, indeed, but not flesh; and in that respect
his happiness exceeds his virtue. Surely that adornment
is best and most desirable which even an angel might envy.

6. There remains still one more remark to be made
about the adornment of the Christian virgin. The more
peculiarly your own it is, the more secure it remains to
you. You see women of the world burdened, rather than
adorned, with gold, silver, precious stones; in short, with
all the raiment of a palace. You see how they draw long
trains behind them, and those of the most costly materials,
and raise thick clouds of dust into the air. Let not such
things disturb you. They must lay them aside when they
come to die; but the holiness which is your possession will
not forsake you. The things which they wear are really
not their own. When they die they can take nothing with
them, nor will this their glory go down with them. The
world, whose such things are, will keep them and dismiss
the wearers naked; and will beguile with them others
equally vain. But that adornment of yours is not of such
sort. As I said, you may be quite sure that it will not
leave you, because it is your own. You cannot be deprived
of it by the violence, nor defrauded of it by the deceit of
any man. Against such possessions the cunning of the
thief and the cruelty of the tyrant avail nothing. It is not
eaten of moths, nor corrupted by age, nor spent by use.
It lives on even in death. Indeed, it belongs to the soul
and not to the body; and for this reason it leaves the body
together with the soul, and does not perish with the body.
And even those who kill the body have absolutely nothing
that they can do to the soul.

LETTER CXIV.

To ANOTHER HOLY VIRGIN.

*Under a religious habit she had continued to hav: a
spirit given up to the world, and Bernard praises her for
coming to a sense of her duty; he exhorts her not to
neglect the grace given to her.*

1. It is the source of great joy to me to hear that you are
willing to strive after that true and perfect joy, which belongs not to earth but to heaven; that is, not to this vale of
tears, but to that city of God which *the rivers of the flood
thereof make glad* (Ps. xlvi. 4). And in very truth that is
the true and only joy which is won, not from the creature,
but from the Creator; which, if once you possess it, no
man shall take from you. For, compared with it, all joy
from other sources is sorrow, all pleasure is pain, all sweetness is bitter, all beauty is mean, everything else, in fine,
whatever may have power to please, is irksome. Indeed, you
are my witness in this matter. Ask yourself, for you will
believe yourself more readily. Does not the Holy Spirit
proclaim this very truth in your heart? Have you not been
persuaded of the truth hereof by Him long before I spoke?
For how would you, being a woman, or rather a young girl
so fair and ingenuous, have thus overcome the weakness of
your sex and years; how could you thus hold cheap your
extreme beauty and noble birth, unless all such things as
are subject to the bodily senses were already vile in your
eyes, in comparison with those which inwardly strengthen
you to overcome the earthly, and charm you to prefer
things heavenly?

2. And this is right. Poor and transient and earthly are
the things which you despise, but the things you wish for
are grand, heavenly, and everlasting. I will say still more,
and still speak the truth. You leave the darkness to approach the light; you come forth from the depth of the sea
and gain the harbour; you breathe again in happy freedom
after a wretched slavery; in a word, you pass from death

to life; though up till now, living according to your own
will and not God's, to your own law and not that of God,
while living you were dead—living to the world, but dead
to God; or rather, to speak more truly, living neither to
the world nor to God. For when you wished while wearing
the habit and name of religion to live like one in the world,
you alone had rejected God from you by your own wish.
But when you could not effect your foolish wish, then it
was not you that rejected the world, but the world you.
And so, rejecting God and rejected by the world, you had
fallen between two stools,[1] as they say. You were not
living unto God, because you would not, nor to the world,
because you could not: you were anxious for one, unwelcome
to the other, and yet dead to both. So it must happen to
those who promise and do not perform, who make one show
to the world, and in their hearts desire something else.
But now, by the mercy of God, you are beginning to live
again, not to sin, but to righteousness, not to the world, but
to Christ, knowing that to live to the world is death, and
even to die in Christ is life. *Blessed are the dead which
die in the Lord* (Rev. xiv. 13).

3. So from this time I shall not mention again your un-
fulfilled vow, nor your disregard of your profession. From
henceforth your purity of body will not be impaired by a
corrupt mind, nor your name of virgin disgraced by disorderly conduct; from henceforth the name you bear will
not be a deception, nor the veil you wear meaningless. For
why hitherto have you been addressed as "nun"[2] and "holy
virgin" when, professing holiness, you did not live holily?
Why did you let the veil on your head give a false impression of the reverence due to you, while your eye launched
burning and passionate glances? Your head was clothed,

---

[1] Compare in this place Imitation of Christ, Bk. i. c. 25. "A religious person who has become slothful and lukewarm has trouble upon trouble, and suffers
anguish on every side, because he lacks consolation from within, and is debarred
from seeking it without." Read also Sermons 3 and 5 upon the Ascension.

[2] This expression is borrowed from the Rule of S. Benedict, in which it is said
that the younger shall call their elders *nonna* (in monasteries for men *nonnus*)
Chap. lxiii.

indeed, with a veil, but it was lifted up with pride, and
though you were under the symbol of modesty, your speech
sounded far from modest. Your immoderate laughter, un-
reserved demeanour, and showy dress would have accorded
better with the wimple[1] than the veil.   But behold now, at
the bidding of Christ, the old things have passed away, and
all things begin to be made new, since you are changing
the care of the body for that of the soul, and are desirous of
a beautiful life more than beautiful raiment.   You are doing
what you ought to do, or rather what you ought to have
done long ago, for long ago you had vowed to do it.   But
the Spirit, who breathes not only where He will but when
He will, had not then breathed on you, and so, perhaps, you
are to be excused for what you have done hitherto.   But if
you suffer the ardent zeal wherewith, beyond a doubt, your
heart is now hot again, and the divine flame that burns in
your thoughts, to be quenched, what remains for you but
the certain knowledge that you must be destined for that
flame which cannot be quenched.   Nay, let the same Spirit
rather quench in you all carnal affections, lest haply (which
God forbid!) the holy desires of your soul, so late conceived,
should be stifled by them, and you yourself be cast into hell
fire.

[1] *Wimple.*   So all the MS. codices that I have seen, viz., at the Royal
Library, Colbert Library, Sorbonne, Royal College of Navarre, S. Victor of Paris
MS., MS. of Compiègne, and others at other libraries, which have " with the
wimple" (wimplatæ), though all editions except two (viz., that of Paris, 1494,
and of Lyons, 1530) have "one puffed up" (*uni inflatæ*).   They ask what
"with the wimple" (wimplatæ) means.   Of course it is a word formed from
wimple or guimple, owing to the easy change of g to w.   In French "guimpe"
or "guimple" is a woman's head-dress, once common with women of noble
birth (as we learn from the old pictures of noble ladies), but the more simple
and modest refrained from wearing it.   So we read in the French poet, contained
in Borellus' *Glossarium Gallicum* :—

> Moult fut humiliant et simple
> Elle eut une voile en lieu de guimple.

Which may be rendered—

> She was a lowly girl and simple,
> And wore a veil in place of wimple.

Now, however, the word "wimple" is scarcely heard outside the cloisters of
nuns.

LETTER CXV.

To another Holy Virgin of the Convent of S. Mary of Troyes.[1]

He dissuades her from the rash and imprudent design which she had in her mind of retiring into some solitude.

1. I am told that you are wishing to leave your convent, impelled by a longing for a more ascetic life, and that after spending all their efforts to dissuade and prevent you, seeing that you paid no heed to them, your spiritual mother or your sisters, determined at length to seek my advice on the matter, so that whatever course I approved, that you might feel it your duty to adopt. You ought, of course, to have chosen some more learned man as an adviser; yet since it is my advice you desire to have, I do not conceal from you what I think the better course. Ever since I learnt your wish, though I have been turning the matter over in my mind, I cannot easily venture to decide what temper of mind suggested it. For you may in this thing have a zeal towards God, so that your purpose may be excusable. But how such a wish as yours can be fulfilled consistently with prudence I entirely fail to see. "Why so?" you ask. "Is it not wise for me to flee from wealth and the throng of cities, and from the good cheer and pleasure of life? Shall I not keep my purity more safely in the desert, where I can live in peace with just a few, or even alone, and please Him alone to whom I have pledged myself?" By no means. If one would live in an evil manner, the desert brings abundant opportunity: the wood a protecting shade, and solitude silence. The evil that no one sees, no one reproves. Where no critic is feared, there the tempter gains easier access, there wickedness is more readily committed. It is otherwise in a convent. If you do anything good no one prevents you, but if you would do evil you are hindered by many obstacles. If you yield to temptation, it

---

[1] This convent still exists under the rule of S. Benedict. It had lately been, as Bernard testifies, the object of a reform when he wrote.—[Mabillon's note.]

is at once known to many, and is reproved and corrected. So, on the other hand, when you are seen to do anything good, all admire, revere, and copy it. You see, then, my daughter, that in a convent a larger renown awaits your good deeds, and a more speedy rebuke your faults, because there are others there to whom you may set an example by good deeds and whom you will offend by evil.

2. But I will take away from you every excuse for your error, by that alternative in the parable we read in the Gospel. Either you are one of the foolish virgins, if, indeed, you are a virgin, or one of the wise (S. Matt. xxv. 1-12). If you are one of the foolish, the convent is necessary to you ; if of the wise, you are necessary to the convent. For if you are wise and well-approved, without doubt the reform which, though newly introduced into that place, has already won universal praise, will be greatly discredited, and, I fear, be weakened by your departure. It will not fail to be said that, being good yourself, you would not desert a house where the Rule was well carried out.[1] If you have been known to be foolish, and you go away, we shall say that since you are not suffered to live an evil life among good companions, you could not endure longer the society of holy women, and are seeking a dwelling where you may live in your own way. And we shall be quite right. For before the reform of the Rule you never, I am told, were wont to talk of this plan ; but no sooner did observances become stricter, than you, too, became suddenly holier, and in hot haste to think of the desert. I see, my daughter, I see in this, and I would you also saw as I do, the serpent's venom, the guile of the crafty one, and the trickery of his changing skin. The wolf dwells in the wood. If a poor little sheep like you should enter the shades of the wood alone you would be simply seeking to be his prey. But listen to me, my daughter; listen to my faithful warning. Whether sinner or saint, do not separate yourself from the flock, lest the enemy seize upon you, and there be none to deliver

---

[1] *Cf.* the French equivalent "Le bon ordre," *i.e.,* the strict Rule of Monastic Life.

you. Are you a saint? Strive by your example to gain
associates in sanctity. A sinner? Do not add sin to sin,
but do penance where you are, lest by departing, not without danger, as I have shown, to yourself, you bring scandal
upon your sisters, and provoke the tongues of many scoffers
against you.

LETTER CXVI.

TO ERMENGARDE, FORMERLY COUNTESS OF BRITTANY.[1]

*He gently and tenderly assures her that he has for her
all the sentiments of pure and religious affection.*

To his beloved daughter in Christ, ERMENGARDE, once
the most noble Countess, now the humble handmaid of
Christ, BERNARD, Abbot of Clairvaux, offers the pious
affection of holy love. Would that, as I now open this page before me, so I
could open my mind to you! Oh! that you could read in
my heart what God has deigned to write there with His

---

[1] She was the wife of Count Alan, and a great benefactress to Clairvaux.
She built the monks a monastery near the town of Nantes (see Ernald, *Life
of S. Bernard*, ii. 34, and according to Mabillon's *Chronology*, 1135 A.D.). The
name of the monastery is Buzay; it is presided over by the most illustrious
Abbot Caumartin, who has communicated to me the first charter founding the
convent. In this charter Duke Conan, son of Alan and Ermengarde, asserts
that he and his mother had determined to build the Abbey of Buzay, but that,
misled by evil counsel of certain persons, they had desisted from their undertaking. At length Bernard, Abbot of Clairvaux, came into those parts. The
House of Buzay was dependent upon his abbey. Bernard, seeing the place
almost desolate, was deeply grieved, " and," says Conan, " rebuked me with
the most severe reproofs as false and perfidious; and then ordered the abbot
and monks who tarried there to abandon the place and return to Clairvaux.'
Conan interposed, and after restoring the property of the monastery which he
had taken away, took steps for the completion of the building. The charter is
signed by Bishops Roland, of Vannes; Alan, of Rennes; John, of St. Malo;
Iterius, of Nantes; and also by Peter, Abbot of the monastery, and Andrew, a
monk. But to return to Ermengarde. Godfrey, Abbot of Vendôme (Bk. v.
Letter 23), urges her to resume her purpose of entering the religious life, which
she appears to have abandoned. The same Godfrey, in the next Letter, speaks
of her as of royal blood.

own finger concerning my affection for you! Then, indeed, you might understand, how no tongue or pen can suffice to express, what the spirit of God hath been able to impress on my inmost heart! And even now I am present with you in the spirit, though absent in the body. It is neither in your power nor mine to be in the presence of the other. Yet you have with you the means whereby you may not yet know, but at any rate guess what I mean. Within your own heart behold mine; and ascribe to me as great affection toward you as you know to be in yourself towards me. Yet do not think that you have more for me than I for you; nor have a better opinion of your own heart than of mine, in respect of affection. Besides, you are too humble and modest not to believe that He who has brought you so to love me and to follow my counsel for your salvation has inspired me also with feelings of affectionate concern for you. So you are thinking how you may keep me with you; and I, to confess the truth, am nowhere without you or away from you. I was anxious to write this short note to you about my journey while on the way, hoping to send you a longer one when I have more leisure, if God will.

LETTER CXVII.

To the Same.

He commends her readiness in God's service, and expresses his desire to see her.

I have received the joy of my heart, good news from you. I am happy to hear of your happiness; and your ready service, now so well known, makes me quite easy in mind. This great happiness comes in no way from flesh and blood, for you are living in lowliness instead of state, in mean, not high place, in poverty instead of wealth. You are deprived of the consolation of living in your own country, and of the society of your brother and your son. Without doubt, then, the willing devotion that hath been born in you is the work of the Holy Spirit. You have long since conceived by the

fear of God the design of labouring for your salvation, and
have at last brought your design to execution, the spirit of
love casting out fear in your soul.   How much more gladly
would I be present to say this to you, than be absent and
write! Believe me, I am annoyed at my business, which
constantly seems to hinder me from the sight of you; and
I hail with joy the chances, which I seldom seem to get, of
seeing you.   Such opportunities are rare; but, I confess,
their very rarity makes them sweet.   For, indeed, it is
better to see you just sometimes than never at all.   I hope
to come unto you shortly ; and I already offer you a foretaste of the joy that shall shortly come in full.

LETTER   CXVIII.

To Beatrice, a Noble and Religious Lady.

He commends her love and anxious care.

I wonder at your zealous devotion and loving affection
towards me.   I ask, excellent lady, what can possibly
inspire in you such great interest and solicitude for us?
If we had been sons or grandsons, if we had been united to
you by the most distant tie of relationship, your constant
kindnesses, frequent visits, in a word, the numberless proofs
of your affection that we experience daily, would seem to
deserve, not so much our wonder, as our acceptance as a
matter of obligation.   But as, in common with the rest of
mankind, we recognize in you only a great lady, and not a
mother, the wonder is not that we should wonder at your
goodness, but that we can wonder sufficiently.   For who of
our kinsfolk and acquaintance takes care of us ?   Who ever
asks of our health ?   Who, I ask, is, I will not say anxious,
but even mindful of us in the world ?   We are become, as
it were, a broken vessel to friends, relatives, and neighbours.
You alone cannot forget us.   You ask of the state and
condition of my health, of the journey I have just accomplished, of the monks whom I have transferred to

another place. Of them I may briefly reply, that out of a desert land, from a place of grim and vast solitude, they have been brought into a place where nothing is wanting to them, neither possessions, nor buildings, nor friends; into a rich land and a lovely dwelling-place. I left them happy and peaceful; in happiness and peace, too, I returned; except that for a few days I was troubled with so severe a return of fever that I was in fear of death. But by God's mercy I soon got well again, so that now I think I am stronger and better after my journey is over than before it began.

LETTER CXIX.

To the Duke and Duchess of Lorraine.[1]

He thanks them for having hitherto remitted customs [or tolls], but asks that they will see that their princely liberality is not interfered with by the efforts of their servants.

To the Duke and Duchess of LORRAINE, BERNARD, Abbot of Clairvaux, sends greeting, and prays that they may so lovingly and purely rejoice in each other's affection that the love of Christ alone may be supreme in them both.

Ever since the needs of our Order obliged me to send for necessaries into your land I have found great favour and kindness in the eyes of your Grace. You freely displayed the blessings of your bounty on our people when they needed it. You freely remitted to them when travelling their toll,[2] the dues on their purchases, and any other legal

---

[1] That is, Simon and Adelaide, not Gertrude, as most write. For the account of the conversion of this Duchess by S. Bernard see *Life*, Bk. i. c. 14. She took the veil of a Religious in the Nunnery of Tart, in the environs of Dijon, as is clear from the autograph Letters of her son, Duke Matthew, who calls his mother Atheleïde. These Letters P. F. Chifflet refers to at the end of his four Opuscula, ed. Paris, 1679. I do not refer to the pretended Letters of Gertrude to Bernard, and Bernard to Gertrude, translated by Bernard Brito, from French into Portuguese and thence into Latin.

[2] *Passagium*, a fixed payment from travellers entering or passing through a country; *droit de passage* or "toll."

due of yours. For all these things your reward is surely
great in heaven, if, indeed, we believe that to be true
which the Lord promises in His Gospel: *Inasmuch as ye
have done it unto one of the least of these my brethren ye
have done it unto me* (S. Matt. xxv. 40). But why is it that
you allow your servants to take away again what you bestow? It seems to me that it is worthy of you and for your
honour, that when you have been pleased to bestow anything for the safety of your souls no one should venture
to demand it back again. If, then (which God forbid), you
do not repent of your good deed, and your general intention
in respect to us is still the same, be pleased to order it to be
a firm and unshaken rule; that henceforward our brethren
may never fear to be disturbed in this matter by any of
your servants. But otherwise we do not refuse to follow
our Lord's example, who did not disdain to pay the dues.
We also are ready willingly to *render to Cæsar the things
that are Cæsar's* (S. Matt. xvii. 26), *custom to whom
custom, and tribute to whom tribute is due* (Rom. xiii. 7),
especially because, according to the Apostle, we ought
not *to seek our gift so much as your gain* (Phil. iv. 17).

LETTER CXX.

To the Duchess of Lorraine.

*He thanks her for kindnesses shown, and deters her from
an unjust war.*

I thank God for your pious goodwill which I know that
you have towards Him and His servants. For whenever
the tiniest little spark of heavenly love is kindled in a
worldly heart ennobled with earthly honours, that, without
doubt, is God's gift, not man's virtue. For our part we are
very glad to avail ourselves of the kind offers made to us of
your bounty in your letter. But having heard of the sudden
and serious stress of business, which, of course, must be delaying you at this time, we think it meet to await your
opportunity as it shall please you. For, as far as in me lies,

I would not be a burden to anyone, particularly in things pertaining to God, where we ought to seek not so much the profit of the gift as advantage abounding to the giver. And so, if you please, name a day and place in your answer by this messenger, when, by God's help, having brought to an end the business which now occupies, you will be able to approach these regions, where our brother Wido [1] will meet you, so that if he finds anything in your country profitable for our Order you may fulfil your promise with greater ease and speed. *For God loveth a cheerful giver* (2 Cor. ix. 7). Otherwise, if perchance the delay please you not, let me know this also: for in this matter I am ready, as reason allows, to obey your wishes. I salute the Duke, your husband, through your mouth, and I venture to urge him and you both, if you know that the castle for which you are going to war does not belong to your rightful domain, for the love of God to let it alone. *For what shall it profit a man if he gain the whole world and lose his own soul?* (S. Matt. xvi. 26).

LETTER CXXI.

To the Duchess of Burgundy. [2]

He tries to appease her anger against Hugo, and asks her assent to a certain marriage.

The special friendship with which your Grace is pleased, as it is supposed, to honour me, a poor monk, is so widely known that whenever anyone thinks your Grace has him in displeasure, he applies to me as the best medium for being restored to your favour. Hence it is that some time ago, when I was at Dijon, Hugo de Bèse urged me with many

---

[1] I think this is Wido [or Guy ?], Abbot of Trois Fontaines, who frequently went to Lorraine. *Cf.* 63, 69.

[2] Matilda, wife of Hugo I., Duke of Burgundy, who was cherishing her anger against Hugo de Bèse. This place was situate four leagues from Dijon, and famous for the Monastery of that name (Bèse) of the Benedictine Order. About this Hugo see Perard, pp. 221, 222.

entreaties to appease your displeasure, which he had
deserved, and to obtain, for the love of God, and by your
kindness towards me, your assent to the marriage of his
son, which, though it did not meet with your approval, he
had irrevocably determined to make, since it was, as he
thinks, an advantage to himself. And for this reason he
has been besieging my ears, not as before, by his own
prayers, but by the lips of his friends. Now, I do not much
care about worldly advantages, but since the matter, as he
himself says, seems to have reached such a narrow pass
that he cannot prevent the marriage except by perjuring
himself, I have thought it meet to tell you this, since that
must be a serious object which should be preferred to the
good faith of a Christian man and your servant. For he
cannot be perjured and yet at the same time keep faith
with his Prince.[1] Aye, and I see not only no gain to you,
but also much danger arising, if those whom perhaps God
has determined to join together should be put asunder by
you. May the Lord grant His grace to you, most noble
lady, so dear to me in Christ, and to your children.
*Behold, now is the acceptable time; behold, now is the
day of salvation.* Spend your corn on Christ's poor, that
in eternity you may receive it with usury.

LETTER CXXII. (*Circa* A.D. 1130.)

HILDEBERT, ARCHBISHOP OF TOURS, TO THE ABBOT BERNARD.[2]

*The reputation of Bernard for sanctity induces Hilde-
bert to write to him and ask for his friendship.*

1. Few, I believe, are ignorant that balsam is known by
its scent, and the tree by its fruit. So, dearly beloved

---

[1] *Legalitati, i.e.*, good faith, which consists in performing promises once made.
[2] In not a few MSS. this Letter, with the answer following, is placed after
Letter 127, and in some even after Letter 252. Hildebert, the author of this
Letter, ruled the Church of Mans (1098-1125), whence, on the death of Gilbert,
he was translated to the Metropolitan See of Tours. This is clear, first from
Ordericus Vitalis, Bk. x., *sub ann.*, 1098, and next from the Acts of the Bishops

brother, there has reached even to me the report of you—
how you are steadfast in holiness, and sound in doctrine.
For though I am far separated from you by distance of
place, yet the report has come even to me. What pleasant
nights you spend with your Rachel ; how abundant an offspring is born to you of Leah ; how you show yourself
wholly a follower of virtue, and an enemy of the flesh.
Whoever speaks to me of you has this one tale to tell.
Such is the perfume of your name, like that of balm, poured
out ; such are already the rewards of your merit. These
are the ears that you are gathering from your field before
the last great harvest. For in this life some reward of
virtue is to be found in the notable and undying tribute
paid to it. This it wins unaided, and keeps unaided. Its
renown is not diminished by envy, nor increased by the
favour of men. As the esteem of good men cannot be
taken away by false accusations, so it cannot be won by the
attentions of flattery. It rests with the individual himself
either to advance that esteem by fruitfulness in virtue, or
to detract from it by deficiency. The whole Church, I am
quite sure, hopes that your renown will be for ever sustained, since it is believed to be founded upon a strong
rock.

2. As for me, having heard this report of you everywhere,
with desire I have desired to be received into the inmost

of Mans, published in the third volume of *Analecta*, where Guido, his successor
in the See of Mans, is said to have been consecrated, after long strife, in 1126.
Hildebert only ruled in Tours six years and as many months. So say the Acts
just mentioned. With them agrees a dissertation by Duchesne, and John
Maan's History of the Metropolitan See of Tours, and so also Ordericus Vitalis
on the year 1125 (p. 832), where he assigns to Hildebert an Archiepiscopate of
about seven years. Hildebert, then, did not reach the year 1136, as *Gallia
Christiana* says, but died in 1132, in which year John Maan places his death.
Horst, in the note to this Letter, refers to another Letter of Hildebert (the 24th),
which he thinks was also written to Bernard. But this Letter, which in all the
editions appears without the name of the person to whom it was addressed, is
entitled in two MSS. "To. H., Abbot of Cluny," which we have followed.
From this Letter we understand that Hildebert had it in mind to retire to Cluny,
if the Supreme Pontiff would allow him. Peter of Blois praises his Letters.
(Ep. 101.)

shrine of your friendship, and to be held in remembrance in your prayers when stealing yourself from converse with mortals you speak on behalf of mortals to the King of Angels. Now, this my desire was much increased by Gébuin, Archdeacon of Troyes, a man eminent as well for his piety as for his learning. I should have thought it my duty to commend him to you, if I were not sure that those whom you deem worthy of your favour need no further commendation. I wish, however, that you should know that it was through his information I learnt that you are in the Church, one who art fit to be a teacher of virtue, both by precept and example. But not to burden you with too long a letter, I bring my writing to an end, though end the above petition I will not until I have the happiness to obtain what I have asked. I beg you to tell me by a letter in reply how you are disposed with regard to it.

LETTER CXXIII. (*Circa* A.D. 1130.)

REPLY OF THE ABBOT BERNARD TO HILDEBERT, ARCHBISHOP OF TOURS.

He repays his praises with praises.

A good man out of the good treasure of his heart bringeth forth good things. Your letter so redounded to your honour, as well as to mine, that I gladly welcomed it, Most Reverend Sir, as giving me an occasion of addressing to you the praises of which you are so well worthy, and as affording me just satisfaction that you have done me so much honour as that your Highness should deign to stoop to me, and to show so much esteem for my humble person. Indeed, for one in high place not to be studious of high things, but to condescend to those of low estate, is a thing than which there is nothing more pleasing to God or more rare among men. Who is the wise man, except he who listens to the counsel of Wisdom, which says: *The greater thou art, the more humble thyself* (Ecclus.·iii. 18) before all. This humility you have shown towards me, the greater towards the less, an elder to a younger. I, too, could extol your proved wisdom in due praises, perhaps more just than those of which your wisdom deemed me worthy. It is of great importance in order to gain assured knowledge of things, to rely on exact acquaintance with facts, rather than on the uncertain testimony of public rumour; and then what we have proved for certain we may proclaim without hesitation. What you were pleased to write to me about myself, it is for you to ascertain. I find an undoubted proof of your own merit in your letter, though it be so full of my praises. For though another, perhaps, might be pleased with the marks of learning therein, with its sweet and graceful language, its clear style, its easy and commendable art, I place before all this the wonderful humility, whereby your Greatness has cared to approach one so humble as I, to overwhelm me with praises, and to seek for my friendship. As for what refers to me in your letter I read it not as describing what I am, but what I would wish to be, and what I am ashamed of not being. Yet whatever I am, I am yours; and if, by the grace of God, I ever become anything better, be sure, Most Reverend and dear Father, that I shall still remain yours.

LETTER CXXIV. (*Circa* A.D. 1131.)

TO THE SAME HILDEBERT, WHO HAD NOT YET ACKNOW- LEDGED THE LORD INNOCENT AS POPE.

He exhorts him to recognise Innocent, now an exile in France, owing to the schism of Peter Leonis, as the right- ful Pontiff.

To the great prelate, most exalted in renown, HILDE- BERT, by the grace of God Archbishop of Tours, BER- NARD, called Abbot of Clairvaux, sends greeting, and prays that he may walk in the Spirit, and spiritually discern all things. ·

1. To address you in the words of the prophet, *Consolation is hid from their eyes, because death divideth between brethren* (Hosea xiii. 14, VULG.). For it seems as if according to the language of Isaiah they have made a covenant with death, and are at agreement with hell (Is. xxviii. 15). For behold, Innocent, that anointed[1] of the Lord, is set *for the fall and rising again of many* (*cf.* S. Luke ii. 34). Those who are of God, gladly join themselves to him ; but he who is of the opposite part, is either of Antichrist, or Antichrist himself. The abomination is seen standing in the holy place ; and that he may seize it, like a flame he is burning the sanctuary of God. He persecutes Innocent, and in him all innocence. Innocent, in sooth, flees from the face of Leo, as saith the prophet : *The lion hath roared ; who will not fear* (Amos iii. 8). He flees according to the bidding of the Lord, which says, *When they persecute you in one city flee ye into another* (S. Matt. x. 23). He flees, and thereby proves himself an apostolic man, by ennobling himself with the apostle's example. For Paul blushed not to be let down in a basket over a wall (Acts ix. 25), and so to escape the hands of those who were seeking his life. He escaped not to spare his life, but to give place unto wrath ; .not to avoid death, but to attain life. Rightly does the Church yield his place to Innocent, whom she sees walking in the same steps.

2. However, Innocent's flight is not without fruit. He suffers, no doubt, but is honoured in the midst of his sufferings. Driven from the city, he is welcomed by the world. From the ends of the earth, men meet the fugitive with sustenance ; although the rage of that Shimei, Gerard of Angoulême, has not yet entirely ceased to curse David. Whether it pleases or does not please that sinner who sees it with discontent, he cannot prevent Innocent being honoured in the presence of kings, and bearing a crown of glory. Have not all princes acknowledged that he is in truth the elect of God? The Kings of France, England, and Spain, and finally the King of the Romans, receive

[1] *Christus.*

Innocent as Pope, and recognize him alone as bishop of
their souls (2 Sam. xvii.). Only Ahitophel is now unaware
that his counsels have been exposed and brought to nought.
In vain the wretch labours to devise evil counsel against
the people of God, and to plot against the saints who
stoutly adhere to their saintly Pontiff, scorning to bow the
knee to Baal. By no guile shall he avail to procure for his
parricide the kingdom over Israel and the holy city, *which
is the church of the living God, the pillar and ground of
the truth. A threefold cord is not quickly broken* (Eccle-
siastes iv. 12). The threefold cord of the choice of the
better sort, the assent of the majority, and, what is more
effective yet in these matters, the witness of a pure life,
commend Innocent to all, and establish him as chief
Pontiff.

3. And so, very Reverend Father, we await your vote,
late though it be, as rain upon a fleece of wool. We do
not disapprove of a certain slowness, for it savours of
gravity, and banishes all sign of levity. For Mary did not
at once answer the angel's salutation, but first considered
in her mind what manner of salutation this should be (S.
Luke i. 29) ; and Timothy was commanded to *lay hands
suddenly on no man* (1 Tim. v. 22). Yet I, who am known
to the Prelate I am addressing, venture to say "nought in
excess;" I, his acquaintance and friend, say, *Let not a man
think more highly of himself than he ought to think* (Rom.
xii. 3). It is a shame, I must confess, that the old serpent,
letting silly women alone, has, with a new boldness, even
assayed the valour of your heart, and dared to shake to its
base so mighty a pillar of the Church. I trust, however,
that though shaken it is not tottering to its fall. *For the
friend of the bridegroom standeth and rejoiceth at the
bridegroom's voice* (S. John iii. 29) ; the voice of joy and
health, the voice of unity and peace.

LETTER CXXV. (*Circa* A.D. 1131.)

To Magister Geoffrey, of Loretto.[1]

He asks his assistance in maintaining the Pontificate of Innocent against the schism of Peter Leonis.

1. We look for scent in flowers and for savour in fruits; and so, most dearly beloved brother, attracted by the scent of your name which is as perfume poured forth, I long to know you also in the fruit of your work. For it is not I alone, but even God Himself, who has need of no man, yet who, at this crisis, needs your co-operation, if you do not act falsely towards us. It is a glorious thing to be able to be a fellow-worker with God; but perilous to be able and not to be so. Moreover, you have favour with God and man; you have knowledge, a spirit of freedom, a speech both lively and effectual, seasoned with salt; and it is not right that with all these great gifts you should fail the bride of Christ in such danger, for you are the friend of the Bridegroom. A friend is best tried in times of need. What then? Can you continue at rest while your Mother the Church is grievously distressed? Rest has had its proper time, and holy peace has till now freely and duly done its own work. It is now the time for action, because they have destroyed the law. That beast of the Apocalypse (Apoc. xiii. 5-7), to whom is given a mouth speaking blasphemies, and to make war with the saints, is sitting on the throne of Peter, like a lion ready for his prey. Another [2] beast also stands hissing at your side, like a whelp lurking in secret places. The fiercer here and the craftier there are met together in one against the Lord and his anointed. Let us, then, make haste to burst their bonds and cast away their cords from us.

[1] Geoffrey of Loretto, a most renowned doctor, afterwards Archbishop of Bordeaux. He took his name from Loretto, a place in the Diocese of Tours, close to Poitou. It was once famous for a Priory, subject to Marmoutiers. This is why Gerard of Angoulême is spoken of to Geoffrey in this Letter as " the wild beast near you." Another derivation is " L'oratoire," a monastery of the Cistercians in the Diocese of Angers.

[2] Gerard of Angoulême.

2. I, for my part, together with other servants of God
who are set on fire with the Divine flame, have laboured,
with the help of God, to unite the nations and kings in one,
in order to break down the conspiracy of evil men, and to
destroy every high thing that exalts itself against the knowledge of God. Nor have I laboured in vain. The Kings of
Germany, France, England, Scotland, Spain, and Jerusalem,
with all the clergy and people, side with and adhere to the
Lord Innocent, like sons to a father, like the members to
their head, being anxious to preserve the unity of the
spirit in the bond of peace. And the Church is right in
acknowledging him, whose reputation is discovered to be
the more honourable and whose election is found to be the
more sound and regular, having the advantage as well by
the merit as by the number of the electors. And now,
brother, why do you hold back ? How long will the serpent
by your side lull your careless energies to repose ? I know
that you are a son of peace, and can by no reason be led
to desert unity. But, of course, that alone is not enough,
unless you study both to maintain it and to make war with
all your might upon the disturbers thereof. And do not fear
the loss of peace, for you shall be rewarded by no small
increase of glory if your efforts succeed in quieting, or even
silencing, that wild beast near you ; and if the goodness of
God, through your means, rescue from the mouth of the
lion so great a prize for the Church as William, Count of
Poitiers.

LETTER CXXVI. (A.D. 1131.)

To the Bishops of Aquitaine, against Gerard of Angoulême.[1]

*He nobly defends the cause of Innocent as the rightful
Pope, against Gerard of Angouléme, who was taking part*

[1] Gerard was the second Bishop of Angoulême of this name, by birth a
Norman, of the Diocese of Bayeux. Ordericus calls him " a most learned man,
of great fame and influence in the Roman Senate " (Bk. xiii., A.D. 1136). This
is shown by the fact that he was Legate of the Holy See in Aquitaine during
almost the whole of the Pontificate of Paschal II. and other legitimate Popes

*with the Schismatic.   He gives a picture of his character,
and exposes his subterfuges.*

To his Lords and Reverend Fathers, the holy Bishops,

until Innocent.   Nor was he wanting in zeal, for, if we can believe William
of Malmesbury (*History of the Kings of England*, Book v.), he had the
courage to accuse William, Prince of Aquitaine, who was disregarding the laws
of marriage, as being another Herod.   But John Besle contends that this was
a calumny against Count William (*History of the Counts of Poitiers*, chap. 32).

Pope Innocent having refused to Gerard the commission of Legate, he shame-
fully abandoned the party of that Pope and adhered to that of Anacletus, who
granted to him the title as a bribe, and proceeded to act, not as a Legate, but
as a disperser, drawing all those whom he could influence to the party of the
schismatic.   That is the reason why Bernard warns the neighbouring Bishops
of Aquitaine to disregard the voice of the seducer, and to follow Innocent, their
legitimate Pastor.   He lays before them these grounds of his right, viz.:
" The high character of the person elected, the priority of his election, and the
solemnity of his consecration."   Yet there were not wanting some persons who
upheld the right of Anacletus, and who brought forward arguments upon the
other side, as appears from the Letter of Peter, Bishop of Portus, the author and
defender of the consecration of this man, to William, Bishop of Præneste; to
Matthew, Bishop of Albano ; to Conrad, Bishop of Sabina ; and to John, Bishop
of Ostia, who all followed the party of Innocent.   This Letter is reported by
William of Malmesbury (*Historia Novella*, Book i.)   The party of Innocent,
however, prevailed ; all the chief leaders, whether ecclesiastical, except Gerard
of Angoulême, and a few others, or secular (if William, Count of Poitiers, and
Roger, King of Sicily, be excepted), taking his side.   But as for Gerard, he
was obstinate in his defence of the schism, and he died unhappily in 1136,
according to Ordericus.   Ernald has related his death in the *Life of S. Bernard*,
Book ii., chap. 7.   But it has been thought by some that this author, by too
great zeal for religion, has invented many things against Gerard, as that he
died suddenly and impenitent without confession and *viaticum*, and he adds
that his body was found lifeless on his bed and enormously swollen, and other
details of the same kind unworthy of a serious writer.   Those who judge
thus rely upon the *Gesta Episcoporum Engolismensium*, in which it is said :
" On the day before his death he said, in his confession to the priests, that he
had sustained the party of Peter Leonis in ignorance that it was against the
will of God ; that he repented of and confessed it.   Almost all that he
possessed he gave to the Church, or distributed to the poor, when dying.
That he celebrated Mass with abundant tears on the Saturday which preceded
the Sunday on which he died, which event took place in the year 1136 A.D.
He had been Bishop for more than 33 years.   As he had wronged one of his
chaplains by his liberalities, he gave to each of them at the end of his episcopate one mina [1] as a benefaction.   That man who, as a magnificent star, had

---

[1] The mina = 100 drachmæ, or one-sixtieth of a talent ; and the drachma
was nearly equal to the Roman denarius, = 7¾d.—[E]

by Divine permission, of Limoges, of Poitiers, of Périgueux, and of Saintes, Brother BERNARD, called Abbot of Clairvaux, sends greeting, and prays that they may be steadfast in adversity.

1. It is during peace that bravery is acquired, in the struggle that it is displayed, in the victory that it triumphs. The time has come, most Reverend and honoured Fathers, to show your courage, not to hide it, nor to let it rest inactive. The hostile sword, which seems to threaten the whole Church with death, hangs most of all over your necks; and it is you whom it threatens most eagerly and most closely, so that you are obliged by the daily attacks of which you are the objects, either to resist bravely or (which may God forbid!) disgracefully to retreat. The new Diotrephes, who loves to bear the first place[1] among you, rejects you from his communion; he refuses to recognize with you him whom the whole Church receives as coming in the name of the Lord. Not him, I say, does he receive, but the man who comes in his own name. I am not surprised at this, for he himself, even in his old age, strives and pants unweariedly to attain a great name. I am not led astray by an uncertain or false rumour in forming this opinion of the man; I judge of him from his own words. In a letter which he lately sent to the Chancellor of Rome,

enlightened the West with his brightness, now rests, alas! under an obscure stone outside the church which he built."

But as this story has no certain support, there is no reason for our rejecting that of Ernald, and especially as Alain, of Autun, who subjected to a severe criticism his books on the *Life of S. Bernard*, does not differ in this respect a nail's breadth from Ernald.

As for Anacletus, he died miserably in 1138, on January 7, as Foulques, of Beneventum, declares, "having occupied his see for the space of seven years, eleven months, and twenty-two days." This agrees with the account of William of Malmesbury, who says (*Hist. Nov.*, B. i.): "Anacletus died in the eighth year of his assumed pontificate (as it is said), and then Pope Innocent began to enjoy the title of Sovereign Pontiff in a peace which nothing has troubled up to the present time." Upon this subject consult also S. Bernard's Letters 144, 146, 147; Sermon 24 *in Cantica*, at the beginning; and the notes on Letter 147.

[1] *Primatum.* He refers to Gerard, who affected to hold a primacy, that is, the dignity of Legate. The allusion is to 3 Ep. S. John v. 9.

does he not supplicate, in terms as humble as they are unworthy of him, to be entrusted with the charge[1] and honourable title of Legate of the Holy See? Would that he had obtained it. Perhaps if his ambition had been gratified according to his prayers it would have been less hurtful than it is, being frustrated. Then, indeed, it would be hurtful to himself alone, or, at all events, to few; but now it breathes discord over the whole world. See what the love of vain glory does! The title of Legate is a heavy burden, especially for the shoulders of the old; who is ignorant of that? And yet it is a severe punishment to this extremely aged man to live without this title for the few days that remain to him.

2. But perhaps he will accuse me of rash judgment with respect to him; perhaps he will say that I venture to judge the secret feelings of his soul on a mere suspicion which nothing authorizes me to do. It is true I am very suspicious on this matter; but I would ask, what man would be so simple as to think otherwise than I have done in a case so clear? To refer briefly to an action that was unmistakable. He is one of the first, if not the first of all, to write to Pope Innocent; he applies for the title of Legate. He does not obtain it. He is indignant, he falls away from him; he passes over to the party of the other, of whom he boasts that he is the Legate. If he had not in the first place made suit for this title, or had not afterwards accepted it from the other, one might have been able to attribute his double dealing to some other motive than ambition; but, as things stand, he has no plausible excuse to make. Let him lay down this mere empty name of Legate, for it has no functions; and I, for my part, will lay aside, if I can, this opinion of him; if not, I will at least acknowledge my reluctant suspicion as being rash. But he will, I know, be with difficulty persuaded to do it. He is not a man to strip himself voluntarily of a title which has long rendered him great among his neighbours, and without which he would appear degraded. We see in him what Scripture calls *the*

---

[1] Many editions read: " To be weighted with the charge and honoured with the title;" but to be " weighted" is wanting in the MSS.

false shame which leads to sin (Ecc. iv. 25). Can there be, in fact, any worse thing, any greater offence than extreme pride in mere dust and ashes, so that it is reluctant, I do not say to be subjected to others, but not to rule over others ?

3. Because of this he quitted the party of Innocent, whom he called his holy Father, and the Holy Catholic Church his mother, and attached himself to his schismatiarch, with whose vain glory he has much in common. They have made mutual alliance, and have conceived an evil design against the people of God : *Scale is joined to scale, so that no air can come between them* (Job xli. 16). The one gives to the other the name of Pope, and the other in return styles him his Legate ;˙and so they flatter each other's vain glory. They console, support, and commend each other in turn ; but each of them does this for his own sake, and not for that of the other, for they are men who love only themselves. With equal zeal they combine against the Lord and against His Christ ; but their motives are not the same. Each one seeks to derive from the other some personal advantage, and (which is abominable) at the expense of Christ's heritage. Are they not attempting under your eyes to ruin His realm, if you will permit it ? That Legate fabricates new Bishops[1] among you for the party of his Pope, that he may not be alone ; nor does he wait until the Sees are vacant by death, but by the aid of the secular power tyrannically intrudes men into the places of Bishops yet living, taking occasion from the ill-will and relentless hatred of secular princes towards the Bishops of their cities. He sets in secret snares with the rich, that he may slay the innocent. By such a door he enters into the sheepfold.

4. Do you suppose that this Legate busies himself with such activity for the sake of his Pope only, and without any personal interest ? He has added, in order that he may boast himself the more, France and Burgundy to the ancient

---

[1] Thus he intruded Ramnulf, Abbot of Dorat, into the See of Lisieux. *Life of S. Bernard*, B. ii. 33.

limits of his legation; and he may add still further, if he
pleases, the Medes, the Persians, and the people of the Deca-
polis. Wherefore should he not arrogate to himself besides
the empty name of jurisdiction over the Sarmatians, and,
in fact, over every place that his foot has pressed ? O,
man no less without modesty than without sense ; mindful
neither of the fear of God nor of his own honour ! He
thinks that he is not found out, while he is the laughing-
stock and amusement of all his neighbours. And rightly
so. For he uses the sanctuary as if it were a market ; and
like a merchant seeking his gain goes here and there to the
sellers, seeking to obtain at the lowest price what he wants
to buy: so he seeks on all sides an ecclesiastical dignity,
and decides at length in favour of that Pope who has consented to make him his Legate. And so Rome could not
have had a Pope, unless he had found one to make him
Legate ? Whence came this privilege to you in the Church
of Christ ? Who has given you this prerogative over
Christ's heritage ? Is the sanctuary of God become your
patrimonial estate ? As long as there was any hope of
obtaining from the lord Innocent what you had the shameless impudence to demand of him, he was to you holy
Father and Pope in your letters. Why, then, do you now
accuse him as a schismatic ? Was it the case that his
holiness, and his legitimate tenure of the Papacy, vanished
with your hopes ? It was wonderful in how short a time
bitter water and sweet proceeded from the same fount.
Yesterday Innocent was catholic, holy, Supreme Pontiff ;
to-day he is schismatic, wicked, and a troubler of the
peace ; yesterday Innocent and Pope ; to-day Gregory,
simple Deacon of S. Angelo. It is from the same mouth,
indeed, but from a double heart, that these contrary sentiments proceed. Deceitful thoughts are in the heart, and
from the heart they have been spoken. But what can you
think of the reserve or self-respect of the man whose double
heart renders uncertain the voice of his conscience, and
with first Yes and then No makes his tongue forked ? He
ill-understands how to provide, according to the saying of

the Apostle, *things honest both before God and before men* (2 Cor. viii. 21), who being an unjust judge neither respects nor fears God or men.

5. It is quite certain that ambition, when it extends into impudence, defeats its own success; and the unscrupulous man, when he makes his object apparent, renders it unlikely to be attained. Ambition is the mother of hypocrisy; it needs obscurity and shadow, and is unable to bear the light. Ambition, the lowest placed of the vices, has always an eye towards advancement; but all its fear is to be perceived. Nor is that wonderful; for it may fail in obtaining its end, unless it escape observation; and the more it pursues glory the less it can be obtained, if it is suspected of the pursuit. What is more inglorious, especially for a Bishop, than to be known for a man greedy of titles and honours, when a Christian ought not to glory, except in the Cross of our Lord Jesus Christ? The ambitious will be esteemed by others only as long as he shall walk in darkness; and the hypocrite will be able to seem righteous and holy to the eyes which see only the outward appearance just as long as his meddling with filthy lucre be kept concealed. But when by impudence, or some imprudence, he happens to show what is lurking in his mind, does not the unmeasured love of greatness which is shown to all eyes turn to his shame and confusion rather than to his glory, and so, in truth, verify those words of the Scripture : *Whose glory is in their shame, who mind earthly things* (Phil. iii. 19); and this : *If I seek my own glory, my glory is nothing* (S. John viii. 54); and that imprecation of the Prophet directed, as I believe, against hypocrites : *Let them be as the grass upon the housetops, which withereth before it is plucked up* (Ps. cxxviii. 6, VULG.). The sentiment of shame has not yet perished in men, so that naked and shameless ambition should be honoured even by them, especially when they meet with it in an old man and a priest, in whom that puerile vanity is the more unbecoming, as increased gravity and holiness are befitting to him; and if he is flattered to his face, he is

turned into ridicule behind his back by all. There is an ambition more delicate and more enlightened,[1] which proceeds at least with caution, if not with pure intention ;[2] if it succeeds in advancing its object, it takes good care to keep its measures secret ; but if not, it still lies close, and does not break the reserve which it imposes upon itself. And such an ambition, if it does not fear God unto salvation, yet for innate modesty retains honourable feeling, because it stands in fear of men, and blushes at public disgrace.

6. But must not the ambition be headlong and the desire to dominate imperious which causes a man not to spare the repose of his old age nor the honour of his priesthood to obtain the precarious title of Legate, which he would not be certain of for more than a year, which makes him tear open again the side of the Saviour, whence issued forth once blood and water for the salvation of men, for joining them together in the unity of faith ? But whosoever tries to divide those whom Christ has joined together for their salvation proves himself to be, not a Christian, but an Antichrist, and guilty of the Cross and death of Christ. What impatient, what unbridled desire ! what unrestrained eagerness ! what blind and shameful ambition ! He is obliged to confess that (as I have said) he began by making a petition unworthy of him to the legitimate Pope ; and, smarting at the refusal he received, he took refuge immediately with the schismatic, and accepted from his sacrilegious hand the longed-for dignity, thus cruelly and shamelessly piercing the side of the Lord of Glory. For he divides the Church, for which that Side was divided upon the Cross. But one day he shall see Him whom he has pierced, and the Lord shall pronounce judgments, who now endures injuries patiently. When the day shall come that He shall do justice to those who are oppressed, and interfere in equity on behalf of the meek of the earth, will He, think you, turn away His ear from His beloved spouse when she invokes His aid against those who have oppressed

[1] *Oculata.* Otherwise, "secret" *occulta.*   [2] *Saltem caute, etsi non caste.*

her ? No ! He cannot be deaf to her complaint : *My neighbours and my friends approached and stood against me ; and those who were beside me stood afar off.   Those who sought my life used violence against me* (Ps. xxxvii. 12, 13, VULG.).   Why should He not recognize the bone of His bone, the flesh of His flesh, yea, rather, the spirit of His spirit?   Is she not for Him that well-loved Spouse, whose beauty has drawn Him here below, whose form He has put on, whom with marvellous condescension He has embraced with tender love, so that they two should be one flesh, as hereafter they shall be one spirit ?   For *although she had known Christ according to the flesh, yet then shall she know Him no more :* because before her face shall be a spirit, Christ Jesus the Lord ; and being closely united to Him, she shall be one spirit with Him ; when death shall be swallowed up in victory ; and that which is weak in the flesh shall overcome by the power of the Spirit ; when the glorious Spouse of the Church shall have her in his sight in her glory, as His dove perfect and beautiful, not having a spot of sin, a wrinkle of corruption, or any such thing.

7. While I linger willingly upon these consoling thoughts I have become almost unmindful of my subject, so strong is my desire to *redeem the time because the days are evil.* The thought of more happy days transports me, but my purpose calls me back, reminds me of the facts, and plunges me into sorrow.   The enemy of the cross of Christ (I relate it even weeping) carries his audacity so far as to drive from their (Episcopal) seats the holy men who entirely refuse to bend the knee before the beast of the Apocalypse, whose mouth opens wide with impious blasphemies against God and against His sanctuary (*Apoc.* xiii. 6).   He endeavours to raise altar against altar, and is not ashamed to confound good and evil.   He endeavours to intrude abbots into the places of abbots, Bishops into the places of Bishops, to thrust out the Catholics, to advance the schismatics.[1]   Poor creatures, and to be pitied, who

---

[1] Ordericus declares (Book xiii., page 825): " In most monasteries two abbots arose, and in bishoprics two prelates strove for the chief authority: of

consent to accept such promotion from the hands of such
a man. He traverses sea and land to make one Bishop;
and when he has made him, he makes of him doubly the
child of hell that he is himself. What do you suppose is
the cause of such furious activity? It is because that precept announced by the angels to mortals, in which glory is
given to God and peace to men, is to him displeasing; and
while he and his party usurp the glory they trouble the
peace. He alone merits glory who alone doeth wonders,
as the Apostle says, *to God alone be honour and glory*
(1 Tim. i. 13). As for man, he ought to think himself
happy, he ought to regard himself as being mercifully
favoured if it is permitted him to enjoy the peace of God
and peace with God; but how can it be thus if men themselves wish to usurp the glory of God? Oh, foolish sons
of Adam, who, while you despise peace and desire glory,
lose them both! It is because of this that the God of
vengeance has now *moved the land and divided it*: *He
has shewed His people heavy things, He has given them a
drink of deadly wine.*

8. Whether we will or no, the truth of the Holy Ghost
will necessarily one day be fulfilled, and that falling away
foretold by the spirit of prophecy, as we read in the
Scriptures (2 Thess. ii. 3), will take place; but woe to the
man by whom it comes. It would be better for that man
he had not been born. But who is that man except the
man of sin, who, notwithstanding that a Catholic had been
elected by Catholics to the holy place, and according to
canonical rules, invaded it for himself, although he desired
it not because it was holy, but because it was the highest
place? He invaded it, I say, by the sword, by fire, by
money, not by the merit of his life or by his virtues; he has
attained to that in which he remains, but he remains only
by the same means that he attained it. That election of

whom the one adhered to Peter (Anacletus) the other favoured Gregory
(Innocent)." So also in the Acts of the Bishops of Mans, Vol. iii., of the
Analecta, p. 338, on the subject of Philip, the intruded Bishop of Tours, of
whom Letters 150 and 151 (of S. Bernard) speak.

which he boasts so much was nothing but the note of a faction, a mere pretence, the occasion and the screen of his evil plan; it is impudent and false to call it an election. If there is in the Church a principle authentic and incontestable, it is that after the first election there is no second. Suppose that there has been one, after which a second is made; yet it is not a second, it is simply null and void. But even although that which preceded was conducted with too little solemnity, and not sufficiently according to ordinary formalities, as the enemies of unity contend, yet ought a second election to have been resolved upon before the manner of the former had been discussed, and it had been quashed by a deliberate judgment? It is that which obliges me to say that the factious persons are those who have hastened to lay their hands rashly upon a rash usurper, notwithstanding the prohibition of the Apostle: *Lay hands suddenly upon no man* (1 Tim. v. 22). They have, without doubt, the greater fault; they are the true authors of the schism, and the chiefs of this great mischief which has been done to the Church.

9. But now they demand judgment, which they ought to have waited for[1] before acting. When that proposition was made to them in fit time they rejected it; they only do this now in order to appear[2] to have the right on their side if you refuse it in your turn; and if you accept it they hope that during the process time may be gained by delays, and in the meantime something may happen in their favour. Or do they despair of their cause, and are they convinced that it can be made no worse than it is, whatever be the issue of the process? Whatever (they say) has been done hitherto, now we seek a hearing; we are prepared to submit to what may be decided. This is a trap. What else is left to you in your wicked undertaking, what other resource have you for seducing the simple, for arming the ill-disposed,

[1] *Exspectasse;* otherwise *expetiisse.*

[2] *Justi,* thus the old copies in most editions for *injusti* used in irony. But in one MS. (Colbertine, No. 1410), reads, *injusti justi vos videamini*—that is, "so that you who are right may appear wrong." One MS. of Beauvais reads simply *injusti.*

and for hiding your own guilt? If you did not say this
what could you say? But now God has already judged
what man seeks too late to reopen; but He has judged by
the evidence of the facts, and not by the wording of a
decree. Is it possible that human rashness would dare to
interpose an appeal from the judgment of God? What if
God should accuse and cry by the prophet, men have taken
away from me the right of judgment?[1] No purpose can
stand against the purpose of the Lord; His word runneth
very quickly, and draws together the peoples and the kings
into one mind, so that they serve and obey the lord Innocent as Pope. Who will appeal from this? It has been recognized and proclaimed by Walter of Ravenna, Hildegar of
Tarragona,[2] Norbert of Magdeburg, Conrad of Salzbourg,
Archbishops; it has been accepted by Equipert of Munster,
Hildebrand of Pistoja, Bernard of Pavia, Landulf of Asti,
Hugo of Grenoble, and Bernard of Parma,[3] Bishops. The
singular merit of these prelates, their manifest sanctity,
and their authority respected even by their enemies, have
easily determined me, who hold a lower rank in merit as in
office, to follow their leading whether it be right or wrong.
I do not speak of the multitude of others, both Archbishops
and Bishops of Tuscany, Campania, Lombardy, Germany,
and Aquitaine, of France, also, and all the Spains, as well
as of the whole Church of the East, whose names are in the
Book of Life, but which the brevity of a letter cannot find
space for.[4]

10. All these with one accord, not induced by money,
not led away by fallacious reasoning, not allured by con-
siderations of worldly relationship, nor compelled by fear

---

[1] This is not found in any prophet; but in *Doctrina SS. Patrum*, Book
against rash judgment, n. 7.

[2] He had succeeded to Ordelric, whom Ordericus (B. xiii. pp. 891, 892) calls
" a very learned old man."

[3] Bernard of Parma, in certain MSS. is placed after Bernard of Pavia, and in
others, particularly in the two Colbertine MSS., his name is wanting altogether.
Ughellus says that he died towards the end of the Pontificate of Paschal II.

[4] These words, " but which the brevity of a letter cannot find space for," are
wanting in two of the Colbertine MSS., but are found in the third.

of the secular power, but submitting themselves to the will of God which they cannot doubt has been made plain, have frankly rejected Peter Leonis, and recognized Gregory for Pope, under the name of Innocent. Of the prelates of our province, not one, indeed, is mentioned by name in this letter ; because I could not name them all, and the special mention of some of them would appear to be a kind of adulation. But I ought not to pass over those holy men, who, though dead to the world, live a better life in God ; their life is hid with Christ in glory, is consecrated entirely to the knowledge of the will of God, and to the endeavour to please Him. Of these, then, the Camaldulian[1] Religious, those of Vallombrosa, those of the Chartreuse, the Cluniacs,[2] those of Marmoutiers,[3] my own brethren in religion the Cistercians, those of S. Stephen of Caen,[4] of

[1] Most of the old MSS. have the name thus, but some have it *Camaudilliensis.* The Camaldulian monks and those of Vallombrosa are two Congregations of the Order of S. Benedict in Italy, and are too well known for it to be needful to say anything about them here (Mabillon's note). The Order was founded by S. Romuald, a noble of Ravenna, who retired in the later part of the eleventh century to Camaldoli, near Arezzo, in the Appennines, and commenced a hermit's life. It has two divisions, the hermits, who are solitaries, and monks who live in community. The habit is a white cassock, scapular, and hooded robe. The Vallombrosan Order is a branch of the Benedictines *of Cluny,* and was founded, also in the eleventh century, by S. John Gualbert, a Florentine. It was confirmed in 1055 by Pope Victor II. The habit is of a very dark grey, almost black.—[E.]

[2] A contemporary author, Ordericus, has described the manner in which the monks of Cluny received Pope Innocent (B. xiii. p. 895): "On learning the arrival of Innocent, the monks of Cluny sent to him sixty horses or mules with all trappings fit for the Pope and the Cardinals, and brought him to their house with great respect. There they entertained the Pope and his followers for eleven days, and caused him to consecrate a new Church in honour of S. Peter, chief of the Apostles, with great solemnity and attendance of the people. Thence he obtained great influence through all the West because he had been placed before Peter [Leonis] by the monks of Cluny. Yet Peter Leonis had been brought up by them, and was a monk of theirs by habit and profession."

[3] Marmoutiers was an important monastery near the city of Tours, over which then presided Abbot Odo, to whom Letter 397 is addressed. Upon this monastery depended many priories, which formed, as it were, a congregation. But Bernard here mentions only the more important monasteries.

[4] Caen is a town on the river Orne, in Neustria or Normandy, not far from the ocean. This abbey was founded and magnificently endowed by William

Tiron,[1] of Savigny,[2] in one word, the unanimous consent of
the brethren, as well secular clergy as monks, of strict
life and approved conduct, following their Bishops as
flocks follow their pastors, firmly adhere to Innocent,
zealously defend him, humbly obey him, and recognize him
faithfully as a true successor of the Apostles.

11. What of the kings and princes of the earth? Do
they not receive Innocent in the same disposition, with the
peoples who are subject to them, and confess him to be
Pope, and the Bishop of their souls? What man is there
of good family or of distinguished rank who does not think
the same thing? And yet those people still protest with
quarrelsome importunity and importunate argument. They
make their accusation against the whole world, and, notwithstanding their small number, endeavour to dictate to
the whole of Christendom, and to oblige it to confirm by a
second judgment an election[3] which has been already judged
and condemned; they began by improper precipitation,
and now wish to reopen the whole question. But, after
all, what means have they of assembling the chiefs of each
order [secular and ecclesiastical], I do not say of the
faithful simply, so as to submit the controversy to their
judgment? Who would be mighty enough to persuade so
many thousands of holy men to pull down again what they
had before built up, and to lend themselves to a deception?
Then where could a place be found safe and spacious
enough for all? For this is a business which belongs to the
whole Church, not the private cause of one person. You
see, then, that you [*i.e.*, the opponents] are demanding a

the Conqueror. Its first Abbot was Lanfranc, Prior of Bec, and afterwards
Archbishop of Canterbury.

[1] The monks of Tiron-le-Gardais in Le Perche, the Diocese of Chartres, were
instituted by the venerable Abbot Bernard, whose Life is extant with notes by
Souchet. James de Vitry praises the devotion of the monks of Tiron in his
History of the West, c. 20. This monastery, with that of Marmoutiers,
flourished under the Benedictine Congregation of S. Maur.

[2] Savigny. There are two monasteries of this name in France, the one in
the Diocese of Lyons, the other in that of Avranches, of which latter Bernard
must be understood to speak here. It was founded in 1112 by the most pious
Abbot Vitalis.   [3] *I.e.*, that of Peter Leonis.

thing which is impracticable, only to bring a false accusation against your Mother Church; or rather you are digging
a pit for yourselves into which you shall be thrown; you
are weaving a snare in which you shall be taken and held,
nor shall you return into the bosom of your Mother. A
pretext will never be wanting to him who wishes to break
faith with his friend.

12. But let it be so. Suppose that God should change
His mind (I speak after the manner of men), should recall
His decree, should assemble a Council from the ends of the
earth, should allow the matter which He has judged to be
submitted for a second judgment, which is not the way in
which God acts, whom, I ask, will they give to Him for
judges? All have taken their side in this matter, and it
will be very difficult to agree upon a judgment; so that so
great an assemblage of men will have the weariness to
assemble for disagreement rather than for peace. And,
finally, I would be glad to know into whose hands that
schismatic would consent to trust the city of Rome, which
he desired so eagerly and for so long a time, which he
gained with so much trouble and at so great a cost, which
he possesses with such pride, and which he fears to lose
with so great shame, lest the whole world should be seen
to have come together to no purpose, if when he loses his
cause he does not at the same time lose Rome; otherwise
why should he who has been despoiled enter upon the
cause? Neither the civil law nor the Canons oblige him
to do so. And this I say, not that I have any doubt of the
justice of our cause, but because I distrust the cunning of
our adversaries. God has already manifested His justice
as clearly as the light and His judgment as the noon-day,
although to him who is blind neither does the light appear,
nor does the blaze of noon-day enlighten; to him light and
darkness are the same.

13. The question is, then, of ascertaining whether of
these two claimants is the rightful Pope. As for that
which relates to them personally, that I may not seem either
to flatter or to detract from either one or the other, I will

say nothing except that which is spoken everywhere, and which, I suppose, everyone believes, namely, that the life and character of our Pope Innocent are above any attack even of his rival; while that of the other is not safe even from his friends. In the second place, if you compare the two elections, that of our candidate at once has the advantage over the other as being both purer in motive, more regular in form, and earlier in time. The last point is out of all doubt; the other two are proved by the merit and the dignity of the electors. You will find, if I do not mistake, that this election was made by the more discreet part of those to whom the election of the supreme Pontiff belongs. There were Cardinals, Bishops, Deacons, or Presbyters, and these in sufficient number, according to the decrees of the Fathers, to make a valid election. Then, as to the Consecration of the person elected, was it not performed by the Bishop of Ostia, to whom that function specially belongs? Since, then, both the person elected is maintained to be the more worthy and the election more discreetly conducted, and the formalities more regularly complied with in performing it; upon what pretext, or rather by what spirit of contention, do they try against right and justice and the voices of all good men to depose him, and to set another Pope over the reluctant and protesting Church?

14. You see, most reverend and illustrious Fathers, under what obligation you are to oppose with all your powers this attempt so malicious, so unworthy, and so rash. It is becoming to the whole Church, but most of all to you and yours, that zeal for the House of God should consume your souls. It is your duty, I say, and that of your flocks to watch and pray, that you enter not into temptation. The more boldly the adversary presses on, and the greater is the stress of battle, in that place is there surely the greater need for bravery and caution. How cruel and how cunning is the foe who has risen against you, you know, I am sure, by your own experience. Alas! what ravages has he not already committed in your neighbourhood, having recourse

in turn to force and to cunning, the constant arms of his
malignity! But shall his malice prevail over your wisdom?
No doubt this is his hour, and the power of darkness; but
the hour is his last, and his power soon passes away. Be
not afraid, nor permit yourselves to be drawn away. Christ,
the power of God and the wisdom of God, is with you; it
is His own cause. Trust in Him; He has overcome the
world; *He is faithful, and will not permit you to be
tempted above that ye are able.* Though the deluded man
appears solidly established, without doubt you will soon
see his fair show of prosperity overcast by general rejection; nor will the Lord leave the rod of sinners long over
the lot of the righteous. But, in the meantime, it is committed to your vigilance to provide with the care and
solicitude that becomes your office, that the good people
of your dioceses should not stretch out their hands towards
this wickedness.

Prayer for Catholics:

*Do good, O Lord, unto those that are good and true of
heart* (Ps. cxxv. 4); and for the schismatics: *Make their
faces ashamed, O Lord, that they may seek Thy name* (Ps.
lxxxiii. 17).

LETTER CXXVII. (*Circa* A.D. 1132.)

To WILLIAM, COUNT OF POITOU[1] AND DUKE OF AQUI-
TAINE, IN THE NAME OF HUGH, DUKE OF BURGUNDY.

*William was of the party of the Antipope Anacletus;
Bernard urges him to abandon it, and to range himself on
the side of Innocent.*

To WILLIAM, by the grace of God, the illustrious Count of
Poitou and Duke of Aquitaine, HUGH, by the same grace,

---

[1] He was the ninth of this name, or, as some think, the tenth, and, by the influence of Gerard, Bishop of Angoulême, he took the side of Anacletus, and persecuted the adherents of Innocent (*Cf. Life of S. Bernard,* lib. ii. c. 6). What
William of Malmesbury (*de reg. Ang.* lib. v.) says about the incest and other
crimes of William, Count of Poitou, must be understood of this man's father,
William VIII., as John Besle has pointed out. For Peter, Bishop of Poictiers,

Duke of Burgundy, sends greeting, bidding him fear Him who is terrible, and who takes away the spirit of princes.

1. I can no longer hold my peace about your mistaken line of action, though you are my near kinsman and dear friend. If any of the people perishes he perishes alone; but the error of a prince involves many, and ruins as many souls as he rules over. Nor are we raised on high, as you know, to destroy our subjects, but to govern them. He by whom kings reign, has put us over our subjects to protect them, not to overthrow them; we are the Church's keepers, not her masters. But since you are known to have discharged that function laudably, and in a way befitting the greatness of your power, on other occasions, I can but wonder by what craft you have been induced to desert your mother and mistress in the time of her dire need, unless, indeed, those counsellors of yours have succeeded in persuading you that the whole Church has been led to recognize Peter Leonis. They are lying men whom, with Antichrist their head, the Truth shall destroy with the breath of His mouth. By the mouth of David He tells us that His Church is spread abroad to all the ends of the earth, and to all the nations of the Gentiles.

2. They have, it is true, the Duke of Apulia[1] on their side; who was banished by the Count, he says, ended his days in exile A.D. 1117. But William IX. succeeded his father A.D. 1126, as the same author says in his *French History of the Counts of Poitou*. *Cf.* also Baronius (A.D. 1135) if more information about his life and all that he did is wanted. He is dealt with at length in *Vita Bernardi* (lib. ii. c. 6). Much, however, that is said of him is fabulous. He was converted by S. Bernard. It is certain, on the authority of Ordericus, his contemporary, who is supported by other influential writers, that William, moved to penitence, set out on a pilgrimage to the shrine of S. James (Compostella), when he was taken ill, " and died on the sixth day of the Passion, April 9th, before the altar of the Blessed Apostle, after being fortified by Holy Communion," about the year 1137.

[1] The Antipope Anacletus, to gain the support of Roger, Duke of Apulia and Calabria, honoured him with the title of King of Sicily (Baronius A.D. 1130, No. 6). Innocent, however, afterwards, having been overcome by him in battle, and ᵠ been taken prisoner, confirmed the title as the price of his freedom. How ⸱tter would it have been had the Pontiff maintained his rights by the ⸱ʳ others, if there really was need to take up arms, instead of going him- ⸱nd being forced to accept disadvantageous conditions. *Cf.* Baronius ⸱⸱ vol. xii.).

I.   27

but they have no other supporter of any power, and him they secured by the ridiculous bribe of a usurper's crown. I ask you, what goodness, or virtue, or honour do they bring forward on the part of their Pope that we should favour him? If what is commonly said of him be true, he is not fit to have the government of a single hamlet ; if it is not true, it none the less is fitting that the head of the Church should be of good repute as well as of blameless life. Therefore, it is safer for you, my dear kinsman, when you acknowledge any one as universal Pope, not to depart from the common mind and agreement of the universal Church, and to receive him that the whole monastic order and all the kings have acknowledged; it is also more to your honour and more expedient to your salvation to receive Innocent as Pope. He appeals to his blameless life, his unblemished character, and his canonical election. His enemies have not a word to say against the two first of these; the third was indeed found fault with, but the unprincipled men who did so have been lately caught in their falsehood by the most Christian Emperor Lothaire.

LETTER CXXVIII. (A.D. 1132.)

To the Same.

Bernard exhorts him gravely to restore to their Churches the Clerks whom he had deprived.

I recollect, most excellent Prince, that I not long ago left you, wishing well with all my heart to you and yours, and ready to lend, whenever I might have an opportunity, all the help that I could to promote your honour and your salvation. These friendly feelings were inspired by my not having returned deprived of the object of my visit to you; by my return, contrary to the expectation of many, bearing a message of peace to the Church, with the rejoicing of the whole earth. But now I cannot imagine with what intent, or by whose advice, that happy disposition in you which the right hand of the Most High had so suddenly worked for the better, has now so suddenly altered for the worse. Why should you expel again from your territories, to the great injury of the Church, the clergy of S. Hilary? Why should you call down upon yourself the wrath of God more heavily than before? Who has bewitched you to depart so soon from the way of truth and safety? Surely he will bear his judgment whoever he may be. *I would that they were even cut off that trouble you* (Gal. v. 12). Return, I implore you, return to a better disposition, lest you, too, be cut off, which God forbid. Retrace your steps; recall the love of your friends, suffer the clergy to return, before you irrecoverably bring upon yourself a terrible foe, Him who takes away the spirit of princes, and is terrible among the kings of the earth.

LETTER CXXIX. (A.D. 1133.)

To the Citizens of Genoa.

He exhorts them to preserve with all possible care the peace that he had re-established among them.

To the consuls, magistrates, and people of Genoa, health, peace, and eternal life.

1. That my visit to you last year was not fruitless, the Church who sent me soon afterwards experienced in her time of need. You received me honourably, and even thought my stay with you was all too short; this was, indeed, conduct worthy on your part, but quite beyond my humble deserving. At all events, I am neither forgetful of it, nor ungrateful to you. May God, who has the power, and whose cause it was, repay to you your goodness! But how can I recompense you for the honour you showed me, except by an affectionate service full of love and gratitude? Not that I take pleasure in favour shown to me, but I rejoice to see your devotion. What joyous days were those; but alas! only too few. Never will I forget

thee,[1] devoted people, honourable nation, illustrious state. At evening, and at morning, and at noon-day did I relate my news and announce my tidings, and I found that the hearers had as much charity as eagerness to hear. We took back the word of peace, and when we had found the sons of peace our peace rested upon them. I had gone out to sow seed, not mine, but God's; and it fell on good ground and brought forth fruit a hundredfold and imme- diately. Wonderful was the rapidity, for great was the necessity. I met with no delay or difficulty; in one day I sowed and reaped and brought back rejoicing sheaves of peace. This was the harvest that I gathered in. To those in exile, in captivity, in chains, and in prison, I took a joy- ous hope of freedom and return to their native land, to the enemy I brought fear, to schismatics confusion, to the Church glory, to the world gladness.

2. And now what remains for me, dearly beloved, but to exhort you to perseverance, which alone wins for man glory, and for his virtues the crown of victory? Without perseverance the soldier does not obtain victory, nor the victor his crown. It lends vigour to the will and perfects all virtues, it is the nurse to merit and the mediator between the battle and the prize. Perseverance is sister to patience, the daughter of constancy, the bosom-friend of peace, the cementer of friendships, the bond of harmony, the bulwark of holiness. Take away perseverance, and obedience loses

---

[1] The men of Genoa made trial of this in the year 1625. When Charles Emmanuel, Duke of Savoy, came up to lay siege to their city, they called on Bernard to redeem his pledge, and vowed as follows :—" We promise to enrol S. Bernard among the tutelary Saints of our State for he engaged in a Letter to us that he would never forget us. We engage to have his day observed as a feast day ; to erect a chapel dedicated to him in our Cathedral or some other Church ; yearly to go in procession, both clergy and laity, and solemnize the sacred rites at his altar, with the consent of the most illustrious Archbishop, and most reverend Bishops, and at which we will piously assist ; lastly, we promise to pay this year and every year for the future by the hand of the Duke, a hundred pounds with each of twelve maidens, as their dowry. In testimony whereof, etc. Given at the Cathedral Church, on Sunday, 25th April, 1625." This was when ruin was staring the citizens of Genoa in the face. The issue proved the worth of their vow. For on the eve of this Festival, Bernard quickly put their enemy to flight, by causing the appearance of the Spanish fleet. Thus writes Manrique.— [Mabillon's note.]

its reward, well-doing its grace, and fortitude its praise. It is not he who has begun, *but he that has persevered unto the end that shall be saved* (S. Matt. xxiv. 13). Saul when he was little in his own sight was made King over Israel, but not persevering in humility he lost both his kingdom and his life. If the caution of Samson and the devotion of Solomon had been persevered in, the one would not have been deprived of his strength, nor the other of his wisdom. I exhort and beseech you to hold fast firmly to this gift of perseverance, the highest mark of honour, the one trusty guardian of integrity. Keep carefully what you have heard joyfully. Remember the words that are written of Herod : *that he feared John and heard him gladly* (S. Mark vi. 20). Well would it have been for him if he had been as ready to act as to listen. It is not they that hear merely who are called *blessed,* but *they that hear the Word of God and keep it* (S. Luke xi. 28).

3. Keep, therefore, peace between yourselves and your brethren at Pisa; keep your fidelity to the Pope, your loyalty to the King; guard your own honour. This is expedient, this is befitting, and this is demanded by justice. I have heard that some messengers of King Roger have come to you ; I know not their object, nor their success. But I must confess with the poet that *I fear the Greeks, even when they bring gifts* (VERG., Æn. ii. 49). If anyone among you is caught (which God forbid) in the disgraceful act of stretching out his hand for filthy lucre, note him straightway, judge him to be an enemy to your name, a betrayer of his fellow-citizens, and a traitor to the common good and honour. If, again, you find any whisperer among the people assuming the devil's occupation of sowing dis-cords, and trying to disturb the existing peace, as he is ever the author and lover of division, then visit such a dangerous fellow the more quickly with severe judgment ; such a disease is the most deadly, because the most inward. A hostile army lays waste the fields and burns your houses, but evil communications corrupt good manners, and a little leaven permeates the whole lump. Sow, plant, and exert yourselves not only not to commit your former misdoings

again, but even by works of righteousness to atone for them
and blot them out. It is written, as you know: *The redemption of a man's soul is his riches* (Prov. xv. 6), and
again, *Give alms and all things are clean to you* (S. Luke
xi. 41). But if you determine to go to war, and, again,
bravely and strenuously to try your strength, to make test
of your arms, I, for my part, think that you ought not to
proceed against your neighbours and friends; it would be
more fitting for you to subdue the enemies of the Church
and defend your crown that has been assailed by the
Sicilians. From them, at all events, it will be more
honourable for you to take possessions, and more just
to keep them when taken. May the God of love and peace
remain with you all always. Amen.

LETTER CXXX. (A.D. 1133.)

To the Citizens of Pisa.

*He praises their zeal for, and devotedness to, Pope
Innocent, whom the Antipope Anacletus had forced
to leave Rome, and who had taken refuge at Pisa.*

To his friends, the consuls, councillors, and citizens of
Pisa, BERNARD, called Abbot of Clairvaux, wishes salvation,
peace, and everlasting life.

May God bless you, and remember the faithful service
and pious compassion and consolation and reverence which
you have shown, and still do show, towards the Bride of His
Son in her evil time and in the days of her affliction. And,
indeed, all this is partly fulfilled, and already there is some
answer to this prayer. Conduct that deserves a reward has
already met with rapid recompense. Now, God is dealing
with you according to your merits, O people, whom He has
chosen to Him to be His inheritance, a people wholly
acceptable, given to good works. Pisa is put in the place
of Rome, and out of all the cities in the world is chosen to
be the home of the Apostolic See. Nor has this happened
by chance or by man's counsel, but by Divine providence
and the good favour of God, who loves them that love

Him, and who has said to Innocent His anointed : "Live at
Pisa, and in blessing I will bless thee. Here will I dwell,
for I have chosen this city." It is because of My support
that the constancy of Pisa does not yield to the malice of
the Sicilian tyrant; that she is not moved by bribes, nor
terrified by threats, nor deceived by stratagems. O, men
of Pisa, men of Pisa, God has done to you great things, and
made us to rejoice. What state is there that does not envy
you? Guard well, O, faithful city, the treasure entrusted
to you, acknowledge the grace of God, study to be found
not ungrateful for the honour bestowed on you. Show all
the honour you can to your Father, and the Father of all,
and to the princes of this world, and the judges of the
earth who are with you ; their presence makes you
illustrious, glorious, famous. But if you know not the day
of your visitation, city renowned above all others, then
shall you be the last of all cities. I have said enough to
wise men. I commend to you the Marquis Engelbert,[1] who
has been sent to help the Pope and his friends. He is a
brave and energetic young man, and, if I mistake not,
faithful. Let my request win him your favour, especially as
I have specially commended you to him, and advised him to
pay great deference to your wishes.

LETTER CXXXI. (A.D. 1135.)

To the Inhabitants of Milan.

*The inhabitants of Milan, who had been reconciled to
Pope Innocent, seemed to be wavering in fidelity to him.
Bernard exhorts them to remain faithful, and reminds*

[1] Who is this Marquis? I think that it is he that, in the life of S. Norbert
(c. 32), is called the brother of the Bishop of Ratisbon. Of this Engelbert one
daughter was betrothed to Count Theobald. This is the passage :—"And so
the ambassadors of Count Theobald having been chosen, Norbert took them to
Ratisbon. The Bishop of Ratisbon was of noble birth, and had a most
powerful friend in his brother, Count Engelbert, who had daughters of marriage-
able age, one of whom was taken and betrothed to Count Theobald. Then the
ambassadors returned to announce," etc. Her name was Matilda (Order. Vit.,
lib. xiii.). Engelbert or Inglebert was also Duke of Carinthia and Marquis of
Friuli.—*Cf.* note to Ep. 299.

them of the recent benefits conferred upon them by the Roman See.

To his friends, all the clergy and laity of Milan, BER-
NARD, called Abbot of Clairvaux, sends greeting in the
Lord.

1. God is dealing well with you; the Roman Church is
treating you well. One acts as a Father, the other as a
mother. And, as a matter of fact, what has not been done
that should have been done? You asked that honourable
persons should be sent you from the Curia, to God's
glory and your own honour, and it has been done.[1] You
asked that your unanimous decision about the election of
your venerable father[2] should be confirmed, and that has
been done. You wished for what is forbidden by the
sacred canons to be done, except under great necessity, to
be made lawful in your case, viz., for a bishopric to be
raised to an archbishopric, and that, too, has been granted
you. You asked that your fellow-citizens should be rescued
from the hands of the men of Placentia, a thing which I
neither can nor will pass by, and this has been done. I ask
you, lastly, what reasonable request that the daughter has
made has the loving mother refused or even postponed for
a time? To sum up all, you will shortly have the *pallium*,
the fulness of honour. But now listen to me, illustrious
people, noble race, famous state. Listen, I say (and I speak
the truth; I lie not), to one who loves you, who is zealous
for your good. The Roman Church is very mild, but she
is none the less powerful. Faithful is the saying and
worthy of all acceptation, that he who does not wish to be
crushed by her power must not abuse her kindness.

2. But someone will say, "Yes, I will pay her the reverence that is her due, but not a whit more." By all means

---

[1] Guido of Pisa, Matthew of Alba, and Geoffrey, Bishop of Chartres, were
sent with Bernard (*Life*, lib. ii. n. 9) to reconcile the inhabitants of Milan to the
Roman Church. They had stirred up a schism because of the deposition of
Archbishop Anselm, who had been elected by them.

[2] *i.e.*, Ribault, who had been chosen by them for Bishop after the deposition
of Anselm.

do so, for if you give her the reverence she deserves, you
give her all, for fulness of power over all the churches of
the world has been given to the Apostolic See as her special
prerogative. He, therefore, who resisteth the power resisteth the ordinance of God. She can, if she see fit,
appoint bishops where before there were none. Where
they exist she can degrade some, exalt others, as reason
bids her, so that she can make bishops into archbishops and
vice versâ, where she sees necessity. From the ends of
the earth she can summon the most exalted ecclesiastics
and compel them to appear before her, not merely once or
twice, but as often as she sees fit. Moreover, it is in her
power to punish all disobedience, if by chance anyone
should endeavour to resist her. This, too, you yourselves
have found to your cost. What good did your last rebellion do you,[1] and the disobedience which your false prophets
wickedly enticed you into? What fruit had you in those
things whereof ye are now ashamed? See what loss of
power, glory, and honour you suffered in the persons of
your suffragans.[2] Who was able to stand up for you and
withstand the just severity of the Apostolic authority,

[1] He is speaking of the rebellion in which, following Anselm of Pusterla, their
Archbishop, the Milanese took the side of Conrad against the lawful Emperor
Lothaire. Sigonius relates the matter (del Reg. Ital. lib xi. A.D. 1128). He
says: "Conrad, supported by several princes, claimed the throne against
Lothaire. Then, elated by temporary good-fortune, he hastened with an army
into Italy, and having made Archbishop Anselm and the Milanese his friends,
he received the crown of the kingdom at Monza, over-ran Lombardy, and drew
to his side most of the States. For this the Archbishops of Mentz, Magdeburg,
and Tréves, by the command of Lothaire, excommunicated him. Honorius,
however, punished not only Conrad but also Anselm, who had crowned him,
and the people who had received him. Cf. Otto of Frisingen (Chron., lib. vii.
c. 17).

[2] By following Archbishop Anselm and supporting Anacletus and Conrad.
The dignity was restored to them on their repentance. And S. Bernard must be
understood to have spoken of this restoration above when he said that the
bishopric had been exalted into an archbishopric out of grace to the Milanese.
For this see enjoyed Metropolitan dignity from the beginning. We must
not omit what Sigonius relates (del Regn. Ital., lib. xi. A.D. 1133): "Innocent
having been twice received courteously and honourably by the Genoese rewarded
them by exempting their Bishop from the jurisdiction of the Archbishop of Milan,
and by placing under him one half of the Bishops of Corsica.

when, provoked by your audacity, it determined to cut off
your members, and strip you of your old and illustrious
honours? And you would at this moment be a hideous
and headless mass if mercy rather than power had not been
directed towards you. Who will have power to forbid
greater disasters still if, which God forbid, you again provoke them? See, then, that you do not again fall away, for
know for a certainty that you will not so easily find a
remedy a second time. If anyone should say to you that in
part you should obey and in part refuse to obey, although
you have felt the full weight of the Apostolic power and
the completeness of its authority, then I ask whether such
a man has not either been deceived or wishes to deceive.
But do what I bid you, for I am not leading you astray.
Give yourselves rather to humility and to meekness, knowing that God giveth grace to the lowly, and that the meek
shall inherit the earth. Be careful to keep the good will of
your mistress and mother now that you have regained it.
Study so to please her for the future, that she may be
pleased, not only to keep safely for you what she has
restored, but also to add what she has not yet given.

LETTER CXXXII. (A.D. 1132.)

To the Clergy of Milan.

*He congratulates the Milanese clergy, by whose endea-
vours the State had abandoned the Antipope Anacletus
and returned to the unity of the Church.*

Blessed be ye of the Lord, for by your zeal and diligence
your state has been set free from error, has abjured its
schism, and returned to Catholic unity. The news of it
has spread amongst Catholics; Sion has heard of it and
rejoiced, and you are glorified before God and the people.
How joyfully does your Mother, the Church, welcome back
such a number of worthy sons, whom she was grieving for
as lost! With how joyous and serene countenance does

God, the Father, receive this sacrifice at your hands! Do now, as sons of peace, what you propose to do for the peace of the earth. And I, brethren, longing to become a sharer and companion of your joy, am coming, according to your request, with our beloved brethren, your messengers. Concerning the things you wrote to me of, I will more fully satisfy you according to reason if it be the good pleasure of God. But since I shall soon be setting out to the Council, I hope it will be no burden to you to postpone them till my return.

LETTER CXXXIII. (A.D. 1134.)

TO ALL THE CITIZENS OF MILAN.

Bernard had been invited to negotiate for peace on their behalf, and gladly accepts the invitation.

I gather from your letter that you have some slight amount of regard for me. And since I cannot find that I deserve it, I believe it to be by the gift of God. I am far from declining the goodwill of a powerful and famous people. I welcome your kindness towards me, and with open arms receive devotedly the devotedness of your renowned State; especially now that you have abjured the error of the schismatics, and returned to the bosom of your Mother Church with the rejoicing of the whole world. Nevertheless, I think that not only to me is it a cause of rejoicing that I am invited to strive to make peace, and that I, a poor and unknown personage, am chosen by a most illustrious city to be its mediator and minister; but I think that it is also an honour to you to be desirous of peace and agreement with your neighbours, when the hostile attack of many States, as is well known to the world, has been powerless to force you to yield for a moment. And so being now hastening to the Council I shall hope to return by way of you, and make trial of your alleged goodwill. May He who giveth the goodwill cause that it be not in vain to me.

LETTER CXXXIV. (A.D. 1134.)

TO SOME NOVICES RECENTLY CONVERTED AT MILAN.[1]

Bernard congratulates these Milanese novices on their conversion, and promises to visit them on his return from the Council.

To his beloved brethren at Milan lately converted to God, BERNARD, called Abbot of Clairvaux, sends greeting, and prays that they may worthily carry out in the spirit of counsel and strength what they have well begun.

Blessed be God who hath made the world's glory to be of none account in your eyes that He might bestow upon you His own. How full of vanity are the children of men, how deceitful are they upon the weights, for, according to the saying of the Gospel, they *receive honour one of another, and seek not the honour that cometh from God alone* (S. John v. 44); surely in this they all are alike deceitful from vanity. But with you it is not so. From this reproach God's mercy has set you free, to make you a sweet odour to God in every place, to be to His glory, to be a cause of rejoicing to the angels, and an example to men.

---

[1] From this title Baronius infers that before the arrival of Bernard at Milan, i.e., before A.D. 1134, a community of Cistercians had removed thither, and had founded a monastery, to which these novices had submitted themselves. But Ughellus (*Ital. Sacr.*, Vol. iv.) thinks that Chara-vallis was the first house of Cistercians at Milan, and he proves it to have been founded about two miles outside the city not earlier than A.D. 1135, and that, therefore, under the name of " novices " in this epistle we must understand those who had been recently converted by the influence of S. Bernard on his way to the Council of Pisa, and who had devoted themselves already to him in mind. The date given by Ughellus for the founding of the monastery is proved from the original inscription and from the first charters of the place, in which it is uniformly called Chara-vallis and not Clara-vallis. See Ep. 281. On the name of this monastery of Chara-vallis Mabillon, in his work entitled " Museum Italicum," writes in the first part (p. 18, § 8): " For the reading Chara-vallis we have some original deeds of the place, and also an ancient inscription cut on the cloister-wall as follows: ' In the year of grace 1135, on the 22nd of January, this monastery was built by S. Bernard, of Clairvaux; in the year 1221 this church was consecrated by Henry, Archbishop of Milan, on the 2nd May, in honour of S. Mary of Chara-vallis.' "

If, indeed, there is joy in heaven over one sinner that repenteth, how much more over so many and over such men as you, and especially over those who belong to such a city as yours. And I, brethren, induced by my great joy, and also invited by you, sent you word by my dear brothers, Otto and Ambrose, whom you sent to me with your invitation, of my decision to come with them. But on second thoughts, thinking it better not to see you for a few brief moments, nor merely in passing, I postponed my visit till my return. I am now going to the Council, but by God's help I will return by your way, and afford your holy purpose such counsel and help as reason shall enable me.

LETTER CXXXV. (*Circa* A.D. 1135.)

To Peter, Bishop of Pavia.[1]

Bernard attributes to God the praises lavished upon himself, but congratulates the Bishop on his works of mercy.

If good seed, sown in good soil, seems to have brought forth fruit, His is the glory who gave the seed to the sower, fertility to the soil, increase to the seed. What have we to do with these? I certainly will not give Christ's glory to another, much less will I claim it for myself. Surely it is *the law of the Lord that converteth the soul* (Ps. xix. 7) and not I; it is the testimony of the Lord that is sure and giveth wisdom unto the simple, and not I. It is the hand and not the pen that is praised for the fair shape of the letters, and if I am to claim for myself what belongs to me in anything I have done, I confess that *my tongue is the pen of a ready writer* (Ps. xlv. 1). But, you say, why then are *the feet of them that preach good tidings called beautiful?* (Is. lii. 7). What are their advantages? much

---

[1] Ughellus has two Bishops of Pavia of this name: one elected A.D. 1130 or 1131, the other after Alphonse and Conrad, A.D. 1148, and it is to this latter that he assigns this Letter. It, however, suits the former better, and, indeed, it follows immediately after ep. 134, which was written A.D. 1134.

every way. First, because they are the children of their Father which is in Heaven, they think that the glory which they offer to Him as tribute is none other's, but His, and being children they are His heirs. Then also they reckon that the salvation of their neighbours is also their own, for they love them as themselves. Thirdly, the labour of their lips shall not utterly perish. For *every man shall receive his own reward according to his own labour* (1 Cor. iii. 8). I have not prevented my lips; thou hast opened thy heart also, and therefore wilt doubtless receive more, inasmuch as thou hast laboured more. I am certain that thy reward awaits thee, for thou hast given drink to the thirsty, and met with bread those that were flying. Nor will thy kindly offices, nor the exhortations to salvation with which thou hast refreshed the bowels of Christ in His poor go unrewarded. We are both fellow-labourers, fellow-helpers of God : let us both hope for our reward in the sight of the souls of the saints saved through us. May God grant that I never forget you, nor you cease to remember me.

LETTER CXXXVI. (A.D. 1134.)

To Pope Innocent.

He asks that Dalfinus, who was prepared to give satisfaction for the injuries that he had inflicted, may receive gentler treatment.

If we were always meeting with calamities, who would be able to bear them? If with prosperity, who is there that would not despise it? But Wisdom, who sweetly orders all things, so tempers with moderation and alternates for His elect the necessary vicissitudes that attend upon the course of their temporal life, that they are neither shattered by adversity nor beguiled by prosperity. The former is made more tolerable by the latter, and the latter receives a keener enjoyment from the former. Blessed be God in all things: our sorrow has been turned into joy, our wounds have been soothed first by wine, then with oil. The robbers and plunderers have been smitten with compunction and brought low. They send back with honour the priest of the Lord, on whom they dared to lay hands; the spoils which they had carried off they energetically collect again, and wholly restore. If any part of them cannot be found Dalfinus will give satisfaction for it according to your good pleasure; he has pledged me his honour to this. If he comes to the feet of your majesty,[1] as he proposes to do, in order to fulfil his promise, I ask that the young man may be dealt with more gently than he deserves. Not that I wish so great a crime to go unpunished, but that the Church, if possible, may be honoured by due satisfaction being given; so that he who gives the satisfaction may not be exasperated beyond the limits of his patience, and may not repent him of having listened to my advice.

LETTER CXXXVII. (A.D. 1134.)

To the Empress of the Romans.

As Pope Innocent did not wish to restore the Milanese to his favour until they had made submission to the Emperor Lothaire, Bernard commends them to the clemency of the Empress.

In bringing over the citizens of Milan[2] I did not forget the instructions given me beforehand by your excellency.

---

[1] It is gathered from this that this Letter was directed to the Supreme Pontiff, who is not seldom styled " your majesty " by others, as by Bernard in epp. 46, 150, 166, etc., also by Odo de Dioglio and others. Still, this title is sometimes given to the prelates under him. *Cf.* notes to ep. 370.

[2] Sigonius (*de Regn. Ital.*, lib. ii. A.D. 1134) speaks of this as follows: " When the Milanese saw themselves excommunicated and deprived of their metropolitan's dignity for following Anselm in his support of Anacletus and Conrad, moved by repentance for their misdoing, they sought, through their Bishop Ribault, whom they had chosen in the room of Anselm, to recover favour with Innocent and Lothaire; and they wrote a letter with this object to Bernard, the power of whose influence they knew to be great. Bernard being summoned

Even if I had not received them I should none the less have aimed to secure your honour and the welfare of your kingdom, as I do always and everywhere as far as I can. As a matter of fact, the Milanese were not received into favour with thy lord the Pope, nor into the unity of the

by Innocent to the Council of Pisa, as he was hastily passing through Lombardy wrote to congratulate them on having laid aside their error, and promised to help them by his intercession and to come to them on his way back. Having arrived at Pisa the Council was opened and its business happily ended, mainly by his sagacity and wisdom. The acts of that Council were many. The chief one was an anathema directed against Anacletus and his supporters. To the Milanese, who had been persuaded by their Bishop to return to their allegiance to Innocent, many honours were given ; Ribault, whom they had themselves elected, was allowed to retain his dignity, and was gifted with the pall, so that the city regained its metropolitical dignity, and a most honourable embassy was sent to them to give them pardon. Guido of Pisa, and Matthew, Bishop of Alba, were sent as legates *a latere*, and with them was joined the man they most asked for, Bernard, to extinguish the schism caused by Archbishop Anselm, and to set the people free from their wickedness by the ministry of religion. The Milanese, when they heard that Bernard was close by, immediately rushed out of the city with great joy, went seven miles to meet him, with such a multitude of all orders and ages, both men and women, that a stranger might have thought that they were abandoning the city to settle elsewhere. Then when the two companies met, they vied with each other in their eagerness to see him, to speak to him, and even to kiss his feet. They plucked hairs from his garments to keep them as remedies against disease, thinking everything that he had touched holy, and supposing that they themselves would become so by having touched him ; and in this manner they brought him with shouts and rejoicing into the city. Then on a day appointed a conference was held. At it they first of all repudiated Anacletus, and acknowledged Innocent as true and Catholic Pontiff. Next they forswore Conrad and publicly recognized Lothaire as their king and lord, and received him, as did the rest of the world, as the august Roman Emperor, and promised on the Holy Gospel that they would give satisfaction for their past contumacy according to the counsel and command of Innocent. Afterwards they agreed to submit to Bernard's decision, and they accepted the penalty which he imposed. While Bernard was at Milan he cured by the power of God, to the great wonder of all, a vast number of sick, who were brought to him, lame, blind, halt, and especially he set free very many who had been possessed by a devil because of the schism. Then by the order of Innocent he set out to Pavia and Cremona to make peace between the States of Lombardy. But being unsuccessful in his efforts at Cremona, he announced their obstinacy to Innocent in these words : "The people of Cremona have hardened their hearts, and their prosperity is leading them to their ruin. They despise the Milanese, and their confidence is their snare. They put their trust in chariots and horsemen, they have frustrated my trust in them, and rendered my labour useless."

Church until they had publicly abjured Conrad, and acknowledged my lord Lothaire as their king and lord, and
received him, as the whole of the world does, as the august
Emperor of the Romans: nor until they had taken an oath
on the Holy Gospel, by the direction and command of my
lord the Pope, that they would give you fitting satisfaction
for the injury that they had done you. I give, therefore,
hearty thanks to the divine goodness which has thus laid
your enemies at your feet without the horrors of war, or
the shedding of man's blood; and I ask that, when the
Milanese seek through the Pope as their mediator for your
favour, we may find you as kindly disposed and merciful as
we have often before experienced you to be; and so they
will not repent of having listened to sound advice, and you
will receive at their hands the service and honour that are
your due. For it is not seemly that your faithful servants
who labour for your honour should be put to shame by you,
as they certainly will be if, after they have held out to
others the hope of indulgence at the hands of your gracious
majesty, they find you inexorable when they intervene on
their own behalf.

LETTER CXXXVIII. (A.D. 1133.)

TO HENRY, KING OF THE ENGLISH. *

He asks for assistance to Pope Innocent from the King.

To the most illustrious HENRY, King of England, BER-
NARD, called Abbot of Clairvaux, wishes health, prosperity,
and peace.

To wish to teach you, and especially about what concerns your honour, would be the part either of a fool, or of
one who knows nothing at all of you. It is enough for me,
therefore, to state the case simply and in as few words as
possible; when a hint is enough many words are superfluous. We are on the threshold of the city, salvation is at
the doors, righteousness is our companion, but the Roman
military want other food than that. And so by righteousness we appease God, by our arms we terrify the foe, but

we have not the bare necessaries of life. You know better than I what should be done to finish the good work that you have begun in your magnificent and honourable reception of my lord, Pope Innocent.[1]

LETTER CXXXIX. (*Circa* A.D. 1135.)

To the Emperor Lothaire.

Bernard exhorts the Emperor to repress the schismatics. He recommends to him the cause of a certain Church at Toul.

To LOTHAIRE, by the grace of God Roman Emperor and AUGUSTUS, BERNARD, called Abbot of Clairvaux, sends greeting and prayer, if the prayer of a sinner be of any avail.

1. Blessed be God who has chosen you,[2] and set you up as

---

[1] What Henry I. did may be seen in the *Life of S. Bernard* (lib. ii. c. i. n. 4). William of Malmesbury also says (*Hist.* lib. i.):—"Innocent having been shut out of Rome, crossed the Alps, and hastened into Gaul. There he was received by the whole Church on this side of the Alps. Moreover, King Henry, who was not easily to be moved from any position that he had once taken, voluntarily acknowledged him at Chartres, and at Rouen loaded him with presents, not only from his own stores, but from the nobles and also from the Jews." Roger of Hoveden, too, relates this same reception (*Annals* A.D. 1131). Further, in the year 1132, according to Fulk, editor of the Chronicle of Beneventum, when the Emperor Lothaire was besieging Rome for the purpose of restoring Innocent, and had not sufficient force to take the city, being supported by only two thousand soldiers, Bernard, who was with him, sought by this Letter reinforcements from the King of the English. These, however, Henry was unable to supply. We learn from a Letter of Hugh, Archbishop of Rouen, to Pope Innocent, what a Christian and pious death he died, A.D. 1135. This Letter is well worthy of preservation, and may be seen in the *History* of William of Malmesbury (lib. i.), and in Baronius (*Annals* A.D. 1135).

[2] Lothaire, Duke of Saxony, was a man well-spoken of by all: *Cf.* William of Tyre (lib. xii. c. 16) ; Otto of Frisingen (lib. vii. c. 17) ; Sigonius, who praises him as well for his piety as for his valour ; Conrad, Abbot of Ursperg, who sings his praises, as a brave general, a sagacious counsellor, and a terrible opponent to the enemies of God and of Holy Church ; Peter the Deacon, who exalts him in wondrously magnificent terms. He says: "Who would not admire the greatness of the Emperor's mind ? He would sit in the Chapter from prime to vespers endeavouring to appease the discussions of the brethren, going without food and drink, while striving for peace and unity. Under the Imperial cloak he served his heavenly King. For, as I myself can testify, when he was

the horn of our salvation, to the praise and glory of His name, to the reparation of the Imperial honour, to the support of the Church in her evil hour, and lastly to work salvation in the midst of the earth. It is His work that the glory of your crown is being daily added to and raised on high, is wonderfully increasing and advancing in all honour and magnificence before God and men. Of His doing surely it was, and of His power that you lately accomplished so successfully[1] such a laborious and dangerous journey, undertaken on behalf of the peace of the kingdom and the liberation of the Church. Indeed, you have most gloriously attained the full height of the Imperial dignity, and, what is still greater, you did so not by a mighty hand, that so the greatness of your mind and of your faith might the more clearly shine forth. But if the earth trembled and was still before so tiny an army, what dread may we suppose will seize upon the hearts of the enemy when the King shall proceed to show the power of his arm? Moreover, the goodness of his cause will animate him, nay, a double necessity will urge him forward. It becomes not me to exhort to battle; nevertheless, I say unhesitatingly that it is the duty of the Church's advocate to protect the Church from being attacked by the madness of schismatics, it is the prerogative of Cæsar to uphold his own crown

engaged on any expedition he would at the early dawn hear mass first for the departed, then for the army, then either for himself, or else the ordinary mass of the day." It is not without reason, therefore, that Bernard praises God for giving the Empire such an Emperor.

[1] This was the journey which, at Bernard's instigation, Lothaire undertook from Germany into Italy, as far as to Rome, although with but scanty forces, for the purpose of placing Innocent on the Papal throne, and of in turn receiving from him the Imperial crown. This last ceremony took place in the Lateran while the Antipope was occupying the Vatican, and holding the strongest positions of the city. *Cf.* Baronius (*Annals*, A.D. 1132); Sigonius (lib. xi. A.D. 1132); *Life of S. Bernard* (lib. ii. c. 2). For all this Ordericus (lib. xiii. p. 896), in describing the journey of Lothaire to Rome, A.D. 1133, says that he bade Peter either to give place to another or submit himself to the judgment of a Council in respect of his election, and that he said the same to Innocent. He says, too, that Peter agreed, but Innocent declined, and that, therefore, Lothaire was angry with the latter, and handed over to Peter the positions he was holding, and left Rome without finishing the business.

against the Sicilian usurper.[1] For as a Jew by descent has seized upon the See of Peter to the injury of Christ, so without doubt everyone who makes himself a king in Sicily speaketh against Cæsar.

2. But if it is incumbent upon Cæsar both to render the things that are Cæsar's to Cæsar, and to God the things that are God's, why are the possessions of God at Toul diminished without Cæsar getting any gain from them? It is to be feared that neglect of trifles may become a barrier to great matters. What I refer to is this. The church of S. Gengulphus[2] in that city is being grievously oppressed, and unjustly, too, it is said; and they say that in some way or other your prudence has been beguiled into opposing my lord the Pope, when he was about to see justice done, by a request from you not to interfere. I implore and advise you to act more prudently, to recall the injurious request, to permit justice to be done before that Church is destroyed to the foundation. I am but a poor

[1] About the rights of the kingdom of Sicily there was at other times great discussion, with which, however, we have nothing to do now. It may be found described in the work of Baronius, if it is still extant, and in the works of those who wrote against him. Bernard rightly speaks of the "Sicilian usurper," inasmuch as he seized the duchies of Apulia and Calabria, committed to the charge of William, his cousin, and kept them from the Pontificate of Calixtus till the year 1136, when Lothaire, on his second journey into Italy, according to Conrad of Ursperg, entered Apulia, and conquered Roger, having kindled the zeal of his soldiers chiefly by telling them that they were fighting against a foe of the Church, and an excommunicate. Cf. Otto of Frisingen (lib. vii. c. 16 and 20); Fazell (lib. 7. poster. decad). Roger, however, repented afterwards under the admonitions of Bernard, and Peter of Cluny, who urged him by letter to seek reconciliation.

[2] For S. Gengulf, or Gangulf, or Jangulf, see Sigbert (A.D. 759): "S. Gengulf flourished in Burgundy, and there gloriously suffered martyrdom." In his honour a noble church was erected at Toul, in Lorraine, about the year 1065, by S. Gerard, bishop of that city, as I have been informed by a Letter from the illustrious and Reverend Andrew Saussay, Bishop and Count of Toul, a man distinguished not less by his learned writings than by his dignified position. So also we find in an ancient MS. in his possession: "An abbey of S. Gengulf was first founded at the southern entrance of the city by S. Gerard, who also gave it an arm of the saint." Udo, another Bishop of Toul, restored the church. This invocation of S. Gengulf was also given to several collegiate churches, as, e.g., in the case of S. Exuperius, at Corbeil, where the Prior, or head of the Chapter, is called abbot. Cf. ep. 178.

Religious, yet I am your devoted servant, and if I seem importunate, it is, perhaps, just because I am thus devoted. I salute the Lady Empress in the love of Christ.

LETTER CXL. (*Circa* A.D. 1135.)

To the Same.

He commends to the Emperor the Pisans, who were entirely devoted to Pope Innocent.

I wonder at whose instigation, or by whose advice, it is that your vigilance has been so eluded, that men who were certainly worthy of double honour at your hands have met with quite opposite treatment. I mean the citizens of Pisa, who were the first, and, at one time, the only people to lift up their banner against your rival. How much more just would it have been had the royal indignation flamed out against those who on some pretext or other have had the audacity to attack a brave and loyal city, at a moment, too, above all things, when many thousands of its people had gone out to fight against the tyrant, to avenge the wrongs of its Lord, and to defend the imperial crown. For, that I may most fittingly apply to this city what was of old said of holy David (1 Sam. xxii. 14), I ask, among all States what one is so faithful as Pisa, going out and coming in, and obeying the King's command? Is not this the people which lately raised the siege of Naples, and put to flight the one powerful enemy that the kingdom has? Is not this the people, too, which, wonderful to say, in one campaign stormed the wealthy and strongly fortified cities of Amalfi, Ravello, Scala, and Atturnia, cities which up to that time had been found impregnable by all who had attempted their capture? How meet and right, how consistent with all reason and justice, would it have been that a faithful city should have been protected against every foe, at all events while engaged in such exploits as I have mentioned ; to say nothing of the presence of the Supreme

Pontiff, who had lately been driven into exile, and received by the men of Pisa with the utmost honour, which they still continue to show ; nor yet of the good service that they have done the Emperor, for which at that very time they themselves were under sentence of banishment. But things have gone by contraries ; those who were hostile have met with favour, and those who have done their duty have incurred wrath. But perhaps you knew nothing of all this before. Now, however, that you do, it behoves you, nay, decency and good policy call upon you, to change your orders and your mind, that so men who deserve especially to be honoured by the King's countenance and bounty may hear and receive from you for the future such things as they have merited. How great is the reward that the men of Pisa can claim ; how great a reward may they still earn ! I have said enough for a wise man.

LETTER CXLI. (A.D. 1138.)

To Humbert, Abbot of Igny.[1]

Bernard blames him severely for having suddenly and rashly abandoned his abbey and his charge.

May Almighty God forgive you. What has made you act thus ? Who would have believed that a man endowed with such good gifts would have so stumbled and fallen into evil ? How could a good tree have brought forth such bad fruit ? How terrible is God in His judgments among the children of men ! I am not surprised at this token of the power of the devil, but I am surprised that God should have allowed one whom I believe to have served Him so faithfully for so many years to fall so grievously. What

---

[1] Humbert joined the monks of Clairvaux from Casa Dei ; then he was made by Bernard first Abbot of the new monastery of Igny, in the Diocese of Rheims. Desiring a life of privacy he resigned his office A.D. 1138, in which year this Letter was written from Italy. In spite of it, however, he adhered to his purpose, and Guerric was chosen to succeed him. He died at Clairvaux A.D. 1148, as we shall see in the second volume, in reference to the sermon that Bernard delivered after his death.

will He do with me, an idle and careless servant, if He
hands over His faithful follower for a time unto the will of
his enemies ?   What reason, I ask you, have you for deserting your charge ?   It is rather to be called an act of impiety,
at which your children grieve and your adversaries rejoice.
I wonder that you were not deterred by the example of
Abbot Arnold, whose similar presumption was shortly afterwards punished with a well-deserved but dreadful end, as
you well recollect.   And he, indeed, as I know well, had
some excuse, but you have none.   Is it that your monks
were disobedient to your commands, or the converts
neglectful of their tasks, or your neighbours by any chance
hostile to you and your house, or were your worldly possessions too small and insufficient, inasmuch that you were
forced to leave those whom you were not able to govern or
to feed ?

Take care, lest the words of God come to apply to you,
They have hated me without a cause (S. John xv. 25).   For
what ought He to have done more for you, that He did not
do ?   He planted for you a choice and beautiful vineyard ;
He surrounded it with the hedge of vowed continency;
He dug in it a winepress of the strictest discipline ; and He
built a tower of holy poverty, the top of which reached
unto heaven.   He appointed you to till it and to take care
of it.   He honoured you in your labours, and, if you permit
Him, He will crown those labours.   But you, alas ! are
pulling down the wall that He has built, and exposing His
vine, laden with fruitful branches, to all that pass by that
way.   Who is to prevent the wild boar out of the wood
from rooting it up, and the wild beast of the field from
devouring it ?   You write to me that you are not afraid to
die under such scandal and the anathema of our lord the
Pope, but I can only wonder how you can think this a
good preparation for your death.   Moreover, even if you
had no other course open to you, might not some other
time have been chosen but that when I am kept away by
the necessities of the universal Church, and so am prevented
from lending any aid to that unhappy community which

you are rendering easy of attack? I beseech you, by Him who was crucified for you, that you cease from tormenting those who have already enough affliction, and desist from adding sorrow to sorrow. To tell you the truth, I am so affected by this grievous rent made in the Church at large that my soul is aweary of life, even if you and yours could manage to live in peace.

LETTER CXLII. (A.D. 1138.)

To the Monks of the Abbey in the Alps.[1]

These monks of the Abbey in the Alps had associated themselves with Clairvaux under the Cistercian Order. Bernard praises and consoles them for the loss of their Abbot, who has been called to a higher rank, and instructs them respecting the election of another.

1. Your good father and mine, by the will of God, has been promoted to a higher place. Let us, therefore, dearly beloved, do what the prophet speaks of when he says, *The sun was raised up, and the moon stood still in her order* (Habak. iii. 11, VULG.). He is the son by which your congregation in the Alps is made everywhere illustrious, just as the moon receives her light from the sun. And as He has been raised up let us stand still in our order, we who have chosen to be doorkeepers in the house of our God, rather than to dwell in the tents of ungodliness. Our Order

---

[1] This monastery was in Savoy, in the Diocese of Geneva, and is now called Annecy. It was founded by Humbert II., Count of Savoy. Its first Abbot was Guerin, who was afterwards made Bishop of Sion, and this was the occasion of this Letter being written, in which Bernard consoles the Alpine monks for the loss of their Abbot. Gaspar Jongelinus (*Notit. Abbat. Cister.*) refers the foundation of this monastery to the year 1136, but that it was founded before this and that the monks had not embraced from the beginning the Cistercian habit, but had after some time affiliated themselves, is evident from this epistle, especially from the words, "How joyfully has the whole Cistercian Order opened its arms to you!" It is evident, too, from what S. Bernard goes on to say, that they had attached themselves specially to Clairvaux. *Cf.* also Ep. 253 to the same Guerin, and Manrique (*Annals* A.D. 1136), where he speaks of the incorporation as having taken place. Also the *Life of S. Bernard* (lib i. n. 67).

is lowliness, humility, voluntary poverty, obedience, peace, and joy in the Holy Spirit. Our Order is to be under a teacher, under an Abbot, under rule and discipline. Our Order is to seek to be silent, to train ourselves by fastings, watchings, and prayers, and manual labours, and above all things to hold the more excellent way of charity; nay, more, to be progressing from day to day, and persevering in these things until our life's end. And this I trust that you are carefully doing.

2. But you have done one work, and all men marvel. Although you were holy, you thought your holiness to be nothing; you sought to share in that of others, that you might be the more holy. Fulfilled is that which is written in the Gospel, *When ye shall have done all those things which are commanded you say, We are unprofitable servants* (S. Luke xvii. 10). You count yourselves unprofitable, and you have been found to be humble. To do what is right, and to think one's self unprofitable, is found amongst very few, and therefore many wonder at it when found. This, I repeat, is what makes you more famous than those who are famed, more saintly than the saints. And wherever this rumour of you has spread, it has filled all places with the sweetness of its odour. This grace, in my judgment, is to be preferred to protracted facts and anticipated vigils, and to every kind of bodily discipline; but godliness is profitable unto all things. How joyfully has the whole Cistercian Order opened its arms to you! with what smiling faces have the angel hosts looked down upon you! They know well that, above all things, Almighty God is pleased with brotherly fellowship and union, for He says by the Prophet, *It is a good thing to be joined together* (Is. xli. 6, VULG.); and by another, *Behold how good and joyful a thing it is, brethren, to dwell together in unity* (Ps. cxxxiii. 1); and again, *If brother helpeth brother both shall be comforted* (Prov. xviii. 19, VULG.).

3. Moreover, this that you have done tends to foster humility. And how acceptable this is to the Divine Majesty is taught us by him who says : *God resisteth the proud, but*

giveth grace unto the humble (S. James iv. 6).   It is shown,
too, by the Master of humility, who says : *Learn of Me, for
I am meek and lowly in heart* (S. Luke xi. 29).   What need
I say, of the special welcome of love given you by our little
flock of Clairvaux, to which you have more specially affiliated yourselves ?   No words can express the mutual
charity that exists between us, and which works in a marvellous way by the pouring forth of the Spirit.   It only remains, brethren, that, after invoking the Holy Spirit, you
hasten to elect an abbot.   For if you were to wait for me, I
am afraid that my arrival may be long postponed, and that
delay would be fraught with danger.   But call to your side
my dear brother, Godfrey, Prior of Clairvaux, to fill my
place in this and any other matters ; and then, according to
his advice, or the advice of those he may send, in case he
cannot come to you himself, as well as of your father
Guerin, choose such an abbot as may be able to labour for
the honour of God and for your salvation.   Forget me not,
brethren.

LETTER CXLIII. (*Circa* A.D. 1135.)

To his Monks of Clairvaux.

*He excuses his long absence, from which he suffers more
than they ; and briefly reminds them of their duty.*

To his dearly-loved brethren the Monks of Clairvaux, the
converts,[1] and the novices, their brother BERNARD sends
greeting, bidding them rejoice in the Lord always.

[1] " Converts " (*conversi*) was the name formerly given to adults who had been
converted to the religious life, and who were distinguished by this name from those
who were offered as children. The lay brethren are here meant ; *cf.* ep. 141 n. 1.
They were present at the election of an abbot (ep. 36 n. 2), just as once the
laity were joined with the clergy in the election of a bishop. Here they are
named before the novices, but in Sermon 22 (de Diversis n. 2) they come after
them ; they were not admitted into the choir. Bernard, moreover, distinguishes
them from the monks. For at that time they were not among the Cistercians
reckoned among the monks, as is proved by the *Exordium Ci·terc.* (c. 15),
although they made some profession. Hence Innocent II., in some deed of
privilege or in ep. 352, here says : " Let no one presume without your leave to

1. Judge by yourselves what I am suffering. If my absence is painful to you, let no one doubt that it is far more painful to me. The loss is not equal, the burden is not the same, for you are deprived of but one individual, while I am bereft of all of you. It cannot but be that I am weighed down by as many anxieties as you are in number; I grieve for the absence of each one of you, and fear the dangers which may attack you. This double grief will not leave me until I am restored to my children. I doubt not that you feel the same for me; but then I am but one. You have but a single ground for sadness; I have many, for I am sad on account of you all. Nor is it my only trouble that I am forced to live for a time apart from you, when without you I should regard even to reign as miserable slavery, but there is added to this that I am forced to live among things which altogether disturb the tranquillity of my soul, and perhaps are little in harmony with the end of the monastic life.

2. And since you know these things, you must not be angry at my long absence, which is not according to my will, but is due to the necessities of the Church; rather pity me. I hope that it will not be a long absence now; do you pray that it may not be unfruitful. Let any losses which may in the meantime happen to befall you be regarded as gains, for the cause is God's. And since He is gracious and all-powerful, He will easily make any losses good, and even add greater riches. Therefore, let us be of good courage, since we have God with us, in whom I am present with you, though we may seem to be separated by a long distance. Let no one among you who shows himself attentive to his duties, humble, reverent, devoted to reading, watchful unto prayer, anxious for brotherly love, think that I am absent from him. For can I be anything but present

receive or to retain any one of your converts who have made their profession, but are not monks, be he archbishop, bishop, or abbot." In the Council of Rheims, held under Eugenius III., the converts are called "the professed" (Can. 7), and although they may have returned to the world, yet they are declared incapable of matrimony, like the monks, from whom, nevertheless, they are distinguished. For the early days of Clairvaux *cf.* notes to ep. 31.

with him in spirit when we are of one heart and one mind ? But if, which God forbid, there be among you any whisperer, or any that is double-tongued, a murmurer, or rebellious, or impatient of discipline, or restless or truant, and who is not ashamed to eat the bread of idleness, from such I should be far absent in soul even though present in body, just because he would have already set himself far from God by a distance of character and not of space.

3. In the meanwhile, brethren, until I come, serve the Lord in fear, that in Him being delivered from the hand of your enemies you may serve Him without fear. Serve Him in hope, for He is faithful that promised ; serve Him by good works, for He is bountiful to reward. To say nothing else, He rightly claims this life of ours as His own, because He laid down His own to obtain it. Let none, therefore, live to himself, but to Him who died for him. For whom can I more justly live than for Him whose death was my life ? for whom with more profit to myself than for Him who promises eternal life ? for whom under a greater necessity than for Him who threatens me with everlasting flames ? But I serve Him willingly, because love gives liberty. To this I exhort my children. Serve Him in that love which casteth out fear, which feels no labours, seeks for no reward, thinks of no merit, and yet is more urgent than all. No terror is so powerful, no rewards so inviting, no righteousness so exacting. May it join me to you never to be divided, may it also bring me before you, especially at your hours of prayer, my brethren, dearly beloved and greatly longed for.

— — - ~

LETTER CXLIV. (A.D. 1137.)

To the Same.

He expresses his regret at his very long absence from his beloved Clairvaux, and his desire to return to his dear sons. He tells them of the consolations that he feels nevertheless in his great labours for the Church.

1. My soul is sorrowful until I return, and it refuses to be comforted till it see you. For what is my consolation in the hour of evil, and in the place of my pilgrimage? Are not you in the Lord? Wherever I go, the sweet memory of you never leaves me; but the sweeter the memory the more I feel the absence. Ah, me! that the time of my sojourning here is not only prolonged, but its burden increased, and truly, as the Prophet says, *they who for a time separate me from you have added to the pain of my wounds* (Ps. lxix. 26). Life is an exile, and one that is dreary enough, for while we are in the body we are absent from the Lord. To this is added the special grief which almost makes me impatient, that I am forced to live without you. It is a protracted sickness, a wearisome waiting, to be so long subject to the vanity which possesses everything here, to be imprisoned within the horrid dungeon of a noisome body, to be still bound with the chains of death, and the ropes of sin, and all this time to be away from Christ. But against all these things one solace was given me from above, instead of His glorious countenance which has not yet been revealed, and that is the sight of the holy temple of God, which is you. From this temple it used to seem to me an easy passage to that glorious temple, after which the Prophet sighed when he said : *One thing have I desired of the Lord, which I will require, even that I may dwell in the house of the Lord all the days of my life, to behold the fair beauty of the Lord and to visit His temple* (Ps. xxvii. 4).

2. What shall I say? how often has that solace been taken from me? Lo, this is now the third time, if I mistake not, that my children have been taken from me. The babes have been too early weaned, and I am not allowed to bring up those whom I begot through the Gospel. In short, I am forced to abandon my own children and look after those of others, and I hardly know which is the more distressing, to be taken from the former, or to have to do with the latter. O, good Jesu! is my whole life thus to waste away in grief, and my years in mourning? It

is good for me, O Lord, rather to die than to live, only let
it be amongst my brethren, those of my own household,
those who are dearest to my heart. That, as all know, is
sweeter and safer, and more natural. Nay, it would be a
loving act to grant to me that I might be refreshed before I
go away, and be no more seen. If it please my Lord that
the eyes of a father, who is not worthy to be called a
father, should be closed by the hands of his sons, that they
may witness his last moments, soothe his end, and raise
his spirit by their loving prayers to the blissful fellowship,
if you think him worthy to have his body buried with the
bodies of those who are blessed because poor, if I have
found favour in Thy sight, this I most earnestly ask that I
may obtain by the prayers and merits of these my brethren.
Nevertheless, not my will but Thine be done. Not for my
own sake do I wish for either life or death.

3. But it is only right, that as you have heard of my grief,
you should also know what consolation I have. The first
solace for all the trouble and misfortune that I undergo is
the thought that the cause I strive for is that of Him to
whom all things live. Whether I will or no, I must live for
Him who bought my life at the price of His own, and who
is able, as a merciful and righteous Judge, to recompense us
in that day whatever we may suffer for Him. But if I have
served as His soldier against my will, it will be only that a
dispensation has been entrusted unto me, and I shall be an
unprofitable servant; but if I serve willingly I shall have
glory. In this consideration, then, I breathe again for a
little. My second consolation is that often, without any
merit of mine, grace from above has crowned me in my
labours, and that grace in me was not in vain, as I have
many times found, and as you have seen to some extent.
But how necessary just now the presence of my feebleness
is to the Church of God, I would say for your consolation
were it not that it would sound like boasting. But as it is,
it is better that you should learn it from others.

4. Moved by the pressing request of the Emperor, by the
Apostolic command, as well as by the prayers of the Church

and the princes, whether with my will or against my will, weak and ill, and, to say truth, carrying about with me the pallid image of the King of terrors, I am borne away into Apulia. Pray for the things which make for the Church's peace, and our salvation, that I may again see you, live with you, and die with you, and so live that ye may obtain. In my weakness and time of distress, with tears and groanings, I have dictated these words, as our dear brother Baldwin [1] can testify, who has taken them down from my mouth, and who has been called by the Church to another office and elevated to a new dignity. Pray, too, for him, as my one comfort now, and in whom my spirit is greatly refreshed. Pray, too, for our lord the Pope, who regards me and all of you equally with the tenderest affection. Pray, too, for my lord the Chancellor, who is to me as a mother ; and for those who are with him—my lord Luke, my lord Chrysogonus, and Master Ivo[2]—who show themselves as brothers. They who are with me—Brother Bruno and Brother Gerard [3]—salute you and ask for your prayers.

LETTER CXLV. (*Circa* A.D. 1137.)

To the Abbots Assembled at Cîteaux.

Bernard begs them to have compassion upon his labours and sufferings, and to excuse his absence on that account. He earnestly desires to die among his brethren, and not in a foreign land.

[1] Baldwin, first Cardinal of the Cistercian Order, was created by Innocent, A.D. 1130, at a Council held at Claremont. He was afterwards made Archbishop of Pisa; *cf. Life of S. Bernard* (lib. ii. n. 49) : "In Pisa was Baldwin born, the glory of his native land, and a burning light to the Church." So great a man did not think it beneath him to act as Bernard's secretary, and his praises are sung in ep. 245, *cf.* ep. 201.

[2] All these were Cardinals. Luke, of the title of SS. John and Paul, was created A.D. 1132 ; Chrysogonus, of the title of S. Maria de Porticu, A.D. 1134; Ivo, a regular Canon of S. Victor of Paris, A.D. 1130, of the title of S. Laurence in Damasus; to him ep. 193 was written.

[3] Bruno is called (ep. 209) the father of many disciples in Sicily. Gerard seems to be Bernard's brother. For Bruno see also ep. 165 n. 4.

In much weakness of body and anxiety of mind, as God knows, have I dictated these words to you—a man miserable and born to suffering, yet your brother. Would that I might merit to have now the Holy Spirit, in whom ye have met together, as my advocate to your whole body, that He might impress upon your hearts the trouble that I am suffering, and bring before your brotherly affections my sad and suppliant countenance just as it now is. I do not pray Him to create new pity in you, for I know how familiar to you all is that virtue, but I do ask Him to give you a keen sense of how much loving pity I now stand in need. For I am certain that if that were given you, tears would unceasingly flow forth from the fount of your love, that groans and sobs and sighs would knock at heaven's gate, so that God would hear and be gracious unto me, and say, "I have restored thee to thy brethren, thou shalt not die amid strangers, but amongst thine own people." I am so worn, indeed, by my great labours and griefs that I am often awearied of life. But I speak as a man, because of my infirmity; I desire my life to be prolonged till I return to you, that I may not die away from you. For the rest, brethren, make good your ways, determining and holding to what is true, honest, and useful. Before all things endeavour to keep the unity of the Spirit in the bond of peace, and the God of peace shall be with you.

END OF VOL. I.

INDEX.

A.

B.

C.

M.

N.

O.

P.